THE SUPPRESSOR

ERIK CARTER

.

ISBN: 9798741547977

CHAPTER ONE

Pensacola, Florida
The 1990s

THE MAN WAS OUT THERE, somewhere, hidden in the shadows and completely silent.

And the man was on the hunt.

Clayton Glover, the prey, squeezed himself tighter against the uneven surface, trying to match the silence of the predator. He inched his face toward the corner, stole a glance.

Nothing.

Just deep darkness pierced by crisscrossed streams of faint light that came in through the warehouse's banks of windows, dust particles dancing within. Row after row of pallet racks, their skeletal steel uprights and beams climbing high above him into the darkness. Boxes and tubes and machinery and tools lined the shelves, all of it macabre and shadowy.

He ducked back into his position of safety, chest heaving. He let his head fall back against the stack of plastic bags behind him, which were full of coarse gravel. The plastic was cold against his sweaty hair. The stones poked at his scalp. He took in choppy breaths, willing them to be quieter, willing himself to shut the hell up.

All of this was happening because of Glover's decision to follow Burton.

Glover wasn't smart enough to be a leader, but he knew whom to follow. People like Lukas Burton—a winner, a born commander. He was the sort of man who could lead a guy like Glover to success, wealth, safety.

But if Burton was so damn great, why was Glover being hunted down now in a darkened warehouse?

And who the hell was the man hunting him?

Prior to the confrontation in the parking lot a few minutes earlier—when Glover had told the man Burton's secret, before he'd managed to escape—Glover had never seen the man before, this large, cruel-looking individual with sculpted features, dark hair, and cold eyes.

He took another look into the warehouse. Still nothing. But how could—

There!

A flash.

The movement had come at the nearest window.

A reflection.

Something moving. Fast. He had just enough time to turn and find the fist hurtling toward his face.

Pain exploded in his eye socket, a burning wave that surged through the back of his head, up his nose, down his throat.

He stumbled back, took a blind swing, and a powerful hand clasped down upon his forearm and twisted. Glover's feet were swept from beneath him, and he was thrown.

He landed hard on the floor several feet away with an impact that sent another pulse of pain through him, this one rattling his bones, erupting in his shoulder.

He slid along the polished concrete, bashed into something wooden. His eyes strained to open. Jagged boards surrounded him, the shattered remains of a pallet.

A moment of nothing. He breathed.

And then a shadow moved in front of him, the dark man loping forward, pistol in hand.

Glover grabbed one of the broken deck boards and swung just as the man reached him.

In a blur of movement, the man caught the board—*caught it*—and brought Glover's swing to a dead stop.

After another streaking motion, the board was wrenched from Glover's grip, and the man threw it into the darkness. It clattered, the racket echoing off distant walls.

The man stood above him and aimed his Beretta 92FS at Glover's chest. A silencer extended the pistol's length.

Glover kicked feebly at the concrete, but there was nowhere to go.

"No! Shit! Please! I ... I told you everything!" He shielded his face, his chest.

But the man's expression said he wouldn't fire.

Not yet, anyway.

The look wasn't there, that look in the eyes that said a person was prepared to take a life. Glover had been around violence his entire adulthood. This guy—whoever the monster was—had a reason for pinning Glover down like this. He wanted to squeeze more information out of him.

"Talk," the man said, the first time he'd spoken. Minutes earlier, in the parking lot, the man had said nothing. He hadn't needed to. The beating he'd given Glover was enough to get him to spill his guts.

Glover gasped.

The man's voice...

It was a growl. Something at the same time mechanical and of the earth—deep in its bowels, forced up between layers of rock and lava.

The man brought the gun down, taking his aim off Glover's chest and to his knee.

Talk, or you'll never walk right again.

Glover's arms pulled in tighter over his face. "I swear to God! *I told you everything!*"

He really *had* told the man everything. There was nothing left to share.

The dark eyes continued to stare down upon him. The pistol's suppressed barrel didn't waver.

Glover's hands quivered in front of his face. He peered through his fingers, making eye contact with the man, a human connection, a plea.

The man's expression changed. But not in the way Glover had hoped.

The look was there now, in the monster's eyes, a veil of subtle changes to the muscles in his face. He bore the countenance of a man ready to go the full distance, to end someone's life.

The desire to kill.

"Whoa, man!" Glover said. "I gave you what you want. I swear that's all I know! Let me go."

Glover's heart pounded. His eyes moistened.

Why? Why was this happening?

This wasn't how things worked. There were codes to be followed. Glover had snitched. And therefore the man was supposed to let him go. That's how this was supposed to work.

The man's nostrils flared. His eyes went wider, took on a distant, hazy appearance—the kill look gathering power, building steam.

He raised the Beretta, away from Glover's knee, going higher.

And then Glover noticed something.

The man's eyes.

They looked ... familiar.

No.

No, it couldn't be.

The man was the same height, the same proportions, similar build, if a bit more muscular. Dark hair, too, yes.

But the face was completely different.

All angles and sharp lines. Brooding chic, like a fashion model or something.

Those cold eyes, too. They were dark brown, not bright green.

So it couldn't be him.

But somehow ... it was.

It was him!

Glover's lips parted.

A slight change in expression on the foreign but somehow familiar face showed that the man knew Glover recognized him.

"It's you, isn't it?" Glover's voice was weak and pathetic, flavored by the tears building in his eyes.

The man didn't reply. The Beretta continued to ascend, past chest level, to Glover's head, and stopped.

"Why are you doing this?" Glover screamed.

The man blinked.

He lowered the gun, glanced to the floor.

But only for a moment.

Then, he looked Glover directly in the eye, that intense glare boring right through him.

"For Cecilia," the man growled.

He raised his gun.

And fired.

CHAPTER TWO

SILENCE JONES EASED onto the front porch, slowly, carefully transferring his weight onto his lead foot. The floor was concrete, an advantage to him—no creaking boards to give him away. But the porch was deep, as large as a back porch, and the surroundings were quiet, so even his careful steps had the potential to make scuffling noises against the concrete.

It had been gray and miserable all day, and now, with evening approaching, a fraction of sunlight was beginning to pierce through the gloom. But that bit of light didn't concern him. Noise was his enemy at the moment. And so far he hadn't made a sound.

Excellent.

He couldn't risk even the tiniest of noises. The person whom he was slipping past had superb hearing.

The individual wasn't another member of Lukas Burton's gang. With Glover's execution a half hour earlier, all of those people had been eliminated. Except Burton himself.

No, the person he was trying to elude wasn't nearly as dangerous as Burton's contingent. She wasn't dangerous at all.

She was, in fact, a little, old, blind woman.

And she was Silence's only companion in this new life he'd been given. She was his next-door neighbor.

The only threat she posed was the fact that she monitored his drinking, and this watchdog quality of hers was an issue at the moment, because Silence most definitely needed a beverage after what had happened a half hour earlier.

And what was still to come that evening.

His mind was reeling, not from finishing off Glover—which should have been profound enough, should have been a monumental, delectable moment for him—but because of the intel he'd squeezed from Glover before putting two rounds through the man's skull.

The information was staggering, something that sent Silence's assignment careening precipitously into the dark unknown, proving that Burton's plan was much grander than anyone could have possibly imagined.

The implications were unthinkable.

The scale, massive.

Which, along with the fact that Silence just killed the second to last of the men who had stolen his fiancée from him, was the reason Silence held a plastic sack with a six-pack of beer.

One drink. Nothing that could impair him. Just something to smooth the edges.

Or, as his next-door neighbor would see it, something to feed Silence's habit, the monster that had emerged in his life since he lost C.C.

She meant well.

Silence would sip his beer while he pondered what he was to do next, how he could solve the new threat that Burton posed.

Because Glover had said that Burton was making his move.

Tonight.

At 8 p.m.

That gave Silence three hours to figure out where to find the man.

But if Silence was going to consume an alcoholic tonic to calm his pulsating, confused brain, he first had to escape the old woman next-door and make it into his house.

She sat only a few feet away, in the shadows of her front porch, her white eyes shining from the darkness like a pair of tiny judgmental searchlights.

He made it to the front door, slowly put his hand on the doorknob, noticed blood on his fingers.

His?

Glover's?

It didn't matter. He'd find out when he washed.

He eased the key into the deadbolt cylinder, turned. No sound. So far so good. The lock was new and well oiled. While his house was built in the 1950s, many of the details, including most of the hardware, had been updated.

Another quarter turn. The brushed nickel beauty continued to work noiselessly. But Silence wasn't optimistic, because he knew there would be that inevitable noise, the *clunk*, when the deadbolt fully retracted into the unlocked position. There was no avoiding it. A person with normal hearing would easily discern that sound, let alone a blind individual to whom hearing was amplified. But maybe Silence could lessen the sound if he—

The beer bottles clanked together.

"Silence?" Mrs. Enfield's little wavering voice called.

Shit.

Silence exhaled. He stepped to the far side of his porch, which terminated only a few feet from Mrs. Enfield's, separated by the gravel drive that ran between the two houses. His neighbor's tiny figure was on the green cushion of her porch swing, the empty white orbs of her eyes looking but not looking in his direction.

"Yes, ma'am?"

"Come over." She waved her hand.

Silence looked at the plastic sack, felt its comforting weight. Sighed. "One moment."

There was a twinge in his throat with that last word, *moment*, a sting substantial enough to make him grimace. Every syllable he spoke brought pain, little movements from what felt like a permanently lodged knife, dulled with time and rust, but still effective. The more he spoke, the more it hurt, but sometimes the pain simply spiked for no apparent reason, as it had with *moment*.

He crossed the porch again, back to the front door. When he opened it, a pleasant gust of chilly air struck him. Humidity bothered him, and he lived in the most humid region of the continental U.S., so he kept his air conditioning cranked.

He headed for the kitchen, which lay right beyond the living room area, in the house's long, shotgun-style layout. The house was built in 1955, and some aspects showed their age, like the floorboards squeaking beneath his feet, but the Watchers had renovated the interior shortly before they moved him in two weeks ago. While Silence had been surprised that they'd been able to locate such a perfect location for him, what really amazed him were the renovations. They'd gone to great lengths to consider Silence's personal tastes—the palette was all black and grays and whites, and the design touches were modern and chic.

He caught a whiff of fresh rubber and plastics as he opened the refrigerator, a glossy black, state-of-the-art model, so new that it still felt unnaturally clean. The other kitchen appliances were also updated and also black, all the same brand. For whatever reason, the Watchers hadn't taken down the old cabinetry, but they'd still continued with their policy of utilizing his tastes and covered the cabinets with dark gray paint. He found this detail charming.

A nice notion, yes, but he would replace the cabinets soon enough.

He took the six-pack from the plastic sack, placed it on the top shelf. Heineken. Six green bottles in a green cardboard carrier, a splash of color in the glowing white, nearly empty environment. The only other item on the shelves was a white, five-by-five styrofoam to-go box. A bottle of ketchup was on the door.

A cold breeze wafted from the fridge, across his sore knuckles, and he stared at the beers. Wanted one. He could quickly drain a bottle, but Mrs. Enfield could—and would—smell it on his breath.

A feeling swept from nowhere, rushed over him. Self-loathing. Disgust. So pathetic, so worthless, this need for alcohol.

Just like the old man.

He closed the door, noticed again the blood on his fingers. It had to go. Mrs. Enfield would inspect his hands, part of what had become standard protocol this second week of his two-week stay in this home.

The bottle of hand soap at the stainless steel kitchen sink had been there when he first moved in, another of the Watchers' efforts to make the house livable. It was from Bath & Body Works and had little scrubbing beads inside, which Silence thought might do the trick on the blood.

They didn't.

He retrieved his bar of Lava brand pumice soap from beneath the sink and scrubbed away. The blood loosened, pink water swirling the drain, and the mystery was solved—the blood was Glover's, not his. He had no open wounds on his tender knuckles.

As he rubbed suds and water through his fingers, his mind went back to what Glover had said, the critical intel that Silence had gotten moments before chasing Glover into the warehouse and executing him.

I don't know the location, Glover had said, his voice shaking. *I swear I don't. All I know is the time: eight o'clock.*

Silence dried off and hovered a hand above the stainless steel fruit basket that was under the cabinets, next to the fridge.

Peaches, pears, apples.

He chose a nice pear. Mrs. Enfield liked pears. This one was perfectly ripe. Nice scent. Nice color, too, not that the appearance would matter much to a blind lady.

He opened the cabinet doors in front of him, those above the fruit basket. The lower two shelves held dishes—something the Watchers *hadn't* provided, something he picked up last week, matte-finish, charcoal gray, little flecks in the glaze —and the top shelf was full of miniature cans of cat food. The brand was 'Malkin Meats, a company that produced 100%-meat cat foods. C.C. had once told him that many dog and cat foods contained a lot of fillers.

His hand hovered over the cans, as it had at the fruit basket, deciding.

Chicken.

He grabbed one.

A few moments later he stepped around the shrubs and onto the porch of Mrs. Enfield's house, a turn-of-the century home, one of many such in Pensacola. The siding was green, the trim a darker green, and the gabled roof was metal with a dormer window. The porch wasn't as deep as Silence's, though it was wider, naturally, as the house itself was wider. To the right of the door was a rocking chair. On the opposite side was another, matching rocking chair and a porch swing.

She sat at the far end of the swing, her designated spot,

smiling at him, legs crossed at the ankles, toes barely reaching the floorboards, rocking the swing gently, hands stacked on her lap. She was black, and her hair was as white as her eyes. Her dress was a dark blue floral-print with frill around the collar.

She patted the open area of seat cushion next to her.

He sat down.

Mew. A little noise from the floor.

Baxter was curled up beneath the small table in the porch's corner, looking up at Silence, eyes squinted with contentment, his little cat motor rumbling away.

He was an orange tabby. And big. Not the most gigantic cat Silence had ever seen—he weighed about fifteen pounds —but he carried his weight on a decently sized frame. His square head, lion nose, and Jay Leno chin made him look not so much a masculine cat than an actual, human man. He looked like he shouldn't spend his days slumbering on Mrs. Enfield's sofa but instead be out there somewhere in the workforce, a fuzzy personal injury attorney, a four-legged retail manager.

And he drooled.

Not a little spittle now and then. Not a few bubbles with indigestion. An ever-present line of drool leaking from whichever corner of his mouth was lower. Currently, as he looked contentedly up at Silence, the drool escaped the left corner of his mouth, a thin trail glistening in the muted, early-evening sunlight that filtered out of the gray sky.

Silence reached down and grabbed the small saucer beside Baxter's left paw, examined it. Flawlessly clean. Mrs. Enfield was good about keeping it washed.

He set it down, pulled the ring on the can of 'Malkin Meats, and tapped out the contents. Baxter dug in, his purring going louder.

As Silence settled back into the swing, he reached the pear toward his companion. "And for you."

She grasped for it. He took her hands, led them to the pear. She smiled.

"Aren't you sweet?" She placed the fruit on her lap. "Have you been drinking?"

"No, ma'am."

"Let me smell your breath."

"Um..."

"Oblige an old woman. Lean over here."

Back in his kitchen, he thought she would have been able to detect alcohol on his breath from a distance. He hadn't imagined she would give him a closeup inspection.

He leaned across the swing, putting his face near hers.

She sniffed. "Good."

She put her hands on either side of his face, rubbed gently over his temples, his cheekbones. Her palms were smooth but dry. She took his hands, examined his knuckles.

"You've been fighting again, haven't you?"

Silence didn't reply.

"You have. Your face and hands are all softened up. What is it you do?"

Silence didn't reply.

"Fine. Better that I don't know anyway." She sighed. "In the two weeks you've been here, you've proven that you're a good man. That's all that matters. I can read people."

Silence could relate. C.C. had always told him he was good at reading people, that it was an excellent quality to have.

"So whatever trouble you get yourself into, it doesn't change who you are on the inside." Her hands returned to his face, poked about his jawline. "You feel thin, though. Are you eating?"

"Yes, ma'am."

"Don't lie to me."

"Could eat more."

"Mmm-hmm."

She took her hands back and faced the street, her milky eyes blinking. Quiet sounds from the neighborhood—a single car listing by a few blocks over, laughter from a cookout, a pair of birds twittering their appreciation of the returning sunlight.

Their street was in East Hill, a nice area of the city, a desired location. People smiled when they declared, *I live in East Hill.* Sentiments like these weren't pomposity, though, because while there were certainly plenty of expensive homes in East Hill—one very expensive one was right across the street from Silence's—there were also plenty of lesser expensive ones.

East Hill was a way of life, an eclectic mix of the expensive and the expressive and the eccentric, all of it peaceful and beautiful. Old oak trees and pristine landscaping dotted comfortable sidewalks. Kids on bicycles. Palm trees. Friendly neighbors. Lawnmowers. The smell of charcoal grills. The smell of propane grills.

And, as Silence lived in the southwest corner of East Hill —right by Old East Hill—he was only blocks from downtown. The Watchers had done a wonderful job when they found this location for him. He literally couldn't have done better if he tried.

A sound broke the quiet. Rumbling bass. And tires crunching asphalt.

It was the El Camino again. Light blue, dull paint. A long crack in the windshield. Rust had taken nibbles from the door, big mouthfuls of the rear quarter panel.

And inside were the same two punks.

The white guy was behind the steering wheel as the car slowly crept by. His left arm dangled outside, smacking loudly against the door in rhythm with the bass. Tattoos on his skinny shoulder and on his even skinnier forearm. Goatee. White tank top. Fedora. Sunglasses.

In the passenger seat was the black guy. Several years younger, late teens. Light-skinned. Lean, not in the same way as his companion, but in a not-yet-fully-grown way. Dark blue long-sleeve shirt. Beanie cap.

They both looked right toward the porch—the white guy sneering, the black guy trying to match his partner's bravado, but with a hesitancy in the eyes that couldn't be completely masked.

The driver removed his hand from the steering wheel, looked away, reached toward the dash. The music quickly faded off.

When he faced the porch again, he sang to the tune of "Three Blind Mice."

"*One blind mouse. One blind mouse. She's all alone. She's all alone.*" He snickered. "Nice house, Granny! Real nice. We know you be livin' all alone, Granny. Who's this? Your boyfriend?"

The white guy snickered again. It was only after he turned to the passenger seat that the other guy joined him in laughing.

Silence had heard enough.

He jumped from his seat, bounded down the steps, down the short sidewalk.

The El Camino's engine roared, and it bolted off.

It was a futile effort on Silence's part. No chance at catching them. Just pure hubris, pure rage.

He stopped in the middle of the street as the vehicle shrank in the distance. The driver's laughter faded away. The El Camino did a rolling stop at the next corner, squealed to the left, and disappeared.

Dammit.

Silence returned to the porch, sat on the swing.

"Same guys," he said.

"That's three times now," Mrs. Enfield said. She rolled the pear between her hands, fingers shaking.

"How find?" Silence said.

Mrs. Enfield's white eyes looked at him, confused. More and more, Silence was discovering that his new abbreviated way of speaking wasn't the clearest form of communication.

"How did they find me?" she asked, clarifying.

On instinct, Silence nodded, then remembered she couldn't see and said, "Mmm-hmm."

"Mrs. Cooper told me they're from one of the rough neighborhoods on the other side of downtown. Must have heard about the little blind lady alone in East Hill."

Anger rumbled through Silence's chest. He exhaled, his frustration crackling in his destroyed throat.

"Not alone now," he said.

She smiled, reached for his knee, found it, squeezed. "That was very brave of you, chasing after them like that. Thank you."

Silence grunted.

"You just hopped right out of your seat, right into danger," Mrs. Enfield said. She tsked. "Yes, son, I'm quite certain I don't need to know what line of work you're in. But may I ask —you seem edgier than usual tonight; why?"

"Have problem to solve," Silence said. He swallowed, lubricating his throat for more syllables. "By tonight." Another swallow. "Or consequences."

Consequences was a big word with a lot of syllables, a painful word. But if Silence's throat wasn't faulty, he would have clarified it adjectively.

Major consequences.

Life-or-death consequences.

National security consequences.

Glover had told Silence how consequential Burton's actions tonight would be.

But Glover hadn't been able to provide a location.

Just the time, 8 p.m.

Silence glanced at his watch.

Only three more hours.

And Silence had nothing to help him figure out what was going to happen. No additional intel. No contacts to reach out to. No stacks of research materials. The only tool available to Silence that evening was his own mind.

Mrs. Enfield had gone quiet again. Finally she said, "Why don't you talk?"

"You know."

"Because of the pain. Yes, I know why you say so few words. What I'm asking is why don't you *talk*? You say so little with those few words you speak. This ... event you mentioned, the thing that happened to you—why not share it with someone, maybe an old, blind widow with no kids, no family, not much longer for this world. You'll feel better. Come, now, share with me."

Cecilia.

C.C.

A pool of blood filled with long, dark hair.

Body still warm, getting colder.

"It was ... very bad," Silence said.

Mrs. Enfield smiled painfully. "On your time, son. On your time." She held up the pear. "Did you rinse it?"

"Yes, ma'am."

Mrs. Enfield nodded and took a bite, then used the pear to make a sweeping gesture at the neighborhood before them. "How did you end up here, Silence?"

Silence looked beyond the porch. Directly across from them was a house he'd learned was built in the '20s, though the average person wouldn't know it to look at it, so thorough were the updates. A two-story addition was in the back, and through the windows there were glimpses of high-end furnishings and a happy family in the living room, a conversation full of laughter.

Beside that was the street's largest house, two stories of modern design—sharp angles, towering windows.

On the corner was another newer house, more traditional, smaller and a bit more modest.

The street was empty but for a woman pushing a baby carriage and talking on a cellular phone. Her conversation was as pleasant, as laughter-filled as that of the family beyond the window on the other side of the street.

"Lucked out," Silence said.

But he said it figuratively. It hadn't been luck that had brought him there. It hadn't been luck that stole C.C. from him, that stole his voice, his name, his future, and his past.

Cruelty had done it.

Cruelty had beaten C.C. to a bloody mess.

Cruelty had murdered her.

And every bit of that cruelty, all the reasons for Silence's new, destroyed life, were connected to Lukas Burton.

Silence considered once more that he had only one tool that night—his own mind—with which to find Burton.

And stop him.

CHAPTER THREE

A THOUSAND MILES AWAY.

Virginia. Somewhere in the Washington, D.C., metropolitan area, the National Capital Region.

A windowless office, smaller than a child's bedroom. White walls with copious scuff marks, particularly around the vinyl base molding. The desk was metal and also less than gently used.

It was a room treated with careless disregard, like an unloved, long-suffering rental car, one of many such nondescript offices in a cluster of glass office buildings surrounding an artificially green pond with a fountain in the center. A business park, conveniently located off the interstate highway.

Far away from any governmental facility.

It was the latest of their meeting places. A six-month lease under the name Clocktower Enterprises, LLC. They didn't stay anywhere for long.

The seat facing the desk was hard, small, and the cushion was less a pancake than it was a crepe, covered with soiled red cloth that felt like burlap. Tony Laswell shifted again, recrossing his legs, taking the pressure off his left ass cheek and putting it on the right.

As he looked at the older man sitting on the other side of the desk—in the slightly posher yet equally budget-friendly swivel desk chair—he considered clearing his throat, obnoxiously, overtly.

But he didn't need to, because finally Briggs responded. "And when did we get this intel, Falcon?"

Ugh. *Falcon*. Briggs was insistent on using their code-names, even when it was just the two of them. Briggs got frustrated when Laswell called him by his real name and furious if Laswell addressed him by the title he used in the outside world.

Still, Laswell suspected this was less about sticking to protocol than it was a power trip on Briggs's part. After all, the guy had named himself *Jupiter*, as in the Roman king of gods.

Ego, ego, ego.

Laswell checked his watch. "An hour ago, *Jupiter*," he said, giving the name a two-handed shove of annoyed sarcasm. "He squeezed the information out of Glover then put a pair of bullets between his eyes."

Briggs nodded, ran a hand through his bone-white hair, and steepled his fingers beneath his nose, squinting slightly. He looked to the side, as though through a window, a spot on the wall where a window might be in a grander office.

Shit. Another one of Briggs's pauses.

Laswell crossed his legs again. A futile attempt. His entire rear end and his lower back were tingling, falling asleep. If Briggs didn't stop mulling things over so much, Laswell was going to get permanent nerve damage; he just knew it.

But that's how Patrick Briggs acted within this organization. Deep. Reflective. Pensive. Out in the real world, Briggs also had to make monumental, life-and-death decisions.

Those decisions, however, were seen in the light of day. They were filtered through public scrutiny. Here, Briggs didn't have the resources he had out there, nor did he have large numbers of associates with whom to share both ideas and accountability.

And for some reason, this made Briggs move slowly.

Very, very slowly.

Thank god Laswell had a flight to catch. Otherwise, this could last all night.

He drummed his fingers on his watch face, willing time to move faster.

Finally, Briggs took his hands from beneath his nose, placed them on his lap. Still looking out the phantom window, he spoke. "And all we have is a time, no location?"

"That's correct, sir. 2000 Central Time, 2100 here."

Briggs eased back a French cuff, glanced at his Rolex, grunted. "If Burton is as big of a threat as we're thinking, our new man has about three hours to stop a catastrophe." Another pause, a shorter one, enough time to release a long, slightly exasperated sigh. "What's he calling himself?"

"Silence Jones."

Briggs pulled his piercing blue eyes away from the wall and brought them to Laswell. "Silence?"

"He insisted."

Briggs turned toward the desk again, tugged at his navy blue suit jacket. He straightened up in his chair. And grimaced. His ass must have been falling asleep too.

Briggs was tall, large, and very fit for someone his age, a dynamic silhouette that paired well with his classically, timelessly handsome face. Excellent posture. Immaculate grooming.

"So Jones would be Asset..." Briggs scrunched one cheek, looked up, searching his mental files. "Asset 23, yes?"

Laswell nodded. "Correct. He's A-23."

"Codename?"

"Suppressor."

"A silencer. I get it. Very clever, Falcon."

"Thank you, sir. I was fairly proud of myself for that one." Laswell shimmied his shoulders, pumped his eyebrows, and twitched his upper lip in a way that made his mustache bounce mischievously.

Briggs was not amused. He never was.

Briggs leaned forward, put his elbows on the desk, getting closer. The cheap desk chair squealed in protest. His blue eyes penetrated Laswell.

"He's too damn old," Briggs said.

"Old? You're one to judge, ya fossil. Besides, if you think Jones is old, what must you think of me? I qualify for AARP now, ya know."

Briggs scowled, didn't respond.

Never, ever amused.

"He's in his thirties," Laswell continued, his tone more serious.

"*Well* into his thirties."

"We have Assets in their forties, their fifties, and—"

"Yes, and all of those individuals *began* in their teens and twenties. They had time for training."

"He's been trained. He was law enforcement."

Briggs scoffed. "City cops aren't trained assassins."

"You know Nakiri trained him as well."

"So you said. And for, what, four weeks?"

Laswell looked away from Briggs's intense stare. "Three weeks."

Briggs shook his head, the disappointed father figure. "This is *your* experiment, Laswell. And it's on you when it implodes."

"My experiment is going pretty well so far, wouldn't you

say? Now that he's eliminated Glover, Suppressor is one kill away from completing his first assignment."

"So our new Asset was a local cop, working undercover in the Farone crime family, when he crossed paths with our very own Nakiri, yes?"

"Correct. The Farone crime family that has since become the Burton gang."

"What was our man's name before?"

"Jake Rowe. He killed four men in eight hours." Laswell paused a half moment for dramatic effect. "*After* being shot."

Briggs nodded, put a hand to his chin. "Mmm-hmm. That might impress me had Rowe not been caught."

"They murdered his fiancée. The man deserves his vengeance."

"I don't disagree. But you should have made him a Benevolent Cause. That's why we do what we do, isn't it? You could have let Rowe slaughter those men, called it a BC assignment for Nakiri, and then we could have put him in witness protection. Yet you turned a local cop into an Asset. What the hell were you thinking?"

"He has it. You should trust my judgment."

Laswell wasn't often defiant with Briggs.

But he was now.

Briggs was right, though—Silence Jones *was* Laswell's experiment. A long shot. And, yeah, maybe Laswell had overstepped his bounds a tad. So he would restrain his swagger, tame his playfulness, be respectful.

Briggs's attention returned to the wall, and the small office was quiet again. No sounds from the hallway past the closed door behind them; the sixth floor of the building was nearly untenanted. Laswell could hear his and Briggs's wristwatches.

Briggs turned. "And now you've turned his vendetta of revenge into his first assignment."

"A test run, if you will."

"The last one remaining for Suppressor to eliminate is Burton himself?"

"That's correct." Laswell checked his watch again. "And if he doesn't do so soon, we're all going to be in for a world of hurt."

Briggs nodded, steepled his fingers beneath his chin. "I want you to tell me exactly how this Jake Rowe turned from a workaday police officer to a methodical killer overnight."

"Yes, sir," Laswell said humbly.

And he started in on the story of Jake Rowe's transformation.

CHAPTER FOUR

THREE MONTHS EARLIER.

Tension pulsed at the man's temples, pinched the back of his neck, as he sprinted down the alley, his mind flooding with conflicting thoughts—this gruesome chore he'd been tasked with; how the hell he was going to get out of doing the chore; and if he was going to get shot in the process.

His name was Jake Rowe.

The man who would become Silence Jones.

The change that was to come wouldn't be solely a reconstructed identity. There were massive physical differences too.

Jake's face was rounder, less defined. Unlike Silence, Jake bore a prominent mole on the right corner of his jaw, which was not sculpted at a sharp angle to his neck like Silence's. Jake's physique was toned—from many self-indulgent hours in the gym—but not yet chiseled.

And Jake Rowe could speak. Clearly and without pain. And he did so fervently, especially when his words tried to keep pace with the tumultuous storm of thoughts in his overactive mind.

In the final months of Jake's existence, he was known by a different name, Pete Hudson, the identity he'd assumed for his undercover assignment within the Farone crime family, an organization that added even further to his list of monikers, gifting him a traditional mobster nickname, one based on his tendency toward loquaciousness.

Loudmouth.

Pete "Loudmouth" Hudson.

The Farone family had changed Jake's life in a short time, and it was the reason he currently found himself bounding down an alley of crumbling asphalt lined with dumpsters and littered with garbage and potholes, the sky sliced and diced by utility lines.

Jake's chest heaved, and his feet ached as they pounded the pavement. His toe caught a pothole. A splash of water on his shoe. His arms windmilled as he stumbled forward a few steps before regaining his balance.

Ahead was his target: Mr. Ranga, owner of the laundromat on the other side of the alley. Indian American. Forties, short and doughy, in a flannel and cords. But even though Jake was in far better shape, Ranga had spotted him early and gotten a jump on him.

Jake looked back. His partner on this job, Charlie Marsh, was behind him by maybe another thirty feet, struggling to keep up. Even though Charlie was several years younger than Jake, he was nowhere near his fitness level and also several inches shorter. His face was tortured, big strands of his wavy hair flopping all over his sweaty forehead. Poor kid. They'd been chasing Ranga for almost three blocks.

They zoomed past a windowless stretch of brick building with a green roll-down loading dock door. There was a wooden fence to the right with an open doorway, and for a moment, as Ranga pulled in that direction, Jake thought he was going to make a run for the exit. Instead, Ranga took a left into a cross alley.

And disappeared.

"Shit, Pete!" Charlie said. "We lost him."

"No, we didn't."

Jake slowed as he approached the corner. A blind corner. He took out his Colt Detective Special, a small revolver that he'd chosen especially for his undercover alias at the beginning of the assignment. A belly gun seemed the perfect weapon for a car thief.

He hadn't wanted to draw on Ranga. But he had to now. His life was in danger.

Charlie's footsteps pounded up beside him, came to a shuffling stop. Jake glanced over, found Charlie's big, kid-like eyes looking up at him. There was more fear in them than should have been in the eyes of a supposed career criminal. Charlie should have gotten out of this lifestyle when Jake told him to, a couple of days ago in New Orleans when he had a golden opportunity.

The damn fool.

"Come on," Jake said.

A deep breath and he cleared the corner, found a similar alley in front of him. Graffiti and mildew stains tarnished the walls. A metal fire escape to the left. A tall chain-link fence at the far end. Wind scraped a crumpled piece of newspaper in the corner. There was the pungent tang of rotten garbage.

But no Ranga.

Maybe Charlie was right. Maybe they had lost him.

Then a small *ping* of something glancing off metal. Jake's eyes went to the roll-off container in the back, a massive rectangular block of rusty steel.

And saw a pair of eyes peeking around the corner.

Jake and Charlie bolted, Jake immediately building a sizable lead once more.

Ranga scrambled for the fence, and Jake saw that the hands at the ends of his wildly swinging arms were empty. Just as Jake had predicted, Ranga wasn't the gun-toting type. So Jake shoved his tiny revolver in his back pocket as he sprinted to the back of the alley.

He made it to Ranga right as the man reached the top of the ten-foot fence. He grabbed Ranga's flannel with one hand, the fence with the other. Ranga raised a foot and smashed it down. Jake pulled back, but not quite in time, and Ranga's shoe scraped against the edge of his jaw. A sharp pulse of pain.

But Jake still had a firm grasp on his shirt.

He yanked hard, using his six-foot-three frame to torque the smaller man off the chain-link. Ranga fell to the asphalt and rolled, taking Charlie out in the process, bringing him to the ground as well.

Jake was the only one standing now, and in the moment when Jake's back was turned to Charlie, when Ranga's eyes went widest, when the man clearly thought he was about to be tortured, murdered, Jake pulled up on the bottom of his shirt, revealing the black plastic box poking out from the elastic of his underwear. The digital recording device. His "wire."

Ranga's quivering eyes flashed to the device then back to Jake.

I'm a cop! Jake mouthed.

A pause from Ranga. Then the tiniest sign of understanding. A small nod. But his eyes didn't look any less frightened.

Jake grabbed two big handfuls of Ranga's shirt. "Listen up you, *piece of shit!* You're gonna have the two grand tomorrow plus twenty percent interest. Aren't you?"

Ranga continued to look at him with those wide eyes. "Twenty percent? I can't—"

"*Aren't you?*"

"Yes! I will, yes!"

Jake feigned a bit of struggle, an excuse to twist his hips to the right, reposition himself so that his back was to Charlie again. He gave Ranga a wink.

"And you'll meet us downtown," he growled and immediately mouthed a few more silent words: *Downtown police station.*

Another moment of hesitation from Ranga. He gave a fraction of a nod before replying.

"Yes, yes! Tomorrow. Downtown," Ranga said, nodding vehemently now for Charlie's benefit.

"Good," Jake said. "Then run along, asshole."

There had been several moments like this where Jake had to either feign tough guy or somehow weasel his way out of the violence that was part of life within a crime family. He didn't know how many more excuses he could make, how many more punches he could fake.

Fortunately, he wasn't going to have to worry about that any longer.

The department was pulling him out of his undercover assignment that night.

———

The interior of Charlie's 1985 Ford Taurus smelled like body odor, French fries, and dry-rotted foam, all of it mixed with a sharp chemical pine smell, courtesy of the tree-shaped air freshener dangling from the mirror. The seats and dash and door moldings were grimy to the touch—dusty in some areas, sticky in others.

"Dang, Pete," Charlie said, slapping the steering wheel with appreciation. "I've never seen you get so hard-edged with a guy. This might just get you back on Burton's good side after what happened in New Orleans."

Charlie slowed for a stop sign, checked left and right, loose strands of his hair swinging across his face, then sped up again, never completely stopping.

"I don't give a damn about Burton's good side," Jake said. "He doesn't run the Farone family. He only thinks he does."

Charlie took one hand from the steering wheel, used it to rub at his forearm. "Burton's gonna make a move, man. Don't you think? I mean, that's what it looks like to me, like he's gonna challenge Sylvester for control of the family. Oh, jeez, Pete, what are we gonna do? If Burton takes over, he'll make life a living hell for us after what we did in New Orleans."

Jake turned to him. "What *I* did in New Orleans. It was me. You were just along for the ride. If any flack comes our way, I'll be the one to absorb it."

Charlie smiled weakly, a bit of relief in his eyes.

"Besides," Jake continued, "I told you to get out of this life while you still could."

In New Orleans a couple of days earlier, when Jake had taken actions that cost Lukas Burton a significant amount of money, Jake had seen an opportunity for Charlie to get out of the criminal life. As a cop, Jake couldn't turn a blind eye to the crimes he'd seen Charlie commit, but he could get the kid out before he got himself hurt. Charlie was a decent soul, the sort of person who had a short life expectancy in the criminal world.

The Taurus puttered louder as it gained speed, pulling onto the I-110 on-ramp. It listed to the side on its spongy suspension, and Jake grabbed the grimy window crank for support.

"Maybe Burton doesn't run the show just yet," Charlie said as they merged into the streaks of headlights and tail-lights, "but he might soon enough. And we'll be in for a world of hurt."

CHAPTER FIVE

JAKE STEPPED into the warm glow of the Farone mansion and was struck by the smells of well-oiled leather, musky colognes, furniture polish, brandy, wine. The place reeked of power and tradition—a jarring difference from Charlie's Taurus, which he'd exited moments earlier, its scent one of scarcity.

The place was old wood, all of it—the walls, floors, ceilings, moldings. Big rectangles of dark brown. The gloss of high-shine varnish. The only break in the rectangularly wooden nature were the arches that topped the doorways and windows, as well as the wrought-iron balustrade that encircled the second-floor balcony, which looked down upon green leather chairs, long sofas, antique tables, spacious rugs.

Several people had gathered in the great hall, and they were split into two groups with a clear demarcation between the unofficial, unspoken divisions.

Ruckus energy emanated from the west side of the room, by the inlaid shelves, heavy with sculptures and paintings and books, where Lukas Burton and his hangers-on had congregated.

Nine of them. Cocky grins. Sharp, spiking belts of laughter. Hulking figures that leaned against tables and walls, ambling legs crossed in front of them. Rough hands squeezing tumblers of liquor.

Burton was in the center of the group, and he laughed suddenly, deeply, booming over the din of the boisterous men surrounding him. His severe, handsome face tilted back, thin lips stretching wide. He smacked one of his companions on the back.

Jake turned back to his own group, eight people. There were laughs on his side of the great hall as well, but they were quieter and flavored by unacknowledged apprehension.

They were near a set of bow windows that looked to the lush, expansive lawn, which was well lit, making it look crisp and bright against the inky nighttime sky and the dark forest on the other side of the road.

Jake looked away from the stars and the wispy clouds, across a courtyard where, fifty feet away, there was another set of windows, drapes open, bright light pouring into the night.

The library.

Floor-to-ceiling shelves full of stately hardbacks. Chairs and little tables. More polished wood. C.C. would be in there somewhere, but he couldn't see her. She must have been lying on her favorite sofa, as she was prone to do.

He pictured her stretched out, covered with a quilt, her dark curly hair splayed on a tasseled throw pillow, eyes squinted with concentration as she studied an esoteric tome —seventeenth-century philosophy, perhaps, or a biography of Houdini's wife, or a Moroccan cookbook.

Charlie approached. He picked at a fingernail. "This is not good, Pete. Just look over there. Burton and his guys might as well be their own gang."

Jake glanced back across the broad no-man's-land of hardwood floor, twinkling with points of light from the chandelier above. The other group's boisterous loitering continued. Burton's arm was draped over Christie Mosley, the only female in the room. Her gray eyes looked out from beneath choppy bangs, shining with the energy she was absorbing from all the other, gawking eyes.

Her dress was a beacon for the attention, a dark brown number that tightroped the line between elegant and trashy, leaning toward elegance, as Christie's noteworthy curves conformed to the surroundings in the same way as the sophisticated glass vase glowing under a spotlight on the shelf behind her—both shapely forms with sinuous lines that pleasingly dissected the austere linearity of the mansion.

Christie was one of two people who were constantly in orbit around Burton. Currently, they both flanked him— Christie on one side, and on the other, Clayton Glover, a pit bull of a man, with a squarish face, prominent nose, and squinting eyes. He smiled up at Burton.

Charlie continued picking at his fingernail. "I'm telling ya, Pete, it's coming soon. Burton's gonna take over the operation. What are we gonna do?"

Before Jake could respond, another man moved toward him. A silver tray with several glasses of white wine and one bottle of Heineken was perched on the outstretched fingers of his white-gloved hand. He wore a three-piece suit—black jacket and tie, gray vest.

The beer was especially for Jake. He didn't care for wine. He also preferred a burger to a ribeye. C.C., as lovingly as possible, described him as having an "unrefined palate."

He smiled as he grabbed the beer. "Thanks, Saunders."

The butler nodded.

Saunders was seventy or so, gray hair, stout frame, English with a pronounced accent, and had been with the Farone family long before Jake's brief tenure. For decades, actually.

His background was mysterious, but Jake knew Saunders had been an RAF mechanic during the war. While he'd served honorably, Saunders spent his hours out of uniform in a not-so-honorable fashion, earning side money as hired muscle for a London crime outfit. From there, he'd hopped across the pond and somehow ended up in Pensacola as the embodiment of some strange fantasy of Joey Farone's—that of having a proper British butler.

Saunders played the part well, tilting his chin up just so, saying "sir" hundreds of times a day. But to an intuitive person like Jake, it was obvious the old man had developed a persona, nothing more. There was a whole lot of spirit—and potentially danger—bubbling under that black suit. Perhaps that was an additional reason Joey Farone hired him.

Saunders recognized and appreciated that Jake saw through the facade. And he displayed his respect by not calling Jake "sir." Instead, Jake was a "mate."

Jake motioned toward Burton's group. "What do you think, old-timer?"

Saunders glanced over, quickly turned back to Jake.

"I think a storm is gathering."

Not exactly the reassurance Jake was hoping Saunders would provide for Charlie.

But, most likely, quite realistic. Saunders was rarely wrong about these things.

The butler headed for the next trio of Farone-loyal, a few feet away.

"Have a good evening, Saunders," Jake said.

"Cheers, mate."

Jake took a sip of the beer and looked back to the other side of the room, and as he did, Burton glanced up.

Their eyes met.

Arms and torsos and glasses of wine and liquor twisted around Burton, but his stare stayed fixed on Jake. A strand of his dark hair fell to the corner of his eye. He didn't move it, didn't budge. A smile came to his lips.

Jake's mind flashed to New Orleans.

You screwed me over, Burton's look seemed to say. *And I won't forget it.*

A staring match. Everything was a power struggle to Burton. Jake didn't mind giving him the satisfaction.

He didn't want to look at the guy anyway.

So he was the first to break the stare.

As he turned, he caught a glimpse out the window, across the courtyard to the library. And there was C.C., by the far windows, looking at him, arms crossed over the front of her gray sweater dress.

He smiled.

She returned the smile, lifted one arm to flutter her fingers.

Five-foot-three-inches of prototypical Italian-American beauty—black curly hair, olive skin, ageless face, dark eyes with long lashes, proportions and curves meeting the perfect ideals of Roman sculpture and mathematics.

Beyond the physical, though, nothing about C.C. was prototypical.

Jake had tried for the longest time to label her essence, and the best word he'd managed was *bohemian*.

She wasn't of the current '90s grunge counterculture, nor was she a hippie. She was unique in the most literal sense of the word—not fashionably special, but genuinely different.

To Cecilia Farone, life was a warm breeze, and she was the vibrant feather drifting on its undulations, dead leaves all around her descending to the cold, dark depths as she rose higher and higher.

The smile she was giving Jake—from across the courtyard, through two sets of windows—projected a mild current of hesitancy. That was understandable. Her genuine smile would likely not return for some time, not with her life changing as much as it was going to very soon.

The room quieted, and Jake turned away from the window.

In walked Sylvester Farone, C.C.'s brother and a contrast to her in nearly every way, an unfortunate-looking man, tall with parted hair, a sloping posture, and a sad mustache. While his suit was on-trend baggy, it was also wrinkled and unkempt, and he wore it as awkwardly as he wore his own body, making it look baggier than the intended style.

Across the room, Burton's group turned to face Sylvester, but they did so casually, flippantly, like a classroom of grade-schoolers from whom the teacher had long ago lost respect.

Burton scooted Christie away with a little smack to the rear end. She shuffled forward, stopped, and whipped around, her long, wavy hair flailing. A devilish gaze from her almond-shaped eyes, and then she turned back around and scuttled her heels backward, stopping a foot in front of him, where she put her hands on her knees and stuck her ass out.

Harder, Jake saw but couldn't hear her say.

Burton grinned back at her, smacked her ass again, giving it some oomph this time. The *crack* carried across the hall.

Christie sashayed from the room, throwing Burton a flavorful smile over her shoulder.

"It's here, buddy boys," Sylvester said in his nasal voice. "The chance we've been waiting for."

He paused, watching Christie as she slinked past him. His wet lips quivered, raccoon eyes going wider, twinkling. She smiled salaciously.

Sylvester cleared his throat, looked back to the others. "We're taking out the Rojas. Tonight. At 7. I have it on good authority that they'll be receiving a shipment of coke from their friends in South America. A shit ton of it, a full semi-truck full of Colombian white gold. They gambled their whole fortune, put all their eggs in one basket, so we're gonna catch them with their pants down at the drop point, intercept the shipment, finish 'em off once and for all, and get all that product as a nice little bonus."

He snort-laughed. His face glimmered with gleeful anticipation, like a sweaty-palmed child clutching a video game controller, about to conquer the level that had thwarted him for so long.

"The truck you're looking for will be a black semi with a green trailer. It'll have 'Garrison Power Tools' in white letters on the side. They're meeting in the parking lot of that abandoned high school on the west side—Wagner High. Burton has located the perfect intercept point for us."

He motioned to Burton, who gave a big, faux-bashful smirk and waved off the compliment. *Ah, jeez. You flatter me. It was nothing.*

"An alley between two of the old warehouse buildings," Sylvester continued. "Across the street from the school. Be there an hour ahead. We'll have them outnumbered and completely unaware. Do me a favor, buddy boys—make it bloody for ol' Sylvester, would ya?"

His gleeful smile quivered. Sweat glistened on his forehead.

Creep.

Murmurs from both sides of the great hall.

Everyone had known coming into this meeting that Sylvester's announcement would be consequential, but they hadn't known it would be *this* significant.

Jake's group slowly dispersed, heading for the doors, but Burton and his cronies resumed their revelry. Shouts and laughter. Clinking tumblers and beer glasses.

Jake looked through the window again, across the courtyard. He found C.C.'s eyes waiting for him.

And they still bore that look of concern.

CHAPTER SIX

MARVIN TANNER SLAPPED a hand against the wall of communications equipment in the back of the van, rocking the entire vehicle.

"Hell yeah!" he said. "We got 'em now! The Farones *and* the Rojas. Two for one."

Harrison, from his position seated behind a bank of small monitors and gauges and multiplex LCD number displays, scowled up at Tanner's hand, where it was planted next to a series of switches.

Harrison was a young guy, black like Tanner, though much lighter skinned, with wild, overgrown hair. He wore an enormous pair of glasses and a blue T-shirt with a logo that Tanner didn't recognize—some rock band, no doubt.

Tanner didn't care for Harrison, and, really, he didn't care for any of the tech guys. But they held a significant bargaining chip—their esoteric knowledge of specialized and entirely necessary equipment—and they weren't afraid of flexing that bit of power, as evidenced by the disdainful look Harrison was giving to Tanner's hand.

The insolent little shit.

Tanner removed the hand, but, not to be outdone, he moved it, along with his other hand, to the back of Harrison's seat.

Harrison inched away as Tanner leaned forward, getting closer to the round metal speaker cover that sat next to a row of dials.

"Can we clear up that interference?"

Harrison shook his head. "It's, um..." He paused, making a few tweaks to the dials. "It's rubbing against his shirt, I think. He's on the move."

Tanner looked at the black-and-white video monitor, the one directly linked to the tiny camera on the outside of the van.

The Farone mansion was an old-fashioned, stone-sided behemoth with lush green lawns. People leaving, going to the brick-paved driveway, walking toward the dozen or so cars parked around the fountain—old, worn-in vehicles that looked terribly out of place.

Tanner leaned back and turned to Agent Pace, the other man in the back of the van with him and Harrison.

Pace was a big guy, late thirties, with a square head and dark, parted hair. Tanner knew he was of Hispanic heritage, but if he hadn't known, he would have pegged Pace as a Native American.

"The Rojas are the principle rivals?" Pace said.

Tanner nodded. "For the last six years or so, yeah. Another lower-level gang like the Farones. Joey Farone was kicked out of New York decades ago when he couldn't cut it with the big boys. He just didn't have it in him to sever thumbs and break skulls. But since he fell into rapidly progressive dementia the last couple of years, the son runs the show, and he's just the opposite of his old man. Sylvester loves the bloody stuff, got a real penchant for torture.

"The Rojas just arrived a few years ago—a splinter of a

bigger outfit in Colombia. They get the heroin shipments from down south, cut it, package it, and ship it. And it's been cramping the Farones' style since they got here. They've collided more than once. The powder keg will be tonight."

Pace pointed to the monitor. "With your undercover man right in the middle of the explosion. Real nice, Tanner."

Tanner clenched his jaw. Damn fed. Pace's personality had begun to grate on Tanner's nerves within five minutes of meeting him, which made Tanner regret his decision to contact the FBI for a consultant.

"I'm pulling Rowe out. Tonight. Before the shit hits the fan," he said through his teeth.

Pace shrugged off his brown sport coat, folded it over his arm. "*If* we can get him out. He's too stuck on that girl."

"'That girl' is bringing down the Farone family."

"Maybe so, Lieutenant," Pace said. "Or maybe our guy's in too deep. Maybe Cecilia Farone is playing him. Don't see him leaving yet, do you?" He pointed at the monitor again.

Tanner looked.

The guy was right. Jake was not among those people leaving the mansion.

Pace shoved his hands in his pockets, jingled his keys. "And Rowe kills the feed every time he talks to her. Do you really trust him?"

The agent was awfully insistent, awfully pushy for someone who was little more than a glorified temporary assistant.

More insolence from a younger person.

Was there any respect left in the world?

Tanner stared him down. "You're a consultant on this case, Agent Pace. You've been here two weeks. You don't know Jake Rowe like I do." He narrowed his gaze. "You're damn right I trust him."

"Isn't the guy, like, a spaz or something?"

Now Tanner was really pissed. Few things bothered him more than gossip—particularly misguided, dangerous gossip about the people he cared about.

Tanner hadn't taken Jake under his wing simply because of his brilliant—if not tumultuous—mind, one that had *detective* written all over it. Jake was a good damn dude, too.

Jake, with his genuine smile. The gym-sculpted physique. His penchant for sharp duds. Unexpected tenacity and grit.

Tanner wasn't about to let some dirty fed just breeze in here and disparage the guy.

"He has some focus issues, but he passed his psych exam with flying colors, for your information. We all have our quirks, shithead."

Pace chuckled, not looking away. Nothing bothered the guy.

A staticky noise from the speaker. Then silence.

Pace snickered, shook his head. A *told-ya-so* grin came to his lips.

Harrison looked up at Tanner. "The feed died."

CHAPTER SEVEN

JAKE LOOKED DOWN at the small plastic slide switch on top of the device, his finger still resting on it. It sat to the left, the *OFF* position.

He sighed and put the device back in its spot at the front of his pants, beneath the elastic of his boxer briefs. He was in a small bathroom off the great hall, and he checked his reflection in the mirror as he straightened his shirt around the device.

This was going to piss Tanner off, his killing the audio feed. It always did. Jake's go-to retort was that *he* was the one putting his life on the line, that if Tanner wanted someone else to go undercover within a notorious crime family, someone who wouldn't turn off his listening device for occasional moments of brief privacy, then by all means, pull Jake out and bring in another guy.

Tanner had yet to bring someone else in.

Jake's undercover time was drawing to an end anyway. What did it matter now?

And Tanner trusted him. For some reason, the old fart

had seen something in Jake—an older recruit and someone with a background atypical to most new police officers—and put him on a fast-track to a detective slot. That's why Jake had initially taken this undercover assignment: building credentials at a lightning-fast pace.

Then the assignment ballooned into something bigger and more time-intensive than anyone had thought it would.

Now, Jake just needed to survive this meeting with the Rojas. The department would pull him from the undercover position, and he would take C.C. with him as he left the Farones. Then, no more future as a Pensacola detective. Hell, a future in Florida even seemed unlikely. Tanner's consultant, Agent Pace, was going to put him and C.C. in witness protection.

And then?

No clue. The future was opaque. Foggy.

And he liked it that way.

C.C.'s bohemian spirit was contagious, and he had embraced the idea of the unknown.

Jake shook his head at the thought as he regarded his reflection. The eyes looking back were emerald green, not his natural color.

One thing was for sure—he and C.C. would need to get out of Pensacola. The metropolitan area had a decent population, but it wasn't huge, and there was a small town vibe to the place. After months of being embedded in the Farones, the removal of his bright green contact lenses wouldn't be enough to avoid recognition from all the Farone-associated people in Pensacola.

He leaned closer to the mirror, examined the contact lenses.

Such a bright green. Damn bright. He couldn't wait to never wear them again.

His attention went lower.

The damn mole.

On the corner of his right jaw.

He ran a finger along it. While he disliked the contact lenses, he loathed the mole. Always had, especially as a kid.

It was another identifying feature the Farone family would not forget.

No, he wouldn't be coming back to Pensacola for a long time. If ever. Tanner would put a good word in for him at whatever police department he ended up at. Heck, maybe Jake would still be on the fast-track to detective.

Or maybe he wouldn't join another police department at all. Jake could begin a new career for his new life. Sure, why not? The only constancy he needed was C.C.

He examined his green-eyed reflection for a moment longer.

And left the bathroom.

———

Jake walked into the library and found C.C. arranging flowers in a vase, her back to him, and when she heard his footsteps, she stopped but didn't turn around.

He took her shoulders, and she rested her cheek against the back of his hand, still not turning.

"You bought me flowers," he said. "How sweet."

She finally faced him, rolled her eyes. There was a slight smile, but it couldn't overpower the concerned expression he'd seen from across the courtyard a few minutes earlier.

She wore a light gray sweater dress, long-sleeve with a V-neck opening, under which was a black shirt. The dress fell to her knees over a pair of green leggings. Ringed over her hips was a lime green belt with a rubbery shine. Green plastic bangle bracelets encircled one wrist.

Grays and greens, all nicely coordinated. She was outlandish but still stylish.

He studied the concern in her smile.

"You heard?"

She nodded.

Jake exhaled, looked to the ceiling. "A hit against the Rojas. *Tonight*. Unbelievable. This really screws with our plans of getting you out of here. Why did this have to happen right now?"

C.C. smiled at him. "Life doesn't happen to you, love. It happens for you. One's identity is forged by the way one meets life's challenges."

He could always count on C.C. for some sage philosophy, even at a moment like this.

"I don't want you to go," she said. "To the hit tonight."

"I know it's gonna be dangerous, but—"

"No, it's more than that." She looked away from him, balled a fist and squeezed it with her other hand. "I have a premonition."

Jake sighed. "C.C...."

C.C. had a lot of premonitions. And hunches. And suspicions. All of them fueled by the zodiac or the teachings of a long-dead philosopher or current trends in the field of metaphysics.

She stepped away, crossing her arms, and his fingers slid off her waist.

"I'm being serious." Her eyes remained downcast as she spoke, moving side to side, as though reading divinations on the floorboards. "Listen to me. There's a bad vibe tonight."

"Babe, I can't go off one of your intuitions. Tanner was listening. He heard all the details about the hit." He patted his belt line, a small clunk as his fingers hit the listening device. "They'll pull me out tonight. That was always the plan

—to use any big event like this as an excuse to get me out. When I call him, we'll make the arrangements, and—"

"It's Burton," she said, finally looking up.

Jake cocked his head. "What?"

"He's up to something. Something outside the family."

Jake shrugged. "Of course he is. I told you what happened in New Orleans. I also told you Burton's more dangerous after what happened there, and that you should leave the mansion. But that's beside the point." He narrowed his eyes at her for a moment. "Everyone knows Burton's trying to get leverage against the Farone-loyal contingent, so he—"

Her arms uncrossed, fists swinging to her sides. "You're not listening to me, Jake!"

Her eyes widened as soon as she said it. Her hands went to her mouth.

She'd used his real name.

Jake sucked in a breath. His heart hammered. He looked out the window, across the courtyard to the great hall. Burton, Glover, and McBride, the last members of their group remaining after the meeting—their backs were turned to the window, and they were in mid conversation.

He looked to the doorway a few feet away, the hallway beyond. Empty.

C.C.'s hands remained on her mouth. Her face had gone pallid, and her eyes were saucers.

"I'm sorry," she said through her fingers.

Jake exhaled and gave her an understanding nod.

She lowered one of her hands, brought the other to her lips, chewed a fingernail. "I'm telling you, it's something more. It started with one of my premonitions, yes, but I took action." She paused. "I followed him."

"Oh, god, C.C...."

"I was safe! I trailed him out to his beach house. There

were men waiting for him. A pair of brand-new Maseratis. Out-of-state plates. New Jersey."

Interesting.

The Farone family certainly had strong ties to the New York-New Jersey area, as the patriarch, Joseph Farone, had originally come from Manhattan, having a brief stay in New Orleans before ultimately ending up in Pensacola. But while Burton was a higher-up even before he formed the schism within the family, the Farones had never directly involved him in high-level matters.

So what were exotic vehicles from New Jersey doing at his place?

Jake didn't have time to ponder it. He needed to figure it out.

A quick glance through the window, and he saw Burton, Glover, and McBride laughing, paying them no attention. Still, Jake turned his back to the window for what he was about to do.

He reached into his pocket and took out his small note-book, a NedNotes brand PenPal. All cops needed a good notebook, but Jake hadn't warmed to the traditional, top-bound variety so many police officers used. At five by three and half inches, the small PenPal suited his needs perfectly. But just as importantly as the size was the fact that the spiral binding was on the side, and since PenPals were one hundred pages thick, the binding was large enough to hold a mechanical pencil. The front covers were durable plastic and came in a variety of colors. This one was canary yellow.

C.C. had encouraged him to use his notebooks in other capacities. She saw them as a tool he could use to help organize his often confused brain space. Her primary recommendation was mind mapping, a diagramming system used to organize concepts visually and hierarchically.

Jake flipped the PenPal to the first clean page. While

undercover, he wrote notes as infrequently as possible, and when he did, he used shorthand abbreviations that only he would understand. Just in case.

He took the mechanical pencil from the spiral binding and wrote: *NJ vhcs Bn*

The standard *NJ* for *New Jersey* and two of his own abbreviations for *vehicles* and *Burton*.

"I need to swing by Burton's," he said as he snapped the notebook shut and stuck the pencil back in the binding. When C.C. started to object, as he had moments earlier to her own Burton investigation, he added, "Hey, if you're gonna spy on him, I get to as well. I *am* the police officer here."

He flashed her a smile.

She wasn't amused.

She crossed her arms, pulling them in tight, as though to warm herself. "I'm telling you, there's something not right about what's happening tonight with the Rojas. I can feel it."

Her chest raised as she took in a breath. She released it and moved closer. Her hands went to his chest, eyes looking up at him. At six-foot-three and five-foot-three, there was a perfect foot of height difference between them.

"You asked me to sell out my entire family, to never see them again. Sylvester is a monster, a psychopath, and I'm glad to do my part to bring him down. But I'm doing it for you. So indulge my quirkiness and don't go to the hit tonight. Find an excuse. Say you ran out of gas. Say your aunt died. Something. Just tell me you won't go."

She had a point.

C.C. was giving up everything she'd ever known. And since Tanner was undoubtedly going to pull Jake from his cover tonight, there really no point in Jake putting himself in danger.

"I won't go," he said. "I *am* going to Burton's, but, okay, I won't go to the Roja hit."

She exhaled, face losing its tension.

"Thank you." Another deep breath. "I love you."

"I love you too."

"Promise?"

"Do I promise that I love you?"

"No. Promise me you won't go to the hit tonight."

He nodded. "I promise."

CHAPTER EIGHT

A NORMAL MAN would have been crumbling under the pressure right about now.

Lukas Burton, however, was not a normal man.

His plan was huge, its scope staggering. But before he could fully coordinate with his new business partners, he had to completely break free from the traditional vestiges of the Farone crime family. So far, he had seven loyal men.

He'd given the other people in the organization plenty of time to join him, to join the winning side.

And now their time was up.

Yet despite the pressure that was building, Burton was calm as a windless sea. More than calm. He was excited. While the Farone-loyal contingent had dispersed as soon as Sylvester had given the instructions, Burton and his men had remained in the great hall, finishing their drinks, laughing, telling loud jokes and slapping each other's shoulders for several more minutes before heading out.

McBride was the last of his troops—as Burton liked to call them—aside from Glover who was still there. He was a big Irish shit with a dirty red beard, lumpish body, and a tattoo on his right cheek, an inch away from his eye. After another rumbling laugh, McBride clamped a hand on Burton's shoulder—more tattoos on his knuckles—and lumbered away, enormous feet clomping on the hardwood.

This left only Glover and Burton.

Burton watched McBride walk off, and then his eyes traced across the living room to the window on the far wall that looked out onto the darkened courtyard. Through the leaves and branches and bushes, he could see another window, a warm glow in the darkness.

The library with its walls of books and leather furniture. And two figures—Pete "Loudmouth" Hudson and Cecilia Farone. Speaking to each other.

For the longest time, their relationship had been a poorly kept secret. They'd given up on that and now communicated freely and openly. Usually they were all laughs, smiles, playful flirtations. Tonight, though, their conversation appeared deadly serious. Burton watched the silent drama playing out before him—short, jerky movements, terse swipes of hands, punctuating their words, knitted brows. Burton had never seen them like this.

"Look at that, Glover. Trouble in paradise," Burton said without taking his gaze away from them.

Glover scoffed as he smoothed a strand of his dark blond hair back into its combed-back position. "Hippie bitch. Hot piece of ass, don't get me wrong, but could you imagine dealing with her? Hudson's an idiot for getting involved with that chick."

Burton felt a pulse in his forehead.

He turned on Glover. "*That's* why Hudson's an idiot? How about he's an idiot because he stole from me?"

Glover's lips parted. He cleared his throat. "What happened in New Orleans? Of course, but I mean ... he can be an idiot for multiple reasons, right?"

Burton glared at him for a moment. "And don't call Cecilia a bitch."

He turned back to the window. Hudson and Cecilia were hugging, a long deep embrace. All was forgiven. Then they parted, still facing each other, two hands interlaced, arms stretching out, a few final words. Then the fingertips broke their bind, and Hudson turned and walked out.

Burton walked off too.

"Where you going?" Glover said behind him.

"Shut up."

Around a sofa, through the center of the great hall, past the kitchen—where Sylvester was seated at the island and looked up from his wine with a goofy, wet-lipped smile and greeted Burton with a *Hey, buddy boy*, which Burton ignored—and to the dim, sconce-lined hallway that led to the foyer.

As Burton turned the corner, Hudson approached from the opposite direction.

Hudson slowed, ever so slightly and only for a moment, before continuing toward Burton, a pathetic attempt at posturing. Hudson was just that sort of guy, a man who thought too much of himself, a man whose posturing had landed him somewhere he never should have been.

Burton wasn't sure how Hudson had landed among the Farones, but this car thief had arrived only months earlier and done so with quite a splash, impressing both the old man and his psychotic son. And, of course, he'd ultimately impressed the daughter as well. The irony of it—the hair-yanking, anger-pulsing frustration of it—was that Hudson somehow managed to thrive while maintaining a frame of right-eousness.

Righteousness.

In a criminal organization.

Insane. Just absolutely absurd.

This was one of many reasons Burton was restructuring

the Farone crime syndicate: they recruited idiots like Pete Hudson.

He stepped into the hall, and Hudson continued in his direction, only slowing when they were a few feet apart. More of that unspoken pissing match.

They looked at each other.

What a big, goofy idiot. Hudson's *gee whiz* face was long with a prominent nose and bright green eyes. Olive skin, dark hair, and a defined but unassuming jawline—all of which gave him an everyman handsomeness that was surely the reason Cecilia had overlooked his dork persona.

"Taking off, Pete?"

"That's right."

"Well, you relax for a bit. It's gonna be a big night for us. I mean, taking down the Rojas? *Whew!*" He gave a little disbelieving shake of the head, a long exasperated sigh. And a slight malicious grin at the corner of his mouth.

Hudson saw right through it, stared back into him. Stone-faced.

Burton lessened the grin, maybe fifty percent, and let dark sincerity pour from his eyes. "You don't think I'm going to forget what you did to me in New Orleans, do you?"

Hudson didn't reply.

"You stole from me, Pete, so I'm going to steal something from you. When I do, I want you to remember something—everyone will be involved, and we'll take our time. Two things are going to happen. One will happen tonight; the other will happen down the line. A chance for me to reconnect with my roots, with Daddy. A real homecoming. Know what I mean?"

Hudson narrowed his eyes.

Good.

Burton had wanted his statement to be cryptic. It wasn't supposed to make sense.

Not yet.

The only disappointment was that Hudson didn't reply. Burton wanted a *What the hell does that mean?* He wanted to frustrate Hudson even more, to engorge his confusion to a mouthwatering level.

But Hudson just looked back at him for a moment longer, then stepped past, went to the door, and exited without looking back.

Burton watched him leave.

CHAPTER NINE

WAVES CRASHED on the sand that, in the daylight, was touted as "the world's whitest." Bathed in bright moonlight, it took on a cool gray hue.

Jake was far beyond the condo towers, in an area of beach houses, moving to the far end where the properties were more spread out and the houses larger, grander. A moist breeze blew off the water. Few people were out.

As he rounded a curve, Burton's house crept into view, an ultra-modern amalgamation of lines and right angles with an off-white facade and long stretches of glass. A grid of handrails traced the staggered balconies. There were two proper floors, and a third was built into the slope of the beach, fronted by a trio of concrete stilts and a zig-zag stair-case that descended from a sprawling porch on the floor above.

All those mammoth windows were dark. Nobody home.

Still, Jake needed to approach this situation very carefully.

He stopped walking and sat in the sand, brought his knees up and wrapped his arms around them, looked out to the waves, a typical nighttime beachgoer reflectively studying the sea. He felt the coolness of the sand on his butt through his chinos. He let a few moments pass then took a pair of compact binoculars from his pocket, looked to the waves and slowly, casually turned his gaze toward the beach, swinging the binoculars slightly upward until Burton's house appeared.

He wasn't sure what exactly he was looking for, but if C.C. was right about the vehicles she'd seen that could mean—

Jake brought the binoculars to a halt.

A busted-out glass door.

On the lowest level, beneath the overhang. A few jagged fangs of glass outlined the doorframe, but most of it lay in shards on the brickwork, leaving a huge open void into Burton's house, a space easily large enough to accommodate a grown adult.

He got up and strode as briskly as he could toward the house without breaking his character of the casual nighttime beachgoer.

Easing his trajectory away from the waves, he climbed up the grade toward the house. He took out his Colt, peered through the busted door from the far side of the concrete slab porch. Saw nothing. Just shadows and glimpses of Burton's high-end decor.

He ran along the side of the darkened house, up the hill, shoes sinking in the soft, unpacked sand, to the driveway. No out-of-state Maseratis. No vehicles at all.

Back down the embankment to the broken-out door. He avoided the shards of glass as he stepped inside, then halted, listened.

Nothing, just the crashing waves beyond.

Gun at the ready, he swept through the house, room by room, closet by closet, finding nothing.

He went to the office. As with the rest of the house, there were modern, chic touches—a lot of polished steel, a pair of abstract sculptures. A wall of windows looked upon the moonlit water, the waves.

He sat at the desk, flipped on the small desk lamp. The desktop was clean, organized, a stack of paper in the center. He picked it up, flipped through the pages, unimpressed. Nothing significant.

To the side was a cherry, two-tier letter tray. He grabbed a stack of envelopes, flipped past the first two.

And stopped.

The Personal Manifesto of Delbert Patterson,
or Musings on the Transmogrification of Societal Frustration

What the hell?
He began reading.

Societies rise, and societies fall. A natural order. Now, technological advances impede this earthly rhythm, and therefore it must also be technology—in the form of heavy armaments—that restore the order.

America refuses to come to a natural end. And so I, and others like me, will bring it to an end.

Jake had to stop for a moment. When he'd left the mansion, he'd expected to find something strange at Burton's, and that feeling had been amplified when he saw the broken glass door.

But an anarchist's manifesto...

Nothing could have prepared him for something like this. He continued to read.

This is not an exercise. This is not a warning. This is certainly not a cry for help. Soon, I will attack all means of American infrastructure that have not yet...

A sound behind him.

He turned in time to see someone lunging from the shadows, a quick glimpse of a silhouette in baggy jeans and a baseball cap. He threw up an arm, partially blocking the punch, but it struck him with enough force to send him into the desk, knocking the lamp to the floor.

The lightbulb popped, and the room snapped back into near darkness, just reflected moonlight coming in through the massive windows.

Jake rolled over the desktop and landed in a crouched position on the other side of the desk. He immediately went for his gun, but the man delivered a swift high kick, knocking it from his hand.

It clattered on the tile.

He looked up in time to see another kick already in motion and got a quick glimpse of the man's silhouette against the moonlight—he was about five-foot seven and tiny, his baggy-style jeans even baggier than their intended look.

The next high kick clipped the side of Jake's face as he tried to stand, sending him rolling across the floor toward the glass wall.

The man rushed in his direction. Jake stretched for a footstool on casters, a few feet away, and shoved it hard toward the guy.

It smashed into the man, bringing him to the floor.

Jake leapt forward, and the man immediately flung him away, using his own weight against him, some sort of grappling move Jake wasn't prepared for.

The man straddled him, got a hand around his throat, raised a fist...

And now, closer to the glass wall, in the moonlight, Jake saw who it was.

Christie Mosley.

"*Christie?*"

CHAPTER TEN

THE GARAGE WAS a massive stretch of subterranean concrete. Mottled twelve-foot walls surrounded a contrastingly smooth, traffic-polished floor that was marred by tire tracks and glistened with oblong patches of white shine from the fluorescent lighting. The damp air carried the scents of vehicle exhaust and rubber.

Behind Tanner was a line of SWAT trucks. He felt their massive, riveted, sharp-edged presence looming over him.

In front of him, seated in folding chairs interspersed among massive pillars and squad cars—which looked diminutive in their proximity to the SWAT trucks—were a dozen men in black tactical gear, sitting tall in their seats, facing him, awaiting his instruction.

Tanner adjusted an elbow pad. He wore the same gear as the others. His eyes moved over the faces looking at him. Most bore steely resolve, but several of them could hardly contain their excitement. Their muscles twitched, knees bounced. Satisfied smirks. Ready for action. The SWAT team didn't assemble often in a sleepy city like Pensacola.

As for Tanner, he'd long ago lost his taste for explosive

moments of violence. He couldn't wait to strip this armor off and get back into normal clothes. A pair of his pajamas would be nice. Yes, the red pair. He'd slip into those bad boys and climb into his warm bed with Martha.

But first he had to get Jake out of his undercover assignment. It had been a long time. Too damn long. The guy was a protégé, and Tanner couldn't help but feel like he'd treated him like a workhorse.

He knew the risks, Tanner reminded himself.

He scanned the faces in front of him again.

To get Jake out, he was going to have to sate the pugilistic desires of a bunch of adrenaline-and-testosterone freaks. He was surprised they could contain their energy enough to listen to him for five minutes.

He sighed.

Then he turned to the whiteboard behind him, which was covered with papers, diagrams, and maps—the plans for that night's operation.

"This is the man we bring in first," Tanner said and pointed to the 8x10 file photo. "Some of you know him. Jake Rowe. He's been undercover with the Farones for months, longest in PPD history. Study the face. Memorize it. He won't put up a fight. Cuff him. Protect him. Bring him in. He's done us all a great service. It's time to thank him for it."

CHAPTER ELEVEN

THE WOMAN CALLING herself Christie Mosley stared in disbelief at the person she'd just captured, the man lying on the floor beneath her, struggling, going red in the face, as she crushed the lower corners of his rib cage between her thighs.

She'd expected it to be one of Burton's "illustrious" visitors. Instead, it was possibly the last person she would have imagined.

It was Pete "Loudmouth" Hudson. And he was damn lucky she hadn't killed him.

Hudson's gaping mouth and wide eyes said that he was equally amazed that she was the person with whom he'd been struggling.

Which made sense.

An hour ago when he'd last seen her, she'd been in the slut dress and high heels, swaying her hips for the benefit of every man in the Farone mansion. Now she wore a pair of loose Levi's, an oversized linen shirt, and a black ball cap with her ponytail sticking out the back.

Plus, she'd kicked his ass. That was probably a shocker for him too.

When she'd slipped into the office, Hudson's back had been turned enough that she hadn't been able to see who it was. She'd watched as he searched the desk, finally grabbing a short stack of stapled paper from Burton's letter tray.

The document was Delbert Patterson's twisted manifesto. She knew this because she'd held it herself only minutes prior to Hudson, having centered the document on Burton's desk and taken a photograph of each page with a state-of-the-art camera—digital with an LCD screen on the back, small enough to fit in her pocket. It wasn't yet available to the civilian public, one of many such technological advantages her organization possessed.

The efficient way Hudson had cleared the house and his beeline for the desk had told her the guy was a pro. No doubt.

But what kind?

She lessened the pressure between her thighs, and Hudson sucked in a couple of deep breaths, the red color in his face receding.

Her fist remained in the air, wound-up and ready.

Pete Hudson was more than a mere car thief, this tall, cute, sheepishly charming "Loudmouth."

And she'd known it the whole time, from the moment he first appeared in the Farone syndicate several months back.

But she'd assumed he was some sort of con artist, a faker who wanted the good life but didn't have the credentials to back it up. He was charming, after all.

Clearly, her assumption had been a dangerous oversight.

Stupid!

She really pissed herself off sometimes.

Below, Hudson wiggled his sides, shaking out the tension. Even with her fist still raised above him, it was clear that he understood the confrontation was winding down.

He'd seen violence before.

A pro.

What the hell was this guy?

She could beat it out of him. That's what her quivering fist was telling her to do.

But that fire of hers was what had landed her in this life to begin with. It had taken her years, but she'd learned how to control it, when to defer to diplomacy. She couldn't stumble now. Not when she'd worked so hard for so long.

Not when she was so close to being finished.

Don't screw this up.

She slowly lowered her fist. Exhaled. And with one swift movement, she rolled off him and to her feet.

Hudson coughed and rubbed his sides. Bloodshot, wet eyes looked up at her. Then a tiny smile tugged at the corners of his mouth—a look of understanding.

In the same way that she recognized him as a professional, his expression said that he recognized the same quality in her.

He grimaced as he rubbed his ribs harder, but the smile remained. "So you're Burton's girlfriend *and* his watchdog."

The Loudmouth could be a coy little smartass when he wanted to. More of that charm of his.

"What the hell are you doing here, Hudson?" she said.

Hudson slowly climbed to his feet. More grimacing. More rib-rubbing. He pointed. "I saw the broken door. What are *you* doing here, creeping around in the dark with what looks like a break-in downstairs?"

She reached out suddenly, pulled up his shirt, revealing the small bulge she'd perceived, the tiny break in the line of his shirt.

A digital audio device, its square top peeking out the top of his underwear.

"I knew it. You're undercover. PPD?"

Hudson narrowed his eyes, still a hint of the bemused grin on his lips. A pause. And he nodded. He slowly reached into his shoe, keeping his other hand in the air for her benefit, and retrieved a badge.

"You got me," he said. "Now, tell me—why does the girl-friend of a smalltime criminal lieutenant know where to find a listening device on an undercover cop *and* have the hand-to-hand combat skills to incapacitate a man twice her size? Who are you?"

Double-speak. And that grin, which became a bit more serious.

I gave you something. Now give me something, he was saying.

Undercurrents of diplomacy in a standoff between two competent forces, unacquainted but aware.

Should she, or shouldn't she?

A half moment passed, then the warring thoughts in her mind reached a compromise: she'd give Hudson a creative bit of semi-truth.

"I'm undercover too," she said.

"No shit. What precinct?"

"I'm not with PPD."

"Escambia County?"

She shook her head.

"Wait a minute!" Hudson said, pointing a finger. "There's a manifesto from some goddamn lunatic on Burton's desk ... You're FBI, aren't you? You're here to—"

"Burton isn't just trying to take over the Farone crime family," she said.

It was time to give the guy a bit more. He knew too much now to keep him completely in the dark. She'd bring him into the mix, allow him to think she was FBI.

"There's a lot more to it, Hudson, and ... Wait. What's your actual name?"

Hudson's mouth twisted to the side, and a moment passed before he replied.

"Rowe. Jake Rowe. PPD narcotics. Who are you?"

"You can continue to know me as Christie Mosley."

Rowe opened his mouth wide in feigned offense. "Well, that's not fair. Give a little, get a little."

She didn't break a smile, but she couldn't help but warm to his disarming, unassuming quality, which paired well with his humble good looks and tall, broad-shouldered body.

No wonder the Farone chick had gone gaga over him.

"Burton's been using the Farone counterfeiting presses to fund some really bad dudes," she said, "like the one who wrote that manifesto. That's why I'm ... um, undercover."

Rowe reached into his pocket and took out a small notebook. It had a bright yellow plastic cover with white lettering that labeled it as a *PenPal*.

She snorted. "You're taking notes?"

He popped a pencil from the spiral binding and started writing. "Trust me. I need to."

"Do you just carry that thing around with you?"

He didn't look up. "Continue, please."

"Nine months ago a guy named Keith Sutton tried to use counterfeit bills to buy a shitload of weapons in Boston. Caught in the act. Escaped police. A couple of days later, on a different side of the country, here in Pensacola, of all places, he was found dead—two bullet holes in his chest and weighted ropes around his ankles. Someone tried to sink him in the bay, but ol' Sutton was more buoyant than they'd counted on. Since the Farone crime syndicate is known for counterfeiting, a connection to the Farones was obvious."

Rowe scribbled away. "Why the Farones? There's gotta be plenty of decent counterfeiters up north."

"It's more complicated than just counterfeit bills. That's why I staged the break-in tonight. There's also..." She trailed off. She was giving him too much. A moment of consideration, and she pivoted. "Just understand that everything is tied to Burton."

Rowe studied her, wanting the extra info she wasn't sharing. She could see him weighing his options. Finally he said, "And all of this relates to tonight's hit on the Rojas?"

"In a manner of speaking. Burton told me tonight's the night he's taking over the Farone family."

Rowe's pencil came to a sudden stop. He looked away.

The guy's long undercover investigation had surely consumed him—his time, his energy, his mental health—and the deep lines on his forehead said that the information she'd just shared had hit him hard.

He'd been at this for several months.

That was a hell of a long time to be undercover.

She should know.

"Which means you need to be especially careful tonight," she said. Rowe's attention returned to her. "And we need to figure out all we can."

"We?"

"You and me. We're a team now."

Rowe shook his head. "I'm not going."

"Come again?"

"I'm not going to the Roja hit tonight. I promised C.C."

She forced something resembling a smile onto her face. "C.C.? Cecilia, you mean?"

Rowe nodded. "My lieutenant planned to pull me out in the event of something like this, to 'arrest' me at the next big hit. I was getting out tonight anyway. C.C. has a bad feeling about the Roja hit; I promised her I wouldn't go."

She could no longer muster a mediating smile.

"Listen, Rowe, you *are* going tonight." She glared at him. "This is much more important than a promise to your little girlfriend."

She paused and again weighed how much she should tell him. She went with her gut instinct.

"Burton has something else in mind, something even

bigger than funding anarchists. This past week, he's been telling me about a bigger vision of his, an idea of using other Farone family resources to get into activities more lucrative than printing fake money."

"What resources are those?"

She shrugged. "That's what *we're* gonna find out, teammate."

She turned and headed for the door.

Without looking back, she said, "Now, come on. We gotta get you back into town."

CHAPTER TWELVE

AN HOUR LATER, Jake was back in Charlie's musty old Taurus. Charlie guided the car to a stop behind the other parked vehicles, then gave a quick flash of his brights before extinguishing the headlights entirely.

The car in front of them flashed its brake lights.

A moment later, so too did another car farther up the alley.

Three vehicles in position, and they'd acknowledged each other, a three-car train idling in a dark alley with Charlie's Taurus as the caboose.

The two-story brick walls loomed high on either side, only a few feet away, marred by mildew and fissures. The broken windows were dusty and dark. Lighting was scant and came from a single fixture above a utility door, left on undoubtedly to curb off intruders, though the patches of graffiti said the tactic hadn't been entirely effective.

The bluish light from this simple security precaution was in contrast to the street beyond, which glowed a faint yellow-orange. Past the street was the wide-open parking lot where the Rojas' truck was to arrive. A beat-up chain-link fence surrounded the lot, and in the distance was the abandoned school, a sprawling two-story brick building, completely dark and overgrown with untended plant life.

Jake took his cellular phone from his pocket, illuminated the green-colored screen to check the time: 6:27.

He pressed the 1 button and held it for a moment. Speed-dial.

Charlie leaned over. "Who ya calling?"

"C.C."

Soon Jake would need to call Tanner, let him know he was in position. But first he was going to come clean to C.C., tell her he'd broken his promise, that he'd had no choice but to break it, that he'd come to the Roja hit.

Charlie chuckled. "Not even married yet, and she's already got you checking in with her. Man, you're whipped. *Wah-PSSH!*"

Jake shook his head and held the phone to his ear.

CHAPTER THIRTEEN

BURTON APPROACHED the backside of Wagner High School—two stories of brick with a grand, tiered entryway, all of it eaten by ivy and surrounded by unsightly bushes and crape myrtles and a few wretched palms. Tangles of weeds crawled out of the deep crevices in the sidewalk.

He trotted up the three limestone steps to the main entrance, which had been covered by a section of chain-link. Someone had cut a gap through the fence large enough for a grown man to fit through, and evidently this had been done some time ago, as the cuts in the wire were as rusted over as the rest of the fencing.

Burton slipped through the hole and tested the door handle. Unlocked. Just as he was told it would be.

Inside, the hallway was a long tunnel of cracked flooring and dangling ceiling tiles, bounded by battered lockers. None of the light fixtures were operating, of course, but there was plenty of ambient city light to illuminate his path.

At one time, this had been a magnificent place. The quality of the workmanship and materials was apparent even as it decayed from existence. Burton imagined teenagers in

1950s garb roaming the hallway, smiling big 1950s smiles, smart kids on their way to futures as doctors and lawyers and engineers.

The public had complained when the powers-that-be boarded up this grand old place. *How can you shut down such a beautiful building? It has so much history. Do we* really *need a new school?*

People with that mindset were being left behind in the emerging world, dying off as much as the twentieth century itself. People like that were the reason people like Burton were prospering. Change was inevitable. And inevitabilities were profitable.

At the back staircase, he took the handrail and climbed the granite steps, which were smooth and scalloped from decades of foot traffic. The tapping of his shoes echoed off the walls as more phantom 1950s kids funneled around him, late for class. He could almost hear the ghost of a bell.

The second floor hallway was as dilapidated as the first. No lockers on this floor, just classrooms. Some doors were closed, some open, some hanging from their hinges, some missing entirely. Burton headed to his designated location, one of the empty doorframes.

As he turned the corner, he saw the man he was to meet, at the opposite side of the room, past a vista of ruined, upturned desks. The man was a silhouette by the windows, his back turned to Burton.

Burton stopped at the doorway and gave the man a warm greeting.

"Good evening, Mr. Roja."

CHAPTER FOURTEEN

IN THE BRIEF pause before the phone attempted to connect, Jake looked past the other two cars, across the abandoned parking lot to Wagner High School, a stately, two-story classic. When Jake had first moved to Pensacola as a kid, the school was still operational—past its prime but still magnificent. Since then, time and neglect had done their parts, eroding its austere character.

Instead of dialing, the phone gave a busy signal.

BEEP, BEEP, BEEP...

Jake frowned.

The Farone mansion had several phone lines, and the one he'd dialed was C.C.'s personal line, which rang in her bedroom and the library. She rarely used the line—as she rarely spoke on the phone—and she didn't own a cellular.

He pressed *END*.

"What's the matter?" Charlie said.

Jake shook his head.

A tickle of guilt wriggled in Jake's gut. He could have called C.C. before he left Burton's beach house, but he purposefully hadn't. He'd thought that if he called her from the Roja hit, explained that he'd *had* to go, the immediacy of the situation would make her less likely to be upset.

That had been cowardly of him.

He entered another number, Saunders's, which rang in the butler's pantry.

An immediate busy signal.

BEEP, BEEP, BEEP...

Another number, one that rang in the great hall and kitchen.

BEEP, BEEP, BEEP...

All the lines busy at once. That could mean only one thing: some sort of technical issue. A fallen tree lying over a cable, perhaps, or a vehicular collision with a telephone pole.

Of all the freaking times for this to happen...

That guilt he'd tasted a moment earlier compounded. Now he wouldn't be able to contact C.C. until after the hit he'd promised her he wouldn't attend.

He exhaled, let his head drop back to the headrest.

He couldn't let that worry him right now. There was a task at hand, something much more immediate.

C.C. was always trying to help him organize his chaotic mind space, and she told him that one thing he needed to do was focus on one task at a time. Multitasking, she'd told him, was highly overrated.

Focus.

The phone was still in his hand, and there was another phone call he needed to make, the one to Tanner.

This call would finalize Jake's decision, would alert his superior that he was ready to be pulled from the operation he'd been working on for months. It would solidify his lie to C.C.

Here we go.

He entered the number.

And pressed *SEND*.

CHAPTER FIFTEEN

TANNER ADJUSTED HIS HELMET, and as he did, he could feel sweat on his scalp. A drop slipped out of his hair, over his forehead, around his eye. The elbow pads, too, were frustrating him, and he adjusted them simultaneously by grinding them into the armrests on either side of his seat.

The interior of the SWAT vehicle was as squarish and bolted as the exterior. The passenger seat where Tanner sat was a series of stitched-together blocks of hard-as-rock cushions. The dash in front of him was a long plane of plastic and metal. The ceiling was riveted rectangles.

The truck sat in the darkness beneath the I-110 overpass. The city beyond was quiet—an empty and forgotten area, with a deserted high school and its equally deserted parking lot to the right and an abandoned pair of two-story brick industrial buildings to the left. No people and no traffic, aside from that rumbling on the interstate highway overhead. A plastic bag fluttered by, urban tumbleweed.

"Eyes peeled, boys," Tanner said. "We're looking for a black semi with a green trailer, 'Garrison Power Tools' in plain, block letters across the side."

He hadn't turned when he'd said it. Aside from the driver to his left, there were four SWAT-gear-clad guys in the bench seats in the back. They were all looking to him for leadership, but he could feel one particular pair of eyes staring at him—those coming from the first position on the bench right behind him.

Dammit.

He turned around, found Pace looking at him. With that smug grin. Even with the strap of his helmet secured tightly around his jaw, Pace's face had a strong yet irksome quality.

"Now or never, huh?" Pace said.

Tanner's eyes lingered on the self-satisfied son of a bitch for a moment, but before he could reply, his cellular phone rang.

The green-colored screen showed: *850-555-8913*.

He immediately pressed *END* to terminate the incoming call, then turned back to Pace. "That was Rowe. He's in position."

He moved his thumb to the green rubber *SEND* button and left it there, hovering a quarter inch above, ready. As he looked down, he saw that the thumb was shaking.

Pace noticed too. His eyes flicked to the phone then back to Tanner, his cocky mug growing a bit cockier.

"Rowe called us, and now you're gonna call him when we see the truck," Pace said. "Then we 'arrest' him."

"That's right. He'll stick to the back, as far away from the others as possible, and we'll cut in before the Farone men can reach the Roja shipment."

Pace shook his grinning head. "Why now? Why'd you wait so long? His girl is gonna give us everything we need to put away her brother and the rest of the Farones. You coulda gotten Rowe out of there weeks ago."

Tanner was starting to understand why the FBI had chosen Pace as the consultant for this assignment. When

Tanner had made the request, he'd assumed the Bureau would send someone from the local Pensacola office or possibly one of the nearby field offices in New Orleans or Atlanta. But Pace had come all the way from Kansas City. Though annoying, the guy was perceptive, and he saw things for what they were. He asked the right questions.

"For the Rojas, that's why," Tanner said. "Our two-for-one. There had been word that something like this was going to happen with the Farones' rivals. Jake got us to this point where we can dismantle both gangs at once."

Pace shrugged. "I don't know, Lieutenant. Seems like you've left the guy out to dry. You said we're gonna cut in before the Farone men can reach the truck, but if you're so sure this operation is safe, why'd you put us in this shit?" He tapped his black armored vest. "Seems to me you're using Rowe as bait."

Tanner shot him a look. "Rowe coordinated all of this. He's a damn hero." He paused. "And he knew the risks."

CHAPTER SIXTEEN

BURTON TOOK a step into the rotting room, and two figures swept out of the darkness from either side of the doorway. Suited behemoths, shaved heads, one with a goatee, both towering over Burton.

He came to a stop, unalarmed. He'd known the men would be there, so he slowly lifted his arms as they patted him top to bottom. When they found him clean, one of them waved him on, and he crunched through the debris to the man at the windows.

Roja didn't turn to face him, just continued to look through the grimy glass to the outside world below. A fraction of a smile played at the corner of his lips.

He was a short, stocky man, whose overall presence reminded Burton a bit of Glover, though Roja's stoutness was of a softer variety—round cheeks with a burly beard and thick, doughy forearms. He wore a dark canvas jacket and oversized jeans with pockets that drooped beneath his ass cheeks. The baggy clothing further squashed his proportions.

Beyond the window lay the decrepit, poorly lit parking lot, then the street, then the alley—a narrow, single-car-width path that led between two darkened industrial buildings. A trio of cars sat in the alley.

Burton knew the vehicles well. He knew who owned each of them. And he knew that there were people in each of the vehicles, despite the fact that none of the vehicles' lights were on.

"That's all the Farone faithful, funneled right where I promised." Burton said. "Satisfied?"

Roja finally turned to him. "Elated."

He waved a hand without taking his eyes off Burton. One of the suited men approached, handed Burton a metal briefcase.

Burton popped it open. Stacks of cash. A quick visual approximation told him Roja had kept his end of the bargain. He wouldn't count it. Not yet. He was showing Roja that he trusted him. It was another real-world lesson in diplomacy. *International* diplomacy. Something Burton was going to need to utilize frequently in the near future.

Roja's smile grew wider, but there was a dark flash of speculation across his eyes. "My empty truck arrives; the Farone men make their move; my men mow them down; and then you and I have a newfound agreement, all the old strife forgotten."

"Entirely forgotten, Mr. Roja," Burton said. "In fact, it'll be dead and buried. Your beef was with the Farone family. After tonight, you'll be dealing with a new group: the Burton gang."

Very diplomatic. More real-world experience.

Roja nodded his approval, hesitancy fading from his eyes, grin remaining. He returned his attention to the window.

And Burton headed for the door.

Roja turned. "Aren't you going to stay for the fireworks?"

"I'm afraid I can't," Burton said. "I have a family matter to attend to."

CHAPTER SEVENTEEN

THE ALLEY WAS UNNATURALLY QUIET. The air was still, lifeless, and humidity had made it palpably thick. Time seemed to have slowed.

And there was a situation.

Jake leaned forward in his seat, looked outside. In front of Charlie's Taurus were the two other cars that had been there when they arrived. None of the other cars had shown up.

He grabbed his cellular phone, which he'd placed in the cup holder clipped to the dash, one of those cheap, plastic, aftermarket jobs. He pressed the button on the top of the phone, and the LCD screen illuminated pale green, displaying the time as 6:22.

The springs in the driver-side seat squeaked as Charlie turned in his direction. "What's the matter, Pete?"

Jake hadn't realized he was frowning at the phone, but Charlie had perceived his tension. Like Jake, Charlie was good at reading people.

"Only half an hour to go," Jake said and pointed through the windshield. "In these three cars we've got all the Farone faithful. But none of Burton's men have shown up."

Charlie gave a small, wobbling smile. "Well, there's still time." He glanced outside, to the left, to the right, back to the left. His long bangs swung with his quick movements. "There's plenty of time, don't ya think?" A nervous chuckle.

Jake peered out his window, leaning down so that he could look up the side of the wall, its red bricks glistening with moisture, its windows darkened.

"Yeah," Jake said quietly. "There's still time."

CHAPTER EIGHTEEN

BURTON RAPPED a knuckle on the doorframe of the office, which was nestled in the far corner of the Farone mansion, another room of deep brown wood, from the coffered ceiling to the polished floor. A massive desk sat in the center of the room atop a sprawling rug.

Sylvester looked up from his position seated behind the desk.

And there it was—that goofy-ass smile of his.

It had a simple purity that was off-putting when you knew the sort of demented things the man enjoyed. Always smiling. You never knew whether the guy was pondering pinball—a hobby he adored—or surreptitiously jacking himself off to the memory of a man's screams of agony.

Freak.

Because of his slithering qualities and his sinister nature, Sylvester had often been labeled a snake. But to Burton, he was a salamander. A long, thin body with spindly appendages. Jerky head movements. Wide eyes and thick, smacking lips. And unlike a snake, which was dry, Sylvester always looked moist. Slimy.

The salamander slithered up from the tall, plush leather chair and waved Burton in with a wet smile.

As Burton entered the room, he took off his jacket, laid it across the tufted chair opposite the desk, and rolled up his shirt sleeves.

Sylvester stood and went to the front of the desk, where he met Burton with a handshake.

"Burton. What brings you by, buddy boy?" He glanced at the clock behind the desk. "There's not much time left before you need to be at Wagner."

"I came to bury the hatchet."

Sylvester rubbed his chin "How do you mean?"

"It's no secret that your daddy has been a father figure to me. So it would only make sense why there are rumors that I'm planning on taking over the family."

Sylvester smiled wider, waved it off, put a hand on Burton's shoulder. "Burton, I—"

Burton reached into his back pocket. "And I want you to know that the rumors are true." He pulled a small knife from its leather sheath and plunged it into Sylvester's chest.

A screeching wheeze. Sylvester's eyes went wide.

"Every word of the rumors is true."

A few sputtering, bloody shrieks.

"Not so much burying a hatchet as burying a knife, I suppose."

Gurgling. Wide eyes.

"Is this gruesome enough for you, 'buddy boy?'" Burton said, pressing harder against the knife. Sylvester gasped. "Are you liking this, you goddamn freak?"

A jolt, and Sylvester's body stiffened. Then went limp. And collapsed in Burton's arms.

Burton lowered Sylvester into the chair. Salamander arms splayed. Back at an angle, slouching. Eyes and mouth open. A smear of blood on his chest.

As Burton tugged on the knife, it suctioned into Sylvester's side. He had to give it two tugs to get it out.

His hand bore a sticky, glistening red glove. The knife, too, was entirely coated in blood, hardly even cleanable.

Screw it. Not worth the energy.

He dropped the knife in the trash can by the desk, then used his clean hand to take the sheath from his pocket and dropped it in the can as well.

He went to the office's tiny half-bath and washed up in the antique porcelain sink. As he lathered off Sylvester's blood, he watched his reflection. His lips wanted to smile, wanted to relish the victory, and he obliged them a bit by allowing the corners of his mouth to rise slightly.

It was a big step, killing Sylvester, both in terms of his overall plan but also for personal reasons. He'd just eliminated Joey Farone's biological son. That brought Burton another rung up the ladder of the old man's good graces. But there was another son—the surrogate son—still higher on the ladder than Burton.

Burton blinked. And came back to himself.

The water rushing over his fingers. His reflected face. The peak of his forehead glistening with a tiny sheen of perspiration.

He couldn't relish the victory for long. And he certainly couldn't dwell on the emotional aspect. Much remained to be done that night. On both fronts. Business and personal.

He turned the faucet off, dried his hands, rolled down his sleeves, re-buttoned them.

Back into the office, to the far side of the room where he retrieved his jacket and put it on.

No, tonight's fun wasn't over yet. Not even close. He needed to meet with his troops for a moment, then continue to the next step.

He gave his jacket a sharp tug, then reached into each sleeve and pinched the cuffs, pulled them out into view.

A final brush to the front of his jacket. Satisfied, he left the office.

———

Burton rounded the corner and entered the library.

Cecilia immediately looked up at him from her reclined position on a small sofa. A steaming cup of tea sat on the table beside her. She frowned. Her knees went to her chest. She closed the book she'd been reading, pinching a finger between the pages.

Burton gave her a warm smile. "Whatcha reading, Cecilia?"

She eyed him cautiously. "It's about accelerationism, the dangers thereof. Technological, social, political."

Burton stepped closer, smiled broader. "Acceleration? You're speaking my language. I'm always looking for the next best thing, another opportunity for progress."

"I've heard that about you, yeah." Her eyes followed him.

"That's why I've come to talk to you. You know, C.C...." He stopped. "May I call you C.C.? That's what your little cupcake calls you, isn't it? I'm gonna call you C.C. You know, C.C., your pop is like the father I never had. But it only occurred to me recently that if Joey Farone is my father, that makes you and Sylvester my siblings. That's what I'm doing tonight—letting my siblings know how very much they mean to me. I just showed Sylvester, *buddy boy*, how much I care. Now it's your turn."

Cecilia stood, slowly placed the book on the table next to the cup of tea. "What is this?"

Burton continued toward her. "Now, we all know about

you and Pete Hudson. Everyone does. Even your senile old man recognizes it. And I don't think I need to tell you that your dad now favors Pete to me, even after all the years I've been with the family. But, I digress. This isn't about me and your dad. It's about you and me."

He stepped closer.

Cecilia backed away. "Stay where you are, Lukas."

He didn't comply, continued forward.

Eyes on him, she reached down to the table, avoiding the tea, finding the phone. She lifted the receiver to her ear.

And her face turned pallid.

Lips, eyes opening wider.

"Oh, need to make a call, Cecilia? C.C.? Sis?" Burton said affably. "I guess you haven't heard. For some darn reason the phone lines stopped working half an hour ago. Almost like someone cut them."

Cecilia shuddered. She turned around, heading for the door in the back. But she stopped in her tracks.

Glover stepped into the doorway. Approached her slowly. Shit-eating grin on his face.

Cecilia looked between Glover and Burton as they closed in. They were within six feet of her on either side.

She backed to the side, to the sofa, and grabbed the mug of tea off the table, both hands. With a quick jerk, she flung the contents into Glover's face.

In the split second before Glover's hands went to his eyes, Burton saw a cloud of steam erupt over his head. His skin instantly pinked. That shit must have been scalding hot.

Glover bent in two, hands covering his face, water dripping off his fingers. He screamed.

Burton laughed.

Cecilia ran past Glover, to the doorway where he'd entered.

But Burton didn't budge. Just watched.

Cecilia made it to the doorway and halted, her shoes screeching on the hardwood, arms flying up.

Two figures casually stepped around either side of the doorway, blocking her path. A white pretty boy with long brown hair and a black pretty boy with big eyes and a square jaw. Cobb and Knox. They slowly entered the room.

Cecilia backpedaled, nearly losing her balance. She looked over her shoulder, eyes meeting Burton's for a moment.

Burton heard several more sets of footsteps enter from the doorway behind him, the one through which he'd entered. He didn't turn around.

The men appeared on either side of him, his other troops. Gamble, Hodges, McBride, and Odom.

A video camera mounted on a tripod was in McBride's fat Irish hands. He went to the back corner of the room, began setting it up.

Cecilia's eyes met Burton's again.

"I talked to Pete before he left," Burton said. "Told him I was going to take my time."

"*Sylvester!*"

"Your brother can't hear you."

Cecila's mouth gaped in silent disbelief, gathering Burton's implication, one that made tears form in her eyes.

Finally.

He'd been waiting on the waterworks, surprised that they hadn't formed yet. This hippie was gonna be harder to break than he'd thought.

The troops circled the room, putting on leather gloves, interlacing their fingers to tighten the fits. Odom took a blackjack baton from his pocket.

Cecilia cupped her hand over her mouth. "Saunders!"

Burton tsked. "I'm afraid I sent Saunders on an errand. Won't be back for at least an hour, probably two."

The troops closed in on her. She stepped back, her calf smacking into the table, hands quivering.

Burton looked over his shoulder to McBride, in the corner with the camcorder.

"Roll camera," Burton said.

CHAPTER NINETEEN

JAKE CHECKED the time on his cellular phone again.

6:57.

In front of him were the same two cars.

Behind, the alley was open.

Charlie leaned across the center console and looked at the screen on Jake's cellular. "Three minutes to go, and still none of Burton's men."

For several minutes Charlie had prodded himself along with forced enthusiasm, nervous laughs. Now, his brow was knitted. His intertwined fingers skittered over themselves, looking through the rear window, the windshield, back to the rear window, then the windshield again.

Jake took a breath. Held it. Released. C.C. had taught him breathing techniques, ways of centering when he felt the tingle of tension coursing through him, when his heartbeat was unpleasant, almost painful.

He felt the breath at his center, what C.C. called his "core."

Released it.

Then he looked out the window to the brick wall beside him as he'd been doing every thirty seconds.

This time he noticed something new.

A figure.

Just visible in the darkness of a window.

His eyes flicked to the side, the next window over.

Another figure, this one holding a rifle.

His heart jackhammered.

And an immediate realization came to him.

"Burton..."

"What?" Charlie said.

Jake turned on him. "We gotta get the hell out of here. This is an ambush!"

"*What?*"

"There are snipers in these buildings, Charlie! Burton set us up."

Charlie looked out his window, squinted. "I don't see nobody."

The cellular phone rang. The number on the screen was Tanner's.

Jake pushed the *END* button—the termination of the call was the agreed-upon signal that the message was received.

"*Shit!*" he said. "The truck's nearly here."

Charlie leaned over the steering wheel, looked through the windshield, squinting. "What are you on about, Pete? The truck's not here yet."

Jake's mind flashed on what Burton had said.

You stole from me, so I'm going to steal something from you.

Then Jake's heart pounded harder as he remembered the next part of Burton's statement, the ominously cryptic part.

When I do, I want you to remember something—everyone will be involved, and we'll take our time.

"Back out of the alley!" Jake shouted.

Charlie's face drooped, his eyes going sad in that childlike manner of his. "Pete ... man, are you going chicken?"

"Charlie, goddamnit, we're sitting ducks! *Go!*"

"But..."

Jake pulled his gun, pointed it at Charlie. "I'm a cop! Go! *Now!*"

Charlie's face sank even lower. "You're a ... a cop, Pete?"

Something in Jake's periphery. He turned. Ahead of them, beyond the other two cars, a tractor trailer pulled into the abandoned school parking lot. Fast. It came to an abrupt halt that smoked the tires and made a *screech* that sounded all the way across the parking lot, echoing off the walls of the alley.

The truck was black. The trailer was green with *GARRISON POWER TOOLS* emblazoned down the side in tall, white block letters.

In the alley, doors flew open on each of the two cars ahead, and the Farone men poured out, guns in hand, darting for the parking lot.

Instantly, the alley erupted with gunfire. Flashes from the upper floors of the buildings on either side. *CRACKS* reverberating off the walls.

Two of the men were struck and collapsed to the ground. The others returned fire to the windows as they dove back into the relative safety of their cars.

"*Back out!*" Jake screamed.

Charlie, panicked now, grabbed the shift knob.

A bullet tore through the windshield.

Charlie's head fell back to the seat. Eyes open. A line of blood snaked from his forehead to his nose.

CHAPTER TWENTY

TANNER GRABBED the armrest on the door as the SWAT truck clipped the corner of a curb, and a jolt of energy struck him like an electric shock. He lifted out of his seat.

The truck flew toward the alley on the opposite side of the street that fronted the abandoned school parking lot.

Flashes of muzzle flare lit the alley. The *CRACKS* carried over the distance, audible even through the thick construction of the armored truck. Shots came from the second-floor and from the trio of cars below, a firefight, an ambush with the poor souls in the cars pinned in a crossfire.

Tanner looked to the mirror bolted on the outside of his door.

Behind, a second SWAT vehicle swerved to the right, going for the semi-truck parked in the center of the otherwise abandoned school parking lot.

THWACK!

A round glanced off the roof of the truck. Shouts from the men in the bench seats in the back.

Ahead, the flashes of gunshots ceased. Both groups of men—those in the buildings and those trapped in the vehicles—were criminals and sensed the threat of the oncoming police raid.

Hispanic men flooded from the buildings' exits, three from each side, all with firearms, some taking potshots at the SWAT truck and the men in the cars. One man held a MAC-10 at waist height, clutching its long suppressor to stabilize the weapon. He sprayed a burst of rounds into the first Farone vehicle. The windshield exploded, shattering into a crystalline latticework, and blood splattered it from the inside.

With the front vehicle immobilized, the middle car was pinned and the only operational vehicle was an old Ford Taurus at the rear. A man was motionless behind the steering wheel, mouth open, a rivulet of blood running down his face from a hole in his forehead.

And beside him, crouched low beneath the dash, was Jake.

The SWAT truck came to a screeching halt. Tanner threw the door open, exited, took cover behind the door, both hands on his weapon.

SWAT team members flooded out of the back of the vehicle and stormed the alley in a single-file line, a snake. The situation they were running into was a logistical shitshow, and tactics quickly devolved into chaos.

Shouted commands. A flurry of arrests, men thrown to the ground, both Rojas and Farones. Others slipped away into the night, cops in pursuit.

Tanner proceeded along the wall. Pace appeared behind him, nodded.

The gunshots subsided. The firefight was quickly dying off. Scumbags had a tendency to run when the cops showed up. Go figure.

Tanner and Pace inched toward the corner of the building, and Tanner squinted through the smoke and debris at his objective—the Taurus in the back.

There was Jake.

Sprawled across the center console, trying to free the dead driver from his seatbelt.

Tanner turned to Pace. "There he is. Let's get our man outta here."

They advanced toward the car, weapons aimed.

"*Freeze, Hudson!*" Tanner shouted.

Jake looked up, spotted them.

He made eye contact with Tanner.

And he shook his head.

There was something serious in Jake's eyes, even more serious than the situation surrounding them. Tanner knew him well enough to know that something was wrong.

Something was about to happen.

He wasn't going to let them take him in.

Jake continued to shake his head, and he shouted, "No!" though Tanner couldn't hear it.

Pace turned to Tanner. "What the hell is Rowe doing?"

CRACK!

A piercing sound. Debris fell on Tanner's head, bouncing off his helmet.

The shot had come from the second floor of the far building. A remaining Roja man, one who hadn't fled like the others. He held a Ruger AC556 Carbine—a nasty piece of work, a full-auto hell-bringer.

The Rojas had come fully prepared to slaughter the Farones.

After pushing Tanner and Pace back, the Roja man swung the rifle to his left.

Bringing it in line with the Taurus at the back of the alley.

CHAPTER TWENTY-ONE

JAKE FUMBLED with Charlie's body as he tried to push it out of the car. He periodically ducked beneath the dash as bullets punched through the sheet metal. Glances out the windshield showed Tanner and the FBI agent, Pace, approaching fast, guns drawn.

Another glance. Tanner was screaming.

Jake gave Charlie's body another tug. It wouldn't move. One of Charlie's dead hands clenched the steering wheel.

He grabbed Charlie's wrist, pulled.

A bullet struck the door, shattering the window.

Jake crouched again as glass rained down.

He glanced up.

Tanner and Pace were almost upon the car, close enough now that he could discern their screaming.

"Pete Hudson, step away from the vehicle!" Tanner said.

The fed leveled his pistol. "Hands up, asshole!"

Jake took hold of Charlie's hand again, yanked hard, breaking its grip on the steering wheel. He threw the body out the door. It rolled once, coming to a halt face up.

Charlie's open, blood-splattered eyes stared into the dark sky, still showing a bit of that saddened, betrayed expression he'd worn just before the bullet crashed through the windshield.

Jake's mind flashed to the recent events in New Orleans that had indirectly caused this. He owed Charlie his life after what happened in Louisiana.

And now he was abandoning his dead body in an alley.

"I'm sorry, Charlie."

He slammed the door shut.

A bullet struck the front quarter panel, a large round from a high-powered rifle. The piercing metallic shriek made his ears ring.

Staying low, beneath the horizon of the windshield, he jockeyed his body into position. Legs over the console, to the pedals. Left hand on the wheel.

A glance to the side. Tanner and Pace. Feet away. Screaming. Guns aimed.

He made eye contact with Tanner.

Tanner's shoulders dropped. His brow released its pinched tension. And his mouth fell open into a look not unlike the one Charlie had given him a few minutes earlier when he found out Jake was a cop.

A look of betrayal.

Tanner had sensed what Jake was about to do, that he was going to flee. Jake could see it in his eyes.

Burton's words came to Jake again, quelling the momentary guilt.

You stole from me, Pete, so I'm going to steal something from you. When I do, I want you to remember something—everyone will be involved, and we'll take our time.

Hurry.

A bullet hissed past the car, and Jake dropped farther below the dash. He pressed the clutch pedal, threw the stick

shift into reverse, then did a quick shuffle of his feet, drop-
ping the clutch and smashing the gas pedal.

The Taurus's tires screeched, and it flew back. Jake gritted
his teeth as he clenched the steering wheel and guided the car
blindly from his crouched position.

SMASH!

He struck the wall. A shower of sparks illuminated
the cab.

A few feet away, a bullet crashed into a dumpster.

To the end of the alley. A gust of wind blew in through the
shattered window. He cleared the threshold and made it to
the street.

He immediately yanked the wheel to the side, bolted up
in his seat, threw the stick into first.

And barreled off.

Heading for the Farone mansion.

CHAPTER TWENTY-TWO

JAKE BURST through the front entrance of the Farone mansion. His shoes squeaked on the parquet floor.

"*C.C.!*"

His Colt was in his hand. He'd cleared the door, his technique piss-poor and reckless, emotion overtaking him. His academy training was now distant and staticky, lost in the swirling storm of his chaotic mind.

The house felt empty, humming with nothingness and the quiet aftershocks of violence. There was an earthy smell, something raw and natural overpowering the warm scents normally associated with the home.

Sprinting. Through the foyer, across the expanse of the great hall, down the dimly lit hallway toward the library. His footsteps echoed to the second-floor balcony, off the wainscoting and the coffered ceiling.

He halted. His shoes screeched again.

A flash of something terrible. Through the doorway of the office. Unmistakable death. Blood.

The leather chair behind the desk, out of place, by the left corner and resting against the back wall. Sylvester. Slouched.

Arms splayed off the sides of the chair. Mouth open. Eyes open. A massive patch of blood on his shirt.

"Shit..."

Jake glanced to Sylvester's chest. Not moving. The blood on Sylvester's shirt was going dark, congealing.

Jake took off.

His breathing was detached. Tingling in his forehead. A flush of cold over his moist skin.

Around the corner, into the library.

The sofa. The gap beneath it showed the floor beyond.

C.C.'s calf. Her green leggings. The bottom of her dress. Motionless.

A wet puddle, glistening in the library's warm lighting.

Jake's hand went to the sofa. He whipped around the corner.

The blood was a pool, and she lay in the center, on her stomach.

A sucking noise from his throat.

She was completely still, as dead as her brother.

Not at peace.

Violence had twisted her body. Perfectly motionless but with the appearance of movement, like unmoving action evoked by a talented painter.

Her left arm reaching up, fingers splayed.

Right arm behind her back, hand cupped.

Legs staggered, bent at the knees.

Dress off her right shoulder, a tear in the side.

Motionless motion, trying to swim out of the blood.

Her face was unrecognizable. Half of it was no longer a face.

Long, curly, black hair fanned out in a circle, matted in the blood. There was a hole in the back of her head. Black. Red. Wet.

Jake stumbled. The gun dropped from his hand, clattered away.

The sucking noise in his throat crackled.

He fell forward, right knee, left knee, onto his stomach. His palms went forward, splashing in the deep puddle of her blood. Not cold. But not warm. His fingers squished into the rug.

He tried to say her name.

C.C.

Popping sounds from the back of his throat. No words.

I love you.

Nothing. Not even the popping sounds.

He lifted his hand out of the blood, shaking, reached for her.

And quickly brought the hand to his face. Vomited. Bile shot through his fingers. He felt her not-warm blood on his cheeks, his lips.

He saw her face. Not her face. Bulging, contused. Half of it skinless. Underlying tissue.

The light feeling swept over his skin again.

Into his head.

Cold.

Bright.

He fell.

CHAPTER TWENTY-THREE

ECHOING SOUNDS SOMEWHERE in the distance.

Small taps. Little pops. Coming at Jake, circling closer, through a tunnel he felt but didn't see.

Brightness, somehow, even with his eyes closed. He opened them.

The tunnel was a brighter area within an expanse of haze that was light and filled with a thick mist that felt both cold and warm, dry and moist, so dense that he saw only inches ahead.

All of it bright. With that spot of brighter bright in front of him. Where the popping noises were.

He reached out, saw his hand before his eyes, details obscured by the haze.

The hand gave a small sense of scale, putting an object between him and the orb of brighter light, which seemed now like a searchlight in the fog, somewhere in the distance.

It was too far away to touch. He'd need to approach. Which meant he would have to stand.

His hand went down, to push himself up, and sank into a doughy, airy surface.

Then he was downtown. Shops, boutiques, cafes. A bright day, the sky a pure, blazing, Florida blue. C.C. wore sunglasses. She was laughing, and he wondered why. On his arm. Saying something.

His hand slid forward in the dough. The mist tickled his cheek. The light was before him.

My God! What—

A flea market, off U.S. 98, outside Pensacola on the way to Destin. A big, permanent setup with open-air shelters shading row after row of vendor tables. The musty smell of twenty-year-old toys and forty-year-old furniture.

C.C. held a yellow dress, black floral print, daisies or something. She'd skipped away from him when she spotted it. She held it to her chest, spun in a circle, hopped.

—*God! What have*—

The mist. The tapping sound. From the brightness.

Tap, tap, tap.

C.C. there now. In the mist. Before him. Blocking his view of the bright spot he was trying to reach. Why would she stop him? He needed to see it.

But suddenly he didn't care anymore. Not with that ethereal face. Her dark brown eyes mellow with contentment. The light now illuminated her from behind, tracing her outline, tinting the edges of her black hair a deep crimson.

She smiled.

Then screamed.

The left side of her face boiled. Pink, purple, shiny. The right side exploded, flesh flying off. The mist turned pink.

Loud footsteps. Vibration in Jake's side, through the floorboards, through the blood-soaked rug.

The taste of vomit, on his gums, burning the back of his throat. The copper smell of blood. Moisture on his arm, his face.

His eyelids snapped open.

Someone was rushing toward him from the library's doorway.

Saunders.

Red, sweaty, rage-filled face.

"My God, what have you DONE?"

Jake's eye's flicked to C.C. Inches away. Her destroyed face.

He looked away, couldn't look at her, back to Saunders.

The old man's barrel chest looked ready to rip out of his three-piece suit. His teeth were bared. Feral.

It was only then that it became clear to Jake: Saunders thought he'd killed C.C.

The notion had been so ludicrous it hadn't immediately gelled in his mind.

He tried to speak.

It wasn't me!

Nothing. Popping sounds from his throat.

Saunders stopped three feet away from him. Sweat dripped down his cheeks, which were blotched bright red and pale white. His arms quivered.

"Mate, tell me this isn't what it looks like..."

I found her, Saunders. I love her!

Small crackles from the back of his mouth.

Saunders's lip quivered. "You son of a bitch."

An explosion of movement, and then pain rippled through Jake's side. A brutal kick from Saunders's wingtip. Jake's mind flashed on the old man's history in the London underworld.

Jake rolled to the side, further into C.C.'s blood, which was now cold.

How long had he been out?

He looked up. Saunders was not there.

And Jake knew where he'd gone. His eyes flicked to the right.

Saunders was pulling at a bookshelf, the one that had a row of books on a concealed set of metal tracks—a hidden compartment that stored a Mossberg 590.

Jake turned. His Colt had settled several feet away from him.

Saunders heaved back the hidden drawer, *SMACK*, grabbed the shotgun.

Jake felt his body move on instinct. No time to think. No time to scramble for his gun.

No time even for a last look at C.C.

There was a pump-action shotgun behind him, one that Jake knew was loaded to full capacity with nine rounds of buckshot.

He sprinted through the doorway, down the dark hallway, footsteps echoing harshly once more. He slipped on the blood-slicked sole of his right shoe, arms flailing momentarily.

His chest burned. His thighs ached. He tasted the cold, sour vomit in his mouth.

And he ran faster than he ever had.

The corner was ahead of him, the one he needed to take to get to the front door.

BOOM!

A deafening sound echoed through the hallway as buck-shot ravaged the wall several feet back. Even so far away, debris peppered the back of Jake's legs, the soles of his flailing shoes. A fragment of wood whistled past his shoulder.

Around the corner. He threw the door open and quickly closed it. Into the thick night.

The Taurus was ahead, achingly far, maybe fifty yards, where he'd left it by the fountain. A few feet from it was the Farones' Bentley, which hadn't been there when he arrived.

No sound behind him yet. Saunders hadn't made it out of the house.

To the Taurus. He threw open the door, fell into the driver's seat.

BOOM!

Searing pain in his calf. Metallic pops around him.

A pellet of buckshot had struck his left leg just as he was pulling it into the car.

Door shut. His body continued to move on instinct, ignoring the pain, forgetting about time. He fired up the engine.

A quick glance back to the house. Saunders, bursting through the front doors, the Mossberg at his shoulder. He racked it.

Jake smashed the gas pedal, dropped the clutch. The tires screamed. The Taurus shot forward.

BOOM!

More pellets *thunked* into the Taurus's sheet metal.

The tires screamed as Jake spun the car around the circular fountain.

BOOM!

Past the fountain, heading down the driveway, toward the dark trees, the empty road.

BOOM! BOOM!

He looked in the rearview. Saunders behind him, emptying the shotgun with abandon. The blasts flaring into the inky night.

To the road. A screeching turn.

And Jake roared off into the darkness.

CHAPTER TWENTY-FOUR

BRIGGS HADN'T SPOKEN the entire time Laswell had described the series of events that led to Jake Rowe's revenge-fueled string of murders throughout Pensacola, Florida. Now that Laswell had reached a good stopping point in the tale—with Rowe taking a pellet of buckshot to the leg—he gave the old man a moment to gather his thoughts.

Fortunately, Briggs had stopped staring at the wall, which was such a weird, off-putting habit. Instead, while Laswell had outlined the events, Briggs had sat nearly perfectly still across the desk from him, listening intently, only small movements of his arms, adjustments of his ass position in the cheap chair.

Laswell had long since given up on fidgeting in his own chair. His ass had fallen entirely asleep, as he'd earlier predicted.

And now, in this quiet moment, Briggs just continued to stare at him, blue eyes locked in, as he processed the information. So intense. Laswell had to look away.

Sheesh, now he wished the guy would just go back to staring at the wall.

Finally, Briggs broke the awkward quiet.

"Rowe was injured when he began his bloody revenge."

He'd said it as a statement, not a question, and though he raised an eyebrow in an almost skeptical manner, Laswell could tell he was impressed.

"That's correct. One of many indicators of his tenacity."

It was like a job interview. By now, Laswell felt like he was selling the idea of Silence Jones to the old man with every sentence. Sure, Laswell had stepped out of line by offering Rowe a position as an Asset without authorization, but that didn't make this conversation any less awkward.

And the ass-killing chair wasn't helping matters either.

"So, yes," Laswell continued, "Rowe was bleeding profusely when—"

Briggs raised a hand. "Wait. Tell me more about the guy, his background."

Laswell settled back into the chair, shifting his weight. The left cheek tingled a bit. Maybe there was a bit of life left in his ass after all.

"He grew up in a small coastal town in Northern California," Laswell said. "Father was a chain hotel manager; mother, a homemaker who gave singing lessons on the side. Moved to Pensacola, Florida, at age eight, when Daddy's company opened a new beach resort. Momma died in a car accident about a year after the move. He was a bright kid, but only so-so in school. After high school, he went to Florida State, average student, got a degree in communications."

"Communications?" Briggs scoffed. "Bullshit degree. That's what they put football players in."

Laswell cleared his throat. "Um, my daughter's majoring in communications, sir."

Briggs straightened in his seat, eyes widening, apologetic words forming on his lips.

Laswell mugged. "Kidding."

Briggs scowled.

The guy really couldn't take a joke.

Laswell continued. "Rowe moved back to Pensacola. Couldn't find work for a while."

Briggs scoffed at this, seemingly a confirmation of his moments-earlier proclamation of communications being a bullshit degree.

"Got a teaching license at Pensacola's University of West Florida. Four years of teaching high school speech while taking nighttime graduate-level courses at UWF. Got his master's. Taught three years at a community college. Then a career change into the police."

"And how long had he been a cop?"

Laswell grimaced. There had been several points in this meeting when he was hesitant, almost embarrassed, to answer Briggs's questions about his hand-picked new Asset.

This was one of them.

"A year."

"*A year?* You assured me this man is fully prepared!"

Laswell inched back in his seat, scratched at his mustache. "Less than a year, technically. But that's not what you asked. You asked if Jake Rowe had prior training, and I told you that he had, that he'd been trained both at a police academy and by Nakiri."

Briggs scowled. "You can be a real manipulative son of a bitch, you know that?"

Laswell smiled broadly, stretching that beguiling mustache of his ear to ear. "Thank you, sir."

Briggs was right. He *could* be a real manipulative son of a bitch. He was a lawyer by training, after all.

But, then, so was Briggs.

Briggs shook his head, sighed. "So why did our speech teacher go cop?"

"Hard to say, really. It would appear to me a bit of an early midlife crisis. A chance for adventure and purpose."

"Teaching wasn't purposeful enough for him?"

Laswell raised his hands. "I'm only speculating here. Records show he lobbied his communications skills to get selected for the undercover position. Not that it would have taken much cajoling, I'm sure."

"He's got balls; I'll give him that."

Briggs looked away.

To the wall.

Oh, no.

But Briggs was merciful. The moment of reflection was brief. He turned back to Laswell. "Continue. What happened after Rowe fled the Farone mansion?"

Laswell grinned. "Here's where things get tasty. Here's where Jake Rowe gets his revenge."

CHAPTER TWENTY-FIVE

JAKE DIDN'T KNOW how he'd gotten there, why or even if he'd chosen the destination.

He hadn't been driving since he left the Farone mansion. Other forces were controlling him—working the pedals, turning the wheel. And those forces brought him to his neighborhood.

For the first several miles leaving the country estate outside of Pensacola proper, on the edge of the metropolitan area, his mind was a complete fog. He couldn't feel his hands, his feet, but somehow he kept on driving.

A few miles later, inside the city, with the other vehicles and traffic lights, his senses faded back into existence. And so did the feeling of dread, the realization of the pain. Whereas there had been detachment, suddenly it was real.

His loss of C.C.

The numb fingers, the dead feet brought him all the way back through town, to the east side, driving for over half an hour, to the quiet neighborhood near the mall and the airport where his rental house was located. The police department had secured the house for what was to be a temporary stay, but as he fell deeper and deeper into his undercover lie, the lease was extended. It became his home, not just a house.

Still, he'd lived there only a few months, and as he approached, the house felt foreign. The tragedy had somehow shined a light on the lie.

This was Pete Hudson's home. Not Jake Rowe's.

As he killed the engine of Charlie's Taurus, putting the stick into first and pulling up on the handbrake, he finally realized why he'd come to the house.

Burton.

At a minimum, Burton would have the place watched— but more likely, he would have posted a man here.

Jake didn't know what his next move was, but he knew it lay on a collision path with Burton.

That's why he'd come back here.

To get the ball rolling.

He'd parked about a block back, giving himself plenty of space. He leaned over the steering wheel, squinting at the simple ranch-style house. Yellow brick. Gray shutters and door. Bushes along the sidewalk and a sparse, sandy, Florida lawn.

The windows were dark. No signs of movement. He recognized all the vehicles parked along the street as neighborhood regulars.

Pain pulsed from his leg, and he glanced at it. Lots of blood, but the pellet hadn't lodged in his muscle. It had nicked the taut skin on his calf, which splayed open to a four-inch gash. It hurt like hell, but it wouldn't kill him. Not yet, anyway. He could very well bleed out if he didn't get medical attention soon.

He'd get it stitched up.

But not yet.

Blood covered his clothing. So much. Most of it C.C.'s. On a quiet street in a quiet neighborhood, could he make it to the house without someone noticing a horror movie character trudging up the sidewalk? He'd take the risk.

Instant fire in his leg as he stepped out of the car. He clenched his jaw and went to the trunk, where he took out the tire tool and the emergency blanket. Using the wedged end of the tool, he pierced the blanket, then tore off a thin strip, wrapped it around his wound, and pulled tight. Another flare of pain, and he bit his tongue to keep from screaming.

He panted as he tugged a knot into place. The pressure was relieving, and it would keep the bleeding down for a while.

He hobbled down the sidewalk, his eyes trained on his house, looking for movement.

Nothing.

When he got to the fence at the edge of the property, he slipped into the shadows. He traced the fence's edge until he was in line with the shallow side of the garage, where there was a seldom-used side door. He quietly unlocked it.

The garage was nearly pitch black, just faint outlines from the light coming in through the crack he'd left in the door, revealing his black Grand Prix in the center of the two-car space, the wood-paneled walls, the extra refrigerator, the workbench.

The workbench...

The car...

A plan materialized.

The room went black as he closed the door. He stepped to the bench and explored blindly until he found what he was looking for—the piece of broken bicycle chain.

He stepped behind the refrigerator, which sat beside the door that led into the house, and took his keys from his pocket. He rested his thumb on one of the rubber buttons on the plastic fob for his car's security system/remote starter.

Keeping his thumb on the button, he looped an end of

the bicycle chain in each hand. He crouched down and squeezed on the chain so tightly that that it hurt, the greasy metal digging into his palms.

He pushed the remote starter button.

The Grand Prix fired up.

He held perfectly still. Waited.

Footsteps from inside his house, drawing near, at a run. The man rushed past him, toward the Grand Prix, threw open the driver side door, and jabbed his Glock inside. He'd left the door to the house open, a patch of light falling in the garage, revealing the man.

It was Cobb. Not a leader among Burton's minions, but no slouch either. White, late twenties, maybe early thirties. Brown wavy hair. Brown beard.

Jake jumped out and wrapped the bicycle chain around Cobb's throat from behind. He clenched down hard.

Immediately Cobb retaliated, waving the Glock like a club. Cobb was well trained. No panic. Firing his weapon prematurely would draw unwanted attention.

Cobb slid his foot behind Jake's, knee twisted behind his leg, and brought them both tumbling to the floor. Jake's head smacked into the open car door as they fell, but he landed on top of their two-man pile, knocking the Glock free of Cobb's grasp. It rattled against the smooth concrete and bashed into the wall at the far side of the garage.

He brought the chain in a full loop around Cobb's neck and pulled tight, Cobb's face instantly reddening.

Jake leaned away from Cobb's clawing fingers, pulled the chain even tighter.

Cobb's cheeks went from red to purple, eyes watering and bloodshot. Droplets of blood ringed his neck where the chain cut into flesh.

Small gurgles from his throat.

Jake gave the chain a tug, a finishing blow.

Except it didn't finish him. Cobb kept slapping.

Weaker. Flatter.

Jake tugged again.

And again.

Then Cobb went limp.

Jake's chest heaved. His breaths wheezed. He didn't release the pressure on the chain for several long moments, staring down at Cobb's face.

He needed to be certain.

A few seconds passed. He put two fingers to Cobb's throat.

Cobb was gone.

Jake sat back on his haunches, pressure going to his knees, and to his wounded calf, which he'd forgotten about during the action, the adrenaline.

A surge of pain.

He grimaced and tilted his head back, looking up at the sheetrock ceiling. His mind went to what Burton had said.

I'm going to steal something from you. When I do, I want you to remember something—everyone will be involved, and we'll take our time.

Jake's attention snapped back to Cobb.

Everyone will be involved...

This was one of the men who killed C.C., destroyed her face, broke her body, left her swimming in her blood.

Now he was very dead.

Jake had murdered him.

And Cobb was only the first. Of several.

He would kill them all.

Everyone will be involved...

He would kill all eight of the new Burton gang.

He studied Cobb's face, frozen in a look of bewilderment. Blood oozed down his neck.

One down; seven to go, Jake thought.

First, he'd make sure there were no other Burton visitors in the house.

He found Cobb's pistol lying against the wall several feet away. It was a Glock 19. Second generation, as evidenced by the checkering on the front and back straps. It held the standard magazine, which meant fifteen rounds if it was fully loaded, sixteen if Cobb had stuck an extra in the chamber. 9 mm. Polymer-framed. Short-recoil. Efficient, reliable, and real-world tested across the globe by countless armed forces, security firms, and law enforcement agencies.

Ideal for what Jake had planned.

He used his new gun to clear the open doorway and the living room beyond. It was alight via the floor lamp that Cobb had turned on. He left it on.

That sense of disconnect returned to him as he moved through the house, clearing each room—the feeling that this was no longer his home. It was Pete Hudson's. Not Jake's. The home of a fictitious character who was now gone forever.

House cleared, he now needed to make a few preparations. He went back to the living room. The answering machine on the end table by his couch flashed a red *1*. One new message. He pressed the eject button, took out the tiny tape, and stuck it in his pocket.

To the office. His simple, old desk—a gray metal job that the police department had picked up at a consignment shop —was on the back wall. He opened the center drawer, grabbed the handheld voice-recorder/microcassette player he'd had since college.

In his bedroom, he gathered two black T-shirts, jeans, and his hiking boots. Stripped. Went to the adjoining bathroom and took a one-minute shower to wash off the blood, which turned the shower's floor pink. His entire being was so numb that the warm water felt like nothing, like he'd been anesthetized—everywhere but his wounded calf, where it burned fire.

Back to the bedroom, where he tore a long strip of cloth from one of the T-shirts, tied it over his wound, dressed, and then slipped back through the house, flipping off the lights.

Into the garage, closing the door behind him, and into the idling Grand Prix. He shut the driver door, seatbelted himself, and hit the garage door opener button.

The ceiling-mounted door began to retract. With the dim light put out by the opener's bulb, he glanced through the car's side window, to body on the floor. When the garage door was completely open, he looked away.

And backed out.

CHAPTER TWENTY-SIX

"HOLY SHIT," the woman calling herself Christie Mosley said. "He killed him."

She held a pair of compact binoculars with one hand and pressed her cellular phone to her ear with the other.

"How do you know?" Falcon said.

"Because I'm looking at the damn body right now."

She'd parked her red Cutlass Supreme across the street and a block back from where Rowe had parked the bullet-riddled Taurus. She'd watched through the binoculars as he'd slipped into the side door of the garage. Several minutes later, the garage door was now open, and a black Pontiac Grand Prix was backing out, its tail lights glowing red, clouds of exhaust from the muffler tips.

And to the side, on the floor of the garage, was Cobb's lifeless body.

The car's hood cleared the garage, and the taillights went brighter as it braked, came to a stop. The garage door began to lower.

"He's leaving now," she said. "Backing out in a Grand Prix."

The car moved again. When it reached the end of the drive, it reversed onto the street.

At the house, the garage door met the ground.

"He's just leaving the body behind."

"Interesting," Falcon said. "Follow him."

She waited for the other car to get to the end of the block then pulled out, not yet turning on her headlights. The other car slowed at the stop sign, and she took her foot off the gas, keeping a good distance between them.

Then the Grand Prix turned to the right, no turn signal.

She accelerated.

A sharp sound from behind her, in the distance. Sirens.

She checked the rearview mirror. At the edge of the tiny crest in the street behind her, there was a faint glow of red and blue police lights, growing brighter.

She rolled to the stop sign and turned right.

CHAPTER TWENTY-SEVEN

"Ah, dammit," Tanner said as he stepped past a uniformed officer and through the side door of the garage.

There was a body on the floor before him.

Which meant that Jake Rowe—the guy Tanner had thought so much of, the guy Tanner had put on a fast track to detective—was now a murderer.

The corpse's name was Cobb. One of Burton's underlings. He lay on his back. Arms splayed. Eyes shocked. A bicycle chain wrapped around his neck, embedded in the skin.

Tanner jolted slightly as Pace cleared his throat behind him, too loud. The fed stepped beside Tanner, shook his head, shoved his hands in his pockets, then jingled his keys. Tanner inched away from him.

Outside was a handful of uniformed cops. Tanner could hear their chatter through the garage door. But the only other person inside with him and Pace was the photographer, crouched beside Cobb's body, yellow block lettering on a dark blue windbreaker.

A flash of the camera lit the garage, a typical middle-class place. This typicality was the reason the department had rented the house—it was the perfect abode for the unas-suming car thief character they'd created.

Which now brought to Tanner a nightmare of red tape and diplomacy. How the hell was he going to explain to the leasing company that a murder had happened on their property?

And the bloodstain on the garage floor—that was gonna be there for a while.

If not forever.

Jake had been a fictitious criminal.

And now he was a real one.

Tanner had been in this line of work for decades and had seen this far too often—a good person dealt a horrible stroke of fate, turned into a violent criminal.

Well-to-do parents of murdered honor roll students. Boyfriends of raped girlfriends.

And now Jake Rowe. One of the most decent and resourceful guys to join his department.

Tanner felt sick. He needed an antacid.

"Self-defense," Pace said. "Rowe comes back, tries to get his wheels; they got a guy waiting for him; Rowe takes care of business."

Tanner shrugged. "Maybe. But where is Jake now? We still haven't heard from him, have we?"

Pace shook his head.

Tanner pointed at the body. "And look at all this blood. It's not from that neck wound. Rowe's hurt. He's bleeding bad. Watch the hospitals."

Pace nodded.

Tanner stepped past Pace to the side door, pulled it open, and stepped into the muggy night. Thankfully, Pace didn't follow. Tanner needed a breather from the guy, a moment alone.

Curious neighbors had congregated outside the crime

scene tape, half a dozen or so. Blue and red lights flashed off oaks and palms. A news van pulled up, stopped.

Shit. The press. Just what Tanner needed.

His thoughts went to Jake, this man who was no youngster when Tanner met him a year ago but who was fresh-faced and wide-eyed in spirit, brimming with convictions and ambitions.

And smarts too.

He wasn't all that book smart, despite having taught some college. Jake was the first to admit that. But he more than made up for any shortcomings with his incredible analytical skill. He could think through anything. That's all he did: thinking. He'd think and think and think until an answer came to him.

His thought process was often convoluted—which was something Cecilia Farone was supposedly helping him sort out—but it always led him in the right directions. He had instincts, and he came to the right conclusions.

But most importantly, Jake had guts. That's what mattered most.

It looked like he was using that courage for the wrong reasons now.

Tanner turned his attention past the gasping neighbors, down the street, to the west. The sun had recently set, and the sky was all pinks and yellows, deep violet clouds. Not too far from where Tanner stood, this would be a beautiful sunset on the Gulf.

Tanner ran a hand along his jaw. "Where the hell are you, Jake?"

CHAPTER TWENTY-EIGHT

THE ADRENALINE or the madness or the fog or whatever had been keeping the pain from Jake's leg had worn off. Now his entire calf felt like a piece of molten stone.

It was as heavy as stone too, and it scraped behind him as he dragged it up the cracked sidewalk. His homemade bandage had soaked through with blood, saturating the jeans, which stuck to his leg, heavy and cold.

He grimaced as he pulled the leg another step farther. The damn thing seemed heavier with each step. Not much farther to go.

The neighborhood was a shithole, the sort of place that was never entirely quiet, even when the streets were dark and lifeless. Laughter in the distance. A bottle clattering on concrete.

At the next crossroad, he took a right onto a short dead-end street with a clump of trees and a buzzing streetlight at the end. Two houses on the right side of the street. On the left side were two more houses and a one-story, ancient-looking brick building with shuttered windows, something that must've been a soda shop or a grocery in the neighborhood's happier days. Now, however, it would seem uninhabited were it not for the single illuminated bulb by the door.

Jake was one of the initiated few people who knew the true nature of the building. Rather, his alter ego, Pete Hudson, was.

He stumbled up to the battered metal door and gave two solid bangs.

A few moments later, the door opened, and Dr. Mayer's face peered out of the gap, blinking the sleep from droopy yet sparkly blue eyes that sat behind a pair of round, old-fashioned glasses. He was an older man with combed-back, gray hair and a jowly basset hound face. His shirt was a button-up, wrinkled from his sleep.

Mayer regarded Jake's leg wound. "Oh my. Let's get you taken care of." He opened the door farther and looked past Jake. "Just you? Sylvester said to stay here all night because there might be many wounded. I figured you'd be showing up hours ago." He glanced at Jake's leg again, scrunched his lips. "I didn't get a call."

Jake took his PenPal notebook from his back pocket, and his fingers stuck to the tagboard backing, which had a splotch of soaked-in blood that hadn't fully dried.

C.C.'s blood. Or his. Or both. He couldn't be sure.

He flipped to the first of the notes he'd prepared.

I couldn't call. There wasn't time

The doctor squinted at the note, then at Jake. "Can't you talk?"

Jake shook his head.

"Took a blow to the neck, did you?"

Jake nodded.

Mayer put his hand on Jake's neck, examined. Jake was

good at reading people, and he could see skepticism in Mayer's eyes. He'd caught Jake's lie.

Mayer stepped back, still squinting at him, hesitant. "I'll need to call. This is ... very unorthodox, you just showing up like this."

Jake took out the Glock 19, pointed it at him, and flipped to the next note.

You're not calling this in

He shuffled inside, crowding Mayer back, and shut the door. A jolt of pain in his leg.

Mayer's eyes went wide, and he put his hands up.

It was a small, dimly-lit space, one unit in the old building —a medical exam area and a tiny bathroom to the side. All of it dingy and utilitarian. Hardly sanitary looking. Hardly even organized. An exam table dominated the center of the room. A cot—for the doctor's use in all-night situations such as tonight—was at the far wall, blankets messed up, pillow askew.

Mayer's lip trembled but his eyes burned fire—not fear, but shock. He'd been in this game for decades and had surely been through many hairy situations.

"Do you know who you're messing with, you stupid shit?" Mayer spat. "I'm Joseph Farone's personal doctor."

Jake flipped to the next note, showed it.

Get what supplies you need. Then we're leaving

Mayer read the note, looked up at Jake with eyes that had gone even darker.

"Leaving?"

Jake jabbed the gun toward the back of the room. Mayer

glanced over his shoulder and saw what Jake had indicated: the door in the back.

"Oh, I see," Mayer said as he turned back around. "You're a damn traitor, aren't you? That's why I didn't get a call. They know you're injured; you can't go to the hospitals; so you come here to grab the doctor, but you gotta get out of here as quickly as possible since they might come here looking for you."

Jake nodded then swiped his gun, a *turn around* command, and led Mayer to the cabinets. The doctor opened one of the glass doors and started taking out supplies: antiseptic, sutures, gauze.

Jake noted one important omission from the doctor's gatherings. Keeping the Glock leveled at Mayer, he yanked the mechanical pencil from the notebook's spiral binding and scribbled out a note.

Grab something for the pain, dickhead

Mayer glowered at him, then grabbed a bottle of lidocaine and a sterile-wrapped syringe.

———

Jake had the Glock pointed at Mayer as the doctor finished his work, wrapping the elastic bandage around the gauze-covered stitches. They were in the wooded patch of earth on the opposite side of the sidewalk where Jake had parked the Grand Prix, a couple of blocks away from Mayer's building. Jake sat on a half-destroyed wooden crate. Bottles and plastic shopping bags and McDonald's wrappers littered the earth around them.

"You know I'm going to call the moment you leave," Mayer said as he made the final pass with the bandage.

Jake shook his hand and gave him a look that said, *No, you won't*. He pointed at the doctor's waistline, where a cellular phone was clipped to his belt, and made a little *gimme* motion with his hand.

The doctor fumed as he handed the phone to Jake, knowing full well what was about to happen.

Jake smashed it on the sidewalk.

He hobbled off the crate. The Glock felt unduly heavy in his hand, and he stumbled to the side, regained his balance. Naturally, Mayer hadn't given him a blood transfusion, and from Jake's bit of medical training as a police officer, he estimated that he'd lost several hundred mils of blood.

He was gonna be woozy for a while.

He kept the Glock leveled on Mayer as he limped to the Grand Prix and got in.

"You stupid shit," the doctor said before Jake shut the door and peeled off.

———

Twenty minutes later. A different shithole part of town. Somewhere he could disappear for a few minutes. Gather himself. Rest his leg briefly.

Before he tracked down and murdered the rest of Burton's men.

He was parked beside an abandoned factory, its chain-link fence rotting and falling over like the fence he'd seen earlier that evening at the abandoned parking lot outside Wagner High School.

That felt like a year ago.

He leaned his head back and exhaled. Closed his eyes. A long moment passed, so long that he realized he might have even fallen asleep.

Eyes open.

He took out his notebook, fingers sticking to the bloody back cover, removed the mechanical pencil, and wrote a list of names, then crossed out the first one.

~~Cobb~~
Gamble
Hodges
Knox
McBride
Odom
Glover
Burton

His eyes lingered on the list, then he flipped to a fresh page and scratched out a quick note.

My name is Jake Rowe

He faced the rearview mirror and held the notebook beside it.

His eyes flicked from the note to his reflection. He tried to speak, breaking it down to the first couple of words.

My name...

Nothing. His lips moved silently.

My name...

Nothing again.

It wasn't that the words just wouldn't come to him. He *literally* couldn't speak. He was giving it his full effort, but no sounds would come out.

He slapped the notebook shut, shoved the pencil back into the binding, and dropped it on the passenger seat where it landed beside the microcassette player.

His hand went to the player. Stopped. Hovered over it for a moment. And then grabbed it.

He reached into his pocket and retrieved the tiny tape he'd taken from his answering machine. He put it in the player. Hesitated. Pushed the *PLAY* button.

There was a beep. And then the message began.

C.C.'s voice.

"Hey, it's—"

He pressed *STOP*.

Her voice.

Oh, my god.

Deep breaths. His eyes went up, staring into the headliner, and his head returned to the headrest. He closed his eyes.

———

And his mind went to a memory, took him back several months.

He and C.C., hand-in-hand, nighttime on the beach, a favorite spot of theirs, a literal common ground for two people who were very different but couldn't get enough of each other.

The moon lay a long, shimmering trail on the black water. The waves weren't choppy, but they were steady and loud. The glistening condos and hotels were ahead of them in the distance. They'd walked to the national seashore—a long stretch of natural, untouched beach—and were now returning to civilization. C.C. had asked him what was on his mind.

And he'd answered her, letting all the disordered, tumultuous thoughts in his head spew from his mouth.

"...which is why I just don't know about all these new diet trends, you know?" he was saying. "It seems to me that if they put something in a green box, say it's low-fat, then people gobble it up. Is that how easily people are persuaded? Green packaging? I mean, come on. Those things are loaded with sugar, and sugar is what's gonna make you fat, not dietary fat. It's like people just assume fat is gonna make you fat because the word's the same. Word-choice, packaging—people are so easily manipulated. It's mind-boggling. And—"

C.C. waved a hand to cut him off, her fingers pinched. "Maybe that was a bad question on my part, asking a 'loud-mouth' what's on his mind. You use ten words when three will do."

Jake chuckled. "You did it again."

"Did what?"

He upturned one of his hands and pinched his fingers together like she'd just done. "You did the Italian hand. For as quirky and individualistic as you are, you still go full pizza pie every now and then."

She smiled, shrugged. "We all take bits and pieces of our experiences to become what we are, consciously and subconsciously. And *you're* changing the subject, mister. We were talking about that wild mind of yours. You're a smart man, love. You really are. But you—"

"I'm not that smart. I was an average student at best."

"Whatever you say, Professor. Book smarts aren't everything, anyway. You ponder things. You see the whole picture. *That's* intelligence. But you think too much."

Jake looked at her, raised an eyebrow. "How can a person think too much? You just said I see the whole picture. Isn't that kind of synonymous with thinking too much?"

C.C. shook her head. "Not at all. Confucius said that life is really simple, but we insist on making it complicated. Try taming your thoughts."

"And how do I do that, exactly?"

"You can start by taking some deep belly breaths. From the stomach, not the chest. Diaphragmatic breathing, like I taught you. It'll calm you down."

"Like this?" Jake took a deep breath and puffed out his cheeks, crossed his eyes.

She just looked at him, not granting his idiocy a response.

Jake let the breath out, chuckling. "C'mon, babe. I don't see how breathing is going to 'tame my thoughts,' as you say. I think a lot, yes. I know it's a problem, but, I mean, breathing? Maybe I could get one of those calming drugs that've been in the news. I've already had my department psych exam, but maybe Tanner could—"

"Jake!"

He turned to her.

"*Shhhhhh*. Give silence a try. Just be quiet sometimes, love. *Shhh*. Silence."

They continued down the beach, not speaking. Just the two of them, just their two sets of footsteps squeaking in the sand. The towers were still far off in the distance.

After a few moments of this, Jake felt C.C. looking in his direction. He turned, found her with a little smile on her face. "Well, how did you like it, being silent for a few moments?"

Jake pointed at the Gulf. "It wasn't silent at all. There was the sound of the waves. Duh."

C.C. scowl-smiled at him. "Quiet your mind, love. You think way too much. Be present. In the moment."

She let loose of his hand and stepped into the waves. Her sarong soaked instantly, to her knees. The cloth floated, tossing with the motion of the waterline, rising and lowering on her legs. She smiled, beckoned for him.

He stepped in, sloshed toward her. "Damn, the water's so warm tonight. Feels like bathwater. It's been so hot lately. And humid. In a couple months, it'll be—"

C.C. put a finger to his lips. "*Shhh*. Quiet. Be here. With me. In this moment. Right now. *This* moment. Silence."

She kissed him.

———

Jake looked at the tape player. His hand shook. He pressed the *REWIND* button. The tape screeched for just a moment as it rewound the brief bit of the message he'd already played.

Then he pressed *PLAY*.

"Hey, it's me."

C.C. stopped abruptly, her breaths audible over the hum of the recording. A moment passed. And when she spoke again, her voice was angry, something Jake had rarely heard, something that sounded wrong coming from Cecilia Farone.

"I saw Charlie Marsh a few minutes ago. He told me you called him. He said you're going tonight."

Another pause.

"You promised me you wouldn't go. *You promised me!* Now you've lied to me. And you know…"

Another pause, momentary.

"You know how important honesty is to me." Her voice cracked. "But I guess if I'm having my quirky intuitions, my hippie feelings, you don't need to be honest with me, huh?" She was clearly crying now. "And now I'm scared out of my mind about you. I know something's going to happen tonight, something horrible. I know it."

Another pause.

"*Asshole!*"

A loud *clank* as she slammed the phone.

A beep indicated the message had ended.

Jake pressed *STOP*, folded his arms across the top of the steering wheel, and put his head on his forearm.

He cried.

CHAPTER TWENTY-NINE

THE WOMAN CALLING herself Christie Mosley stared through her binoculars at the black Pontiac Grand Prix, a block away.

She'd seen Rowe lay out over the steering wheel, and she'd begun to settle back into her seat, assuming that he'd fallen asleep.

But now she saw swift movements from his back, rising and lowering. Shaking.

He wasn't sleeping at all.

He was crying.

Her cellular phone rang.

"Yes?" she said, propping it against her shoulder, not taking the binoculars from her face.

"Straight from the Pensacola Police dispatch," Falcon said. "Farone family brutally murdered—brother and sister."

"Oh ... my god."

That's why Rowe was weeping.

"Your boyfriend," Falcon said with a heavy, sarcastic emphasis on *boyfriend*, "must be making his power moves. You can't follow Jake Rowe all night. If Burton's plan is going into full swing, you gotta get back to him." A pause. "What's the current status on Rowe?"

She watched as Rowe continued to shake on the steering wheel. Suddenly he slammed a fist against the car's dash. The weeping continued.

And somehow she felt compelled to maintain his privacy.

"He's ... he's regrouping in his car."

"Give it another hour," Falcon said. "Then we need you back with Burton."

"Roger that."

The call ended. She placed the phone in the cupholder.

For a moment longer, she watched as the figure in the distance wept, head now directly on the steering wheel, arms draped.

She lowered the binoculars. And exhaled.

———

A half hour later and a few miles away, she parked her Cutlass Supreme and watched as Rowe's Grand Prix rolled to a stop outside a ho-hum apartment complex of two-story, motel-style buildings. The ground-level units had a small porch; the second-floor units had balconies with thin black handrails. Copious palm trees. A pool area in the center of the parking lot. It must have been a nice place at one point, but neglect had stolen most of its luster.

Her cellular was at her shoulder again. "All right, we're at Shallowbrook Apartments now. I've been here before. This is Odom's place. Burton had him store some coke here a few weeks ago."

The Grand Prix's driver-side door opened.

"Rowe's walking up to one of the buildings," she said. "He just stashed a Glock 19 under his belt. Shit, he's lost his damn mind. He's gonna whack Odom. You know that, right?"

"Obviously," Falcon said. "Don't interfere."

CHAPTER THIRTY

GLOVER TRIED TO CONTAIN HIMSELF, tried not to snicker.

He was in the Farone library with Burton, and standing before them was the old butler, Saunders, looking flustered, sweaty. At their feet was Cecilia Farone's destroyed body, lying in the puddle of blood where he and Burton and the others had left her.

"It was inconceivable," Saunders said, running a hand over his forehead. "You just wouldn't believe it."

"*Pete Hudson?* Are you sure?" Burton said, shaking his head. He looked at Cecilia's body again, quickly turned away, shuddering.

Again, Glover stifled a snicker. Burton was good at putting on an act. Too good. Chilling.

"As I live," Saunders said. "He was laying here with her in the blood. Like something out of a horror movie. Those are his."

Saunders pointed at a line of bloody footprints leaving the pool surrounding Cecilia, going out the doorway. They were large, as were Pete Hudson's feet, and the spacing was broad —he'd been at a run.

Burton nodded, sighed, and looked down at Cecilia again.

"Well, I did see her and Pete having an angry conversation after the meeting." He pointed to the Mossberg, leaning against the wall. "Where's the body?"

Saunders raised an eyebrow. "Pardon?"

"Hudson. Where'd you dump his body?"

Saunders shook his head. "There is no body. He got away."

Burton's mouth opened. He turned on Glover.

Glover had contained his snickering, but now he couldn't hide his shock. Like Burton, his mouth went wide. He heard himself gasp.

Pete Hudson was alive. Out there somewhere. On the loose.

Anger stormed in Burton's eyes. His realistic yet thin facade of civility rarely wavered, but few things enraged him as much as losing control of a situation.

Burton's smile quivered back into place. "Hudson got away, did he?"

"But I got him in the leg," Saunders said and motioned toward the Mossberg.

"Hurt bad?"

Saunders shrugged. "Grazed him. He's not going to die, but he's bloody well hurting."

The old man suddenly looked away, distraught. His hand returned to his forehead.

"I can't believe it," Saunders said. "Pete killed Sylvester *and* Cecilia. In one night..."

Burton glanced at the body. "Well, Hudson is a ruthless bastard deep down. Don't let that goofy smile fool you. I've had chats with the guy. Total psycho. Have you called the police?"

"I did. I hesitated, but ... I didn't know what else to do. The phone lines weren't working, and I couldn't find a cellular in the entire house. He must have taken them all. I had to drive into town, to a payphone. I got back right before you arrived."

"And you reported Hudson?"

"Of course."

Burton smiled. "Very good." He reached behind his back and took out his Smith & Wesson Model 29, aimed it at Saunders's chest.

Glover gasped.

On the ride over, Burton had told him the plan of action. This hadn't been discussed. This was not on the agenda.

"Burton, what are you doing?" Glover said, the first time he'd spoken since they returned to the mansion.

Burton ignored him.

Saunders brought his hands up slowly. But he didn't panic, just narrowed his eyes at Burton. The old guy had been through a lot. He wasn't easily rattled.

"What the hell is this?"

"I need information from you, Saunders," Burton said. "Where's the second press? I only know of the money-printing press. I need to know where the other one is."

Saunders's eyes went to Cecilia's body and back to Burton. "It was you, wasn't it?"

"Answer me."

"Piss off. The police will arrive any moment."

CRACK!

Burton fired. The round was horribly loud, amplified by the wooden walls, the stacks of books. Glover's hands went to his ears.

Saunders howled and clenched his thigh, both hands, blood oozing between his fingers. But he didn't fall. Tough old salt.

This was definitely not on the agenda.

"Looks like Hudson circled back to the mansion," Burton said. "Decided he should silence the only witness. He managed to put a round in your leg. But did he finish you off?"

Burton aimed at his head.

"*Okay!*" Saunders screamed. His faced dripped with sweat. "Okay! The business park on Alexander Street, in Warrington." He groaned. "Suite 109."

Burton nodded. "Thanks, Saunders."

CRACK!

A spout of blood from Saunders's forehead. He crumpled to the floor, a couple of feet away from Cecilia. A stream of bright, fresh blood raced out onto the carpet and mixed with the thick darkened blood already there.

Saunders's mouth was open, teeth exposed.

Glover felt his hands shaking.

Burton turned to him, smiling. He looked down, saw Glover's shaking hands, scoffed.

"Come on, pussy," he said and walked off.

Glover glanced at Saunders's body then followed Burton.

CHAPTER THIRTY-ONE

JAKE TURNED his notebook to the correct page, then stuffed it into his back pocket.

The apartment buildings encircled a courtyard with a rundown gazebo in the center. Each building's second story had balconies with a shared staircase between two apartment units. Jake cut through the courtyard, avoiding the mismatched patches of light—some warm-hued, others cool-hued—from the black lampposts, crossing thick, poorly kept centipedegrass. Many of the units had their screen doors open, and Jake heard snippets of nighttime home life as he passed—laughter, a New Kids on the Block song playing through a tinny speaker, the clatter of silverware, copious televisions.

Odom's building was ahead. Jake retrieved the Glock. He climbed the stairs quickly, stepping as lightly as possible, but the tired boards still moaned under his weight.

At the balcony, the door to his left was closed and dark. Through the other door, he saw the bluish light of a television set, its brightness level waning and waxing. Like so many of the apartments, Odom's sliding glass door had been opened to a screen door. There was the muffled drone of television voices, two characters having an urgent conversation.

He dispatched with stealth and threw open the door.

There was Odom. On his couch. In nothing but his tighty-whities, watching *L.A. Law*. The TV was the only source of light.

Odom was in his late forties, one of the oldest members of Burton's gang. White, long, and lean. His cavernous cheeks sported a gray-and-brown beard.

Instant recognition in Odom's blue, deep-set eyes. "Oh, Jesus Christ ... You were supposed to die."

Jake yanked the notebook from his pocket, showed the note.

Did you hurt her?

Odom squinted at it, confused for a moment before a malicious sneer materialized on his lips.

"What's with the note? Cat got your tongue, Loudmouth?"

Jake jabbed the notebook forward, scowled.

Odom's sneer grew wider.

"You're damn right I hurt her. We all slapped her around for a while. Tell ya what, though, I wanted more. That was a fine piece of ass you had there, Hudson. But Burton wouldn't let us. Crazy son of a bitch really thought of her as a sister, I think."

Odom's eyes flicked to the small, ratty table beside the couch. Peeking out of a stack of car magazines and *Playboys* was the butt of a revolver.

Jake darkened his expression and shot an eyebrow up, telling Odom that he'd seen what the man had hidden in the magazines.

With a series of swipes from the Glock, Jake motioned for

Odom to raise his hands, stand up, and move away from the revolver. Odom did as instructed.

Then Jake motioned for him to get on his knees.

Odom continued to sneer, but Jake could see genuine fear now, as though Odom hadn't considered Loudmouth Hudson a genuine threat to this point, even after the man had barged into his apartment aiming a gun.

Odom went to his knees, hands up.

Jake motioned for him to put his hands on his head. Odom acquiesced.

"Just blast me right here, huh? All these people in the surrounding apartments to hear it? Not even gonna use a silencer to cut down on the noise?"

The man had a point. Jake hesitated.

Odom suddenly dove for the couch, plunging his hands between the cushions, and pulled out a small pistol.

Two guns stashed within feet of each other in the living room. This guy was loaded to the teeth.

Jake lunged at him. Got his hands around his neck. Swung his side into Odom's arms, getting out of the path of the gun.

Odom tried to maneuver the pistol back around, and Jake swept laterally, clamped his hand on Odom's wrist, torqued it in the opposite direction. Odom went to the floor as Jake stripped the gun from his hand—a front disarm technique Jake learned at the academy.

One of Odom's big boots swept at Jake, catching him behind the knee and bringing him to the floor beside him. Jake wrapped his legs around Odom's waist and rolled them away from Odom's pistol.

They crashed into Odom's recliner. Jake was behind Odom, and the Glock weighted Jake's hand, ready and willing.

But Jake gave a thought to what Odom had said.

It *would* be a mistake to put a round through Odom's head

in the apartment complex—not just because of the potential of being found out, but also because there could be an errant bullet. Someone else could get hurt.

Or killed.

So instead of shooting Odom, he would strangle him.

Odom's neck was in the crook of Jake's elbow, and he gagged as Jake pulsed his bicep. Fingernails dug into Jake's arms. Odom swung a fist backward like a hammer at Jake's ribs, missing once, connecting on the second attempt, which nearly stole Jake's breath.

But Jake had a powerful advantage, and through his taut arm he felt the beginnings of Odom's death. He felt the man's panic. His desperation. His dissipating strength.

A recent memory flashed through Jake's mind. One from only moments earlier: Odom's sneering face, his gleeful confirmation that he had been one of many who had taken part in ending C.C.'s life, that he'd wanted to sexually assault her as well.

No, strangling Odom wouldn't suffice.

Jake jerked his arm hard to the side.

Crack!

Broken neck.

Panting, Jake rolled off him, his head coming to rest on the matted carpet next to the coffee table. For a few moments, Jake remained like this, breathing hard and looking up at the popcorn texture of the ceiling.

Then he got to his knees. And looked down at Odom.

Eyes open. Tongue hanging from his mouth, onto his scraggly, disgusting beard.

Jake flipped his notebook to the list and crossed off another name.

~~Cobb~~
Gamble
Hodges
Knox
McBride
~~Odom~~
Glover
Burton

The pencil stayed on the page for a moment as he looked at the list.

Two down; six to go.

He stood, went to the bedroom in the back, a room just as shitty as the living room. The bed was unmade, its tussled bedding faded and old. There was the sour smell of body odor.

To the closet. Where he knew Odom would have a stash of weapons.

Odom didn't disappoint.

On the closet floor was a steel weapons case. The numerically-coded lock was unlatched. He tipped its door open and found a small arsenal.

Plenty of the items could be helpful for Jake's mission, but there was only one object item he was searching for.

A suppressor.

There were several in the case. Most of them were shit, some of them even homemade-looking. But he found a decent one. Tested the threading. It fit.

He started to close the case. And stopped.

A blackjack baton. About eight inches long with a flexible, braided leather handle and a battered, black-painted, lead bulb on the end.

Jake picked it up.

Blackjacks had been outlawed in his department for some

time—before he joined—but he learned about them during his training. It was a brutal weapon used in close-quarters combat. The weighted end was effective at knocking people out.

They were also known to split open scalps.

He thought of C.C.'s destroyed face.

The lead bulb at the end of Odom's blackjack was covered with blackened blood, not quite dry, still sticky.

Jake nearly dropped it before he tightened his grip around the leather handle.

He hurled it across the room.

The weighted end impaled the wall, fissures in the drywall. The handle quivered.

He left the bedroom, and as he walked past Odom's body, he held up the suppressor.

Thanks for the tip, he thought as he shoved it in his back pocket and left.

———

Screams. Lots of screams.

And panicked people funneling around Jake from both sides, going for the exit.

Old Reno tavern was as divey of a dive bar as Jake had ever seen. Flickering neon beer signs lit the gloom, which smelled like cigarette smoke and perspiration and desperation.

The patrons flooded around him in a panic he'd created when he walked in and fired a round into the floor. Even the bartender—who seemed the type who would unflinchingly poke a deadbeat's eyeballs out—had run away.

The only person who remained stationary was the man sitting at the bar, staring at Jake with wide eyes, a beer bottle in front of him. Shaking. A fat, redheaded slob with tattoos.

McBride.

As the last of the bar's patrons pushed past Jake, he approached McBride.

The man's curly red hair poked out the bottom of a beanie, from which a drop of sweat rolled out, over his forehead, down his round nose. His hand was six inches from the beer bottle. Tattoos on his knuckles. Shaking.

"Oh, shit ... Oh, shit..."

Jake could just hear a faint melody. Sad music. A doleful Bill Withers song. He didn't need any extra sadness. He considered putting a round through the jukebox, then also considered how hillbilly that would look. *Shootin' the jukebox.* He let it be.

A revolver stuck out of the back of McBride's jeans, right by his exposed, sweaty ass crack. Jake grabbed the gun. A Smith & Wesson. He tossed it over the bar.

The notebook was already turned to the correct note when Jake pulled it from his back pocket. He slapped it on the bar in a puddle of water and booze.

The list. Cobb's and Odom's names crossed off.

~~Cobb~~
Gamble
Hodges
Knox
McBride
~~Odom~~
Glover
Burton

Jake tapped his finger next to *McBride*.

McBride shook harder. "Come on, Pete. Please. I was just doing what Burton wanted. You know that, right? He's the big cheese. All us guys gotta do what he says."

Jake raised the Glock. The weapon was now several inches longer with the addition of the suppressor, which he pressed into McBride's forehead. He felt the other man shake through the gun's handle.

He looked McBride in the eye.

Then he squeezed the trigger.

CHAPTER THIRTY-TWO

GLOVER HATED the look and feel of Burton's beach house.

It was so jagged and uncomfortable. Everything was lines and planes and flat surfaces and glass and metal. Sure wasn't cozy.

Yet Burton loved the place, took great pride in it, as though it was an extension of his success. And, of course, it was. No one else outside the immediate Farone family could afford a place like this.

Glover leaned against the smooth marble countertop in the kitchen, a phone receiver to his ear. The house felt even more uncomfortable than usual because no lights were turned on. There was only the moonlight coming in through the copious glass, reflecting off the waves and sand beyond. Just past the kitchen, in the living room, Burton stretched out on a vast, angular sofa, tumbler of scotch in hand, staring out to the beach. His stillness was disconcerting.

When they'd arrived a few minutes earlier, they discovered that there'd been a break-in. They immediately cleared every room, switching on lights as they went. Afterward, Burton had him turn all the lights back off.

Burton was like that—when he got pensive, he liked darkness. Glover supposed that jibed with the cold nature of his home.

For several minutes, they'd sat together in the long, uberchic sofas in the living room, in the darkness, looking out into the waves. When the phone rang, Burton had waved Glover away to answer it.

Glover hung up, rushed into the living room. Burton didn't turn away from the waves.

"Someone blasted Odom in his apartment," Glover said. "And McBride at Old Reno."

"Someone?" Burton scoffed. "It's Hudson. And he came here looking for me." Burton pointed to the floor, indicating the break-in on the lower level. He took a sip. "What about Cobb?"

"Never reported back," Glover said.

Burton thought for a moment.

Glover waited. It was best to remain quiet when Burton got like this. And Glover had never seen him this bad.

Finally Burton said, "Bring everyone in."

CHAPTER THIRTY-THREE

Tanner popped three chewable antacid tablets into his mouth.

Tropical fruit.

None of the three were the same color, and supposedly each had a different flavor, but he chewed them all together into a disregarded mush. It all tasted like chemical shit anyway.

Tanner's stress level had steadily climbed all night, which meant that so, too, had his stomach acid.

Why were things always so much worse when there was a personal element?

And why, when there was a personal element, would your brain not give you a damn break?

Tanner's brain kept reminding him of that thirty-second moment, in the break room, three months after Jake had joined the force.

A half-minute slice of life.

Jake had told him that his father had never been a bad man but had never been a great man either. That when Jake's mother had died, his father crumbled, turned to the bottle.

That Jake had been emotionally on his own since he was nine years old. That his father's half-absence and eventual death left him searching for strong men from whom to model his own development.

That Tanner was one of those male role models.

Tanner sighed. He took another sip of stale coffee, sloshed it around his mouth to clean the chemical pineapple taste from his teeth.

Jake, goddamn you. What the hell are you up to?

Tanner put the coffee mug on the scratched laminate of his desk and leaned back in his chair, interlacing his fingers behind his head.

His office was a gray box with a single window. The desk filled most of the floorspace. Frames covered the side walls— certificates, his college diploma, training class photos, ceremonial photos.

The corkboard on the rear wall had, for months, been plastered with photos and notes about the Farone investigation. Increasingly, in the last two months especially, the right-hand side of the board became dedicated to Burton's schism within the Farones.

Which now constituted the entire gang, it would seem, after the massacre in the alley.

There was a sucking sound.

A damn annoying sucking sound.

Pace.

Sucking air between his two glossy, blazingly white front teeth.

He sat on the corner of Tanner's desk, and he was using Tanner's phone. *Argh!* Tanner didn't appreciate having this fed's face pressed up against the phone he used every day, and he sure as hell didn't want his fed ass smashed against his desktop.

This close, Tanner could smell the guy's cologne. It was as clean and shiny as his teeth.

Cocky son of a bitch.

Pace hung up. "Odom's lady friend found him dead in his apartment, broken neck. Cobb, McBride, and now Odom. That's three of Burton's men confirmed murdered."

Tanner sat forward, removed his hands from the back of his head. The old office chair squealed as it straightened, and it squealed a second time as he pivoted the chair to look at the photos on the Burton half of the corkboard behind him.

"Shit," he muttered.

"It's because of the Farone girl," Pace said through that smartass grin of his.

Tanner narrowed his eyes. "How do you mean?"

"Rowe was in love with her, and everyone in the Farone organization knew it. Someone anonymously calls us, tells us that Rowe was the one who beat her to a pulp tonight, and yet the members of Burton's gang start showing up dead, on the same night, murdered one by one. Rowe didn't kill Cecilia Farone. It was—"

Tanner stuck up a hand, looked away from him. "It was the Burton contingent, and now our man is out getting his revenge. Thank you for the wonderful insight, Mr. Federal Agent. How did I ever get by without you?"

Pace chuckled, unfazed. "Then tell me this: why didn't Rowe go for Burton first?"

Tanner pointed to the photos behind them. "Because they had a rivalry. That's why Burton killed his lady." Tanner ran a hand along his mustache. "He's saving Burton for last."

CHAPTER THIRTY-FOUR

IT HAD BEEN a fifteen-minute drive from Pensacola to Pensacola Beach. In theory, there had been plenty of time for Jake to cool off.

But he hadn't.

The same rage roiled in his gut, the same clouded vision that he both perceived and didn't perceive.

And by the time he took the curve around the road to reveal Burton's ultramodern beach house, he still felt venom pulsing through him.

Several cars lined the horseshoe driveway. He recognized all of them. Burton had called in the forces. In the middle of the night. Word must've gotten out about Jake's killing spree. Just as Jake had predicted. That's why he'd come here.

To get them all in one fell swoop.

Jake stopped two houses up, parked on the side of the road, edging the wheels into the packed sand of Burton's neighbor's lot.

He stepped out of the Grand Prix. Onto the road. And started toward Burton's house.

As he took out the Glock, he made a quick mental calculation—an assumption that Burton would have a man waiting for him.

The assumption was immediately validated.

There was a figure at the side of the house, a dark outline at the peak of the beach's embankment. The man stood by the concrete stilts, holding what looked like a shotgun.

Jake crossed the road, approached the house from the opposite side.

As he came around the corner, where the embankment met the flat bottom of the primary floor, he peeked beneath and saw the other man.

It was Knox—twenty-something, black, mocha skin tone, square jaw with the strong, scrubbed-clean features of a would-be Hollywood actor. He held a pump-action, much like the Mossberg Jake had faced back at the Farone mansion.

Jake went farther down the embankment, soft white sand silencing his footsteps, and he eased onto the concrete patio area, which held a propane grill and an upscale set of lawn furniture.

Knox's back was turned to him, still facing the road. If Jake could stay quiet enough, this would be a clean kill.

Too late.

Something caught Knox's attention.

Knox spun around, the shotgun swinging with him, aimed in Jake's direction.

Jake lunged forward, his left boot slipping on the sand-covered concrete. Knox's finger tensed on the trigger, but Jake's shoulder collided with his ribs before he could squeeze. Knox buckled.

The Glock struck the shotgun's barrel with a metallic *clank*. Both weapons dislodged. The men's arms tangled as momentum carried them forward, off the concrete, away from the house.

Jake landed on Knox as they thudded in the sand. He

reached for Knox's neck, missed. Knox swiped Jake's arm, pulled at his hair. Fire from his scalp. His face snapped back.

A fist connected with Jake's side. The pain registered muffled and distant. Unimportant. He immediately threw a punch of his own, cracking his fist across Knox's jaw, throwing the man's head to the side.

The grip on Jake's hair released, but Knox took the blow well, his face snapping right back around. His big, dark eyes locked on Jake. A line of blood trickled from his upper lip.

The shotgun was a few feet away, half-buried in the sand. Jake reached. His fingertips grazed the stock. The gun shifted.

He threw another punch at Knox, missing the face, hitting the shoulder on the follow-through. He pulled their combined weight through the sand toward the shotgun. Reached again. Grabbed it.

And smashed the stock across Knox's head.

A sickening, wet *thwack*. Knox's jaw had broken. The lower half of his handsome face was rearranged. He looked like he'd crawled out of a cubist painting. A horrible moan. Hands to his cheeks, patting at himself dumbly, weakly.

Dazed. Little strength left.

That would make this easier.

Jake wrapped his hands around Knox's neck, and Knox slapped back with his remaining energy. All ten of Jake's fingers squeezed tight, thumbs digging into the esophagus.

Sputtering noises escaped Knox's lopsided mouth, from somewhere deep inside him. Spittle gurgled from his lips.

The sounds faded. His arms padded Jake weakly.

And he was still.

Jake leaned back, his hands remaining on Knox's neck—no longer squeezing, but resting.

His chest heaved.

As it had been with the other kills, Jake hadn't realized how exhausted he was. Adrenaline and rage had fueled him.

He needed to keep moving, to get into the house and continue his mission. But he'd give himself a moment, just a few seconds, to catch his breath.

Which was a mistake.

A metallic *click* from behind. An unmistakable, telltale noise. He didn't turn around.

A jolt of pain as the barrel of the gun jammed into the back of his neck.

Then a sharper pain to his head that made his eyes shut and his body drop back to the sand.

CHAPTER THIRTY-FIVE

PRESSURE ON JAKE'S upper arms. And his wrists. His thighs. His ankles.

There was a sharp snapping noise. Irritating. Almost painful.

He opened his eyes.

A pair of fingers snapped an inch from his face. Each snap brought another pulse of pain to his throbbing head.

It was Burton. Smiling.

And in a flash, Jake took in the entire situation.

He was tied to a small wooden chair in the center of Burton's living room, on the dark gray area rug, next to the square, concrete coffee table, all of it encircled by the long planes of Burton's stylish sectional sofas.

At the far wall, a few feet in front of him, Burton's home theater projector screen had been extended. It was aglow with the bright blue standby screen. Otherwise, there were no lights on in the room, just moonlight coming in through walls of glass.

There were four other men in the room, all standing: Burton, Glover, Gamble, and Hodges, the remaining members of Burton's contingent, the ones Jake hadn't killed yet.

With the theater screen in front of him, Jake's overactive brain flashed on a strange, out-of-place notion: that this scenario—tied to a chair, surrounded by adversaries—was one that a big-screen hero in a typical action movie would face with steely, unflinching resolve.

But here in the real world, Jake felt fear, deep down inside. Dread. Lots of it.

Burton leaned over, getting closer to his face, smiled. "Hello."

Jake couldn't speak, but he wouldn't have replied even if he could.

"Earlier I told you I'd take my time," Burton said, "that I'd involve all of my troops. I want you to know that I kept my word. I mean, you saw the condition of poor Cecilia's face. Or, what remained of it, I should say."

Snickers from the other men.

Burton put his hands in his pockets and rocked back on his heels. "What do you have to say to that?"

Jake lunged at him, the ropes tugging all over his body. The chair legs pulled at the rug's thick pile. He tried to scream. His lips moved rapidly, but only popping sounds came out.

Burton cocked his head.

"Wait a minute ... you actually *can't* talk, can you, Pete?" He chuckled, glanced at his men, then back to Jake. "You can't talk because you saw Cecilia. I know what this is. It's called selective mutism. Usually happens with children. Happened to a little cousin of mine, couldn't speak for two years after she saw her daddy get squashed by a city bus." He looked at the others. "We scared him speechless, boys!"

Laughter.

Jake had never heard of selective mutism, but from the

way Burton described it, he knew this was exactly what was afflicting him.

Burton paced in front of him. "Now, you're probably thinking we're gonna kill you. And you're correct. But first ... gee, how do I put this?" He drummed his fingers on his chin, looked toward the ceiling in mock concentration. "First, we're going to torture you."

That same fear rushed over Jake, that same non-action-movie-hero dread, a stronger wave of it, this one with a powerful undertow.

Burton's eyes widened with faux concern.

"Why, you look frightened, Pete! Don't worry. I'm not gonna poke things in your eyes. I'm not gonna cut you or burn you." He gave a smile. "I'm just gonna make you watch a little movie."

CHAPTER THIRTY-SIX

BURTON WAS GOING to enjoy this.

Oh, was he ever going to enjoy this.

He stepped away from Hudson, looked at Gamble. "Get the tape ready."

Gamble went to the projector at the other end of the living room.

Burton faced Hudson, tied to a folding chair, trying his damndest to look tough, but with palpable, wonderful fear showing on his lips and in his eyes.

Burton's hands went behind his back. He gave Hudson a warm smile.

"You see, Pete, I took a precaution. I saw the urgent conversation you and Cecilia had before the Roja hit tonight. I figured it could very well be that she was looking out for you, telling you not to go to the hit. One of her premonitions or something. She always was a sweet little hippie to you, wasn't she?

"So I thought, you know what, I'll record it—if he doesn't go to the hit, then I'll have a videotape to show him."

He glanced to the back of the room. Gamble had put the

tape into the VCR connected to the projector. He was fiddling with the settings.

Hurry up, damn you.

Burton stepped toward Hudson, leaned down, getting close to his face. Hudson was still fighting to hold on to the stoic facade, but Burton could see anguish wriggling under his skin. Sweat beaded his forehead.

"But you went to the raid and *still* survived," Burton said. "You're nothing if not a survivor. So it all worked out just splendidly, because now I get to show you what exactly happened to your dear little C.C."

Hudson squirmed in his chair now. He could no longer contain his fear. Lips trembling. Eyes blinking rapidly.

It was savorous, Hudson's anguish. Burton could almost see it, like a cloud emanating from his sweaty figure, wafting up toward the ceiling, disrupted by his torturous writhing. Burton smelled it, sucked it in, took in a big gulp through his nostrils, still smiling at him, always smiling.

In New Orleans, Pete Hudson had cost Burton tens of thousands of dollars out of the startup fund he was using to form his new operation. In recent hours, Pete Hudson had taken four of his seven men. And, months earlier, Pete Hudson had stolen the favor of Burton's surrogate father, the man who Burton had stood beside, supported, risked his life for even as the old man lost his mind.

Yes, Burton was going to enjoy destroying Pete Hudson's soul.

"It's ready," Gamble said from the rear of the room.

Burton straightened up and nodded at Gamble.

He turned to the screen, which came to life. A flash of white; the bright blue standby image returned for a moment; *PLAY* appeared in white letters in the upper righthand corner.

Then the video began.

First, there was McBride's fat, Irish ass on the screen, but when he shifted, the scene was revealed—Cecilia in the middle of the Farone library, surrounded by Burton's troops, all wearing black leather gloves and dangerous smirks.

Hudson moaned.

Earlier, Burton had tried to position himself perfectly, to get himself into the most photogenic position for the final image. He wasn't sure how the end result would turn out, of course, but seeing it now on the big projector screen made him smile. He'd done well—positioned like a born leader at the left side of the screen, standing tall, a commanding presence watching as the circle of his men tightened around Cecilia.

Burton turned back to Hudson. "I look good, don't I? Like a freakin' movie star." He turned to the other men, who had taken positions on either side of Hudson's chair. "Don't I?"

Laughs from his troops.

Hudson averted his gaze from the screen, burying his face in his shoulder. Hodges grabbed him by the hair, twisted his head forward, *Clockwork Orange* style.

"That's right," Burton said. "Pete's gonna watch our movie, fellas. All of it. Don't let him look away."

On the screen, Burton's troops tightened their circle around Cecilia. Odom twirled his blackjack baton aimlessly in his hand.

Cecilia shook, stumbled.

Burton's on-screen doppelgänger was smiling just as much as his current persona. The other Burton looked at the camera and winked.

The circle of men closed within feet of Cecilia. And stopped. A moment of relative stillness. Just Cecilia trembling, slowly turning in a circle, looking at the faces.

Then Knox backhanded her hard, spinning her around, sending a line of blood flying into the library.

Hudson screamed.

CHAPTER THIRTY-SEVEN

THE WOMAN CALLING herself Christie Mosley was in her Cutlass Supreme outside the beach house that belonged to the man to whom she'd been posing as a girlfriend for months. The beach road was quiet and dark, very little traffic moving past to interrupt her view as she looked through her binoculars at the massive banks of windows on the first floor of the house, the main tier of its staggered, geometric design.

The scene she'd been watching play out, for several minutes, in Burton's sprawling living room was illuminated by two faint light sources—the moonlight pouring in through all the massive panes of glass, reflecting off the waves beyond; and the projector screen at the far wall of the living room, where a video was playing.

A pillar blocked her view of the screen, and the interior of the house was so dark that she saw everything in shadows, silhouettes. Four men on their feet; one bound to a chair.

Though she couldn't fully distinguish his features, the man in the chair was clearly Jake Rowe. And what was happening to him looked horrible.

Her cellular phone was on the passenger seat. She placed a

speed-dial call, turned on the speakerphone feature, left the phone where it was.

"Yes?" Falcon said, scratchy through the speakerphone.

"They're torturing him."

"How so?"

"It's hard to tell. He ... He's clearly tied to a chair. Thrashing all over the place. Violently. They're holding him back, but..." She squinted. "But they're not beating him. They're hardly touching him, just the occasional slap."

"Electrocution, perhaps."

"Maybe. Or maybe poisoning, but ... Oh, god. It's getting bad. He's convulsing like crazy."

She checked the clock on the dash.

"It's been ten minutes of this. I need to do something."

"You'll do nothing. This isn't your fight. You won't jeopardize everything we've worked for."

"They're gonna kill the guy!"

"So be it. Stand your ground."

She watched as one of the figures stepped behind Rowe, both hands on his head, which had fallen to his chest. The man yanked him back up straight, and Rowe began to shake again, even harder, the entire chair thrashing.

Oh god...

Falcon must have been correct. Electrocution. It had to be.

Rowe continued to thrash.

Her stomach roiled. Her legs twitched, wanting to bolt. She didn't know how much more of this she could take.

More importantly, she didn't know how much more Rowe could take. Whatever they were doing to him, he wasn't going to last much longer.

CHAPTER THIRTY-EIGHT

JAKE COULDN'T TELL how much time had passed. In his training at the academy, he'd learned that in times of high stress, the perception of time can be distorted.

Maybe an hour.

Maybe five minutes.

Maybe half an hour.

Knox had struck her first. Backhanded her.

She'd spun around, twirling to the opposite side of the circle of men, where Gamble had caught her, grabbed her arms.

McBride approached. An uppercut to the stomach that folded her.

Gamble pulled her back upright. Shoved her away.

Hodges grabbed her next, hands moving up and down the sides of her dress, grabbing her breasts. Burton shouted at him, anger replacing his smile momentarily. Hodges cowered, shoved C.C. away.

She'd avoided the next man's grasp, Odom's, and she punched him in the mouth. Her strength was clearly zapped, and her form was pitiful, but she'd caught him by surprise, a blow that snapped his head back.

The other men laughed.

And Jake welled with pride, somewhere deep within the swirling mass of pain in his gut.

Odom looked at the others as they laughed, mortified. He swung his blackjack at her face, crushing her eye socket, tearing the skin.

Jake screamed at this. Turned away. Someone punched him hard in the ribs. Saliva exploded from his mouth.

Someone else grabbed his head from behind, forcing him to face the screen, callused fingertips pressing into the corners of his eyelids, prying them open.

Blood dripped from the side of C.C.'s face.

Cobb next. Broke her nose.

She fell.

They picked her up.

McBride.

Gamble.

Hodges.

Glover—he was given extra time with her, benefits of being Burton's second-in-command.

They threw her to the left side of the circle.

Then the right.

Burton watching. The smiling supervisor. Shouting encouragements. And also shouting the occasional admonition when the men touched her just so.

To the left side of the circle. Right. Back and forth.

On the floor. Lifted up.

Laughter.

Wet sounds of flesh-to-flesh, progressively wetter.

An arm around her neck, choking her out. She smacked blindly at the man.

Hodges slapped her. He'd only slapped. No punches, no kicks, some distorted sense of chivalry.

Gamble wasn't afraid to punch. He gave her a blow to the forehead that sent her back to the floor.

They didn't lift her up this time. Instead they kicked.

Jake yelled out again.

A searing burn across his cheek as someone backhanded him.

Glover embellished his kicking routine—more of the benefits of being Burton's primary lieutenant—turning it into an Irish-style dance, laughing. He and McBride, the two Irish members of the group, shared a chuckle.

Odom loped over to C.C., raised his blackjack—

And Burton caught his wrist, gave him a shake of the head, pushed him back to his place in the circle.

"That's enough," the on-screen Burton said to the other men.

C.C. was nearly motionless. Slow rising and lowering of her torso.

Alive.

Somehow that was a comfort to Jake. Why? He knew how this ended.

Surely she'd been unconscious by then. He prayed she was.

For several minutes, there had been terrible screams. Then there had been nothing but the dull thuds of the blows as she'd been thrown among the men, on her feet, alive but dead.

Now there was no sound coming from her. Not even moaning.

Burton stepped away from the others, closer to the camera, looking right into Jake from the screen. He smiled.

Then he went to C.C., squatted. He brought his face inches from her ear. Whispered something.

He took out his revolver and placed it against the back of her head.

Somehow Jake's voice returned.

"*No!*"

Burton fired his weapon. C.C.'s body went limp. The other men laughed.

The real-life Burton stepped up to Jake, blocking his view of the video.

"Oh, so you *can* talk."

For once, the creepy smile left Burton's lips. No false pretenses now; his face was simply dark.

"New Orleans was a mistake, Pete. It's a bad habit of yours: stealing from me. You stole in New Orleans, you stole my troops tonight, and you stole my adopted poppa before that." He paused. And quieter he said, "This is where it ends for you. Say hi to Cecilia for me."

He straightened up and brought the smile back, turned to his remaining men.

"Boys, our friend Pete can talk again." He began clapping. "Come on, now. Give him a hand!"

The other men applauded. Dark eyes penetrated Jake from all sides.

"Let's give ol' Loudmouth an appropriate ending, shall we? We shut him up for a few hours; now let's shut him up permanently." He looked past Jake. "Grab his hair, Gamble."

A tearing sensation at Jake's scalp as his head was pulled back.

Burton stepped forward. He ran his index finger along Jake's outstretched throat. Then he made a pair of criss-crossed swipes right in the center of Jake's neck and looked him in the eye.

"X marks the spot."

Burton pulled back a fist, jaw clenched, arm quivering

with wound-up energy, preparing for a blow destined to do a lot of damage.

And with a blur, it was delivered.

The fist cracked into Jake's throat.

Inconceivable pain. Tearing and crunching. The sensation of air sucking, distorting, wheezing. Scalding needles. Slicing razors. A boiling in his stomach and a blinding light in his eyes.

And a strange thought.

A notion.

One that was simple and pure.

He was going to die.

Everything went white.

CHAPTER THIRTY-NINE

AS HE THOUGHT about the last moment of his previous life, Silence ran a hand along his throat, grimacing slightly with the pain.

He looked out to the street while his finger traced his Adam's apple. The quiet neighborhood of East Hill had become slightly less quiet since he'd first sat down with Mrs. Enfield. Ahead and to the left, windows were now alight in the biggest of the houses, whose modern, squarish, geometrical design reminded Silence a bit of Burton's beach house. More and more people were walking the sidewalk, all laughs and smiles, heading west toward downtown and the upcoming festival.

The sky had been gray all day, but as dusk approached, the waning light peeked through the gloom, just slightly, as though coaxed from its hiding by the joy percolating from the imminent festivities. The streetlights had kicked on a few minutes earlier, joining the party.

Sounds were already drifting over from several blocks away—music and whistles and horns—even though the festival's official start time wasn't for another hour and a half.

Pensacola liked its outdoor events, and start times were more general guidelines than strict deadlines. -*Ish* was appropriate for most situations. 8ish. 6:30ish. Pensacola Beach was located on a barrier island, so it made sense that Pensacola proper's leisure activities had a sense of island time.

As he watched a trio of middle-aged women pass by—dressed to the nines, chatting and laughing—he pressed slightly into his neck, tickling the pain embedded in its core.

It had been a mere instant when Burton's fist had connected with his throat. A fraction of a moment—that's all it takes to change things completely. Silence had always looked at life as a forward-progressing line. To change its direction, you simply place a peg in front of the line, bounce it off its previous course by a few degrees. Want to change your life again? Place another peg in your path.

But other people could lay pegs in front of your lifeline as well, zapping the control you had over your destiny. Burton had placed a large peg in front of Silence's line and sent it careening off into a dark region of life he was never meant to explore, stripping Silence of his sovereignty.

If Silence could just go back and somehow remove that single peg, he'd have control. One minor correction—that's all it would take to set things right again.

C.C., if she were there, would smile at him serenely now, and in a mediating, non-patronizing way she would tell him that his concerns were unfounded. She would say that wishing for the ability to change the past was silly and a horrible waste of life. She would say that he had no control, that he never did. No one did. Control was not meant to be. It was not a part of destiny.

She would tell him to let go.

Life doesn't happen to you, love. It happens for you, she had told him.

He felt something on the back of his hand. Mrs. Enfield's dry, old fingers. She pulled his hand from his throat.

"Stop messing with it."

How could she sense these things?

He lowered the offending hand and placed it on the soft, warm, rumbling mound draped across his right thigh. When he looked down, Baxter looked up, and the moment they made eye contact, the cat's purring spiked.

Baxter's eyes were squinted with contentment, and his head was tilted to the left, which was thusly the side of his face from which his ubiquitous line of drool was leaking—directly onto Silence's thigh. A gross, wet, warm little puddle, on a very nice pair of charcoal wool pants with a subtle plaid texture. Versatile, comfortable. Only a week old, and already one of Silence's go-tos.

And now, evidently, their versatility extended so far as to be a cat bib.

He rubbed Baxter's big head. The purring spiked again.

"You've gone quiet on me again," Mrs. Enfield said. "Dark quiet." She pointed at his throat. "I'm thinking that whatever gave you your bullfrog voice is also the reason you won't open up to me. Yes?"

Not only could Mrs. Enfield see without seeing, but she was also incredibly perceptive.

And insistent.

Silence wasn't particularly bothered by her insistence—it came from the best possible place—but still he didn't reply.

Mrs. Enfield nodded. "On your time, Silence. On your time."

She turned her blind eyes slightly to the west, listened, and shook her head.

"Darn Tristán Festival. I swear it gets less family-friendly each year. Soon, it'll be nothing but a big drunken fest. I wouldn't take kids there past 9 p.m., I'll tell you that much."

Of the many festivals Pensacola hosted each year, the Tristán Festival was one of the biggest and one of several that celebrated the city's proud historical heritage, chiefly the fact that, in 1559, Pensacola was the first European settlement in America, courtesy of Spanish explorer Tristán de Luna.

The Tristán Festival was an annual two-day event, with a first day devoted to a Mardis Gras-style parade and a costume contest, which crowned a King and Queen Tristy. The second day was a more adult-oriented, nighttime affair. The main drag through downtown was closed off from vehicular traffic, and what began as an arts and crafts festival eventually—and sooner than later—turned into a "drunken fest," as Mrs. Enfield had put it.

She groaned. "And those whiz-jets will be flying over, too. I appreciate their service, but at my age I just can't take the noise."

The "whiz-jets" were the Navy's Blue Angels aerobatic team who performed aerial stunt shows all over the country. Pensacola was known as "The Cradle of Naval Aviation," as Naval Air Station Pensacola was the primary training location for naval aviators. The Blue Angels and all things naval aviation were more sources of great pride for the city, and the aerobatic team performed a flyover at the beginning of each year's Tristán Festival.

Silence noticed something in his periphery. A vehicle stopped at the far corner, in the opposite direction to downtown and the festival.

The El Camino. Engine idling. The white guy dangled out of the driver-side door, sunglasses and fedora, looking their way.

"What is it?" Mrs. Enfield said.

"Our friends."

Bass pumped out of the car. The white guy laughed.

Silence transferred Baxter to the center of the swing and

stood up. He approached the steps, thinking the punks would drive off like they did the last time.

But they didn't.

So he stepped off the porch.

Mrs. Enfield called out. "Silence, where are you going?"

He didn't respond.

As he moved down the quiet sidewalk—quiet but for the rumbling music pounding out of the El Camino—the white guy stared at him, grinning, laughing, watching over the top of his sunglasses. Beyond him, the younger guy was also laughing, jeering, and he seemed more emboldened than last time.

When Silence was a few feet away, the driver turned to the kid in the passenger seat, said something. The music died, and both men exited the car.

The black kid stepped around the hood and stood beside his leader. He was tall, and the white guy was short, creating a disparity of easily six inches.

Out of the car, under a streetlight, the kid looked even younger than Silence had originally thought. His mustache was scraggly, cheeks smooth.

"Whatcha want, old man? Huh?" the white guy said through his sneer. One of his teeth was gold. "Did your sugar momma send you to scare us off?"

He turned to the younger guy, snickering, received a sycophantic chuckle in return.

Silence said nothing, just stepped closer.

He looked down upon the white guy, blocking the streetlight, throwing him in shadow. The man took a half step back, a shoe shuffling on the asphalt, losing his balance. A flash of embarrassment swept over his face. A bit of his street cred had just evaporated right in front of his protégé. His face shifted a fraction to the right, checking to see if the kid had noticed.

The man forced the confident sneer back onto his lips.

"Ooooh, we got a tough guy here. Big, tall son of a bitch. Think you scare me, old man?" He reached behind his back. "I'm gonna—"

There was a flash of movement, and Silence didn't realize that he'd done it.

Truly, he *hadn't* done it. Not consciously, anyway. Instinct. A skill branded into his subconscious. Recently.

There was something cold and heavy in his hand. The white guy's gun, a battered old Smith.

It had been so fast, Silence hadn't even felt his arm move, let alone seen it.

Nakiri's training, that he'd completed two weeks ago. The *brutal* training. Hours and days and weeks of torment.

The shit actually worked.

The white guy's hand remained at chest level, index finger extended, lower fingers curled, aiming an invisible firearm at Silence. He looked at the hand with wide-eyed shock.

Silence considered turning the guy's own gun on him. But then he remembered how, moments earlier, the guy had cowered away from him without Silence even having to say a word.

Which reminded him of more of Nakiri's training, the concepts of escalation and intimidation.

He needed to contain this situation, not escalate it.

The opponent was already frightened of him. And the guy was clearly a novice—all bravado, no discipline. A tiny peacock fluffing its tail as wide as possible.

Intimidation was the only tool Silence needed in this situation. He could practically see Nakiri nodding respectfully.

He shoved the revolver in his pocket and glared at the white guy.

"Name," Silence said.

The man jumped at the destroyed quality of Silence's voice.

And when he didn't immediately reply, Silence repeated, louder, "*Name!*"

The man jumped again. "Doughty."

Silence faced the younger guy, whose eyes were saucers, arms shaking. If there was any doubt that this kid was in over his head, it was erased now.

"L-L-Lee. Lee, sir."

Silence patted Doughty's revolver in his pocket and gave the man a dark stare. "Keeping this." He pointed to the El Camino. "Leave."

Doughty's eyes went to Silence's pocket, as if for a fraction of a moment he had the courage to protest, then he opened the driver-side door.

Lee moved around the car, back to the passenger side.

"Not you," Silence said.

Lee stopped.

Silence could sense the kid's quality, his confused decency. C.C. had always told him he was good at reading people.

So Silence was going to go out on a limb, take a chance.

Lee was on the sidewalk, at the front corner of the El Camino's hood. He looked at Silence, the saucer-eyes even wider, then at Doughty who stood in the open driver-side door, one leg in the vehicle.

Doughty turned to Silence, more of his pride crumbling away. His gaze snapped back across the hood to Lee. "Get in the car."

Lee made eye contact with Silence.

Silence shook his head.

"Get in *the damn car!*" Doughty said.

Lee looked back and forth between them. Stopped on Silence. And finally turned to Doughty, shook his head.

"Shit!" Doughty said and dropped into the cracked vinyl seat. "Goddamn idiot."

He slammed the rusty door. His eyes met Silence's, burning. The car bolted off and screeched around the corner ahead. The bass came to life, so loud it rattled the rotting body panels.

The El Camino disappeared.

Silence went to the sidewalk. He put his hands in his pockets and looked down upon Lee. The kid was tall but not nearly as tall as Silence.

"Talk," Silence said as quietly as his voice would allow.

He'd considered saying something more intimidating, something to scare the shit out of the kid. But his throat was hurting bad after the second, louder time he'd growled at Doughty. And, of course, Lee was already scared, shaking. So instead, Silence had said the same one-word command he'd given to Glover—this time in an entirely different tone.

Which brought forth an intriguing notion, one that C.C. would have been very much in agreement with: *Less is more.*

Silence was tall, big, and had severe features and a demonic voice. He didn't need to say much to impart the intimidation that Nakiri had preached. He could say one syllable, *Talk*, and let other people do all the speaking, lowering the number of sounds channeling through his painful throat.

A good idea. He'd remember it.

Lee's lower lip trembled. His skin was a pale caramel color, dotted with freckles. He wore his beanie far back on his head, his hairline propping it up.

"I just follow him around, man. He told me he could help me out, that two people are better than one, you know? He's from Mobile. Just a thief, a petty criminal, but he's trying to make a name for himself here in Pensacola. There's this mob family. They're called the Farones. And there's this other group he's been hearing about, the Burton gang. You've probably never heard of these groups, have you, someone like you in your nice clothes in this nice neighborhood?"

Oh, you'd be surprised, Silence thought.

But Silence played dumb. He shook his head.

"Well, Doughty thinks if he can make a name for himself around town, he'll impress them, get a foot in the door. And he wanted a partner. See, I met him at the gas station after school let out one day, and—"

Silence held up a hand.

Had the kid really just said "school"?

"Age," Silence said.

Lee cocked his head. "You mean, how old am I?"

Silence nodded.

"Seventeen."

Silence sighed.

Even younger than he'd thought.

And the kid had gotten himself involved with an out-of-state petty thug whose biggest aspiration in life was joining up with Burton.

Silence was glad he'd followed his gut instinct. He needed to divert this kid's life path, put a peg right in front of a line that was barreling toward a horrible future. He needed to do so immediately. But how?

Due to Silence's size, strength, and his monster voice, Nakiri had told him that intimidation would be one of his strongest traits. This had proven very effective moments earlier with Doughty.

However, Nakiri had also said, *Never forget about deception. When situations are critical or when adrenaline is flowing, when bullets are flying, it's easy to not consider finesse. But don't forget about it.*

Silence pointed to the street ahead of them where Doughty had taken off. "You're done with him."

He flicked back his sport coat, revealing a flash of his shoulder holster, the Beretta within.

Lee gasped. "Shit, you're a cop! Yes … yes, sir. I won't talk to him again. I mean, the guy's a loser anyway. I … I'll never contact him again. I promise."

Silence nodded. He grabbed a quarter from his front pocket, took his wallet from his back pocket. He handed Lee the quarter and a twenty-dollar bill, then pointed down the street in the opposite direction of where he'd pointed moments earlier.

"Pay phone. Two blocks down." Sharp pain in his throat. He paused. Swallowed. "Call taxi." Swallowed. "Never come back here."

Lee clutched the bill in both hands, nodded fervently, then spun around and took off. He wasn't going to blow this second chance Silence had given him.

"Thank you," the kid called over his shoulder.

Silence watched him retreat down the sidewalk, then turned back for the house.

A few moments later, he stepped up to Mrs. Enfield. He didn't sit back down beside her, though, just stopped and stood next to her. Doughty had delayed him, and now he had to double down. He had to get back to his house.

And move on to the next step toward stopping Burton.

Mrs. Enfield smiled up at him, and her face seemed calm, but her quivering hands gave her away. She was a resolute woman and prideful in the best possible way.

Silence knelt down, laid one of his big hands over both of hers, pressed against the shaking.

"They're gone?" she said.

"They're gone."

She pulled one of her hands out from beneath his, placed it on his cheek. "Thank you, Silence."

Baxter had returned to his spot beneath the table. Silence picked him up, placed him on Mrs. Enfield's lap, then stood.

"Have to go." He swallowed. "Work to do."

"Be safe."

She'd said it with triple-filtered purity. There was no hiding from this intuitive woman the fact that he was in a violent line of work. She didn't want the responsibility or liability of knowing exactly what it was he did—and he couldn't blame her—but she'd also quickly grown to care genuinely about him.

It wasn't a platitude, what she'd said. She meant it. She wanted him to be safe.

"I will," he said and left.

In his house, he went straight for the kitchen, where he first put Doughty's gun in a drawer, then moved on to his primary objective: the refrigerator. He grabbed one of the bottles. Cold and heavy, dappled with moisture.

His mind flashed on Mrs. Enfield, the genuine concern she'd just shown him, her vigilance about his drinking.

He would drink this one beer. Only this one.

He glanced to the far end of the house, where the two bedrooms were. Fresh drywall—unfinished and unpainted— framed the left doorway. The wall had just been put back up a couple of days earlier, and there was still work to do. Beyond that unfinished wall, in the bedroom, was the object that was going to help him find Lukas Burton.

Silence had known his entire life that his mind space was chaotic, but it wasn't until this last year that he understood it was a genuine issue. C.C. had pointed this out to him. And she'd given him several techniques with which to help manage the storm of his mind, things like mind mapping, meditation, breathing exercises, self-reflection.

Since her death, since he'd become a literal new man with a new face, a new voice, and a new name, he'd taken C.C.'s teachings even more seriously than he had when she was alive.

And when the Watchers had given him a $50,000 seed with which to begin his new life, he immediately spent half of that on an item that became an extension of C.C.'s teachings, an item that she would have never imagined he would use.

It was in the back of the house, one of the two bedrooms, right across the hall from where he slept.

And he was going to need it if he was going to stop Burton tonight.

Clutching the Heineken, he left the kitchen, crossed the living room, entered the short hallway, and turned into the bedroom on the left.

There it was.

It filled nearly the entire floorspace of the small room. For the technicians to assemble its large pieces, Silence had to hire contractors to tear down then reinstall the wall and doorway.

A massive, white, glossy pod, split in two, hinged at the back. Sleek and smooth. It looked like something from a sci-fi movie, an escape module, or a giant robotic clam that traveled back in time from the future. In its idle state, there was a gap between the two halves, from which came blue fiberoptic lighting, making the entire room glow.

It was an isolation tank. A floating pod.

Otherwise known as a sensory deprivation chamber.

Ten inches of water inside, kept at the skin-receptor-neutral temperature of 93.5 degrees and loaded with eight hundred pounds of Epsom salt, enough to make anyone float. When the door was shut and the light extinguished, things went pitch-black. The combination of the darkness, the floating, and earplugs created a nearly stimulus-free environment.

Sensory deprivation.

It was the most nothingness one could possibly create for oneself.

And people used this carefully crafted environment to experience the transcendent, the ultimate form of quieting one's mind.

It had cost him twenty-five grand. It had been there for a week. And he'd yet to use it.

The only other item in the room was a folding chair, left-over from the day the technicians had installed the pod. When they'd left, he'd sat in the chair to stare for a while at his bizarre investment.

Now, he sat in the chair again and ran the cold beer bottle between his palms, staring at the pod as he had the first day.

People would tell him he was crazy for spending half his startup cash on a quirky technique he'd never even tried.

Tanner would have said he was crazy.

His dad would have, too.

But C.C. wouldn't have.

He twisted the cap off the beer bottle, took a long swig.

Good. Very good.

He'd drink this beer. Then he'd get in the pod.

And find his answer.

Another gulp, this one bringing cold pain to his neck. He rubbed it, remembered how Mrs. Enfield had chastised him for messing with it.

When she'd scolded him, he'd been thinking of the moment Burton had crushed his throat. At that point in time, he hadn't yet been introduced to the Watchers. He hadn't received his new name or face.

Nevertheless, *that* was the precise moment he became a new person.

He'd died then. Figuratively speaking.

And he would have died literally as well had it not been for her, the woman he'd known as Christie Mosley.

She saved his life.

CHAPTER FORTY

THE WOMAN CALLING herself Christie Mosley fidgeted anxiously in her seat as she stared through her binoculars at the windows of Burton's beach house—the sprawling living room area and the hideous events within.

She'd seen Burton—who she unfortunately knew intimately enough to recognize by a mere silhouette—punch Rowe in the neck, a devastating blow, one so hard that Rowe's chair flew back.

"They punched him in the freaking throat!" she shouted at the cellular phone on the passenger seat. "The chair tipped over. He's on his back, and ... oh, shit, he needs help."

"Hold your position," Falcon said. He'd lost every trace of his often misplaced whimsy. Now his voice was deadly serious, anger threatening to burst to the surface.

The figures converged on the overturned chair. Sharp, fast flashes of movement among the shadow figures.

"They're kicking him..."

"Listen to me, you hold your damn position!"

"Oh, God, they're kicking the shit out of him." She

paused. Gave it another moment of consideration. And then said. "I gotta go."

"Don't you—"

She pressed the *END* button, dropped the binoculars onto the passenger seat by the phone, grabbed her holstered Beretta 92FS, drew the weapon, and bolted out of her car.

Humid, slightly cool air. The sound of waves crashing beyond the house. A screaming seagull.

Across the street. Up the steps to the all-glass front door. She could see all the men clearly now in the living room beyond—Hodges, Gamble, Glover, and Burton converged in a circle, kicking at Rowe. Thin, blue nylon cords tied Rowe to the overturned chair.

If Rowe's throat injury was as bad as it had appeared through the binoculars, he only had moments left.

She tried the door handle. Locked. Reached into her pocket. As Burton's "girlfriend," she'd been afforded a key. She unlocked the door, threw it open.

And started firing.

The men looked up in shock.

Burton managed three words before she squeezed off the first round.

"Christie, what are—"

Her first shot struck Gamble in the forehead. A plume of blood.

Slight reposition. Trigger.

Hodges's shoulder exploded. He screamed. She squeezed twice more, putting two rounds through his chest. He collapsed a couple of feet away from Gamble.

Burton and Glover had crossed the room, running up the floating staircase to the second floor.

She fired three more times, the rounds cracking into the steps, the wall, sending debris clattering into the room.

Instinct and training pulled her after Burton and Glover.

For only a split second, not even enough time to move her feet. Because there was a more pressing objective.

She ran to the chair, dropped to her knees.

"*Shit!*" she screamed and fought the urge to look away.

Rowe was in goddamn horrible shape. She'd seen a lot in the last twelve years of this "job" of hers, but this was the worst. That unassuming, handsome, *aww-shucks* face that she'd known for the last several months as Pete Hudson, and more recently as Jake Rowe, was simply gone.

Gone.

They'd kicked it into nothing. Tissue and blood and flaps of skin.

But he was still alive. Unconscious with slight movements in his chest and horrible puttering, wheezing noises coming from his lips.

The guy was a freaking survivor.

His skin was turning blue. She looked at his throat. It was collapsed, a deep indentation in the center.

Only moments left to save him.

She frantically scanned the room for something she could use.

There.

A legal pad and pen on a small table in the back.

She sprinted to the table, grabbed the pen, sprinted back to Rowe, dropped to her knees.

The pen was metal—a gold Cross pen. A godsend. Metal was better than plastic for what she had planned.

She fought to keep her hands from shaking as she disassembled the pen.

Then she traced her finger along Rowe's throat and found his Adam's apple, a task that should have been simple but was a challenge with the mangled condition of his neck. From there, she slid farther down to the cricoid cartilage.

The spot between the two—between the Adam's apple and the cricoid cartilage—was her objective.

She took her pen knife from the pocket of her jeans, snapped open the blade.

And sucked in a quick, deep breath.

She'd never done this before.

An emergency tracheotomy.

She brought the blade to Rowe's battered flesh and pressed down with a good amount of pressure. The sharp blade pierced the flesh cleanly. Blood raced out, snaked down the side of his neck.

A horizontal incision, a half inch long and a half inch deep.

His neck now open to her, she saw the yellowish cricothyroid membrane. She placed the blade on the membrane, pierced it.

Blood spurted on her face.

And a horrible wet gasp came from Rowe's open throat.

She stuck the metal tube from the pen into the now accessible airway, put her lips around it and sucked to verify that air was moving through the tube and into Rowe.

Lumpy, warm fluid filled her mouth.

She turned, spit. Blood and nastiness speckled the rug.

Airway clear.

She'd done it. Shit, she'd actually done it.

No time to revel in glory. There was still very imminent danger in her environment, on the floor above her. She looked back to the stairs where Burton and Glover fled, mangled by the rounds she'd squeezed off.

She sliced through the nylon ropes, swiped them off Rowe's arms and legs, then hooked him under the armpits and dragged him to the front door.

CHAPTER FORTY-ONE

GLOVER HAD BEEN in a lot of crazy situations in his life of petty crime, especially in recent months since joining up with Lukas Burton.

But he'd never been in a situation *this* crazy, one so crazy that even Burton took a moment to calm down, to develop a plan. Glover hadn't seen the man like this—so lost, so out of control.

They were in a darkened spare bedroom on the second story of Burton's house. A guest room with, like the rest of the house, large floor-to-ceiling glass. This room was on the north side of the house, and so it looked out on the water of the sound as opposed to the Gulf on the opposite side of the island. There was a queen bed with dark gray bedding, perfectly flat and smooth. A sleek dresser.

And a gun locker.

Burton unlocked it and pulled the metal doors open, reached inside and grabbed a pair of Heckler & Koch MP5K submachine guns, handed one to Glover.

Glover looked at the weapon in his hands then looked at

Burton. "*Goddamn, man!* Christie... I mean, what are we gonna—"

Burton shoved him to the side. "Shut up!"

He looked away, thinking, fingers playing on the banana-shaped magazine of his HK.

Finally he said, "All right, we can't just go running back down there. We'll take the side route." He pointed to the sliding glass door and the balcony beyond where there was a set of steps that led down to the sand. "The way she took down our guys ... She's been trained."

Trained?

"You think she's a cop?" Glover said. "Christie? Like, undercover?"

"That'd be my guess. Which means—"

There was a muffled sound of a car engine firing up outside, followed quickly by the *chirp* of tires.

"Shit!" Burton said and ran out of the room.

Glover chased after him.

———

Glover squeezed the HK between his legs, needing both hands to grasp the Jaguar's leather passenger seat as Burton jerked the car around traffic on the quiet, sand-strewn street, honking at the lackadaisical nighttime traffic and beachgoers. The tires squealed. The smell of hot rubber filled the cab.

Burton swerved around another car, and a set of taillights appeared farther down the street—another car that was driving fast, erratically.

"That's Christie's Cutlass," Burton said. "She's going for the bridge, headed back to Pensacola proper."

The street in front of them was now open. Burton smashed the gas pedal. The Jaguar howled. The gap between the vehicles shrank.

The Cutlass swung right, onto a cross-street.

Burton continued straight, flying past where Christie had turned.

Glover looked out the window as they passed the street. "What the hell are you doing? She went that way."

The Jaguar's engine roared as Burton gave it more gas.

"Setting a trap," he said.

Glover looked at the submachine gun pinched between his thighs. "How do you want me to handle this? I mean, that's your girl."

Burton didn't take his eyes off the road, only tightened his grip on the leather-wrapped steering wheel.

"Finish the bitch off."

CHAPTER FORTY-TWO

THE WOMAN CALLING herself Christie Mosley clenched down hard on the steering wheel of the Cutlass Supreme that had been her vehicle for the last several months.

It had been a good car, but she'd never had to test it like this.

The tires screeched as she swerved past a car parked halfway on the street. She stole a glance to the rearview mirror.

The street behind her was empty.

Burton had been back there moments earlier, before she'd taken the latest corner.

He wouldn't have backed off. That wasn't his style. He was up to something.

She looked to the passenger seat.

Bloodied and unconscious, Jake Rowe undulated with the movements of the vehicle. Though she'd seatbelted him in, his completely lifeless form moved violently. Her eyes found the glinting metal tube coming from the center of his throat, swinging precariously. She put a hand on his shoulder to stabilize him, looked through the windshield, then another fast glance to the rearview.

Still no Burton.

Ahead was a red stop sign and a main, well-lit crossroad: Via Del Luna Drive, the road that would take her to the bridge and back to Pensacola.

She came to a stop, waited for traffic to pass, then turned left onto the lazy, two-lane street, the main beach road. She immediately accelerated and swerved around the loitering minivan in front of her, then bolted off.

Suddenly, a car cut across from one of the side streets ahead.

Burton's Jag.

"Shit!"

She tightened her grip on Rowe's shoulder and yanked the steering wheel to the side. The Cutlass shuddered as its entire mass spun around, tires squealing. Headlights blasted through the windshield, making her squint. The surrounding cars laid on their horns, some of them darting to the shoulder.

She slammed on the gas again, taking off in the opposite direction, against traffic for a moment until she reached the small path of road that crossed the median strip.

A glance to the rearview showed the Jaguar coming up fast.

Ahead, the houses' lights gave way to empty, dark, undeveloped beach. She was headed away from Pensacola Beach, to the state park, even farther from Pensacola proper.

Another look to the rearview. The Jag was right behind her. Glover emerged from the passenger-side window. He held a submachine gun of some sort, a MAC-10 or an MP5K, maybe.

He took aim.

Then there was a golden glow of muzzle flare in the darkness.

Loud metallic thuds as the rounds struck the side of the Cutlass.

Whack! Whack!

The Cutlass rocked to the side. The tires screeched. She battled the steering wheel, forearms burning. A rusty tailgate came up fast in the glow of her headlights—an old, slow-moving Chevy truck. She yanked the wheel to the left.

More shuddering from the tires. Around the truck. She released Rowe's shoulder, reached under the passenger seat, retrieved her Beretta.

Whack! Whack! Whack!

Rounds struck the rear bumper. There was the *crack* of a taillight shattering.

She turned in her seat, fired three times. The rear window shattered, crumbles of safety glass raining down. The cab amplified the roar of the gun. Her ears rang into silence.

The Jaguar's windshield spider-webbed as one of her rounds struck. It swerved off the road, whacking into the sidewalk, hopping into the air before landing with a crunch and a squeal of the tires.

This bought her a bit of time. The distance between the two cars grew as the last of the houses passed by. They were now at undeveloped beach. Dark. Black sky peppered with stars. Moonlit ocean.

She spotted a state park parking lot ahead.

And an idea came to her.

She tore into the lot.

CHAPTER FORTY-THREE

BURTON EYED the red Cutlass Supreme greedily, laughing at the blunder Christie had just committed.

Wow. Unbelievable. And to think—for a moment there, he even believed she was some sort of spy or something. *Ha!* How foolish of him.

Whoever she was, she certainly wasn't a local. A local would never get their car stuck in the sand. And he couldn't see a federal agent being that unworldly either.

She'd definitely had some serious training, but now his mind was forming new hypotheses. She must have been a hired gun for one of the new enemy factions he was gaining as he built up his criminal enterprise from the shell of the Farone organization. Maybe, even, she was a friend of the Rojas—a double-cross to his double-cross.

No matter who she was or whatever kind of training she had, he had her pinned now.

A sitting duck.

He smacked Glover's shoulder. "Look at that! The dumb bitch got stuck in the sand."

Glover laughed too.

Ahead of them, the Cutlass rocked back and forth, the reverse light coming on and off, the typical response of someone unaccustomed to parking in sand. Nine times out of ten, once you were stuck, you were stuck for good. Trying to rock the vehicle out was only going to make the situation worse.

Burton slowed down, pulled to the opposite side of the road, several yards behind the Cutlass, grabbed his MP5K from the back seat, and motioned to Glover.

They got out and approached Christie's car, HKs aimed. Burton watched both sides of the vehicle. She might not have been a federal agent, as he'd briefly thought, but she'd proven back at the house that she was a skilled shot—and unafraid to take lives. He would need to be very cautious with her.

A roar of the Cutlass's engine. It barreled backward toward them.

It wasn't stuck in the sand after all.

She'd been faking it...

"Shit!" Burton shouted as he dove to the side, the bumper coming inches away from clipping his leg.

Something small and round flew out of the Cutlass's driver-side window, and bounced on the street with a metallic *clang*, rolling within a few feet of the Jaguar.

The Cutlass swerved violently, tires billowing smoke. It screeched all the way around to the opposite direction and bolted off.

Then Burton looked back to the small object on the ground by his Jag.

It was a grenade.

He leapt to the side as a massive explosion destroyed the car. His ears rang, and a wave of heat flushed his skin, his hair. A fireball lit the darkness.

Pieces of metal and plastic and safety glass fell from the

sky, peppering him, as he crouched in the sand at the side of the road, arms clasped protectively over his head.

He panted. Slowly uncovered his head.

The heat was intense, and his forehead broke out in sweat. Crackling, snapping sounds mixed with the sound of the distant waves, like the world's largest beachside bonfire.

He slowly stood up.

The Jag was in flames, a roaring metallic candle lighting the empty road and beach.

He loved that damn car.

Glover stumbled toward him, coughing, his face black with soot. He bent over, put his hands on his knees, looked up at Burton.

"*A grenade?*" Glover shouted, exasperated. He tried to stand, and a coughing fit bent him over again.

Burton looked off into the distance. The taillights of the Cutlass grew smaller as it zipped away, returning to the lights of Pensacola Beach.

Okay, maybe she *was* a federal agent.

"Who the hell are you, Christie?" he said.

CHAPTER FORTY-FOUR

JAKE'S EYES OPENED.

His visibility was a thin strip bordered with a white, cross-hatched texture. Bandages. He felt them on his forehead, nose, the tops of his cheeks.

He was in a tiny hospital room. Very dark. The walls were close on either side of him, and the space was cramped with beeping machinery, whose various lights—LED greens and reds and blues—were the only illumination.

He looked down, and his chin nearly fell to his chest like a sphere of steel. His neck was weak, helpless against the weight.

From his downcast position, he saw that his lower body was covered with white sheets and bordered by the handrails of a hospital bed. There was pressure across his thighs, like something heavy lying across them. His arms were outside the sheets, covered to his fingertips with bandages. His left forearm was in a brace.

Something brushed his chin, his lower cheek, and as he moved his jaw, he realized that his hearing was muffled, ears covered with bandages. His entire head must have been covered. He raised his right hand to investigate.

And it came to a halt, sending a medicinally numb current of pain through his arm.

His heavy head drifted downward again. He looked.

His arm was hovering a few inches off the bed, ascending no farther, tethered like a kite to the handrail by a thick, double-looped cable tie, a style that Jake recognized from the police department—it was a plastic handcuff. A flex cuff. The other arm was secured to the opposite handrail.

He took in a shuddering breath.

The EKG monitor *beeped* more rapidly.

His eyes fluttered.

And then they closed.

————

He returned.

To C.C.

Months earlier.

They sat on a bench in the shade of a massive live oak tree with massive branches that drooped from the combined effects of weight and time. Tendrils of Spanish moss lilted in the gentle breeze. Behind them, past an expanse of bright green grass, was the Farone mansion, bathed in sunlight, its towering walls partly covered with creeping ivy and lined with palm trees and manicured hedges and shrubs.

They'd been discussing something of supreme impor‑ tance: the films of Mel Gibson. When C.C. had placed *Bird on a Wire* higher than *Lethal Weapon*, Jake could continue the conversation no further.

Jake turned to her with a smile. "For someone so quiet, you're awfully opinionated."

"Quiet people can't have opinions?"

"I would think if someone had an opinion, he or she would voice it."

"A 'loudmouth' like you *would* think that. Ghandi said to, 'Speak only if it improves upon the silence.'"

Jake gave her that smug, incredulous look that frustrated her so: one raised eyebrow, a superior twist at the corner of his lips. "Ghandi was one of the most outspoken individuals of this century, ya know..."

She shot him her own look of superiority. "Exactly. Think about it."

Jake opened his mouth but couldn't form a retort. As she did so often, she'd taken him aback, and he wasn't certain whether he was admiring her quirkiness or impressed by her steadfastness.

"Never underestimate quiet people, love," she said. "Mouthy people like you assume the quiet ones aren't listening. But we are. Quiet people are the ones you need to watch."

"You must not have been paying attention all these months if you think I've underestimated you. If you haven't noticed, I kinda like ya."

She rolled her eyes then looked across the grounds. "That's what worries me about the world now. It's getting so loud. So many voices. So much chatter. Sowing division. There's no time for quiet anymore. Self-reflection has become a punchline."

Jake put his hand on her knee. "Don't feel like you need to change the world all on your own, C.C."

She turned back to him, happiness and warmth returning to her face. "I have something important to tell you."

"Doesn't that negate what you just said about being quiet?"

"Shut up, smartass," she said but smiled softly.

When a moment passed and she hadn't told him this

important thing she needed to say, a rush of anxiety shivered through him.

Maybe she was about to give him bad news. The *worst* news. The news he'd been dreading.

The whole time they'd been together, he'd had a nagging feeling that someday she'd wise up, realize how disproportionately amazing she was, leave him.

But what she said then was, "I love you, Pete."

He released the breath he'd been holding. And waited a moment before he replied.

"I love you too."

"You do?"

He nodded.

"Then why the pause?"

He studied his knees, hesitated again. "Because there's something important I need to tell you also."

He picked an oak leaf off the bench, pinched it between his fingers.

"I'm not who I've told you I am. My name isn't Pete Hudson."

CHAPTER FORTY-FIVE

W HEN J AKE WOKE AGAIN, things felt different.

Somehow he knew that time had passed.

A lot of time.

The visual, too, was different. While his environment hadn't changed—the same dark hospital room cramped with beeping machinery—now there was a man standing in the shadows at the foot of his bed.

Jake jumped.

The plastic strips securing his arms snapped tight, digging into his wrists. A washed-out, drugged-up wave of discomfort swept over him.

The man took a step closer, looking directly at Jake, hands in the pockets of his suit pants. White. Fifties. Tall with an athletic physique, no hint of a middle-aged gut. Thick mustache that he wore in a cool, don't-give-a-shit sort of way that, on his strong face, made him look rather like Tom Selleck, the post *Magnum P.I.* years.

"Welcome back," the man said in a deep voice spiced with a bit of strange, seemingly inappropriate whimsy, accented by a small smirk. "I suspect you think I'm associated with Lukas

Burton. Don't worry about that, buddy. You're very, very far away from Pensacola, Florida. Your guardian angel whisked you a thousand miles north after she saved your life."

Jake tried to reply.

And he was immediately stopped, as though his voice smacked into a concrete wall.

Even with the pain medication clouding his system, a searing slice of pain had torn right through his throat, gnashing, ripping.

He jerked again. His wrists snapped in their binds.

"Don't speak," the man said. "Not yet. You need more time. Burton did a number on your throat."

Burton.

The punch to the throat.

Yes, that was the last thing that had happened. That horrible, crushing destruction that had sent his world into a white cloud of nothing.

Jake had been dead. He had to have been.

Then how was he here?

The mustached man continued to grin. "I had them take you out of sedation for a few moments. I want to implant a few things for your subconscious to ponder while you're knocked out for a few more weeks. Let's start with this."

He reached to the top of the beeping monitor beside him and grabbed a plastic-framed hand mirror, stepped to the side of the bed, and held the mirror a couple of inches from Jake's face.

Pure bandages. A mummy head with a thin open strip in the middle where his dark eyes looked back at him. Someone had removed his bright green contacts. The eyelids were pink, shiny, bloated. They didn't look like his eyes.

The man stepped away, put the mirror back on the monitor, then smiled down at him, his mustache twisting to one side.

"You're never going to look like or sound like or be the man you were before. You need to understand that. It's been a few weeks since your incident. This isn't a hospital; you're in a private facility in northern Virginia, three stories underground. The person who rescued you is one of my, um, employees." He paused. "You killed four people, Mr. Rowe. That's a serious crime, about as serious as they come."

The man stepped to the door in the back. There was a small shuffling sound, and suddenly a patch of light flooded the room.

Jake squinted. The light actually hurt.

The man had cracked the door open. His back was to Jake, leaning his face out the gap in the doorway.

"Go on," the man said to someone on the other side, and then the door closed, darkness returning.

A *beep* from one of the machines.

Immediately, the inside of Jake's left forearm cooled. The drop in temperature coursed through his body.

He exhaled and felt peaceful. In fact, he felt really damn good. He sensed C.C. nearby, heard her laugh.

His eyes fluttered.

The man approached him again, closer than he'd been before, stopping right at Jake's side and looking down at him. "You're facing life in prison. Or the electric chair. But my organization is willing to offer you a second chance. I just wanted to put that idea in your brain."

Jake's head fell back onto the pillow.

His eyes shut.

CHAPTER FORTY-SIX

As Jake's mind slowed once more, at first there was a blank nothingness.

Only for a moment.

And then he was alive again, in a memory.

He was on one side of a table with C.C., and on the other side was Tanner. Two of the most important people in Jake's life, meeting for the first time under terrible circumstances.

With Jake getting sucked further and further into his undercover role, this was the first time he'd seen Tanner in weeks. Meetings with the police were tough to arrange when people thought you were a mobster.

Jake looked at the older man, studying him in a glance. Decency exuded from Tanner, so much that Jake sometimes thought his grumbling was a compensation tactic. Wouldn't want to appear soft. His skin was a deep, warm brown, and his eyes had a sad wetness to them that was complementary to and yet at odds with his grumpy countenance.

They were in an empty office in the police headquarters. Nothing but the table and chairs in the center of the room and a pendant light hanging above. The air was musty and tasted way too dry for Florida. The place felt like an interrogation room, though it wasn't. There was even a window—covered with battered Venetian blinds—where the quintessential two-way mirror should be.

None of this was helping C.C., who was already uncomfortable as all hell, turned in on herself, eyes downcast, the reluctant center of attention who must have felt like she was being interrogated. She wore one of her typical quirky outfits —a pair of vintage flared jeans and a T-shirt with the logo of a Georgia peach orchard—and the splash of wackiness was at odds with both the surroundings and the situation.

Not only could Tanner have picked a better place for them to meet, but Tanner himself was only making things worse with the way he kept leaning forward on the table, inching into C.C.'s personal space, his exasperated huffs every time C.C. offered any form of resistance.

His shoulder holster wasn't helping matters.

Jake knew where Tanner's insistence was coming from— the months of work he and Jake had put into this investigation and the opportunity to bring Sylvester Farone and the rest of the crime syndicate down for good—but he couldn't fathom how Tanner could have such little tact, leaning toward her in his authoritative manner.

C.C. squirmed back in her chair, as far as possible, knitting her fingers on the table's laminate surface.

"Miss Farone," Tanner said. "If you really want to end the suffering your brother is causing, this is the only way."

Tanner uncrossed and recrossed his arms. His shirtsleeves were rolled up, as was his custom, revealing thick forearms with striations. Once upon a time, Tanner had been a gym rat, like so many cops. These days he retained a lot of his former mass, though it was softer than it had been in the old '70s photos Jake had seen. He'd also added mass to his midsection.

C.C. nodded, bit her lip, looked to the linoleum floor.

Jake didn't want to push her much harder, especially after how bothered she was getting by Tanner's insistence, but after a moment, he gave her a gentle prod.

"Babe?"

She looked at him, lips parted, eyes uncertain.

Tanner leaned in even closer. "Ma'am, with all due respect, what's the issue here? You're uncomfortable with the way your brother conducts his business—the torture, the gruesomeness. And you've already been assured that the legitimate part of the family fortune will be yours."

C.C. shot him a look. "*Money?* That's not what I'm worried about." There was no quicker way to get a rise out of C.C. then to accuse her of being money-hungry. "I'm concerned about my father."

Tanner finally leaned away from her. He dropped a knuckle to the table, clearly all he could do to keep from lashing out in frustration. "I already told you that—"

"Tell me again!"

A reluctant smile came to Tanner's face. "The DA has assured me that given your father's mental condition, the state won't waste taxpayer money pressing charges."

"And you can get him into protection with me and Jake? Transfer him to a different nursing home?"

"Of course."

C.C. nodded. "Sylvester. My brother … If I do this, if I bring evidence against him, promise me you'll treat him with as much leniency as you can."

Tanner started to reply, but Jake thought it better if he replied here, something more reassuring than Tanner would give. He simply said, "We promise."

Tanner scowled at Jake, and Jake gave him a look that said, *Be cool.*

C.C. placed her hand on Jake's knee, turned to him.

"We've been together a few months now. Not that long, I suppose. You said you love me. Did you mean it?"

"Of course."

"Maybe I was just a part of this sting of yours. A tool. Something for you to—"

"Absolutely not."

Tanner cleared his throat. "Ma'am, you and Jake can iron out the details of your relationship another time. What I need from you now is confirmation. Can we count on you?"

C.C. looked off to the blinds.

Tanner shot Jake a look, eyes widening, lips pinching tight.

Jake gave him another *Be cool* look and a short chop of a hand.

Tanner leaned in a bit closer to C.C. and forced another smile through his tightened lips. "What's the hesitation, ma'am?"

"You're asking me to send my brother to prison. He may be a monster. Twisted. Evil. But he's still my brother."

She paused.

"He's still my brother."

———

Jake woke with a jolt.

Darkness around him. Beeping medical equipment. Small, bright lights of different colors.

He was back in the tiny hospital room.

Not a true hospital room, though. The mustached man had told him that this was some sort of private facility.

How long had he been out this time?

He took a few deep breaths and relaxed his bandaged head back into the soft depths of the pillow.

His thoughts returned to the memory from which he'd

just awoken. Tanner had been insistent that day with C.C., and it had frustrated Jake. But the old-timer had been doing so for admirable reasons. There wasn't any bad in Tanner.

Sure, he was a grumpy old fart. A Luddite. A grouch. But he was a good cop and a good man. When Jake first joined the police department, he had gravitated toward Tanner immediately, someone to model, someone so different from his father, a man who had been passionless even before he became a drunk.

And now Tanner was surely hunting Jake down.

That's how good cops act. Impartially. Tanner wouldn't care that Jake had been a protégé. To Tanner, Jake would now be nothing more than a suspect, a man who'd murdered four men.

Jake wondered if Tanner sympathized at all, knowing that Burton had killed C.C. Or maybe he *hadn't* determined that Burton had killed her.

Maybe no one knew she was gone.

Maybe Tanner thought Jake had killed her.

He wondered what Tanner was thinking right now.

CHAPTER FORTY-SEVEN

TANNER RECLINED in the old squeaky chair, his back turned to his desk, looking at the corkboard that had recently been redecorated. For months, it was plastered with information about the Farone crime syndicate and the emerging Burton gang. But in recent weeks, the dominating motif was Jake Rowe—charts and bulletins and lookalike reports from as far away as North Dakota.

Jake's face stared back at Tanner from a half dozen spots among the materials.

Behind Tanner, leaning casually, putting his fed ass on the corner of his desk yet again, was Pace.

"It's been over a month, and we haven't heard squat," Pace said. "Face it—either Burton or the Farones finished Jake Rowe off. He tangled with the mob, and they sent him sleeping with the fishes."

He said the last part in a thick, *Godfather*-worthy Italian accent.

Tanner didn't believe that Jake had been snuffed out. No. Not for a moment.

All Jake had was his training and a single year with a

badge. No one would ever call him street-smart either. And with his strange thought process and tendency to over-analyze, Jake's head spent more time floating among the clouds than it did rooted in the here and now.

But he was a survivor. Jake found a way. That's why Tanner had invested so much in the guy, placed him on the fast-track to detective and jeopardized his own reputation by doing so.

Neither Burton nor the Farones had gotten the best of Jake Rowe. Tanner knew that.

"No," Tanner said. "He's still out there. Somewhere. I can feel it."

CHAPTER FORTY-EIGHT

BURTON STROLLED through the large office suite that the Farone family had secretly maintained for many years. It was so secretive that most non-family members of the organization—even high-ranking individuals like himself—never knew of its existence.

But Burton had a way of rooting out the truth.

The facility was no longer a secret to him.

It was his.

Whereas the other, well-known location printed counterfeit cash, this one produced more elaborate documents—driver's licenses, social security cards, birth and death certificates.

And passports, Burton's chief interest in the place.

White walls. Drapes that were permanently down, tacked to the bottoms of the windows. A drop tile ceiling with rows of fluorescent lights.

The floor was filled not with cubicles and desks and swivel office chairs but with large plotters—elaborate, expensive devices used for sophisticated printing jobs, some of them humming, some of them screeching, the sounds melding into a surprisingly comforting din.

A chemical scent perfumed the air, and it was also surprisingly pleasant. Maybe this was simply a case of association—perhaps Burton had grown to associate the tangy scent of ink with his upcoming successes.

Success aside, since Burton took over the press some weeks back, there had been copious hurdles to overcome at the converted office space. To gain his power, he'd had to kill off most of the Farone contingent in one fell swoop—that fateful night when he'd made his arrangement with the Rojas. In the process, though, he'd also killed off most, if not all, of the people who knew how to operate this facility.

And it was a challenge to get his guys to figure them out. First, they weren't the smartest of fellas. Second, Pete Hudson and Christie had killed off all but one of his original lieutenants, leaving only Glover. And third, the new underlings he'd brought on were idiots.

He stepped behind one of them, a scrawny, white trash-looking guy in a threadbare, yellow-stained T-shirt. His name was Maxwell.

Burton silently held out a hand; he didn't need to say anything. Maxwell handed him a passport.

They'd used Glover's photo on the test run. Next to Glover's image on the inside of the passport was the biographical information. He was listed as *Reagan, Ronald*, and his address was *123 Fake Street*.

Burton turned the document over in his hand, squinting at it.

They were getting closer. But they weren't quite there.

His cellular phone rang. He pulled it from his pocket, flipped it open.

"Burton."

It was his most important client, the one whose need for the passports was most pressing.

Burton looked at the passport in his hand as he replied, turning it over, studying it. "Wonderful to hear from you, my friend. Yes, certainly we're getting closer. The fonts are flawless, as is the ink match. We're very close on the security features, which I know was your primary worry. At the moment, the issue slowing us down is the covers."

He closed the passport, ran his thumb across the cover's blue texture. Too smooth. It needed to be slightly rougher.

His client expressed concern about the timeliness of the order.

"Don't fret. We're still figuring these machines out, but it'll get done in time. I've got some real quick learners working for me."

He looked at Maxwell as he said that, whose dull-looking face was again squinting at the screen.

Never hurts to stretch the truth a tad, he thought.

But despite some of his more lackluster talent, Burton wasn't lying when he said the order would be ready on time. Burton knew how to persuade people.

His client asked if there was anything else that might impede progress.

"Nothing will get in the way," Burton said. "The only distraction left for us here is a few remaining Farone-faithful, a couple pods of them still embedded in the region."

He grinned at the thought of slaughtering them.

"But I'm tying up those loose ends very soon."

CHAPTER FORTY-NINE

JAKE HADN'T REALIZED he'd woken up.

But somehow, as his senses returned, he found himself propped up in the bed, pillows behind his back, looking about the small dark room, at all the medical machinery. For how long? He'd simply faded back into existence, which made him suspect that they—whoever "they" were—had brought him out of sedation again.

He glanced at the plastic handcuffs binding his arms to the bed's handrails and saw that both arms were now free of bandages, except for a tiny, fresh-looking patch of gauze on his right arm, about two inches squared. His arm hair had been shaved and was growing back in.

Gone, too, was the cast on his left forearm. He pressed the forearm's bulge of muscle into the handrail, and, as he expected, it was doughy from atrophy. Curious, he also pressed his right forearm into the opposite handrail. While it wasn't pure mush like the left, it had also gone soft. He'd been in this bed for some time.

The only remaining bandages were in a small mound

taped to his right shoulder. If the dressings had been removed from his upper body, then maybe…

He bent at the waist and leaned his face toward one of his restrained hands, touched his cheek.

Yes, his face was now bandage-free as well. His fingers explored. Scratchy stubble, but only a couple of day's worth. Someone had been shaving him. The skin surrounding the stubble was smooth and supple, almost rubbery.

He traced along his cheekbone, which bulged from his face. Must have lost a lot of weight for the bone to protrude so severely. It felt strange, foreign.

He reclined again, and this brought a tiny ache from his right arm. He looked. The pain had come from the patch of gauze midway up the inside of his forearm.

Light flooded the room, and he squinted. The mustached man entered, closed the door behind him. He stopped at the foot of the bed, put his hands in the pockets of his suit pants, and gave a big smile.

"Welcome back, Mr. Rowe. I hope you're feeling well, all things considered. Have you tried to speak?"

Jake shook his head.

"Try now."

As Jake smacked his dry lips and prepared to speak, a pulse of discomfort came from his throat. It felt like a thicket of thorn bushes had sprouted there during his medical slumber, swelling his esophagus, the thorns slicing into him. He worked up some saliva, swallowed, and then spoke.

"Testing," he said.

As soon as the word left his lips, he recoiled. The thorn bush sliced him up.

The mustached man's eyebrows drew together, vicarious empathy.

"Hurts like hell," Jake said, which was a stupid thing to do.

A fresh thrashing from the thorns, pain sharp enough to water his eyes.

The other man's mustache twisted into a little grin. "And it will continue to hurt. The medical staff tells me it'll get somewhat better with time, but you'll always feel it."

Jake rolled his head back. "Great."

A shot of pain. He grimaced. Swallowed.

Just shut up, he told himself.

The man stepped closer. "I haven't introduced myself. You can call me Falcon. My organization saved your life. We're the ones who run this facility."

He pulled a hand from his pocket and gestured to their surroundings.

"And we want to offer you a second chance at life. Or, to put it more accurately, we're offering you a second life altogether.

"I'll cut to the chase. As you're someone who works in bureaucracy, I'm sure you can agree that there are plenty of ways individuals elude justice, plenty of cracks to fall through. If a person knows the right people, if a person has enough money, he or she can get away with murder. Literal murder. But other horrible things as well. Often it's the system itself that allows it. Corruption.

"And so individuals like me have set up an underground operation to right wrongs, to dole out justice to people who have escaped it. A secret group hidden in plain sight, watching it all, monitoring the government's actions—local, state, and federal, even foreign affairs, things like CIA operations. When someone eludes the justice they so sorely deserve, we go in and administer that justice. Usually as a death sentence. We call ourselves the Watchers."

Falcon looked at Jake now, awaiting a response.

It was a lot to consume at once, this concept of a secretive group embedded throughout American government with a mission of righteous murder, and Jake's immediate reaction was one of loyal skepticism.

He worked up some saliva, swallowed. "Treason."

The word hurt his throat, but not as much as the previous times he'd spoken. He'd lubricated the thorn bush more effectively.

Falcon chuckled. "Treason, you say? The first case I worked was a small-town mayor in North Carolina who tortured and killed the brother of his political opponent and had the police chief—his father-in-law—pin the murder on his opponent. One of our men broke his neck. Is that treason?

"Just last month, we uncovered a human-trafficking ring in Oklahoma, operating out of a Native American reservation, using legal loopholes regarding what is and isn't federal ground to transport people. This had gone on for almost a decade. We ended it in one night. With two bullets. Treason?"

The man had a point. Even in Jake's brief tenure as a law enforcement officer, he'd experienced the foggy gray areas within the law—people who should have been arrested but weren't; corruption and injustice.

"What do you..." Jake said and stopped to swallow. "Want..." Another swallow. "From me?"

His throat crackled with pain. He needed to learn to use less syllables.

Falcon rocked on his heels and mugged broader. "We want you to be an assassin, Mr. Rowe. What we call an Asset. You've proven that you can kill. Four men in one night. Shit, man."

Even with all the pain in his throat and the numb quality throughout the rest of his body, Falcon's request made Jake's stomach instantly roil with anxiety.

An assassin?

When he killed four of C.C.'s murderers, it was an act of passion-fueled rage. One night. And it ended with Jake himself being killed.

Since then, he'd been brought back to life—a life drifting in and out of drug-filled memories and dreams. He'd had no chance to come back to himself, to reacquire reality.

But he didn't need to have his full wits about him to understand that he was no professional killer.

The very thought of it...

Insane.

There was a look of recognition in Falcon's eyes, as though he could see Jake's hesitancy, and before Jake could respond, he continued.

"There are four tiers to the Watchers' organization. Let me show you."

He stepped to the side of the bed, to a table, and picked up a small book. Jake recognized it. It was his PenPal notebook—yellow plastic cover, inky bloodstain on the back. He hadn't seen it yet during any of his conscious moments in this medical room, as the table was hidden behind one of the larger pieces of medical equipment.

Falcon made an *eww* face at the bloodstain, carefully avoiding it as he opened the notebook with only two fingers. He took the mechanical pencil out of the spiral binding and started writing.

Jake didn't appreciate him marking up his personal belongings. But given the situation, he decided he should remain quiet. It was good practice, anyway. He would need to stay silent as often as possible with this painful throat of his.

After a moment of writing, Falcon put the pencil back in the spiral binding, smiled at his handiwork with over-the-top pride, and handed the notebook to Jake. There was a simple diagram with words connected via lines.

It reminded Jake of the mind mapping technique C.C. had taught him.

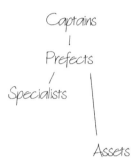

Falcon put his hands back in his pockets. "Everyone in the Watchers, aside from the lowest tier, the Assets, has a day job. 'Hidden in plain sight,' remember? At the top of the pecking order, we got the Captains, the big guns. There are only a few of them, and they all work in government.

"Beneath the Captains are the Prefects, like me." He patted his chest, smiled with more of his animated pride. "Also members of government. We supervise the Specialists and the Assets. If we do well enough, and if a slot opens up, we can eventually become a Captain."

He stepped beside Jake, pointed at the word *Specialists* in his diagram.

"Next we have Specialists. The lifeblood of the Watchers and by far the greatest in numbers. Some work in government; some are in the private sector. These are the weapons-providers, the bankers who funnel our funds into secret accounts, the attorneys who find the loopholes we need, the logistics professionals who'll provide your housing and transportation.

"But most importantly, among the Specialists are the

investigators, the ones who scour through countless records and reports to find people who have escaped the justice they deserve, the people we eliminate.

"Now that brings us to the lowest rung, the bottom of the barrel, the low-end of the pecking order. The Assets. You."

Falcon grinned and tapped his finger on *Assets*, way on the bottom of the page.

"Notice that while both Specialists and Assets fall directly below Prefects, I've put Assets well below Specialists. Should you choose to accept our offer, you won't report to the Specialists, but they'll be your superiors. Don't forget that.

"Assets are the ones who get their hands dirty. All of the fact-finding and resource-management of the Specialists; all of the leadership of the Prefects; all of the decision-making from the Captains ... eventually it all boils down to field work carried out by assassins. We call you Assets because, I'll be frank, you don't have a high survival rate. You folks are tools used to get the job done. If you live, super!, but statistically speaking, the odds aren't great."

Wonderful, Jake thought.

"Unlike Specialists, Prefects, and Captains, who've all been selected for high moral character, Assets have been rescued. They're people who became violent criminals—typically murderers like you—but did so for righteous reasons.

"When we find a person like this, we have a decision to make: Was the person fully justified? Or was their crime so violent that it skirted the line between righteous and wicked?

"If we decide the crime was fully justified—say, a woman who killed her husband after he beat their daughter to death —we hook the person up with a new identity, a new life, and set them free. We call this a Benevolent Cause, a BC. Kind of the reverse of what we normally do, in that we're getting someone *out of* their punishment.

"But if the crime was particularly brutal, it's not right to just set the person free. In this case, we do one of three things: we let the system have them, we arrange alternate justice, or we offer them a path to freedom in the form of joining us as an assassin."

Falcon stopped then. His perpetual grin went away, and his face became as serious as Jake had yet seen it.

"You murdered four people. Over several hours. Yes, they took your girl, and of course I sympathize. Had you blasted a guy in the heat of the moment, I absolutely would have made you a Benevolent Cause, put you in witness protection, gotten you a new start somewhere else in the country.

"But you just kept on killing. And killing ... and killing. And you were a cop, man! That's why we're offering you this opportunity. Join us as an Asset—or we'll leave you to your fate, which, by the way, is grim. Remember what I told you the first time we met? Life in prison or the electric chair, no doubt about it."

Jake didn't reply.

"As an Asset, we'll give you a new identity, just like we do for BCs," Falcon continued. "Typically we move Assets across the country, far away from where anyone would ever recognize them. But we had a unique opportunity with you. Burton's guys really tore the shit out of your face. Just really destroyed you. So when the plastic surgeon put you back together—that would be one of the Specialists we just talked about—he reconstructed you into a whole new man." He chuckled. "The doc's a big shot out in Beverly Hills. You got some world-class work done and didn't even know it."

He took the mirror from the top of the monitor. Paused.

"This is going to be startling. You're a new person. You need to be prepared."

Jake nodded.

Falcon brought the mirror closer, turned it to face him.

And Jake gasped.

Falcon was right. Nothing could prepare him for this.

He breathed rapidly. His heart instantly jackhammered. And for some reason, he crawled back in the bed, as if he could escape the reflection.

"Calm," Falcon said. All trace of that consistent smug, coy quality of his was gone. "Deep breaths. Calm. *Calm*."

Jake's feet kicked at the mattress as he pushed away from the mirror.

This wasn't him in the mirror. And yet, as he moved, the reflection moved with him, this face of sharp angles, bulging cheekbones, a prominent jawline, square chin. His nose was smaller, straighter. His lips were much fuller and more full of color, and overall his mouth was narrower.

"Calm," Falcon said. "Breathe."

Jake complied, took a deep breath.

Falcon extended the mirror toward him, offering it. He gave an encouraging nod.

Jake squeezed the shake from his fingers and took the mirror.

He turned his face, studied it. While his forehead and the area between his eyebrows were perfectly smooth with no lines to indicate a furrow, he still looked rather pouty, like this new face was going to be stuck on a permanent state of brood. Like a Calvin Klein underwear model.

His hand was still shaking, but his heartbeat had slowed.

He sighed.

Well, he *did* wear Calvin Klein underwear. Perhaps it was fitting.

Wait

The mole.

He brought his face down to his tethered hand and ran his fingers along the right corner of his jaw. Smooth skin interrupted only by his stubble.

At least they got rid of the damn mole.

"Ol' Sawbones really went to town on you, didn't he?" Falcon said, smug once more. "I think he really enjoyed himself. Probably the first time he's ever had a clean slate like this. I mean, your face was pretty much hamburger when we found you. Doc turned you into some sort of pretty boy Adonis."

Falcon laughed heartily, hands on his knees. After a moment of this, he straightened up and took the mirror from Jake, placed it back on top of the monitor. He returned his hands to his pockets.

"So with your new, completely unrecognizable face, we're gonna leave you right where you are, in Pensacola. Assets are spread throughout the country, regionally, and we've needed someone in Florida for some time. We've stretched our Atlanta Asset really thin for several years. You're gonna be our Florida man." He laughed. "You've heard about that, right? The whole 'Florida Man' thing?"

Jake nodded.

Of course he had.

Florida was a quirky place that attracted a lot of quirky people. As such, the "Florida Man" phenomenon had arisen— a preponderance of whacky headlines, rather embarrassing to residents of the Sunshine State, that were then collected and shared nationally and internationally.

Florida Man Tackles Gator to Regain Stolen Can of Beer

Florida Man Attempts Robbery Using Green Plastic Water Gun

Florida Man Backs Trailer Into Police Headquarters

Falcon had started chuckling again. The guy sure did laugh a lot.

"You'll cover most Florida assignments. But that doesn't mean you'll always be in the sand and sun. We'll need you elsewhere, as needs demand. So you might be in Tampa for a week. Then the Keys for a month or two. Then you might find yourself in the middle of Montana for a while. Make sense?"

Jake nodded.

"And before you get any bright ideas about taking advantage of our generosity and making a run for the border or something, do know that we're always watching you. We *are* the Watchers, after all. There's a GPS dot in your arm."

Jake looked at the small bandage on his forearm.

Ah. Mystery solved.

"Now, it's a tradition of ours to let Assets choose their new first name," Falcon said. "What'll yours be?"

Jake thought.

And a name immediately came to his mind.

A word.

"Silence," Jake said.

Falcon pursed his lips, clicked his teeth. "Silence? What the hell kind of name is that? Maybe Ryan? Sam? Gordon?"

C.C. in the ocean, to her knees, the waves tossing the bottom of her sarong, beckoning him toward her, the water, so warm.

Quiet, she'd said. *Be here. With me. In this moment. Right now. This moment. Silence.*

Jake swallowed.

"Silence," he said again.

Falcon shrugged. "Silence it is." He sighed, stroked his mustache. "You're not gonna be a problem child for me, are you? I put my neck out to bring you in. All right, all right. I usually throw some mundane, standard last name to go with the first name a new Asset chooses. Let's call you..."

He trailed off and looked toward the drop tile ceiling. His mustache twisted as he thought.

"Jones. Silence Jones."

Silence Jones.

It had a ring to it.

"You'll be Asset 23. Or, A-23."

C.C. would have been alarmed. Among her many esoteric interests was numerology, and a few months ago she'd told him about the 23 Enigma, a phenomenon that suggested the number twenty-three had a negative aura.

A cursed pair of digits...

That was a hell of a number to be assigned as an assassin with a short life-expectancy.

"I also have the great honor of bestowing codenames," Falcon said. "You know, typical tough-sounding things, like sports teams or fighter pilot call signs. 'Shark.' 'Maddog.'" His eyes twinkled with a thought. "And since you're gonna call yourself Silence, your codename will be Suppressor."

He grinned broadly.

"Silencer. Suppressor. Get it? Eh? Eh?"

Yes, yes. Another name for a gun's silencer was a suppressor.

Amusing, but not as hilarious as Falcon seemed to think.

"Here's our offer," Falcon continued. "You killed four men. Join us as an Asset, or go to prison. Simple as that. The offer is provisional upon passing your training, of course, as well as successful completion of your first assignment. And, because I'm such a generous fella, I'll sweeten the deal even more—your first assignment will be finishing what you started: we need you to eliminate Lukas Burton.

"This is your last chance to bail, no strings attached. Do you accept our offer?"

The man in the hospital bed, the man who been Jake

Rowe, the man who was now in a strange, momentary limbo between identities, considered the proposal.

They wanted him to be an assassin.

Could he do that?

Could he be a killer?

Immediately his mind offered hesitancy, put a wall in front of him, reminded him that he didn't even kill spiders he found in his living room.

But then he thought of the Watchers' mission that Falcon had just described. Benevolent killings. Righting wrongs.

He thought of people he'd encountered during his one year as a police officer. Bastards who'd gotten away with rotten, horrible things. People who couldn't be touched, even when they looked you in the eye and told you without telling you that they'd done it.

That's right, they'd say with a cold expression, pinched eyebrows, a cocky grin. *I did it, and there's nothing you can do about it.*

C.C. had once told him her view on sponsored killings, a view that had surprised him. Murder, she'd said, was supposedly the most irrefutable, universally accepted offense among all cultures of humanity. And yet all nations went to war. And many nations had policies of capital punishment. One person's justified killing was another person's murder, and the definition wasn't as clear-cut as people would hope, C.C. had said.

He leaned his face toward his tethered hand again and ran his fingers along his cheek, felt the sharp ridge of that prominent cheekbone. This face wasn't his. But, then, the name wasn't his either. *Silence Jones*. This future, also, wasn't his, a future without C.C.

The old face, the prior name, the future with C.C.—all of that had been Jake Rowe.

If he was a new person, then he could take on a new life.

He could become a righteous assassin.

And, besides, they were giving him his chance to finish off Burton.

With resources and support.

He looked at Falcon. Swallowed.

"Let's do it."

Falcon grinned.

"Welcome aboard, Silence Jones."

CHAPTER FIFTY

LASWELL PAUSED, giving Briggs a chance to digest all that had been said. The point in the story at which he'd initiated the new Asset—*Welcome aboard, Silence Jones*—had seemed like a natural stopping point.

He just hoped Briggs wouldn't take too long processing the information. The old guy had gone back to staring at the wall.

And the cheap chair was still putting Laswell's ass to sleep.

As Briggs pulsed his templed fingers, which were under his chin, propping up his face, Laswell thought again about the moment he welcomed Silence aboard.

He'd again been impressed with the character of the man that he'd chosen as the new Asset. Silence hadn't celebrated, nor did he have any sort of downtrodden look on his face. He just stared back at Laswell, accepting his new future without emotion.

Earlier, Laswell had told Briggs about Silence's training with Nakiri, so now Briggs was completely up to speed. In theory, this meant that Laswell might have to wait indefinitely in the torture chair until Briggs finished processing and broke his wall-stare.

Fortunately, Laswell had an excuse to get out of there. He had a plane to catch.

He checked his watch.

"Well, sir, now that you're all caught up, I gotta get my ass on a plane to meet up with our new Asset in Pensacola."

Briggs looked away from the wall, his bright blue eyes zoning in on Laswell. "Your Florida man only has a few hours left to avert a disaster."

Laswell didn't respond. Briggs hadn't asked a question, after all.

Briggs sighed, then stood up.

Laswell followed suit. He stretched his arms over his head, then poked at both of his butt cheeks. Nothing. Completely asleep. Dead to the world.

Wonderful.

And now he was about to set the ass back down for a couple more hours for the flight to Pensacola. Fortunately, he was flying private. Maybe the high-end accommodations would help to wake his butt up. Literally.

Briggs stretched as well, then walked around the desk, past Laswell. As they left the small office, Briggs flipped off the lights and locked the door.

The hallway had thin, matted carpet and flickering lights in the ceiling. All the other doors were shut except for one at the end, which was cracked open. There was the muffled voice of a man talking about stock prices.

"You'd better be right about Silence Jones," Briggs said as they headed for the elevator.

"I am."

Laswell knew he was right.

It wasn't Silence's experience and certainly not his training that made Laswell so confident. It was his grit.

Silence's X factor, the same quality that Jake Rowe's lieutenant at the Pensacola Police Department had seen in him.

It was the quality that had led an unassuming, older, first-year police officer, former teacher to dispatch four hardened criminals in a single night.

Yes, Silence Jones would be a quality Asset.

––––––

"Your drink, Mr. Beaty."

Laswell had been resting his eyes. He blinked them open, smiled at the flight attendant—who wore a navy blue skirt suit, a scarf around her neck, and a gleaming smile—and took the tumbler from her, cupping the paper napkin to the bottom.

He had the rear of the Learjet all to himself, and the private airline—SkyTrail Aviation—was pampering him. They knew him as Humphrey Beaty, CFO of Clocktower Enterprises, LLC.

He eased back into the leather seat, which was soft, plush, gently used. Yes, this seat was much kinder to his ass than the chair back in Virginia. There was life in his cheeks again.

He took a sip of scotch and thought back to when Silence joined up a few weeks ago. Now Laswell was going to rendezvous with the guy once more in Pensacola. Prefects almost never went into the field. For Laswell, this was only the second time.

But this was not a normal assignment—both in how it was being handled and, more importantly, with the implications of its successful completion.

And as much confidence as Laswell had in the new Asset —all that bravado he'd given Briggs about sensing Silence's good qualities, his ability to dispatch people easily, learning the skills of a killer in one night—this was still jeopardizing

Laswell's own position. Everything in the Watchers was based on trust, and that trust came from a place just below a person's ethical standards. Silence Jones was a gamble for Laswell. But Laswell could feel it. Feel it in his bones. This man was an Asset, through and through.

Nonetheless, Suppressor had pushed the limits of his first assignment. He'd been tasked with settling Lukas Burton weeks ago, but the man was still alive.

There was no time left. The ticking clock was about to stop ticking. It was only a matter of hours until Burton was to make his move. And while Suppressor hadn't deduced exactly what Burton was up to, he had determined that it held critical national security implications.

Which meant the nation's safety rested in the hands of one untested Asset.

Laswell took another sip.

A generous one.

He placed the tumbler in the cupholder. The ice cubes rattled against the glass.

His mind drifted back once more to when he welcomed Silence Jones to the Watchers—and how he'd immediately introduced Silence to his trainer.

CHAPTER FIFTY-ONE

LASWELL WINKED at the man in the hospital bed before him, the man who had just become Silence Jones, Suppressor, Asset 23.

"And now, Mr. Jones, I'd like you to meet your new best friend for the next few weeks. Asset 17. Name of Nakiri."

He leaned back and opened the door, motioned for the person waiting around the corner, and allowed her to step past him and into the room.

Suppressor's growly voice let out a single word of surprise. "Christie?"

He immediately recoiled, eyes squinting, brow furrowing.

Laswell shook his head. That damn throat was gonna be a constant problem for Suppressor. Laswell wished he'd brought some cough drops for the guy.

Nakiri went to the bed.

"Holy shit. They did a hell of a job on you, Rowe." Her eyes roamed over him, going lustful. "You went from David Schwimmer handsome to Johnny Depp hot."

"You can forget the name Jake Rowe," Laswell said. "Nakiri, meet Silence Jones."

Nakiri blinked twice. "Silence? You named yourself Silence?"

Laswell answered for him. "Mmm-hmm. But you'll know him as Suppressor." He turned to the bed. "And you'll know her as Nakiri. You've no need for her name, just her codename."

Nakiri's eyes gave a dark sparkle as she grinned at her new protégé. "We're going to have a lot of fun training, Suppressor."

Suppressor tilted his head, eyes narrowing to cautious slits, as though confused by Nakiri's stony countenance.

But Laswell understood. He knew exactly where Nakiri's dark revelry was coming from.

He cut in before she could say anything else. "And after that, you'll start your first assignment, your trial run."

Nakiri cleared her throat. Obnoxiously.

Laswell glanced at her, then back to Suppressor. "Correction: you'll finish the assignment that Nakiri started. Clearly her cover was blown when she started shooting people at Lukas Burton's place. You have a new face, an inside understanding of Burton, and a strong desire to eliminate him. You'll be finishing the Pensacola assignment."

Nakiri shot Suppressor a frigid glare.

"But don't think that we're simply giving you a chance to finish your revenge," Laswell continued. "Burton's goal is a lot bigger than we originally thought. Huge." He waved a hand at Nakiri. "Get him up to speed."

She bristled, doing little to conceal it. While Nakiri wasn't the most difficult Asset he'd ever commanded, she was at the apex of the list. Copious spirit. Ponderous pride. And this situation bruised that pride a deep shade of purple.

She retrieved a file folder from the canvas messenger bag she was carrying and took out the photos she'd shown Laswell earlier in the day, those of Keith Sutton. One was a security photo of the lean, baby-faced man in his corporeal state; the other showed his bullet-riddled corpse after the police fished it out of Pensacola Bay.

"This is the man I told you about back at Burton's beach house," Nakiri said to Suppressor. "Keith Sutton, the guy who tried to buy arms with counterfeit bills in Boston, found a couple days later bobbing in the water outside Pensacola like a bloated human buoy. Originally we thought Sutton was just your average workaday thug, but since you've been asleep, we've discovered he has more significant criminal ties than the Farones and Burton's new gang.

"He worked for a criminal syndicate out of Warsaw with connections all over the globe—Europe, China, the Middle East. Wanted by Interpol, the EU, several individual nations. Why he'd gotten his counterfeit cash from Burton and not someone more established, we're not sure. But Burton's counterfeiting operations are expanding. He's printing documents worth a hell of a lot more than paper money—passports, birth certificates, death certificates, forged contracts."

Laswell stepped beside her. "Which means we need to move even faster than originally thought. Because whatever Burton is doing, it's escalating rapidly. Not only has he upped his game with counterfeiting, but he's consolidating power. He's having his second-in-command, Clayton Glover, wipe out all the low-level groups that had ties to the Farones. Now there are only two more contingents remaining in the Pensacola region. We don't know where they're hiding, but we believe Burton does, and intel says he's closing on those groups tonight. Once he's eliminated them, there will be no one left to challenge his power."

Suppressor swallowed, a pronounced movement. The new Asset was adapting quickly, learning how to lubricate his rotten throat.

"And then?" Suppressor said.

"Then he moves onto his ultimate goal, whatever he's doing with all his sophisticated counterfeiting," Laswell said. "Burton's meticulous about covering his tracks, but our Specialists are just as meticulous. We've been able to glean some particulars. Whatever Burton's planning, it's huge, and it's happening in approximately five weeks. Which means we need to get you back to Florida with some time to spare; which further means that your training will be only three weeks. Fast and brutal. All while you're still recovering."

Nakiri rapped a knuckle on the bed's handrail.

"Fun and excitement await you, cupcake." She gave Suppressor another devilish grin. "Let's begin."

CHAPTER FIFTY-TWO

GLOVER WAVED A HAND, and four men moved out of the trees and toward the house.

This was great. Simply amazing. The power, prestige, and respect he'd wanted and deserved for so long.

It was all because he'd chosen to follow Lukas Burton, the smartest decision he'd ever made.

Everything was changing for Glover. Changing fast. Even his clothing, of which Burton had given him advice. He wore an expensive pair of gray pants and a striped, button-up shirt. He'd rolled the sleeves up. Uber cool. He felt sharp and intelligent and powerful.

Before him was a two-story, old-fashioned house. Something very Southern looking, which seemed appropriate, as it was on the outskirts of Biloxi.

He watched.

There was a pause. A breeze teased the branch in front of him.

And then shots from the building, cracking through the night. Little blasts of light in the windows.

Glover smiled.

And quickly the smile dropped.

Because someone ran from the house into the small wooded area to the side. It wasn't one of his men.

Glover gave it a moment. None of his men emerged from the house.

Shit.

Evidently he was still going to have to do some dirty work from time to time. That was fine by him. He would've missed it, anyway.

He took out his gun and ran to the edge of the trees. Stopped. Listened.

Rustling leaves. Footsteps, getting away. There was an open parking lot on the other side of the copse. No time for stealth, so Glover just crashed right into the trees. The man was before him, almost to the parking lot and its lights.

Glover raised his gun and put two rounds into his back. The man fell into a pile of branches and leaves, a crunching sound that registered surprisingly loudly after the bark of the gunshots.

More footsteps, coming from the house. He turned.

It was his men, scrambling for the car.

Then distant sirens.

He pivoted, about to dart to the car, and felt something on his shin, looked down.

His nice pants had ripped. A one-inch tear at the cuff.

"Damn."

———

Later, he had the same group of three men with him. They'd become his personal squad, another sign of his growing prestige, his upward mobility.

Not bad.

The last scraggly stronghold for the Farone family was a

mobile home in the woods outside of Crestview, Florida. How ironic. The great legacy, the legends, the mansion, the Italian-American heritage—all of it coming to a close outside a ratty trailer in the woods in rural Florida.

His men had the final guy pinned against a tree, squirming, sweating through a wrinkly dress shirt that stunk of days of life on the run.

Glover stepped up to him. "How many more Farone men are left?"

"Just me. I swear," the man said, shaking. "You've killed them all."

Glover shook his head. "Not all."

He put a gun to the man's forehead and fired.

His men hooped and hollered, but Glover remained resolute. The leader. The mature one. The one in control.

The man slid butt-first down the tree trunk. A wide path of blood chased after him.

Glover took his cellular phone from his pocket and dialed Burton.

CHAPTER FIFTY-THREE

HE WATCHED from his bed as Falcon slipped out of the door, shutting it behind him.

That left just him and Christie.

Or Nakiri, rather.

She drummed her fingers on the bed's handrail, giving him another one of those mysterious smiles. "Are you ready to begin, Silence?"

Silence.

A foreign sensation breezed over him. *Silence Jones.* That was his name now.

He'd have to get used to it.

He nodded.

Nakiri said, "Eight-zero-six-four-five-four-one-six-two-nine."

What the hell?

Silence raised an eyebrow at her.

"I'm going to say the number again, and you're going to repeat it to me. Eight-zero-six-four-five-four-one-six-two-nine."

She hadn't said it blazingly fast, but certainly too quickly to remember.

He strained. "Eight-zero-six..."

Nothing. He shook his head and swallowed. The syllables had hurt.

Nakiri scowled at him. "Wrong."

She took her hand off the handrail and closed it over the bandages on his shoulder.

And squeezed.

Hard.

Pain rippled through him like an electric current, past his shoulder, through his chest, into his arms and legs. Whatever wound remained under those bandages was far from healed. His wrists snapped into the plastic handcuffs. And he screamed, which brought reciprocal pain from his throat, horrible and hot.

She released the pressure, but kept her hand on his shoulder.

"Eight-zero-six-four-five-four-one-six-two-nine. Repeat it."

"Eight-zero." He swallowed. "Six-four..."

He trailed off.

"Wrong."

She squeezed.

Silence screamed again at the wave of pain, wrists yanking the plastic handcuffs tight, but he bit his lip to keep the sound in his chest, below his awful throat.

Nakiri smiled. "Adaptation. No scream means less pain. I like it. Now, come on. You gotta be able to do this. You can't rely on that silly notebook. No crutches for Assets."

She motioned toward his PenPal, sitting on the monitor beside them.

"You'll have to use your memory in the field, dummy. That's what they used to call people who can't talk—*dummy*.

You're gonna be my little dummy for the next three weeks. Now ... eight-zero-six-four-five-four-one-six-two-nine."

"Eight-zero-four—"

"Wrong!"

She went to squeeze the shoulder again but stopped herself short, the tiniest shimmer of sympathy crossing her eyes. A cold smile formed on her lips, and she removed her hand.

"To be continued."

Silence's entire body quaked. His flesh was cold and wet. He sensed his wrists, looked, and saw angry red lines from the plastic ties.

Nakiri looked him over, from top to bottom.

"Let's keep things brief today. It's late, and it's your first day. Only two lessons. We'll come back to lesson one momentarily. Moving on to lesson two."

She traced the back of her hand along his cheek, a tickling sensation that ran across his scruff beard. Her skin was softer than he would have thought, her fingers smaller, delicate even.

He tilted away.

What the hell was she up to?

"Falcon tells me you've only been out of sedation for a few brief moments before tonight," she said. "To you, it must seem like yesterday that Cecilia died, hmm?"

Silence nodded.

"An Asset with an open-ended romantic connection." She tsked. "Now, we can't have that." Her gray eyes locked in on him. "With that voice of yours, you'll never go undercover. Unlike me. Do you know how many times I had sex with Burton? How disgusting it was? How many times before Burton I've had to put myself in situations like that? It's different as a woman, even as an Asset.

"You and me—we need to clear any sexual tension at the beginning of this journey we're about to share. We're gonna be working closely together. Touching. And, believe me, there's *always* sexual tension, no matter how devoted a person is. You'll be interacting with other non-Cecilia women in the field. I need to know that you won't cower away from a woman's touch."

Her hand moved.

Oh.

Now Silence understood what was happening.

Her fingers traced down his neck, tickling even more, prickling his skin, over his chest, pausing to run her finger under the collar of his gown, down his side, past his waist.

She took hold of him.

And Silence knew he was learning a lesson right now, just not the lesson Nakiri intended. If he really was going to be in situations with "touch," as she called it, he would need to use his mind and his memories to disappear.

And remain faithful.

Because what Nakiri didn't understand was that Silence's attachment to C.C. wasn't because she'd recently passed. He'd promised himself to her. For life. And he meant it.

C.C. taught him how to use his mind, and he would use his mind to escape this.

Surprisingly, this situation he was in with Nakiri had triggered a memory. He would use it.

He thought of C.C.

And he was gone.

———

Months earlier.

The beach.

It was early spring, so the sun was warm, but the humidity wasn't stifling. A pleasant breeze rolled off the water. Locals and off-season tourists stretched on towels and splashed in the waves. Pleasant conversations. The smell of suntan lotion clouded the air. The white sand was an endless carpet before them, lined with condo towers and emerald green waves, stretching to the horizon, where it disappeared beneath a brilliant blue sky.

"I'll be happy when you can get rid of those contacts," she said, pointing at his sunglasses. I like your real eyes a lot better. The real you."

He'd taken the lenses out for her a couple of times during private moments.

"The 'real me' includes *this*." He poked the hideous brown blob on the corner of his jaw.

She swatted him. "Stop it. I like everything about you."

"Even the mole?"

"Even the mole. Even your lame jokes."

He took her hand and brought her to a halt. She spun on him, her polka dot sundress twirling.

For a moment he hesitated, but then a bigger part of him took control.

"How would you like to have the brown eyes and the mole and the lame jokes all the time?"

He reached into his pocket, grabbed the small ring, and got on a knee.

"Will you marry me?"

Her mouth opened. No words came out. Just a vigorous nod and a tear that escaped the bottom of her sunglasses.

Jake smiled and slid the ring onto her finger. He stood, put his hands on her waist, his forehead against hers.

Applause.

Jake turned.

People on the beach-towel-draped balconies of the condo tower beside them had seen it all. Cheers, whistles, commotion.

Jake and C.C. waved back.

He took her hand and examined the ring, a carved piece of brown-and-tan shell.

"Hope it fits," he said. "I got it from that surf shop back there."

He pointed to a small building past the condos, next to a pizza joint.

She twisted the ring around her finger.

"It's a little loose, love."

He turned in the opposite direction. "Then let's exchange it. Come on."

She didn't budge, shook her head. "No. I'll just add some masking tape or something."

"It's only temporary," Jake said. "Until we get everything here wrapped up. I mean, it was only a couple of bucks. I'll get you a real ring some day soon."

Her stare had stayed fixed on her hand as he spoke. She ran a finger along the ring. "Please don't. This works for me."

He smiled. "I know it does."

———

The crown of Jake's head had burnt. He should have applied more suntan lotion.

It was dark. They'd spent the entire day at the beach. That week had been a particularly stressful one in their combined efforts of working with the police department to put an end to her brother's brutalities. They'd needed sand therapy, and Pensacola Beach had generously provided some.

There were no more condos or surf shops or beach bars.

They were at the undisturbed, natural beach of the national seashore. Entirely alone.

Moonlight shone off gentle waves that lapped a few feet in front of them where they sat at the edge of the surf, right where wet sand met dry sand.

They'd chatted for over an hour about everything and anything and nothing before reaching a point of silence.

Finally, Jake spoke again. "You know, I've always found it interesting how your life relates to the rest of your family."

She shifted toward him, pulling her knees tighter to her chest. "How do you mean?"

He shrugged. "I mean, you're so peaceful and into such thoughtful, esoteric topics, but all those hours in the library are contingent on the safety provided by your family's violence."

She looked back at him. Blinked. Readjusted the arms wrapped around her knees. Then looked to the sea. "Maybe I've been sheltered. Maybe I live in arrested development. But I used my privilege to expand my mind. To make a difference in the world, one must first take care of oneself."

Her eyes narrowed, as though scanning the dark horizon for a distant ship.

Jake considered filling the quiet moment. But didn't.

"And one must always take advantage of one's opportunities," C.C. said. "It's wrong not to. I'm playing the hand I was dealt. I could get some normal job, be another cog in the wheel. An opportunity was provided to me, and I capitalized on it to have the sort of life I want. If that makes you uncomfortable, I don't give a damn."

Oh, shit.

Anger looked improper on the ideal lines of C.C.'s face. Jake had managed to piss her off for the first time on the same day he'd proposed.

His mind space was so chaotic that when he got to talking, sometimes words just spilled out. Stupid words, often enough. Regrettable words.

"I'm sorry," he said. "Really, I didn't—"

She smiled. "*Shhhh*. I know you're sorry. I can see it. That's one of the things that I love about you: your sincerity."

Jake ran a hand through his hair, his chin lowering. "Oh, man, I really screwed this up, haven't I? On the day I gave you your little shell ring."

In reply, she kissed him.

She moved herself onto him, fingers pressing hard into his back, her breasts squeezed against him through her thin sundress, nipples hard. They tangled for a few moments. Then her hand went below his waist, grabbed him.

He took her wrist, stopped it, and pulled away from the kiss.

"Whoa, now! Easy, tiger. What happened to waiting till we got married?"

She smirked, a coy twinkle in her eyes. "Well, aren't we presumptuous, Mr. Rowe? I'm not going back on what I said. I'm a woman of my word." A purposeful bat of the eyelashes. "Just relax, love. Let go."

———

A half hour later.

They lay against a sand ridge, facing the water, the star-speckled sky, both fully clothed, both covered in a sheen of sweat.

She was on his chest, hand on his shoulder. His heartbeat was finally slowing to a normal rate.

The sea had gone quiet. The rhythmic hum of the waves coaxed his eyelids closed.

"Just a little preview," C.C. said without leaving his chest. "Something to tide us over until the real thing. Okay?"

Jake tried to reply. He opened his mouth, but all he accomplished was a stupid smile.

C.C. lifted off his chest and looked down at him. She grinned.

"I guess there's one way to shut you up."

CHAPTER FIFTY-FOUR

THE PLACE SMELLED LIKE SHIT, like literal feces.

Burton was good at faking smiles, but he had to work extra hard to keep a pleasant look on his face as he traveled down the long, supposedly sterile corridor, which was built wide to accommodate wheelchairs and had stainless-steel railings along the walls. At the far end of the hall was a fish tank and beside it a little table with an arrangement of dusty silk flowers and a mound of easy-to-digest cookies. The floor had been recently polished, but the pungent odor of industrial-strength cleaner did little to cut through the scent of shit wafting out of the rooms.

Burton always looked to the future, constantly searching the horizon for the next great opportunity. If his life could be summed up in a single phrase, it would be *Keep moving forward.*

Forward, forward, forward.

Progress, progress, progress.

But this place, which he'd visited three times now in the last several years, always brought a sobering set of opposing realities to his grand vision. Ultimately, places like this were endpoints of forward momentum. The future held decay and death. It was inevitable. If he kept pushing onward, was he only shortening the time he had left before he, too, was rotting in a chair in a room in a shit-smelling tomb of a building?

He shoved the thought from his mind.

A nurse approached from the opposite side of the hallway, pushing a wheelchair that held a hunched, living corpse with pallid-gray skin riddled with imperfections and moles and sores. Cataract-ridden blue eyes looked up at Burton. There was a smile.

Burton forced his own smile broader, managed a nod, and turned into the room.

It was a narrow space full of white. White walls, a white drop tile ceiling, and white furnishings. A small TV sat atop a white set of drawers, and there was a pair of chairs beside the adjustable hospital bed.

Joseph Farone had been a small man his entire life, but his station had made him appear larger than he really was. Now that Mother Nature had stolen that station, he looked his size. Tiny. And even more frail now with his degrading mental health affecting his physical health. He was the picture of a little old Italian man in the same way that his daughter was the quintessential cute Italian chick. He had a kind old face with a big nose, wrinkled skin that had darkened with age. A shock of white hair, slightly thin on top, spiky and worn combed-back.

His eyes were clearer than the creature Burton had just seen in the hallway. Bright blue eyes. Crisp. They had the same stern but sparkling quality that Burton remembered from so many years ago, eyes that had seen promise in the teenage version of Burton, which had led Joseph to take

Burton in, include him in the family, and give him a better life.

Still, Joseph's rapidly progressive dementia was growing steadily more rapid. It had been six weeks since Burton had visited, and those bright eyes looked even more lost in confusion than when he'd last seen them. Gone.

Burton pulled a chair closer to the bed.

The gleaming blue eyes looked up at him. Joseph smiled, not like a father but like a young child, like a dog expecting a pat to the head.

"How you doing, old man?"

Joseph didn't reply, only smiled broader, dumbly from his position propped up by a pair of pillows.

"I know it's been a long time since I've visited, and I apologize for that. I've been a busy bee. You're gonna be so proud. I've taken over your entire operation. Can you believe that? And I've already transformed things. No more of the petty mafia shit. Drugs, extortion, protection rackets. How antiquated. The twenty-first century is almost here. I've contemporized the operation, gotten more done in a couple of months than you accomplished in decades. Pretty impressive, huh?"

Joseph smiled at him. He reached for the nightstand, grabbed a tiny canvas with a few scratches of paint, held it for Burton to see.

Burton glanced at it. "You made this, old man?"

Joseph smiled, patted his chest.

"Me," Joseph said in his disproportionately deep and booming voice, which sounded scratchier than the last time Burton had heard it.

"I see," Burton said and took the small painting, looked down upon it. "Joseph 'Joey' 'The Jaguar' Farone, painting with all the skill and vigor of a two-year-old."

Joseph laughed then.

Burton joined him in the laugh, which made Joseph laugh even louder and more enthusiastically.

Burton put his hand on the old man's tiny shoulder, squeezed, leaning over him as he laughed.

"Whew!" Burton said, wiping away an invisible tear. "Funny stuff, huh? Want to know something else that's funny? I killed your son and daughter."

Joseph continued to laugh. He pointed to his painting.

Burton laughed louder. "They died like the two clowns they were."

Joseph's laughter faded away, and he looked at Burton, confused.

"Like clowns," Burton repeated.

This brought a smile to the old man's lips.

"Oh, you like clowns, do you?"

Joseph laughed again. Burton joined him.

"I couldn't catch your other son, though," Burton said between laughs. "I like to think you favored Pete Hudson because you were loony by the time you met him, but the truth is, I don't blame you either way. I mean, Cecilia certainly favored him over me."

He chuckled. Joseph joined him.

"You took me in when no one else would. You were a father to me. But this son could never impress you, could he? I was never enough. Not even as impressive as a random car thief that showed up a few months ago."

Burton was no longer laughing. He reached behind the old man, took him by the shoulders, and pulled him away from the bed while he grabbed one of the two pillows.

"I've nearly wiped out the entire Farone crime family," Burton said. "There's only one member left."

He put the pillow on Joseph's face. Pressed down.

Joseph struggled. Minuscule strength pushing back against Burton's hand. Just as weak as he looked.

It only took a few moments.

Burton removed the pillow.

Joseph's eyes and mouth were open, head tilted to the side. Burton pulled the tiny body away from the bed and put the pillow behind him, turned the old man's face toward the ceiling, and brushed his eyelids closed.

Something tickled Burton's cheek, and he wiped it away, rubbed it out of existence, his momentary weakness.

He pushed the call button on the bed's hand railing.

Waited.

And looked at the body.

There had been a single tear. That was all he needed. He'd already erased it. He was fine now.

Footsteps behind him. He turned.

A rotund nurse entered the room. "Is there something I can—"

"Hurry!" Burton said, waving frantically. "He stopped breathing! *Please hurry!*"

She rushed past him. "Oh my goodness, Mr. Farone!"

She pressed another button. An alarm blared. She looked at Burton. "You need to leave. I'm sorry."

He nodded solemnly.

Three more personnel rushed into the room, and he stepped out of their way, pressing himself against the side of the wardrobe by the door.

A final look into the room. Six people crowded over the Jaguar's bed. Shouting at each other. One of the nurses performed CPR. Burton caught brief glimpses of the old man in the small gaps in the action.

Then he turned the corner and entered the hallway.

Yes, he'd shed a tear for dear ol' Father.

Now it was time to celebrate.

He was free of the old man's presence. Unworthiness no longer tainted Burton. He'd been purified, and now he was ready to proceed. Onward to the future.

Forward movement.

Progress.

He smiled.

CHAPTER FIFTY-FIVE

NAKIRI, the woman who had been calling herself Christie Mosley, looked at this man lying in the hospital bed before her, the man who had been calling himself Pete Hudson, who had actually been Jake Rowe, who was now calling himself Silence Jones, to whom Falcon had given the codename Suppressor.

And he disgusted her.

What the hell was Falcon thinking bringing in a thirty-something-year-old inexperienced local cop as an Asset, knowing there was less than a month to train him?

Foolishness.

Falcon was a good man and a good Prefect, but he often made reckless choices that aligned with his cavalier, smartass, goofy-uncle attitude. Someday, one of his off-the-cuff decisions like this was going to get somebody killed.

It hadn't happened yet. But it would.

Maybe Falcon had recognized the rashness of his decision and put Nakiri in charge of training to counteract his imprudence. An attempt at checks-and-balances. If so, she was taking that responsibility seriously, if not personally; she was doing her damndest to fail the trainee.

On his very first evening of training.

Suppressor stifled a scream as Nakiri pressed into the bandages on his right shoulder.

"Wrong! Eight-zero-six-four-five-four-one-six-two-nine."

Suppressor's forehead was wet with exertion "Eight-zero-six..." He swallowed. "Four-five-one—"

"*Wrong!*"

She clamped down.

Another silent scream as he bit down on his lip. Sweat dripped from his nose.

She released the pressure. "Eight-zero-six-four-five-four-one-six-two-nine."

"Eight-zero-six..." He panted. Swallowed. "Four-five-four-one..." Panted. Swallowed. "Six-two-nine."

She tensed her fingers. Stopped.

He'd gotten it right.

Well, what do ya know?

"Good," she said. "Did you notice something about the number I gave you?"

Suppressor just stared at her, chest heaving.

"You need to be perceptive, Suppressor. That's something else for you to work on." She narrowed her eyes. "Ten digits. Just like U.S. phone numbers. You need to be able to memorize ten-digit numbers the first time you hear them."

She took her pen knife from her pocket, snapped open the blade.

Suppressor pulled back into his pillows, eyes going wide beneath his sweaty brow.

Nakiri smirked. "Relax. I'm not *that* mean."

She cut the plastic handcuff on his right wrist, leaned over the bed, pressed herself against him just so, batted a pair of bedroom eyes in his direction, then cut the right handcuff.

Suppressor rubbed his wrists.

She yanked back his cover and sheets, glanced at where she'd busied herself a few minutes earlier, below his waistline, gave him a salacious grin, then undid the large strap restraining his legs.

"There," she said. "Other than the IVs, you're completely untethered. But don't go getting any ideas. You're three stories underground, and this place is monitored." She held up the loose strap. "Just consider this like getting the training wheels off your bike."

She flipped her eyes to his crotch again.

"This undying thing you've got for Cecilia Farone—you know you've just projected a perfect image onto her because of your own low self-image, right? Weak people do shit like that. You would've become anything she asked you to become. Pitiful.

"But you liked our lesson in touch. You can't possibly deny that. The proof's in the, er, pudding. Keep a dead woman rattling around in your brain for all eternity if you want, but it won't change what's happening in the present, in the real, *living* world. You'll find there are lots of gray areas within morality. That's where we exist, all the Watchers, but especially us, the Assets. We live in that gray area."

She gave him another one of her coy grins and walked to the door, opened it, looked back.

"Get some rest. Training resumes tomorrow, bright and early."

———

The next day.

Suppressor was walking well, better than she would've expected. When Falcon had told her the guy had fortitude, he'd clearly been referring to Suppressor's mental toughness.

But evidently he had physical resolve as well. His knees were rather weak, and he squinted a lot, but otherwise he was walking around fairly normally.

They were in the crumbling area outside the building where the underground medical facility was housed: a tower in an abandoned attempt at a commercial park off the interstate in Alexandria, Virginia. All broken concrete and weed-filled cracks and untrimmed trees.

Squinting, Suppressor looked about the surroundings. "I've been..." He stopped to swallow. "Here?"

Nakiri grinned at him. "What, did you think you were under the Pentagon or something? We work where we have to." She looked him over. "How's the pain? Are your legs holding out?"

He pointed to his throat, frowned.

"Your throat hurts worse than your legs?" she said.

He nodded.

"You'll have to learn to live with that one, buddy," she said. "Time for your next lesson."

She stopped. And he did too.

With their last turn, they were now in an abandoned alley full of trash and downed power lines and overturned dumpsters.

"You seem like a quality guy. A future family man, had you not murdered a handful of people. But even if Cecilia was still alive, you wouldn't be having a family. Falcon told you, didn't he?"

Suppressor gave a confused shake of the head, shrugged.

"All us Assets have been spayed or neutered." She pointed at his crotch and made a pair of scissors with her fingers. "*Snip-snip!* You're shooting blanks from here on out, dummy."

His reaction was confusion, not a shred of disappointment. He really was *that* committed to the dead chick. Crazy fool.

"A right of passage, like our GPS dot," she said and held up her right arm, twisting it. "Anyway, I digress. My point is, you're such a good guy, I'm wondering if you really have what it takes to get down-'n-dirty as an assassin."

She paused.

"Hit me."

Suppressor cocked his head.

"Hit me," she repeated.

"Why?"

"Because you need to learn to hit anyone, to be prepared for anything. You were always such a gentleman to Cecilia. I know you don't want to hit a woman. Find a way."

Suppressor hesitated.

"You have to be able to do this. Go." She patted her cheek, turned her face, gave him a nice, open target.

Suppressor grimaced, raised his hand.

And lightly slapped her.

Nakiri laughed. "Whew! I'm lucky I'm still standing, Rocky." She laughed louder. "We'll work on that. Come on."

———

Three days later.

Back in the hospital room. 9 p.m. Another day of physical training in the books.

Suppressor collapsed onto the small bed, gasping. The bandages on his right shoulder were gone. Now there was just a large Band-Aid. Like Nakiri, the medical staff was working every day, feverishly, to get the guy ready in time.

"You'll have to work on your stamina, Silence Jones," she said. "I don't give a shit if you've been in a hospital bed for weeks on end. We need you trained. Fast."

She dug in her backpack and pulled out a stack of magazines, tossed them onto his lap.

"Have fun," she said.

Suppressor lifted one of the magazines, opened it. After a moment he glanced up at her, arched an eyebrow.

"Logic puzzles," she said. "We're not just training your body. Gotta work that mind too. I want five complete and correct puzzles by the time I get back tomorrow morning. Find a way."

Suppressor pointed at a red circle in the graphics on the front cover. In white letters it said, *ANSWERS IN BACK*. He grinned at her.

Well, now.

A little sass out of the new Asset.

Nakiri reached into her bag again, pulled out the stack of torn-out pages she'd removed from the backs of the magazines.

"Nice try."

————

Two days later.

A private boxing gym. A crummy old place worthy of a 1970s-era film, filled with dust-covered equipment that looked unused since the '70s, fittingly enough. It was one of many such Watchers facilities that had been carefully chosen and utilized.

They were in the ring. Nakiri wore a pair of punch mitts, and Suppressor wore a pair of boxing gloves.

He also wore a tank top, and she noticed that his arms were more toned than she'd have thought after so much time in the bed. He was firming up quickly, which was probably a benefit of all those hours he'd spent in the gym in his former life. Through the years, Nakiri had noticed that despite the fact that muscle goes away when not utilized—*use it, or lose it*, as they say—some hard-earned mass becomes permanent.

This was good news for Suppressor. He had to not only get back into shape in a brief period of time, but she was going to get him into the best shape of his life.

At the moment, though, the guy was breathing hard. He gave another punch, halfheartedly. She barely felt it through the padding.

"Harder!" she shouted. "Harder, damn you!"

Suppressor punched again, feebly, and then stopped, panting. He put his hands on his knees and gasped.

"Too weak," he said and grimaced, swallowed, another pair of deep breaths. "Almost two months."

"Oh, so that's it?" she said. "You've been in a hospital bed for almost two month, so that makes you too weak to throw a few punches?"

Suppressor nodded.

And with his head hanging the way it was, she whacked the back of it with her punch mitt.

"Stand up, *you lazy shit!* You've had people bringing you back to life, working around the clock on you for those 'almost two months.' Doctors, nurses. Meals handed to you literally on a platter. What are you going to do when you're in the middle of a desert? What are you gonna do when your target finds you, captures you, beats you, electrifies you? Come on, you sack of shit!"

Suppressor took one more breath and extended to his full height, towering over her, chest heaving.

She scowled at him, wriggled out of the punch mitts, and threw them to the mat. A step closer, a few inches away from him, looking straight up so he could see the rage in her eyes.

His gloved hands hung like lifeless pendulums off his long, feeble body. She tore open the laces, ripped the gloves from his hands, and threw them onto the mat like she had with the punch mitts.

She took a step back, placed her arms at her sides.

"Hit me!"

Silence raised a fist.

"Hit me, pussy! Close your fist and punch a woman. Find a damn way!"

Suppressor's fist hovered for a moment. Then he lowered it.

She moved back into his space, looked up at him.

"This is why we train your mind more than your body. With enough pressure, anyone can learn to kick and punch and stab a knife and shoot a gun. But an Asset's mind keeps them alive in the field, Suppressor. Right now, you're a dead man walking, a man so bloated with ideals that he'll trip and die. You're not prepared. There's no time left. And I'd be a fool to pass you."

She stormed off.

CHAPTER FIFTY-SIX

Several days later.

Silence was back outside the building. Except this time he wasn't with Nakiri; he was with Falcon.

Crumbling asphalt surrounded them. It was colder now, too. And wetter. In the mornings there had been light snows, and in the afternoons, it had turned to rain, which now trickled down the rotting brick of the building across the street. Everything around them was empty and quiet. They were the only living things aside from a pair of birds and a squirrel doing a tightrope act on a drooping phone line at the end of the block.

Falcon had his overcoat buttoned tight as he sucked on a Marlboro.

"Assets are killers. Human weapons. But they're thinkers as well, because more often than not, we're going to need you to investigate before you start pulling your trigger. Your notoriously analytical mind is one of the main reasons I brought you onto the team, Mr. Almost Detective." He took a drag from his cigarette. "That said, have you figured out who I am yet?"

Silence raised an eyebrow.

"Assets aren't technically permitted to know the identity of their Prefects, but if the Prefect is a public figure—which many of us are—it's almost a moot point. I'll simply say that it would be just *peachy* if you figure out who I am, but don't be a *sad sack* if you can't."

He'd put a heavy emphasis on three of the words. Falcon was speaking in code.

"Tell me, Suppressor, what do you think of your trainer?"

"Bitch," Silence said.

Falcon laughed, coughed on his smoke. "I can see why you'd say that. She tells me she's been pretty hard on you." He coughed again, cleared his throat. "Don't forget, she gave you an emergency tracheotomy, got you to a Pensacola hospital, snuck you out the next morning, and drove you across the country. She has rough edges, maybe a few more than the average person, but her heart is where it should be. That's why she's a Watcher."

He took another drag from his cigarette, held it for a long moment, then let the smoke drift out the corner of his mouth.

"Allow me to lend a little perspective. We got Nakiri when she was twenty-four. You remember that news story about the woman who chopped her cheating husband's dick off?"

Silence nodded. Of course he did. The story became a media storm, a progressively common trait in the modern world, something that had concerned C.C. greatly. It concerned Silence, too.

"Well, our girl did something similar," Laswell said. "Before the Watchers, she had been a middle-American homemaker and a part-time employee at a local bakery. Her husband—let's call him Bob—was an insurance agent and a pillar in their small town. They'd had a perfect little life, and she was an old-fashioned, doting wife. Hard to picture, isn't it?"

Silence nodded.

"There were three years of bliss, then she suspected Bob was cheating. He denied, but he couldn't hide it, not with small-town gossip being what it is. The doting wife tolerated his behavior for a year or so until her niece came to her in tears one afternoon. The kid said Uncle Bob had been forcing her to do things. For months. That sent our girl over the edge. She went to the cops, worked with them for two weeks, in the afternoons while Bob was at work."

Falcon stopped, blew out another cloud of smoke. He looked away, chuckled, and Silence saw thoughts and memories sparkling in his eyes.

"Do you know what a nakiri is?"

"Knife," Silence said.

"Right. A big ol' kitchen knife, for chopping vegetables. That's what she used." He took another drag, released. "The night before the warrant was to be served, our girl had a change of heart, didn't think prison was a strong enough punishment for Bob. Her niece was only ten years old. *Ten*. So she slipped out of the bedroom while Bob was sleeping, went to the kitchen. She chopped his dick off, fed it to him, then tortured him for a while before she sliced his throat all the way through the jugular. The body was never found. She fled, and we got to her right before the police."

"Shit," Silence said.

"Mmm-hmm." Falcon looked at the end of his cigarette and saw that it still had a half inch left. "You know why she has such an axe to grind with you, right?"

"Took her assignment," Silence said.

Falcon shook his head. "It's not just that you took her assignment. You spoiled her debt."

Silence raised an eyebrow.

"Each Asset has a debt to pay, your alternative to the prison sentence we saved you from. Fulfill the debt, and we pull that GPS dot out of your arm, give you a fat bank account, and send you somewhere peaceful—beaches, mountains, whatever you like. If you've survived, you've sure as hell earned the luxury.

"For most Assets, the debt is simply a number—a quantity of assignments to complete. Nakiri has been at this for twelve years. Her debt is twenty assignments. Before going undercover as Burton's girlfriend, she'd completed nineteen." He fixed a look on Silence. "See where I'm going with this?"

Silence nodded.

"Pensacola was to be her final assignment," Falcon continued. "And she failed. She broke her cover, aborted her mission to rescue you. She deliberately defied me. I'd told her to let you die."

"Thanks," Silence said.

Falcon shrugged as he examined his cigarette again, saw that it had expended, and flicked it away. He blew into his hands, rubbed them together, and shoved them in his pockets.

"Nakiri had put months into the Pensacola job, by far her longest assignment. She was *this* close to being finished, and she gave up her freedom to save your life. And now I've given the assignment to you, and told her to train you."

Nakiri's hatred toward Silence had been a cloudy sphere of confusion for him. Now it was spotlight bright.

"What's mine?" Silence said.

Falcon turned to him. "What's your debt?"

Silence nodded.

The older man looked away again, down the deserted street. "I'm still working on that. But I'll tell you this much: it's not going to be a standard debt. It won't be a number of assignments. Yours is going to be custom-tailored, more personal."

Personal? Silence didn't like the sound of that. Abstract notions didn't play well with his overactive brain. A simple number would have suited him much better.

Falcon turned to him and grinned. "You look like you're giving this a lot of thought. Don't get ahead of yourself, Suppressor. You still have to complete the training."

CHAPTER FIFTY-SEVEN

IT WAS Silence's third week of training.

He and Nakiri were back in the gym, outside the ring.

And he was struggling to maintain his composure.

A twenty-pound kettlebell quivered before him in his right hand. It had been there for minutes, held straight-armed, elbow locked. His muscles burned fire.

Nakiri stood a few feet away, chomping gum, stopwatch in her left hand. She wasn't looking at either the watch or at Silence; instead her eyes scanned a copy of *Cosmo*, cradled in her free hand. Her feet were crossed, and she tapped the toe of her left Doc Marten while she read.

"There are lots of different types of muscular strength," she said, thumbing to the next page. "We're training you for endurance and stamina. All those fitness-center-sculpted muscles you had looked really hot, but we need something a lot more practical. And deceiving. I mean, take me, for instance. 110 pounds ... give or take a little, ya know. You would have never guessed how strong I was when I kicked your ass at Burton's beach house, huh? Christie Mosley, Burton's feisty, sexy little girlfriend."

She gave a Betty Boop pout, brought up her shoulders, stuck her ass out.

Silence thought back to how easily she'd taken him down at Burton's. There had been a few quick exchanges, and then he was on the floor, squeezed between her thighs in a move that had completely incapacitated him.

No, he certainly hadn't anticipated that from Christie Mosley.

His arm gave out.

Nakiri squeezed the stopwatch.

Beep.

She looked at the watch's screen and couldn't conceal a small, impressed grin. She'd given him almost no credit for his achievements through the weeks, so he was going to take her smile as a compliment, despite how quickly she removed it from her face.

She flipped a page in the magazine, popped a bubble between her teeth. "Next arm."

———

That evening.

Silence sat at the edge of his bed, wearing a pair of flannel pajamas and facing a Macintosh computer that was set up on a small table and connected to a phone jack. A diagonal strip of light from the crack in the doorway sliced over the bed and his legs.

The Internet connection speed, Nakiri had told him, was 56K. Silence wasn't much of a tech head, but he knew that 56K was blazing fast. The Watcher's technological advances were staggering, ahead of the curve, already with a foot in the twenty-first century.

He'd been staring off to the wall, lost in thought, and the computer's flying toasters screensaver had kicked in. Refocus-

ing, he moved the mouse, and the Netscape browser reap-
peared. It was open to the website he'd navigated to moments
earlier: the Atlanta FBI Field Office. He was supposed to be
working on a practice after-action report—an AAR—but
instead he'd logged onto the Internet to sate a personal
hunger.

Falcon had spoken in code the previous night: *It would be
just* peachy *if you figure out who I am, but don't be a* sad sack *if you
can't.*

He'd put heavy emphasis on *peachy* and *sad sack*.

And Silence had figured it out.

Peachy: the Peach State, Georgia.

Sad sack: SAC, Special Agent in Charge.

He clicked the personnel page hyperlink. And immediately found Falcon.

A vertical column of photos cut down the center of the
page—headshots of men and women in dress clothes posed in
front of a blue backdrop with an American flag to the side.
At the top of the column was Silence's Prefect.

He clicked the image and opened Falcon's individual page.

On the left side of the screen was Falcon's photo. He wore
a sharp, conservative suit jacket with a bright red tie, sitting
bolt straight. There was a slight grin under his mustache, but
nothing like the flippant smirk to which Silence had become
accustomed.

Opposite the photo was a list of biographical information.

ANTHONY LASWELL
SPECIAL AGENT IN CHARGE

B.A. Philosophy, University of Iowa, 1962
Juris Doctorate, Cornell University, 1965

U.S. Army Judge Advocate General Corps, 1965-1969
Vietnam Service Medal

Special Agent, FBI
Columbia Field Office - 1969–1970
Indianapolis Field Office - 1970–1977
Dallas Field Office - 1977–1988

Special Agent in Charge, FBI
Atlanta Field Office - 1988–present

Silence smirked.

A sharp voice made him jump.

"Hey!"

Nakiri looked through the gap in the door.

"What's with the grin, dummy? Lookin' at pornography? Back to work!"

She left.

———

Two days later.

They were in the middle of nowhere. Surrounded by snow. As a California boy turned Florida boy, this was as close to a frozen tundra as Silence had ever been. The temperature was somewhere around the freezing point, and the fact that the snow wasn't very thick—only about an inch of fresh powder that had fallen through the night—made things even more bleak, as everywhere mud brown showed through the white.

He and Nakiri trudged across a desolate cornfield, empty but for a few rotten stalks. There were dark outlines of forests on the distant horizon. Another woods was much closer, only a few feet ahead of them. Their destination. They'd walked half an hour to get there.

Nakiri wore a long, stylish coat, to her knees, cinched in tight, hugging her notable curves. A toboggan hat and gloves —matching—completed the look. Over her shoulder she'd slung a duffel bag, and propped against the other shoulder was a scoped Remington rifle, flawless and brand-new looking. She cupped its butt with a gloved hand.

Silence carried nothing.

And he wore only a pair of boxer briefs.

He took another look at his quivering arms. They'd turned a grayish blue. Through his skin, a network of veins and muscular striations were clearly visible.

He felt a disconcerting confluence of pain and numbness. If he kept moving forward steadily, kept an even pace and rhythmic motions, his body seemed almost detached from his senses, teasing him with a reprieve. But if he moved even a little in the wrong direction—say, by stepping on a clod of earth hidden in the snow or tripping over a frozen cornstalk —icy pain jolted through his entire body.

His skin prickled, felt ready to crack. His nipples had constricted into tiny, hard dots on his quivering pecs. Even his eyelids and eyeballs were cold. He spasmed every few steps.

The only saving grace was that his feet were so frozen and wet that he no longer sensed anything from them, not even the ice-pain. At least part of him wasn't hurting, though the numbness itself was getting painful.

They reached the edge of the forest, and as Silence glanced down, he saw briars and sticks and branches poking out of the thin layer of snow. He also saw his bare feet. Which had turned blue.

Nakiri put her hand on his shoulder for a second, and the ice-pain surged through him, both warm and frigid. She quickly took her hand back and pointed to the briars he'd been studying.

"Don't worry," she said. "Like I told you before, I'm not *that* mean."

She pointed again, farther away, to a small path in the woods.

The trail was less cumbersome on his feet than the corn-field had been, but it wasn't exactly like walking on a cotton rug.

And walk they did.

For probably another mile.

Until the woods opened up into a crude shooting range— a cleared-out section with a row of wooden stands spaced evenly against a berm.

Nakiri didn't stop them until they were about twenty-five yards away from one of the stands.

"Stay here," she said.

As she walked to the stand, she pulled a piece of paper from her pocket. After she'd affixed it to the wood, Silence saw that it was nothing more than a sheet of white printer paper with a rough black circle sketched in the center.

"Firearms qualifications," she said with a smile as she returned.

Silence's teeth rattled. "Haven't shot once."

"You're right," she said. "All our firearms training has been bookwork. And this will be your one and only qualification. You can go train with guns on your own time, like the reading list I gave you. I'm here to harden your body, but more importantly to harden that dummy mind of yours. I keep telling you, Suppressor, the mind will be your most valuable weapon."

Silence was just about sick of her head games. He looked away from her, to the empty, skeletal branches above.

"Where are we?" he said.

He swallowed. His voice was even hoarser than usual, the frigid air amplifying the pain.

"We don't work for the government; we correct its mistakes," she said. "But we do work *within* the government. We work where we can, when we can, and one of our Specialists was able to find an open day in the schedule of an undisclosed CIA training facility in rural Virginia." She gestured broadly, dramatically at their surroundings. "Aren't you a lucky boy?"

Silence pulled his arms tighter around his chest and looked at the rifle propped against her shoulder.

"Shoot in cold." He swallowed. "I get it."

Silence reached for the rifle, and Nakiri took a step back and laughed.

"Well, thanks for setting up your next lesson so well, Suppressor. Because this," she said, holding the Remington out on display, "is part of your training on preparedness and dealing with disappointment and lack of resources in the field." She twisted the gun in her hands, looking it over. "I'm just carrying this around because it's so darn pretty. Nice, isn't it? Do you know what it is?"

"Remington 700."

"It's a Remington Model 700*P*, to be exact. A beautiful weapon. Too bad you won't be shooting it today."

She reached into her pocket and retrieved something small and metal, something that fit in the palm of her hand.

"This'll be your firearm, dummy."

She held a tiny, rusty, derringer, something obscure, possibly even homemade. A single-shot, break action .22.

Now Silence saw why the target only twenty-five yards away—he'd be shooting a tiny, inaccurate, rusty, single-shot while his body shook violently.

He took the small gun from her, cracked it open. It was empty.

"Round?" he said.

Nakiri smiled at him. "Sure, you can have all the rounds you want."

She reached back into her pocket and took out a Ziplock bag filled with shiny new .22 LR cartridges. She unzipped the bag then smiled and held it high, shook it, the rounds jingling inside.

As Silence reached for the bag, she swung it upward. All of the rounds flew out, their brass casings twinkling in the muted gray light.

They landed in the snow.

And vanished.

"Oh, and by the way," Nakiri said, "you'll be shooting from the prone position. Might as well get down there and find your first round."

Now Silence fully understood.

This was going to be even worse than he thought.

As he got on his knees and lowered himself to the ground, he thought that he couldn't possibly feel any more pain in his numbed body.

He was wrong.

The cold hit his chest and stomach like a blast, and he shuddered as it stole his breath. His wet fingers trembled as he saw a tiny glisten of brass in front of him, peeking out of the snow beside a twig.

He plunged his pink-blue hand into the snow, pinched the cartridge between two half-dead fingers. His hand shook harder as he brought the round into the snapped-open derringer, inserted it, and snapped the tiny gun back together.

Nakiri propped the Remington against her shoulder, then shoved her other gloved hand into her pocket and used it to pull her formfitting coat in even tighter. She shivered.

"Begin," she said.

———

The target had five holes in it, none in the black center. Silence's hands had become so numb now that he couldn't feel the cartridges nor the gun, couldn't feel any of it as the derringer barked out another small *crack* and left another hole in the paper.

Two inches away from the black circle.

He'd spotted another cartridge a few moments ago, this one a foot away from his shoulder. It was the last one of which he knew the location. He would have to start hunting for them soon.

He reached into the snow, squeezed his hand numbly around where he knew it to be, and retrieved it, then inserted it into the derringer and snapped the gun back together. His arms shook, and for a moment, he wanted to let the desperation roll over him, to fuse with the cold and consume him, swallowing him into the muddy forest floor.

But then he thought of C.C.

She would have a way to get past this obstacle. She always knew the right ways to break through issues of the mind.

C.C. would tell him to breathe. From the stomach. Diaphragmatic breathing. She would say that he should visualize heat, that he should use his mind to substitute heat for the cold.

He took a deep breath. Held it. Closed his eyes.

Nakiri behind him: "What are you stalling for, Suppressor? Hurry your ass up."

He replaced her voice with C.C.'s.

Feel the moment, love. Don't reject it. Embrace it.

He opened his eyes. Exhaled. And squeezed the trigger.

Crack!

A small hole appeared in the black part of the target.

Beep.

Nakiri pulled her hand from her pocket. Resting in her glove was the digital stopwatch that Silence hadn't known she'd brought with her. Her eyebrows raised as she looked at the time.

"Eleven minutes. And only seven rounds." She looked at the target, shoved the stopwatch back in her pocket, turned away from him. "Those are both records."

She grinned. Then scowled.

"One good shot doesn't mean shit, dummy."

She shrugged the duffel bag off her shoulder and threw it in the snow beside him. And when he just stared back at her, she gave him a little motion with her chin that said, *Open it.*

Silence brought his dead fingers to the bag and unzipped it.

A large bath towel. Jeans. Multiple shirts. Boots. Multiple pairs of socks. Fresh underwear. A jacket.

He grabbed the towel and dried off, instantly feeling warmer. Then the jeans. With his hands and arms and legs as lifeless as they were, it took nearly as long to get dressed as it had to hit the target. But when he was done, he was warmer, like he'd climbed into a sauna.

Nakiri stepped up to him.

"Now ... hit me."

Silence stared at her.

More of her mind games. He felt his nostrils flare.

Of all the shit she'd put him through, he hated this the most.

"Still can't hit a woman. You have to be able to do this. Didn't you ever apprehend women as a cop?"

"Of course." He swallowed. "Never punched one."

"Why's that? Because we're so pretty and sweet?" She primly placed a hand under her chin, looked up and to the side, batted her eyelashes. "Let me tell you, Suppressor, you're going to face a lot of awful women in this job. And you'll have to throw a few punches."

She gave him a dark look.

"I shouldn't pass you. You don't have it, Silence Jones. You weak-minded idiot. Weak, weak, weak. Hell, I should have failed you long ago. You stole my assignment, my ticket out of this life. I should go to Falcon right now and tell him what a worthless sack of shit you are."

Her chest rose. An exhale whistled out of her nose, puffing a cloud of vapor in the frigid air. She narrowed her eyes.

"I've put you through some real hell. Any man in your position, no matter how chivalrous, would knock my lights out. There's something else holding you back. And I know what it is."

She stepped closer. A dark smile played on the corners of her mouth. Her eyelids lowered farther, and her gaze deepened. Bedroom eyes.

"This goes back to our first day of training. When I touched you. You have a connection with me now."

She put her hand on his chest, and he brushed it away roughly.

Another sultry look from her.

"That's it. We have a bond, don't we, Silence? That's why you won't strike me. And maybe the bond is giving you conflicting thoughts about your girlfriend."

"Fiancée."

Nakiri shrugged. "I never saw a ring on her finger. Whatever you want to call her, the thought of Cecilia is sullied now, isn't it? Because not only did I play with your ding-dong, but I've been with you every step of the way during the most difficult time in your life. You're closer to me than you *ever* were to her, whether you like it or not."

She put her hand on his crotch, and he smacked it away again, harder than before, strong enough to make a slap sound that echoed through the trees.

"Cecilia told me her secret," Nakiri said. "She and

Christie Mosley didn't have too many moments together, but for some reason, your fiancée decided to open up to me one night. A little girl time. She told me she was saving herself for when you two got married. Not your typical born-again virgin, was she? Aren't they usually the church-going types? Which got me to wondering—maybe it wasn't even by choice. Maybe you were too dickless to do anything with her."

She grinned. Then leaned closer, getting on her tiptoes, placing her lips right beside his neck, so close that he felt the heat of her breath on his frozen skin.

"And maybe you're worried that since you enjoyed how I touched you, then maybe, just maybe, *she* enjoyed it. Cecilia. I mean, I wasn't there, but I gotta imagine that those rough-and-tumble guys didn't just slap her around. You watched the video. Tell me, did they touch her? You know, *touch* her. Did they rub their big, strong hands all over that tight little born-again body? Oh, yeah, baby. That little gray dress she wore that night."

She took a step back and smiled up at him, eyes twinkling darker.

"Maybe she even liked being slapped around. The rough stuff. God knows you weren't man enough to give it to her. All those tough guys feeling her up. Maybe her dying moments were spent living out the sexual fantasies you were never gonna fulfill."

She smiled wickedly.

"Maybe she just loooooved it."

Silence felt something in his numbed body, little tingling sensations in his face. Quivering fury.

He slugged her.

Right to the eye socket.

She flew back, head snapping behind her, hair flailing, landing on her back in the snow.

Silence instantly knelt, reached out for her.

She leaned up, groaning, and planted her hands on either side of her. She looked at his outstretched hand, slapped it away.

One of her eyes was pinched shut, the other scowling.

Then she grinned.

"Training complete," she said.

CHAPTER FIFTY-EIGHT

TRAINING COMPLETE.

Nakiri's words rolled through Silence's mind as he took another sip of the Heineken and leaned farther back in the metal folding chair, his long legs draped in front of him, feet resting inches from the shiny, curved plastic wall of the pod.

He glanced at his hand, resting on his lap. It was blue. The beer bottle it held was blue. His legs were blue. The light coming from the gap in the pod painted everything.

When his training ended in the snowy woods in Virginia, it had been another opportunity for him to fortify his new identity. Before that, when he'd seen his new face, he hadn't felt entirely like a new man. Neither had he felt like a new person when he'd taken the new name and agreed to be an assassin. He'd thought that when training was over, *then* he'd be transformed.

But when Nakiri said it—lying in the snow, looking up at him with that combination of physical pain and mentor approval and maybe even a bit of pride—when she'd said *Training complete*, still the new identity hadn't fully adhered to him.

He'd long ago concluded that his previous life ended when Burton killed him at the beach house, but since then he'd been in limbo. He'd consciously accepted his new name, his new identity—but somehow his subconscious hadn't.

C.C. had taught him that to move beyond one's troubles, one must stop thinking about oneself.

And that's exactly what he needed to do, because his disorganized mind had drifted into selfishness when he had to focus on something extremely critical.

He had to figure out how the hell to find Burton. Failure would have consequences for the entire nation.

Silence took a diaphragmatic breath. Held it. Released.

Then a sip of beer.

Two calming techniques—one of C.C.'s, one of his own.

To figure out what to do about Burton, Silence would have to crawl into that thing in front of him, the alien-looking half-sphere he'd been staring at for several minutes. If the hype was true—and he sure hoped it was, given how much he'd paid for the thing—then a transcendental experience awaited him inside.

That's why he'd gotten it. The ultimate way of calming the storm that was his brain. The nearest facility where he could have paid for an individual session was all the way in Atlanta, which is why he'd dropped half his startup funds on the thing.

Still, he didn't know what to expect. He would finish the beer before he got in. One calming technique at a time.

As he straightened up in the chair, he felt the open, skeletal presence of the half-finished wall against his back— the brand-new studs, the rear side of the hallway-facing drywall, and the original structure above and below. The smell was a mixture of fresh sawdust and decades-old timber.

Another sip of beer. Almost gone. If his first couple of weeks with Mrs. Enfield were any indication, he wouldn't be able to rely on alcohol much longer. She was going to hound him, which meant he was going to have to ditch this calming technique.

Not that he minded. In only a couple of weeks, booze had become a crutch. He thought of his father—drunk and crying, in an undershirt, curled in a recliner.

This was the last time Silence would rely on alcohol. He would kill the crutch.

He looked at the bottle.

In fact, he'd kill it right now.

The glass thunked against the hardwood floor as he put it down.

Another look at the pod. Its glowing blue mouth acknowledged him—whether it was a smile or a scowl, he couldn't tell.

Let's go.

He was supposed to do this naked. So he stripped.

He stuck his hand in the blue gap, and pulled open the lid. The ten-inch pool of water before him was perfectly still.

The supplies he needed were on the little ledge at the front. First, he inserted the flanged silicone earplugs. Then he opened the jar of petroleum jelly and smeared it over the nicks on his knuckles and face. This kept the salt water from burning.

One more look at the unnaturally blue pool, then he got in.

The 93.5-degree water felt pleasant, but not out of the ordinary.

Until he reclined.

He lay back in the water and instantly bobbed. This made him grin like an idiot, despite how silly he felt, despite the seriousness of the situation he was in. Silence had never been a floater. It felt funny.

There was a moment of struggle to get his bearings and

pull his big frame into an upright position. When he finally stabilized, he grabbed the lid and pulled it shut.

And he was sealed in.

All was blue. The arched ceiling created by the underside of the lid was surprisingly high.

Silence lay back in the water, and as soon as his ears submerged, there was, well, silence. The flanged design of the plugs had already cut down on almost all sound, but the combination of the plugs and the water made things unnaturally, unbelievably quiet.

The waterline fell at his chest, around his neck, halfway up his head. He bobbed, gently tapping the sides as he drifted around. He'd been told that bobbing would quickly subside when he stopped moving.

The black speakers were a few inches behind his head. Even though it could be used in a sensory deprivation manner, the pod also had options that involved the senses. The speakers could be used to play gentle music, and the light could be left on.

He reached to the buttons on the wall to his right, pressed the center button, and the blue light vanished.

And it was dark. Really, really dark. Pure black.

He held perfectly still, but pushing the button had created more movement in the water, and his naked body bobbed again and touched the walls—when he'd brush one side, he'd drift to the other side, then the bottom, then the top.

Which frustrated him. How was he supposed to have this transcendental, sensory-free experience if his sides kept brushing the walls? The dealer had told him that Silence's height—six-foot-three—was at the high end of the comfort scale for a standard pod. He'd gotten the *XL* model. Did he need the *XXL*? Was there an *XXL*?

Soon, though, the bobbing subsided, just gentle undulations. He wondered what caused these. His heartbeat, maybe. Or the movement of the Earth. Or the small, unavoidable motions he didn't know he was making.

He blinked.

Which made him realize he'd lost track of whether his eyes were open. It was *that* dark. And relaxing.

Still, it wasn't working.

Where was the transcendental experience?

Ugh. He wanted to climb out. This was silly. Ridiculous. And also dangerous, given the seriousness of the situation, which sent a flood of panic over him.

C.C. would tell him to relax, to breathe, to give it a chance to work.

He took a deep breath. Diaphragmatic.

That's what he was supposed to do, anyway, to get this thing to work—in the pod, one is supposed to focus on one's breathing and stop thinking.

He couldn't stop thinking. It wasn't in his nature, and his entire purpose of doing this float was to think his way through his problem.

Burton.

There was something to all of this that Silence was missing. But what? 8 p.m. tonight. That was the time Glover had given, the time that Burton was to meet with an unknown connection, someone with incredible power. A meeting that had devastating ramifications.

But *why?*

Why were they meeting?

His eyes opened. They'd been closed, and he didn't realize it. He didn't see the ceiling above him, but he knew it was there.

He wasn't in a sensory-free environment. He was in a damn plastic bubble in one of his bedrooms, the one with a half-finished wall.

He was in a twenty-five-thousand-dollar bubble.

This was silly.

Valuable time was ticking away.

This wasn't working.

Dammit!

No transcendental experience. No hallucinations. No out-of-body clarity to help him reach his conclusion.

Nothing.

What would C.C. think?

He blinked.

C.C.

He saw her.

Smiling. Looking up from a book. On one of the sofas in the library. Her spot. Shapely legs crossed in front of her. Her favorite blanket—a gray-and-blue quilt—tucked under her arm.

She fell from the sofa.

Onto the hardwood floor.

And rolled twice. Stopped. Her face was gone. Blood and tissue. The area where her mouth should be opened up. And the monster version of C.C. screamed.

Jake screamed too.

Jake, not Silence.

He ran toward her, his feet thudding on the floor, never gaining, treading in place as she grew farther and farther away. Smaller. Disappearing down a wooden tunnel that stretched farther and farther before him. She was a red blur. Then a dot on the horizon. Gone.

He reached, couldn't grab her.

Silence's eyes opened.

He gasped.

His legs twitched, which brought movement back to the water, making him bob again. His left shoulder gently brushed the wall.

This thing actually works.

But he needed to refocus, to come back to the assign-ment. He was Silence, not Jake. And he had to stop Burton. Not just for revenge, not just for C.C.

Massive ramifications. Countless lives at risk.

Focus.

Burton. Focus on Burton.

Where had he left off?

Before he could answer himself, his eyes were closed again, and he slipped into another memory. His last moments in Virginia. After all his hard work—*Training complete.*

He was back in that dreary little room as he received the details of his first assignment, just before he returned to Florida and killed Clayton Glover.

CHAPTER FIFTY-NINE

THE ROOM WAS FILTHY.

A kitchenette on the lefthand side revealed its previous identity as a break room—battered cabinetry with drooping doors; a teetering refrigerator, whose doors dangled as much as those of the cabinets; a cobweb-coated stainless-steel sink.

Silence was alone, at the long table in the center of the room. He'd found one of the cleanest chairs, but he'd still had to wipe away dust and chunks of ceiling tile.

The decayed quasi-neighborhood was visible through the grimy window. A man prodded a shopping cart along the far sidewalk, the only sign of life. The sky was a lighter gray than it had been, and a bright spot at its peak showed the sun's location. The temperature had risen a few degrees in recent days.

A late model Cadillac sat near the sidewalk that led to the building, the subdued sunlight glistening off its immaculate black shine. The windows were tinted pitch-black. Vapor puffed from its exhaust tips.

Falcon burst through the door in the back of the room, an

unlit cigarette dangling from his lips. He came to an abrupt stop, scowled, and gave the small room a visual sweep.

"She's late. Dammit, Nakiri." He groaned, and his shoulders dropped an inch. "She's one of my problem children. You seem pretty bullheaded yourself. You gonna give me troubles too?"

Probably, Silence thought.

But he said nothing. He wasn't gonna lie, but more importantly, he didn't want to speak. Overall, his throat was improving, but it had good days and bad days. Today was a bad day.

Falcon strolled around the table, his shoes crunching the rotten linoleum. He stopped for a moment to look through the window at the urban wasteland, then flopped his briefcase on the table, pulled out the chair across from Silence, and wiped it clear of debris.

Silence glanced at Falcon's suit—dark blue, pinstriped. There was no way that perfunctory chair-cleaning was going to keep the dust off that expensive wool.

Falcon saw something in his expression and gave his customary grin, the corner of his mouth lifting both his mustache and the unlit cigarette.

"I know what you're thinking: why the hell do the Watchers keep such a shithole place? As you could see from the medical facility below ground, we're not short on funds. But we have to keep up appearances if we're going to remain hidden in plain sight." He pointed to the window, the rough neighborhood beyond. "It's not always glamorous."

He pointed to the cigarette.

"You mind?"

Silence shook his head, but he minded. Smoke bothered him.

Falcon reached into his pocket and took out a cheap gas station lighter. A couple of flicks, and the end of the cigarette glowed orange. He smiled with genuine contentment as he inhaled.

Suddenly switching gears, he pivoted forward, clicked open his briefcase, and retrieved a holstered pistol. He shoved it across the table in Silence's direction.

Silence stopped it with a palm, popped the gun from its holster, examined.

"Your new buddy," Laswell said and took a drag from his Marlboro. "Beretta 92FS, 9 mm, standard Asset sidearm. Fifteen and one with the standard mag; up to thirty-two and one with high-capacity. Open-slide. Short-recoil. And, naturally, threaded for a suppressor."

Silence was already more than familiar with the popular weapon. Like Cobb's Glock 19 that Silence carried during his killing spree, this was a weapon trusted around the world by police and military forces. If he hadn't already learned all about the weapon during his police training, Nakiri had relentlessly pounded the information into his brain in recent weeks.

It was matte black, ideal for the work he'd be doing. The weight of it was pleasing. So was the shape of it, the feel.

He put it back in the holster.

Falcon blew smoke from the corner of his mouth and checked his watch.

"Dammit, where is she?" He took another drag. Sighed. "You made it through training. Do you feel ready?"

Before Silence could reply, the door behind him flew open, and there was the tap of heels rapidly crossing the ruined floor. Nakiri came to the table, threw down the peacoat she'd had hooked over her arm, then tore off her oversized sunglasses, revealing a shiner on her left eye. Purple and yellow and glistening. She pointed at it as she approached.

"Oh, yes, he's ready."

Falcon turned to Silence and grinned. "I'm glad you're learning to do what's necessary. True indiscrimination."

Nakiri went to the other end of the table. She wore jeans and a long-sleeve, V-neck top. After the now customary cleaning of the seat, she flopped down into the chair. Dust ballooned up, twinkling in the sunlight coming in through the window.

She looked across the table at Silence with a slightly softened version of her standard severity. He'd passed a test, and now he was a contemporary of hers, but she still needed him to know he was a piece of shit.

Falcon looked back-and-forth between them, that little grin of his disappearing. Silence had noticed how this attitude of Falcon's could quickly shift into professionalism. There was a clear delineation between civility and playfulness, no matter how goofy the guy could appear.

"Burton had Clayton Glover finish off every last piece of the Farone family," Falcon said. He paused to look at Silence, his expression changing again, this time to something like hesitance, almost pity. "And then he finished off Joseph Farone himself. I know the old man took a shining to you. Sorry to have to report this, Suppressor."

Silence nodded.

A twinge in Silence's gut, another taste of loss in a period of time when he'd lost so much. But it was slight. And it disappeared as quickly as it had materialized.

He remembered what Burton had told him in the hallway of the Farone mansion, the night he murdered C.C. Burton said two things were going to happen, the second of which would occur down the line and be a chance for him to reconnect with his "Daddy."

Burton had followed through. He'd reconnected with Daddy. Murdered him.

After everything Silence had gone through recently, after

all Burton had taken from him, he was surprisingly blank. He wondered if it would always be like this, if he'd been permanently numbed.

Falcon watched him, eyes squinting slightly as though processing a thought before he said it. "You've been trained. You've healed. Now it's time for your assignment. As badly as you want to get your revenge on Burton, you know he's involved in some bigger shit as well. And you need to know more about him."

Nakiri leaned in Silence's direction and almost put her forearms on the dusty table before thinking better of it. She crossed them over her chest instead.

"That's right. You don't think I hung on that piece of shit's arm for months and didn't get any intel, did you, dummy? Burton wanted us all to think he'd been an orphan from unknown parents, handpicked and groomed by Joey 'the Jaguar' Farone. Most of that's true. All except the parenting part.

"His biological father was Jacques Sollier, an international terrorist, active in the mid '60s through the '70s. No one knows whether he was French, French-Canadian, French-Algerian—the guy was a ghost. Bombings in Poland. Assassinations in East Germany and the Balkans. A real opportunist: no-affiliation, highest-bidder-gets-the-job sort of stuff. Moved around Europe with near impunity." A piece of ceiling tile dropped onto her lap. She scowled and brushed it away. "Sollier's specialty was utilizing shipping ports—transporting weapons and explosives and hostages and himself. Evidently he died doing what he loved—they found him with a few holes in his chest behind a utility shed at the Freeport of Riga. Neither the Latvians nor Interpol ever found who did it. My guess is they didn't try too hard."

Falcon squashed out his cigarette on the sole of a brogue

and flicked the butt into the pile of broken cinderblocks in the corner.

"Sollier fathered a child on one of his trips to the States," he said. "Abandoned the kid and the mother, one Carolyn Burton. Momma got herself murdered a few years later. Kid goes into foster care. And you know the rest.

"Now ... let's talk about the present. Nakiri blew her cover with Burton." He pointed toward her, and though he didn't look at her, she still averted her eyes. "So we've been monitoring him from a distance while we pieced you back together. The guy's a pro. He's meticulous about privacy, security. All we've been able to glean is a numerical code: *CG247*.

"But his lieutenant is a whole lot sloppier. Clayton Glover might be moving up in the world, but he's still a scumbag. Every other Friday, like clockwork, he goes out to a crappy part of Pensacola, where a suited man 'escorts' a lady to his Acura."

There was that mischievous twinkle in Falcon's eyes again. He looked at Silence.

"We're getting you back to Florida. Two weeks from today, we know where you can find Glover. Until then, we'll move you into your new house, and you're to proceed with the assignment. Understood?"

Silence nodded.

Nakiri bounced in her chair. "Oh, yippee! Dummy's about to be sent off on his very first assignment. My heart overflows." She wiped away a fake tear. "That would be the assignment you stole from me, Falcon."

Silence was impressed with how cool Falcon was remaining, how impassive in the face of Nakiri's overt insubordination. He didn't scowl or frown or even issue one of his trademark smartass smiles. He just stared back at her.

"I have one more assignment, then I'm out," Nakiri continued. "But, by all means, take your sweet time arranging it, leave me dangling as long as possible while you coddle the rookie."

She bolted up, the chair legs screeching on the old flooring.

"When you have a new assignment for me, you just let me know."

She whipped around, headed for the door.

"Oh, I have an assignment for you," Falcon said.

Nakiri halted. Turned on her heel. A pause. Then she took a couple of cautious steps back toward the table.

"You do?" A quivering smile came to her lips.

"Well, not so much an assignment as a bit of consultant work," Falcon said. He flicked his eyes in Silence's direction. "You're going with him."

"*What?*"

"He's only had three weeks of training. He needs support and a watchful eye. From his teacher." Without turning around, he pointed to the window behind him, toward the idling vehicle. "The Caddie's waiting to take you both to the airport."

Nakiri stormed around the table, heels snapping tiles, stopping inches from Falcon.

"You..." she said and trailed off. When she continued, her voice was quieter. And it cracked. "You are an *asshole*."

Nakiri's chest heaved. She stared down at Falcon, and her lower lip moved as though she was about to say something else. No words came out. A moment passed. Then she spun around and stormed to the door.

She glared at Silence as she breezed past him.

The door heaved open so hard the doorknob punched through the drywall.

And she was gone.

Falcon turned to Silence with that smile of his, shrugged.

"You kids have fun," he said.

CHAPTER SIXTY

Two weeks later.

Glover was giddy with anticipation as he sat in the leather seat of his Acura. He shifted anxiously. His pants were getting uncomfortable.

He drummed his fingers on the leather-wrapped steering wheel of the brand-new vehicle and wondered who they might be providing tonight. Candy or Tiffany or Tina? Candy was his favorite, and he liked the wordplay that came with her name. She really was a tasty treat.

This was yet another perk of his continued ascendency. A massive perk. The one time he'd done something like this in his previous life, before meeting Burton, the chick had horrible acne, sunken eyes, and a bony figure—a damn crackhead. Glover had been certain she was diseased, but he'd proceeded anyway and spent a few fretful months wondering what if.

This, though ... this was a whole different world, the difference between McDonald's and a five-star steakhouse.

He looked out the window.

Well, it wasn't *all* glamorous, not the environment, anyway. There was an empty parking lot, and beyond was the warehouse, closed for the weekend—a well-kept and clean place, if not blandly utilitarian. By contrast, the surrounding neighborhood was urban waste. Shitty houses. Litter-speckled gutters.

It wasn't the most inviting of environments, and it certainly wasn't sexy, but this was the sort of place you had to go sometimes for this sort of thing. No matter how sophisticated.

There was a rap of a knuckle on the passenger window, and he turned, smiling.

The smile dropped.

A man's torso, on the other side of the window, face hidden by the car's roof.

What the hell?

Every other time, the handler would sit in a car parked down the street and let the girl out. She would then take the sidewalk to the Acura, give a quick tap on the passenger-side window, and get in. A safe and secure transaction, assuring both his safety and that of Candy or Tiffany or Tina.

He hadn't dealt directly with any of the handlers since first setting up this arrangement. This initial transaction had occurred at an upscale cocktail lounge, not in a car parked by a warehouse in this gross part of town.

Glover growled, and he tried to maintain his professional countenance as he pressed the window button and leaned across the center console.

The man wasn't the one he'd met at the cocktail lounge, nor was he Ramone or Gus, the other two guys who sometimes dropped off the girls. This man was quite tall, well over six feet, with chiseled features, olive skin, and dark, choppy hair with bangs falling into his eyes.

"Who the hell are you?" Glover said.

The man raised a pistol and pointed it through the window.

CHAPTER SIXTY-ONE

Nakiri sighed out her frustration.

Why was she here?

She was in a rented Honda Civic, a block away from the action, in a cruddy industrial area of town on an equally cruddy, gray day.

If she had to come back to Florida, it could at least be sunny. Gah! The sun was out, like, ninety percent of the time in Pensacola this time of year.

There weren't even any palm trees in sight. It was just a rundown, decrepit, could-be-anywhere part of the city.

Worst of all, she was here as a babysitter.

Falcon had betrayed her. Humiliated her. Not only was this Pensacola job to have been her final assignment that would have completed her debt, but now she was being forced to watch as someone else—a complete rookie, hardly trained—took over. She just had to *sit here* and watch, making her not an assassin but a glorified nanny. That big son of a bitch down the street was costing her in more ways than she had ever considered.

And now she watched as the lumbering doofus kept his

Beretta pointed through the open passenger window of Clayton Glover's Acura.

Suppressor hadn't said anything; he'd just pulled out his suppressed pistol as soon as Glover had rolled down the window. That much was good. She'd taught him the power of intimidation, and with his destroyed voice and big frame, he was naturally intimidating. She told him to use his devil voice sparingly, at choice moments.

Of course, since speaking was painful for him, he was quick to agree to this tactic.

But now, at his first real-world encounter, he'd been quiet for some time. Just staring at Glover with Glover staring back, confused. Yes, it was a good idea to use the voice sparingly, to create dramatic pauses, to create a sense of fear and confusion.

But this was just awkward...

What the hell was he doing?

Gun still aimed at Glover, Suppressor reached into his pocket.

The notebook.

The nasty, bloodstained, water-warped notebook.

Oh, for shit's sake.

"Don't use that stupid notebook, dummy," she muttered. "Use that growly monster voice of yours."

Still, she was impressed with how quickly Suppressor had taken action. He must have written a note for Glover in the few moments before he approached the Acura. This showed a modicum of resourcefulness.

She'd taught him to adapt to the needs of a situation.

A tiny smile tempted her lips, but she rejected it.

Don't go getting proud of yourself, Nakiri.

CHAPTER SIXTY-TWO

SILENCE LOOKED DOWN, for a split second, to his PenPal notebook, the note he'd prepared for Glover.

In that fraction of a moment, there was movement—a streak from the driver's seat—and Glover scrambled out of the car.

Silence considered blasting him right there, before Glover cleared the doorjamb, but he remembered what he'd been told—that he had to get information out of Glover before eliminating him.

Glover scrambled over the short, brick wall into the empty parking lot of the warehouse beyond. He sprinted, his squat, powerful legs propelling him forward. Silence had always thought Glover a brave man, if nothing more.

Now he was showing true cowardice.

Silence sprinted around the Acura's hood, to the wall, over it, and into the parking lot behind Glover.

Black asphalt, clean and relatively new, with bright white stripes and yellow rubber parking blocks. The hard pavement pounded through the soles of his shoes. He would need to remember to wear thicker soles in the field.

Glover headed for the warehouse, but even though his legs were pumping like pistons in a straining engine, Silence's long gait closed the gap rapidly.

Glover stole a glance over his shoulder. Sweat-sheened forehead. Panic in his eyes. His combed-back, blond hair had lost its style, flopping in his face.

The other man's thudding footsteps were loud and clear in Silence's ears as he drew nearer. A couple of feet away. He reached out. His fingers tickled the edge of Glover's gray dress shirt. He clenched, got a fistful of cloth.

And came to a sudden stop.

Silence's shoes scraped to a halt, and with one solid tug he yanked Glover back.

Forward momentum brought Glover's legs out from under him, still kicking. For a moment, Glover was horizontal, floating a yard above the blacktop.

And then he came crashing onto his back.

A wail wheezed from Glover's mouth.

Then Silence was upon him, on his knees, pounding away at Glover's face.

He hadn't planned on immediately beating Glover, but there had been a quick flash across his mind, something that propelled him into immediate action. His mission and the need to complete his first Watcher's assignment vanished from existence.

Glover's fist smashing into C.C.'s jaw. He'd gotten the most time during the beating, the benefits of being Burton's second-in-command.

Silence hurled his right fist.

Crack!

Glover's mouth snapped shut, and when it reopened, his lips were bubbly red. Silence threw a left. Then a right. Glover's head was a toy ball rolling back and forth on the blacktop.

He could destroy Glover's face. It was already swelling,

contused. He could destroy it like Glover had helped to destroy C.C.'s face, like he'd help to destroy Jake Rowe's face.

But Silence had made a promise.

To the Watchers.

They'd given him a second chance at life.

He stopped.

Glover sputtered. Looked up at Silence. Bloodshot eyes.

"Who..." He coughed. A bloody bubble popped at the corner of his mouth. "Who are you?"

Silence didn't reply.

"You're here about Burton, aren't you?"

Silence nodded. The note he'd prepared had demanded that Glover tell him what Burton was up to, but apparently he wouldn't need the note.

Interesting.

Nakiri was really onto something about the whole intimidation thing. Evidently a man got really intimidated when you beat the shit out of him.

Silence would remember that.

"I'll tell you ... I'll tell you everything. Okay?"

Silence nodded.

"Burton's been printing passports for weeks. And he's getting them to his buyer tonight. I don't know the location. I swear I don't. All I know is the time: eight o'clock. I don't know the specific client either, just that the guy's working with terrorist cells out of the Middle East."

Terrorist cells...

Just hearing the words made Silence pull back, stunned. He knew Burton had large ambitions, but what Glover had just said could mean only one thing: Burton was helping terrorists get into the United States.

The implications were staggering, and—

A flash of movement from the ground.

Glover swept his leg, knocking Silence's feet out from

under him. Silence fell backward, hit the ground hard, on his back.

Silence cursed himself. During training, Nakiri had hounded him mercilessly about his tendency to leave himself open to leg sweeps.

Don't forget your feet, dummy.

Yet here he was, moments into his first field experience, already on his back.

Shuffling sounds in front of him. Then footsteps, at a run.

Silence rolled to the side, looked across the parking lot. Glover was getting away, headed for the warehouse again.

Silence scrambled to his feet, bolted off.

Ahead, Glover threw open a dark red metal door and rushed into the warehouse. Through the now open doorway, Silence could see darkness, no lights on.

As he ran the last few feet, Silence pulled out his Beretta again, cleared the threshold, and entered.

Towering walls of pallet racks—loaded with boxes and crates and plastic-wrapped machinery—seemingly endless as they faded away into the darkness at the back of the building. Steel uprights stretched to a high ceiling. A path cut through the center of the space.

Countless places Glover could be, a million nooks and crannies from which he could jump out.

Silence thought back to Nakiri's lessons on stealth. This was one of the skills he'd taken to most readily, which had come as a surprise to her—and to Silence himself—because of his size.

Though the rows of massive, round lights floating high above him were unlit, some of the ambient, gloomy light from the outside oozed in through the windows—big grids of opaque glass and iron muntins. The light came in as hazy streaks, sparkling with dust particles, illuminating a box of nails here, a pallet full of laminate flooring there.

Silence clung along the edge of the aisle, turned a corner, cleared both sides of the row. Nothing. Just a tower of cardboard boxes and a cluster of steel drums.

He proceeded to the next row.

And heard something.

A tiny scratch.

His hearing seemed to have been enhanced since he'd been forced into quietude—like a heightened sense picking up the slack for a weakened one, like blind Mrs. Enfield's ability to see without seeing.

The noise had come from another row up, around a corner loaded with pallets full of plastic bags of coarse gravel.

He slipped into a shadow, turned the corner.

And there he was.

Glover cowered with his back against a stack of gravel bags. His eyes flicked toward Silence, and Silence perceived movement in his hands, the earliest stages of an attack.

Silence literally beat him to the punch.

More of Nakiri's training sizzled through his brain, a newly subconscious impulse.

His fingers tightened, and his fist swung faster than his brain recognized, cracking across Glover's cheek.

The noise it made was revolting.

Bizarre.

Wet and hollow, punctuated by a small, almost delicate *crack* that Silence felt through his knuckles. He'd chipped the corner of Glover's cheekbone.

Glover stumbled back, eyes pinched shut, swung blindly. Silence easily dodged the blow.

He clasped his hand around Glover's forearm and twisted hard while at the same time getting his leg behind Glover's knees. Glover's feet flew up, and with a shove, Silence sent him flying down the aisle.

Glover struck the polished concrete hard and slid several

feet back, bashed into an old, discarded pallet that exploded with the impact. Pieces of wood clattered on the ground.

Silence lunged toward him, closing the distance.

A flash of movement. A streak of wood.

And Silence felt something in his palm.

A reaction so fast Silence didn't perceive it. Glover had swung a broken piece of the pallet, and Silence had somehow caught it.

Another instinctive, instantaneous, unfelt action, and the board was torn from Glover's hand. Silence threw it into the darkness. A moment later came the echoing racket of it landing somewhere in the distance.

Silence aimed his Beretta at Glover's chest.

Glover's boots scratched at the floor as he pushed himself farther back into the destroyed remains of the pallet. His shaking arms shielded his face.

"No! Shit! Please! I ... I told you everything!"

Had he? Had Glover *really* told him everything he knew?

Silence wasn't so sure.

"Talk."

Glover's mouth fell open, and he gasped. His eyes bulged as a look of disbelief fell over him, as though Silence's peculiar growling voice was inconceivable.

And while the voice had clearly intimidated Glover, Silence's command to *Talk* had simply made the man cower more. Maybe Silence needed to add a little extra incentive to his one-syllable command.

He aimed the Beretta lower, at Glover's knee: crystal-clear non-verbal communication.

Glover kicked hard at the floor, pressing himself further into the broken boards. "I swear to God! *I told you everything!*"

Okay. Silence believed him. There was sincerity in his fear. Silence had siphoned every bit of useful information from Glover.

Time to switch gears. His work for the Watchers was done.

Now, a little me time.

It was time to kill another one of C.C.'s murderers.

Glover had kicked C.C. while she was on the floor. He'd turned it into a dance. Hands on his hips. Legs flailing. Laughing.

Glover's lips quivered, and his eyes went wider, filled with tears. He knew what was about to happen. His hands were still held protectively over his face, and he extended them toward Silence, pleadingly.

"Whoa, man!" Glover said. "I gave you what you want. I swear that's all I know! Let me go."

Silence took deep breaths. Through his stomach, not his chest. Diaphragmatic breathing. Proper breathing. C.C. had taught him this.

A flash of sweat chilled his forehead. His skin prickled. The hair on his forearms stood up.

He raised the Beretta, slowly, moving away from Glover's knee, tracing up his body.

Then a strange look came to Glover's face.

Recognition.

Glover's eyes moved over Silence's body, leaving his face, skittering back and forth, like a typewriter, moving down, assessing all the details before snapping back up to his face, locking in on him again.

"It's you, isn't it?" Glover said in a tiny voice that wavered with his rapidly accumulating tears.

Somehow Glover had figured out that this tall figure before him was the man he'd known as Pete Hudson. Glover had seen through the plastic surgery, through the difference in eye color.

Silence didn't reply. He continued to slowly raise the Beretta until it was aimed at Glover's head.

He stopped.

"*Why are you doing this?*" Glover screamed.

Silence stared at him.

And he lowered the gun, glanced at the floor as he remembered it again.

Glover had laughed. He'd laughed as he kicked C.C. to death.

Silence's eyes went to Glover's, which peered out at him from the gaps between the fingers of his shaking, outstretched hands.

"For Cecilia," Silence said.

He raised the Beretta, lined it with Glover's forehead, and fired twice. A double tap. Just like Nakiri had taught him.

Glover's body didn't spasm. There was nothing particularly dramatic about his death, nothing on par with its significance. Just a bright red double-hole in the plane of flesh at the top of his head along with a splatter of blood and brain on the floor and the broken boards behind him.

Silence observed the stillness.

He holstered the Beretta and knelt beside the body, then took his notebook from his pocket and crossed Glover off the list.

~~Cobb~~
~~Gamble~~
~~Hodges~~
~~Knox~~
~~McBride~~
~~Odom~~
~~Glover~~
Burton

Seven down; one to go.

Silence savored the thought for only a moment. Then he refocused on the larger task.

He glanced at his watch. It was almost five. Three hours

to figure out what Burton was doing with terrorists and where Silence would need to go to stop him.

And he hadn't the slightest clue where to begin. There was a connection, somewhere in all the information he'd gathered from this assignment. He just couldn't see it. Not at all.

C.C. always told him to schedule his time, another way for him to organize his tumultuous brain. He would need to plan his three hours carefully.

He would call Falcon and report the intel he'd gathered from Glover. Then he would grab some beer, something to help calm his mind—one drink, nothing that would inebriate him. Then he'd go home, drink the beer, and get in his brand-new sensory deprivation pod for the first time. If the rumors were to be believed, this would be the key to opening his mind.

But first, one more task in the warehouse before he left Glover behind.

He flipped to a clean page in the notebook and started writing.

CHAPTER SIXTY-THREE

Two hours later.

Tanner grunted as he stared down at the body—hunched in on itself, two bullet holes in its forehead, a half inch apart, the tight grouping of an execution-style murder.

The body was Clayton Glover.

And his death was a piece of macabre modern art, an exercise in juxtaposition. Ten square feet of the squeaky-clean warehouse's efficient design and purposeful organization disrupted by jagged boards in a blast pattern surrounding a corpse, all of it haloed by a massive pool of blood.

There would be an investigation. Of course. But Tanner knew who'd killed Glover.

Jake.

Damn you, Jake.

The first responding officer had said that the warehouse was dark when he arrived, but since then, the business owners had been contacted, and now the massive lights in the ceiling were ablaze, flooding the space with blue, sterile light that illuminated the lofty pallet racks and glistened on the highly polished floor.

Tanner liked that the place was so isolated. No gawkers. No press. No weeping family members. Just the crime scene unit diligently milling about in their blue windbreakers, swapping college words in hushed voices as they scribbled notes, took photos, and nodded at each other.

And Tanner and Pace—standing to the side, hands in their pockets, suit jackets tucked back, staring at the body.

One of the windbreaker-wearing technicians was crouched in front of the body, taking a measurement. Glover's unblinking eyes stared into the steel rafters far above. His head was tilted slightly to the left, and a motionless stream of dried, black blood snaked out of the extra holes in his forehead, feeding the puddle on the polished floor.

"We got something here," the tech said. He wore latex rubber gloves, and pinched between his thumb and forefinger was a small piece of lined notebook paper, folded in thirds. The tech gently unfolded it, then frowned at it for a moment before looking up at Tanner, perplexed.

Tanner scowled at him. "What?"

"It's addressed to you," the man said.

Tanner felt Pace's eyes upon him, and he turned to look at the annoying fed. For once, Pace wasn't being annoying, though. His face was pinched with concentration.

The technician put the unfolded paper in a clear polyethylene evidence bag, which he sealed and handed to Tanner without standing.

Two words were scrawled on the side facing Tanner. He could see, through the paper, a longer note on the other side.

Lieutenant Tanner

Tanner recognized the print immediately.

He looked at Pace. "This is Jake Rowe's handwriting."

He flipped the bag over.

Sir,

I'm going to kill Lukas Burton. 8 p.m. He's working with someone connected to international terrorist cells and will be attempting to meet the man tonight. It would be wise of you to contact the FBI.

This will be the last you hear from me. You've always been good to me. And I appreciate it.

—Jake

Shit.

Tanner sighed.

Jake, dammit. What are you doing?

He reluctantly put his finger under the letters *FBI*, and pointed it out to Pace.

The smartass grin returned to Pace's lips. It hadn't left for long.

"It's been three months, and Jake's still on his killing spree," Tanner said, tilting his head toward Glover. He gave the note a little shake. "Even confessed it. This isn't heat-of-the-moment passion. No temporary insanity here. He's a coldblooded killer now."

Pace took the evidence bag from him, glanced over the note, looked up, said nothing.

"And I'm not letting him get away with another murder," Tanner said. "We're stopping this son of a bitch. Tonight."

CHAPTER SIXTY-FOUR

LASWELL HAD NEVER BEEN to Pensacola, Florida. As he stepped out of the Learjet, down the airstairs, a blast of thick, moist air struck him.

Holy hell, Suppressor was right. He'd told Laswell—via a series of abbreviated, gravelly sentences—to be prepared for the brutal humidity of the Florida Panhandle. Laswell hadn't felt stickiness like this since the last time he was in New Orleans, which made sense, given New Orleans was only a few hours due west. As Laswell understood it, the two old cities also shared architectural similarities—features such as downtown balconies with filigree ornamentation.

A jetliner roared overhead as he stepped onto the concrete, and a warm gust of wind buffeted the chain-link fence a few feet away. Pensacola International wasn't a large airport, so while they'd taxied to a private hanger, the main terminal was just ahead, brightly lit, lush with a variety of palm trees. *Welcome to Florida*, the trees seemed to say as their fronds tossed in the strong breeze.

Laswell had noted that Florida points of entry were both welcoming and proud of the state's reputation. The Interstate highway welcome centers offered incoming travelers free orange and grapefruit juice. He'd always found that detail quite charming.

The sun was far in the western sky, and the horizon was starting to fade from gray to pink. The flight attendant waited for him at the bottom of the stairs, smiling broadly, blonde hair tossing, one outstretched arm gesturing grandly toward an idling limousine.

Nice.

SkyTrail Aviation was a real class act. Such a pity he'd never see them again.

Laswell nodded at the flight attendant, stepped past her to the limo, then nodded at the suited limo driver—a twenty-something guy, also wearing a massive smile—who held the rear door open for him and introduced himself as Ricky.

Laswell squeezed through the doorway, into cold air conditioning, and plopped into another comfortable leather seat.

A moment later, the limo eased to a smooth, crawling start, and Ricky's voice came through the intercom.

"You're heading to Bayfront Auditorium, correct, sir?"

"Correct."

Back in Virginia, Laswell had probed Suppressor for locations in Pensacola where he could go should he need to make a trip down south. Pensacola Bayfront Auditorium, he'd been told, was a massive building that sat at the very end of a pier downtown, right in Pensacola Bay, surrounded by water on three sides. It was a very public spot, and located right in the thick of things. A perfect Watchers location. *Hidden in plain sight.*

"Very good, sir," Ricky said. "But please understand that since that's downtown, it's going to take us quite a while. A lot of traffic. We got the Tristán Festival tonight."

"I'm in no hurry."

But, really, there was a time concern. A big one. Massive. He checked his watch. It read 7:47, which made it 6:47 there in the Central time zone.

A little over an hour until Burton's deadline.

He took his cellular phone from his pocket, flipped it open, and dialed Suppressor. One ring, then a message.

Your call has been forwarded to an automatic voice message system. To leave a message—

He flipped the phone shut.

The bastard had turned his phone off.

Off!

An hour before all hell broke loose.

Laswell's fingers curled into fists. And he thought of Briggs, the older man's insistence that Laswell was making a huge mistake with Silence Jones.

He pushed the thought from his mind and dialed Nakiri.

"Yes?"

"Where is he?"

"Don't know. Tried him twenty minutes ago, and the call went straight to voicemail."

"Same here. *Shit!*" Laswell sucked in a breath, forced it back out through flared nostrils. He thought for a moment, and decided that the best thing to do was stick with the plan. Rationality always trumped emotion.

"You're an observer tonight, Nakiri," he said. "Assets don't work in pairs. If Suppressor can't finish the job, you finish it for him. But if he gets himself in trouble, that's his own damn fault. Understood?"

"Yes, sir."

"Good. Be prepared."

He hung up and looked out the window. The limo was moving at a steady click down a four-lane thoroughfare lined with businesses and lush with trees. The traffic issues Ricky had mentioned were not yet apparent, but from the maps

Laswell had studied, he knew they were still a few miles outside downtown.

In the distance, the pink streaks in the sky grew brighter. What had evidently been a gray, miserable day was going to have a magnificent sunset.

And possibly a calamitous ending.

If Laswell's brand-new Asset putzed out.

What the hell was Silence Jones up to?

CHAPTER SIXTY-FIVE

Silence floated in nothingness.

The skin-receptor-neutral temperature; the entirely dark environment; the buoyant water; the potent earplugs—all of it had come together to do its job.

He'd truly been deprived of his senses.

And sucked out of reality.

Images had come and gone, his mind flipping through the slideshow of the last year of his life. Trying to stay on track, to focus on the task at hand. But he kept seeing slides of C.C.

And often the same slide.

The one that showed her lying dead in a pool of her blood.

He forced the image away. There was an objective he was to conquer. Stopping Burton.

So he had to stay focused.

The solution to the issue was in his mind. Somewhere. A detail in the fog. A whisper of a memory. It had to be there.

His mind went to New Orleans. How he, as Jake Rowe, had foiled Burton's plot there, the beginning of Burton's deeper hatred for him—the hatred, Jake feared, that had led to C.C.'s murder.

But did it have anything to do with the task at hand, with stopping Burton's plans with the terrorists?

He didn't think so.

No. No, it didn't.

Stay focused.

What would C.C. say he should do?

She would tell him to focus.

Focus, love.

Burton. The smile, always there, smeared on his face, framed by locks of his dark hair. Nothing about him was real. Always hiding something. The twitching energy in the eyes.

Silence was back in the chair. Tied down. Burton's living room, facing the projector screen. His view alternated between two Burtons at once—the flesh-and-blood one at his side and the video image on the screen, both of them grinning, four dark eyes twinkling. C.C.'s screams. The group of men closing in on her. Odom twirling his blackjack.

Focus.

Charlie had warned him. Charlie Marsh, the overgrown kid brother, waves of hair flopping down into his eyes. He'd told Silence—had told *Jake*—that he shouldn't have crossed Burton in New Orleans, that Burton's plan was huge.

Charlie looked up at Jake, standing by his side in the warm opulence of the Farone mansion.

Charlie wasn't a smart man, but he was intuitive. And he was right. More right than he'd known.

Before the bullet had crashed through his skull. In that dark alleyway.

Jake had been in the passenger seat. The musty smell of Charlie's Taurus. Ambushed. Set up. Burton had led them to a trap. He'd taken Charlie from Jake. Insignificant compared to taking C.C., but a loss still. Burton had taken so much from him, and—

Focus, love.

Focus. Yes. Refocus. Breathe. He took in a deep breath, through his stomach, a diaphragmatic breath, exhaled.

His body bobbed in the water, his toe brushed the back wall, and he left the trance. He was back in the pod.

For only a moment.

Then he was with Charlie again. In the mansion.

I'm telling ya, Pete, it's coming soon, Charlie had said. *Burton's gonna take over the operation. What are we gonna do?*

Burton had done more than take over the Farone crime syndicate. He'd done more than destroy half the family.

He'd moved the operation down avenues it would have never ventured on its own—first by funding anarchists and then by conspiring with international terrorists.

Charlie vanished. C.C. took his place. A different area of the mansion. The library. A look of dread in C.C.'s eyes, telling him she had a premonition about the Roja hit, making him promise her that he wouldn't go.

He promised her.

Then he'd broken the promise.

In the Grand Prix. Later that night. The tape player in his hand. Shaking. Listening to the message.

C.C.'s voice playing from the scratchy speaker—crying, betrayed. He'd broken a promise to her. Angry at him, only the second time ever. Screaming her last word at him: *Asshole!*

The last thing she'd ever say to him. Anger. A swear word. He fell to the steering wheel and wept. For the longest time, he'd—

Focus, love. Focus.

Exiting the library, right after he'd given C.C. the promise that he would soon break. Walking down the sconce-lined hallway, about to leave the mansion, his shoes sinking into plush carpeting. A silhouette appeared at the end of the hallway, close to the foyer, where Jake was headed. It was Burton.

Grinning.

That goddamn grin.

Silence who had been Jake who had been Pete stopped a couple of feet in front of Burton, a smaller bubble of personal space than one would normally give, letting Burton know he wasn't intimidated.

Then Burton spoke in riddles.

Two things are going to happen. One is going to happen tonight, Burton had said. *The other is going to happen down the line. Soon enough, though. A chance for me to reconnect with my roots, with Daddy. A real homecoming. Know what I mean?*

The first thing that Burton was referring to was C.C.'s murder. Clearly.

The second...

Tonight? The terrorist plot?

Was this the connection Silence was seeking?

Is this it, C.C.? Is this the connection? Babe, is this it?

Focus, love.

There was something about what Burton had said then, in the hallway. His malicious smile had been even darker than usual.

He hadn't just been taunting Silence about his plan to murder C.C. There was the second thing too, the thing that was going to happen "soon enough."

Burton had said "Daddy."

A chance for me to reconnect with my roots, with Daddy.

Of course. Joey Farone. Burton had killed Joey Farone, someone who had taken Pete Hudson in, who had blessed his relationship with his daughter.

And it had happened well after C.C.'s murder, after Burton had wiped out all vestiges of the Farone family. It had happened "down the line."

Silence exhaled. Moved. Heard the lap of a small wave against the pod's wall. The 93.5-degree water felt colder.

Shit. There was no connection. He'd lost the thread. And, with it, hope.

Keep going, love, C.C. said. *You're almost there. Stay focused.*

He allowed the water, the pitch-black nothingness to consume him again.

Back to the hallway. Staring into Burton's sneering smile. The memory had gone back in time a few seconds, like someone had pulsed the REWIND button.

A chance for me to reconnect with my roots, Burton said again. *With Daddy. A real homecoming. Know what I mean?*

And Silence was gone. Out of Florida. Out of the heat and humidity. Into a cold, decrepit room. Broken linoleum floor. Dangling ceiling tiles. Gray skies and a ruined urban landscape visible through the windows. He was back in Virginia. Two weeks earlier. With Falcon and Nakiri. Receiving his final briefing before Laswell shipped him back to Pensacola.

They'd given him more information about Burton, intel they'd acquired from Nakiri's undercover work posing as the man's girlfriend.

His biological father was Jacques Sollier, Nakiri had said. *An international terrorist, active in the mid '60s through the '70s.*

Burton's "Daddy."

Not his figurative father, Joey Farone, as Silence had been thinking. The man's *real* daddy.

Sollier's specialty was utilizing shipping ports, Nakiri had said. *Transporting weapons and explosives and hostages and himself.*

As a major Gulf Coast city, Pensacola had a port.

And Pensacola was also hosting a very popular, very busy festival that night. The Tristán Festival. Almost all of the city's attention and resources would be focused on the event.

Including the police presence.

Whatever Burton had scheduled with his contact, it was

set for 8 p.m., which was only a half hour after the official start time of the festival.

When everyone's attention would be far away from the port.

Burton was reconnecting with his roots, with his "daddy," Jacques Sollier, by dealing with international ne'er-do-wells at a seaport.

Which meant Silence needed to get his ass to the Port of Pensacola.

He'd found the connection.

Good, love. Good.

Silence's eyes snapped open.

Darkness surrounded him. Pitch black. There was the gentle sound of water.

No hesitation. He pushed the button beside him, and the bright blue light faded up as he threw open the lid.

He stood in the pod, dripping wet and buck naked. The tiny, bare bedroom with a half-finished wall glowed blue. His flesh goose-bumped in the cranked-high air conditioning.

He took the towel from the chair, quickly dried off, and put on the outfit he'd stored for the occasion—black boots, a pair of black Levi's, a white T, and a black canvas jacket that he'd gotten at a high-end men's store downtown. The jacket was sturdily constructed, but just as importantly, it provided a tactical advantage—unzipped, it made the outfit city chic; zipped, the change provided its real purpose, a sturdy top layer to an all-black tactical outfit.

Through the house, the floorboards squeaking. The weight of the Beretta felt good against his ribs in its shoulder holster. The suppressor was in his pocket.

He threw the front door open. Locked it.

The thick air struck him. It wasn't warm. In fact, the temperature had dropped. But it was more humid than it had been earlier in the day. Florida air did that sometimes—got thicker as it grew colder.

The sounds from downtown were louder now. Things were picking up even before the fun officially began. Shouts, music, laughter, car horns.

Mrs. Enfield was on her porch swing again. "Silence?"

"Will be back," he replied as he headed away from the house. He said it too loudly. A slice of pain in his throat made him groan.

Across his deep porch, down the steps, onto the sidewalk.

The Mercury Sable that had been his ride for two weeks since returning to Pensacola—compliments of the Watchers —was parked in the drive between his house and Mrs. Enfield's. He rushed toward it, checked his watch.

7:06.

It would take him about five minutes to get to the docks. He had time. Plenty of time. But Nakiri had taught him that there was never enough time, so he would need to—

"*Hey!*"

A figure stalked toward him, from the street. Arms at mid-chest level, holding a sawed-off shotgun.

Doughty.

Silence's immediate reaction wasn't panic or shock or even dread.

It was frustration.

He'd *just* figured out the connection, how to stop a terrorist plot against the nation; how to complete his first Watchers assignment, securing a future for himself in this new identity he'd obtained; how to get his revenge against the man who murdered his fiancée and destroyed his life.

And now he was being confronted by a damn street thug.

But quickly those thoughts were replaced by a more rational, primal sense of urgency. He was in danger. Doughty had caught Silence completely off-guard. No time to go for the Beretta. If he did, this guy would cut him down.

He put his hands up.

"You made me look like a fool, old man!"

Doughty continued toward him, steps long and purposeful, crunching in the gravel. His lower lip trembled. His eyebrows were a V.

A small voice came from the side. "Silence? What's going on?"

Mrs. Enfield, a few feet away, her wrinkled hands clasping her porch's railing, white eyes blinking rapidly.

Shit.

"Step back, ma'am," Silence said.

A slice in his throat. He swallowed.

Doughty glanced over, sneering. "Well, hey there, Granny. I'll get to you when I'm done with your boyfriend here."

He looked back to Silence, kept pressing forward.

"You done messed up bad, old man. I killed a dude two years ago. Got away with it, too. And I'm not afraid to take another."

The determination in Doughty's eyes was as genuine as the shotgun in his hands. Silence had destroyed the punk's pride earlier, and for a man like this, a man of pure ego, that was tantamount to kicking him in the nuts.

This was a dangerous situation.

But Silence had learned how to stay cool under unexpected pressure. One day during training, Nakiri had shown up two hours early, unannounced—she'd barged into his room and fired three rounds from her pistol into the small stretch of linoleum flooring between his bed and the medical equipment. The sound had been deafening, and the glint in her eye made him certain she'd lost her mind and was going to kill him. He'd jumped back so quickly, the IV ripped from his arm.

Be prepared for anything, she'd said with a maniacal grin as she holstered her Beretta. *Never flinch. Don't be rattled.*

Months before that, C.C. had given him similar, albeit gentler, advice. A torrent of duties in his undercover assignment had overwhelmed him, many of the duties dangerous and testing his moral limits. She'd given him a quote: *If you remain calm in the midst of great chaos, it is the surest guarantee it will eventually subside.*

He'd asked if that quote was from the Dalai Lama. Or Deepak Chopra, perhaps. Nope. An actress. Julie Andrews. Insight comes from a wide variety of sources, she'd told him.

With the wisdom he'd gained from rage-filled Nakiri and peaceful C.C.—by way of Julie Andrews—a gun-toting punk who just crawled out of an El Camino was a threat but nothing to get rattled about.

He kept his gaze locked on Doughty, who was within feet.

He studied the eyes. Doughty meant business. Silence was good at reading people, but he'd slightly underestimated this guy earlier—Doughty may have been undertrained, but he wasn't lacking in carry-through.

"I'm not afraid to blast you right here, right now," he said, and Silence believed him. He stopped walking, within a couple of feet, close enough that Silence could see the saw-blade markings on the tip of the shotgun's barrel. "And you think that—"

A flash of Silence's hand.

Mrs. Enfield screamed.

Again, Silence had moved without knowing. The cold steel of the shortened barrel was in his hand, and without pause, his fist flew toward Doughty, cracking him across the jaw with a wet crunch.

Doughty crumbled, torso twisted, face in the gravel.

Silence tossed the shotgun into the bushes beside his

house, crouched, reached for the worn pattern in the back pocket of Doughty's jeans—the bulge of a wallet.

The wallet was even more worn-out than the jeans, its leather slick and corners rounded. It was jammed with candy bar wrappers, credit cards, receipts, but only a few greenbacks.

He removed the driver's license.

MANUEL DOUGHTY
455 PREVUE AVENUE
APT 302
MOBILE, ALABAMA

Still crouched, Silence leaned into Doughty's groaning face, put the license an inch in front of his eyes.

"Keeping this." He swallowed. "Know where you live." He swallowed. "Don't come back here."

Doughty's eyes snapped open. He bolted up. A fist caught Silence on the jaw.

Mrs. Enfield screamed again.

Silence shuffled in the gravel and fell to his back.

Doughty jumped on him, and, as before, Silence flushed with frustration, but not fear. The man's weight felt like nothing as Silence caught him by the shoulders and slammed him back to the ground.

Doughty's arm went up, a pathetic attempt at a strike. Silence twisted the arm behind his back.

Doughty yelped.

Keeping Doughty's wrists in his hand, Silence slid over, stones grinding his knees through his jeans. He straddled the other man and pressed his face into the gravel as he pulled the arm farther and farther back. Popping noises. Tendons, cartilage beginning to tear.

He heard Mrs. Enfield. Muffled, distant.

Silence envisioned what could have happened had he not been there. The old, blind woman in fear. Or hurt. Or dead. In a huge puddle of her blood.

C.C. in a pile of her blood. Dead. Because of men like this, like this piece of human filth that Silence was pressing into the earth, this piece of shit.

He could rid the world of this waste, rub it out of this reality. For Mrs. Enfield. For C.C.

One more thrust of Doughty's face into the gravel, then he repositioned, grabbing a handful of greasy hair. He lifted Doughty's face two inches off the ground, and smashed it down.

THUD!

A line of bloody snot shot out of Doughty's nose. His eyes were closed.

Silence's fingers were taut and hard, buzzing with the endurance strength Nakiri had beaten into him.

He raised the head again.

THUD!

More blood, a glob of it that came out in a cough.

He'd heard bone crack that time.

Doughty whimpered.

Silence tightened his machine grip in the filthy hair, brought the head up again.

Felt something on his back.

Something tiny and soft.

A small voice. "Silence..."

He looked up. His teeth were bared, grinding. A bead of sweat raced down the sharp angle of his cheekbone.

Mrs. Enfield. Standing right beside him. Blind eyes looking down at him with her hand on his shoulder. Slowly shaking her head.

"Silence. Stop, baby. Stop. Leave him be."

Silence stared at her.

Her head continued to shake. *No.* Returning his gaze somehow.

He turned his head an inch to look at her hand, minuscule on his broad shoulder.

Then to Doughty. The man's eyes were closed. Squirming. Coughing. Lips wet with blood.

Silence wanted to eliminate him, this man who would harm a woman like Mrs. Enfield. A little, old woman. A little, old hand on his shoulder.

But did Silence really want to kill?

Mrs. Enfield's head still moved side to side. And just like the lessons that had surfaced a few moments earlier—those from Nakiri and C.C.—he'd just received a new lesson from Mrs. Enfield: *the importance of mercy.*

He leaned into Doughty's face. The man's eyes opened. Wide. Stared at him. Shaking.

Silence spoke through his teeth. "Get. *Out!*"

Then several things happened at once.

Doughty scrambled in the gravel, got to his feet, crossed the street to his El Camino, and was gone. At the same time, Silence felt soft pressure on his back, a gentle lifting force that did nothing to actually lift him but still guided him. He was on his feet, walking, though he didn't feel himself moving. All he felt was a bony, dry hand in his, squeezing gently, leading him onto a creaking porch, sitting him down on a swing, bringing his head to her shoulder.

His thoughts became a tempest. Nothing connected. He felt himself tumbling into chaos, threads of reason slipping through his fingers, losing control.

What would C.C. tell him to do? Would she tell him to meditate? To take deep, diaphragmatic breaths?

Mrs. Enfield ran her hand along his cheek and leaned her face against the top of his head.

Silence felt himself shake.

His arms trembled first. Then his stomach. Then his chest.

Heaving, lurching movements. His eyes pinched shut, but no tears came out. His mouth widened, lips motioning, no vocalizations, the only sounds were shudders.

It felt just like that night in the Grand Prix, after listening to the final message from C.C., weeping on his steering wheel.

The same, but different. Crying without crying.

Mrs. Enfield continued to stroke his cheek. Her other arm was behind his back, rocking with his convulsions, hand squeezing his shoulder.

"*Shhh,*" she said. "It's okay. *Shhh.*"

She hummed. He didn't recognize the song. It sounded old-fashioned. And sweet.

A killer. An assassin. That's what he was to be. Someone who lived in violence. His future was to be one of revenge. Not just revenge for C.C.'s murder. Revenge for all sorts of wrongs, for justice eluded.

He would be a shadow. He would bring pain and death.

That was no existence. That wasn't an identity.

One of C.C.'s quotes flashed through his mind, one attributed to Confucius, though possibly misattributed.

Before you embark on a journey of revenge, dig two graves.

Revenge flew in the face of C.C.'s peaceful teachings, her aggregate of wisdom from around the world and through the ages. Humanity had concluded that revenge was a poison.

But then his thoughts went away from C.C. To Nakiri. And Falcon. The Watchers. Its mission. Violence, it would seem, was sometimes the only answer to injustice.

Another of C.C.'s quotes, this one from German poet Heinrich Heine.

We should forgive our enemies, but not before they're hanged.

She'd given him this quote shortly after telling him how

destructive revenge could be. She'd smirked as she'd said it. An opposing viewpoint. Contradictions. She always saw things from all sides.

Violence was needed to stop Burton, this man who was on the verge of a terrorist plot against the nation.

Violence was needed to stop others just like Burton, so many others.

Then, as his shaking subsided and his moment of uncertainty drifted away, listing out of Mrs. Enfield's porch and into the pink sky, he realized that he still wanted revenge.

C.C. was right—revenge was a bane. But he still wanted it.

Needed it.

Just as he needed to be a protector, a person who corrected gross injustices.

An Asset.

A Watcher.

Mrs. Enfield's hand slowed, and the song she'd been humming faded away.

He straightened up and faced her, found her milky eyes waiting for him.

"Better?" she said.

He grunted a *Yes*.

"I told you, Silence, I don't need to know exactly what it is you do. Because I know you're a good man. Whatever's happening tonight, I know it's important. You got the energy pouring off you in waves. You do what you need to do. And come back safe to me."

He took her hand, squeezed it, then stood up.

"Yes, ma'am."

He stepped off the porch and headed for his car.

It was time to see Burton.

CHAPTER SIXTY-SIX

SILENCE WOULD HAVE PREFERRED complete darkness when he and Nakiri arrived at the Port of Pensacola.

As it was, the sky was streaked with blazing purples and brilliant pinks, dark but still giving off plenty of light, which had a surreal golden quality. But it would die off soon, at the 7:24 sunset. That was why the festival's start time was 7:30—to coincide with Nature's light show. Six roaring jets would tear through the sky to help ring in the festival, giving Mother Nature a helping hand with the theatrics. The Blue Angels flyover.

Silence tugged the zipper of his black canvas jacket, cinching it tight, hiding all hints of the white shirt beneath. Next to him, Nakiri was also decked out in black tactical gear. Hers was formfitting and sleek. Like Silence's clothes, hers could easily be adapted to night-out-wear if she tossed on a belt or a scarf.

They approached the fence—ten feet tall and topped with barbed wire. Beyond were warehouses and a pair of big ships and lots of large, metal machinery covered with chipped paint and illuminated by bright lights. Though he couldn't see it,

Silence knew that in the distance—the southwest corner— was the area that stored the intermodal shipping containers. His objective.

A green metal sign with white text stared at Silence from its position, secured on the chainlink fence.

NO TRESSPASSING
The Port of Pensacola is a Border Entry Point. All Persons, Effects, Vehicles, and Vessels are Subject to Search in Accordance with State and Federal Statutes.

Nakiri held up a black, scratchy looking blanket.

"Did you bring one?" she said.

Silence shook his head.

She tugged at the top of the blanket, which was actually two blankets, and threw one hard at his chest.

"Figured you wouldn't," she said. "Be prepared, dummy."

They shook out the blankets and tossed them over the barbed wire, climbed, and threw themselves over the fence. Silence landed with a thud, his impact absorbed by the thick rubber soles of his boots and the tuck-and-roll technique he'd learned both at the police academy and through Nakiri's instruction.

Silence pointed across the facility. "Cargo containers." He swallowed. "Southwest corner."

Nakiri nodded and pointed in the opposite direction, to a large warehouse.

"I'll be watching."

Silence headed toward a patch of shadows behind a fenced cluster of machinery, big, round, metal things. The shadows fell to—

Nakiri's voice. "Wait."

He stopped, turned around.

"Good luck, Suppressor," she said.

He nodded, and for a moment they looked at each other. The warm breeze was strong, and it blew the long bangs off her forehead, completely revealing her gray eyes.

She blinked, and for a moment it looked like she was going to say something else. Instead, her chin dipped, and she turned, darted toward the warehouse.

Silence watched as she slipped behind a metal shed, then he took off. He traced the edge of the fence and looked into the sprawling facility, scouting his options. A pool of orange-ish light to his left. A pool of fluorescent light with a blue hue to his right. Neither of them were great options, but the patch of fluorescent lighting was smaller, so he headed in that direction, staying as close to the water's edge as he could, as the cargo containers he was headed toward were right off the water.

Strange machinery and devices everywhere—large mechanical things he didn't understand. Though he'd lived near the sea his entire life, he'd spent his time splashing in the waves, not floating on the surface. He had very little nautical knowledge. It was a deficiency he would need to address for his new career.

As he rounded a building, his destination was before him: the back corner of the port, which was filled with shipping containers. Massive rectangles of corrugated metal—browns and greens and blacks—all of them about nine feet tall, most with patches of corrosion. The grid pattern in which they were arranged created a little, rusty city—complete with streets and big, flat walls—and the system was so efficient that it only took him moments to locate container *CG247*. Its metal surface had originally been painted red, but there was as much rust as paint now. It sat two containers away from the water's edge.

Here was where Silence would wait.

Here was where it would happen. His revenge.

No.

Not just revenge. So much more than that.

Here was where he would stop Burton's plan, his dealings with international terrorists.

C.C. would tell him to not let his ego rule him, to think about the greater good before himself. Mrs. Enfield would tell him to be sharp and stay safe. And Nakiri would tell him to get his shit together.

Focus, he told himself.

He unholstered his Beretta, then took the suppressor from his pocket and screwed it into the barrel.

CHAPTER SIXTY-SEVEN

THERE WERE DRUNKS EVERYWHERE.

"Oh, God," Tanner grumbled.

He had both hands on the steering wheel of his Lincoln. It was his personal car—Martha's car, really—but he kept a removable dash-mounted blue light in the back seat at all times. Just in case.

The Lincoln slowly crept down Jefferson Street, a road that ran parallel to Palafox Place, which was the main drag through downtown. Palafox was closed to vehicles for the night.

And with good cause.

The second evening of the festival was still a few minutes from its official beginning, but the ruckus had clearly been going on for quite a while. Hours, it would appear. Even Jefferson Street was creeping with traffic, slowed by laughing beverage-clutching goof-offs.

He passed over another cross road and leaned forward, looking past Pace in the passenger seat toward Palafox. A solid mass of bobbing heads, many of them stumbling. Lots of shouting and slovenly laughter. People hanging off the second-story, New Orleans-esque balconies. Beads and noise-makers and neon glow necklaces and plastic yard glasses.

Bunch of drunks. It seemed like the drinking started earlier every year. They could at least hold off on the booze for a few hours for the children's sake. Fortunately, Tanner didn't see too many youngsters in the crowd.

An oversized, ten-foot beach ball bounced past, skipping along the blanket of people to the sound of delighted squeals.

Tanner grumbled again.

Idiots.

All Tanner needed was a beer on Friday nights. And coffee throughout the week. It kept a guy out of trouble.

The smartass in the passenger seat wasn't nearly as disgusted as him. "Looks like a good time," Pace said through his stupid smile.

Tanner pointed through the windshield at a guy a few feet ahead, waving a bright orange plastic flag at the corner of a gravel lot loaded with cars. At his feet was a sandwich sign.

"Look at that," Tanner said. "Ten dollars to park in Pensacola. *Gah!*"

Pace finally wiped the stupid smile off his face, and his eyebrows knitted as he took in the festival's surroundings with a more critical eye.

"Why would Jake Rowe be planning on killing Burton here with all these witnesses? Makes no sense. Unless our guy *wants* to get arrested."

"The note said 8 p.m.," Tanner said. "Half an hour after Tristán's start time. The festival happens once a year, and *this* is the night Jake goes for his revenge? No, I don't believe in coincidences. It'll happen here."

But as Tanner gave it some more thought, he hated to admit that Pace could be right. The fed had asked another good question—why the hell had Jake chosen tonight?

For a moment, Tanner's mind mulled over Jake's great

sense of decency and honor. Pace had sarcastically implied that Jake wrote the note because he wanted to be arrested. But maybe the sarcasm was misplaced. Maybe Jake had such a sense of honor that he really did want to be arrested after he completed his revenge.

It made sense, and for a moment, Tanner was starting to believe it. Until he spotted something.

In the distance.

Of course...

His lips parted.

"What is it?" Pace said.

Tanner didn't reply, just twisted around to the backseat. He grabbed the emergency light, slapped it on the dash, flicked it on, and smashed the horn, swerving past the creeping car in front of him.

CHAPTER SIXTY-EIGHT

THE BRIEFCASE in Burton's hand felt empty.

It was anything but.

The items inside were feather-light, though their symbolic weight was ponderous.

In his other hand was something quite weighty. It was a Maglite—a heavy-duty, anodized aluminum flashlight that, when loaded with big, heavy batteries, became quite substantial. He would need it momentarily.

He was walking through the Port of Pensacola, having gotten access through his special friend who he was about to meet at the shipping containers. An ugly, dreary day had turned into a smoldering beauty of a sunset, which cast a rich aureate glow on everything and gave the utilitarian environment an unduly magnificent aura.

He nodded at the workers. Some of them in jeans and dingy sweatshirts; others in coveralls. Worker bees, toiling while others partied a few blocks over; rough men with rough stares.

Which made Burton wonder about his old man, Jacques Sollier. Were the ports in Europe—where Jacques spent so much of his time—as rough around the edges as those in the States? Probably not. Everything was classier in Europe—the people, the culture, the quality of life. Burton was often envious of his father, this man he never knew, this man who'd lived the good life in Europe. He imagined Jacques spending an afternoon at a street-side café in Paris, or maybe taking a cruise through the Grecian isles.

And Burton was stuck in America.

Specifically, he was stuck *here*. Burton had made a name for himself in Pensacola. He had one of the nicest houses on the beach; he drove expensive cars; his name was spoken with reverence among the criminal element. But he was still in Pensacola. Like he'd always been. His entire life.

Was he really so different from the dock workers he'd just scorned?

Unworthiness fell upon him then, thick and heavy, like a dense fog. It did that sometimes.

But, as always, he shook it off, literally, a quick side-to-side of his head.

He'd have none of that dreary nonsense. Not tonight. Not at his moment of greatness.

He was getting out of this. He would earn a more prosperous, more erudite life. And eventually he would surpass Jacques Sollier. It would take time, but Burton would always have the satisfaction of knowing that he'd reached his dream life through sheer grit.

That dream life was achingly close now, drawing closer with each step he took through the port. Things were escalating, evolving.

Forward, forward, forward.

Progress, progress, progress.

There was a rumble overhead, something the uninitiated might mistake for thunder, a harbinger of rain that would spoil the nearby festival.

But Burton knew better. It wasn't thunder.

He smirked.

And waited for it.

The sound grew louder. Louder. Until it became a scream.

Six F/A-18 combat jets roared overhead in a tight delta formation, perfectly spaced, contrails streaming behind them in the blazing purple-and-orange sunset. The roaring sound sliced through the sky with a warbling, almost straining quality, as though a demon had ripped a hole in the heavens and strained to tear it asunder. The formation banked to the west, heading back to the Naval Air Station.

There was an eruption of distance-muted cheering from the crowd gathered on Palafox. The Tristán Festival had officially begun.

Which meant Burton had exactly half an hour before his designated meeting time.

He spotted his destination ahead: the large shipping containers.

Almost there.

He smiled.

He stepped into one of the aisles in the grid-style arrangement of the massive containers, and immediately the environment became darker. A press of the Maglite's rubber button, and a sphere of clean light joined the faint illumination trickling into the aisle. He went past a half dozen containers before the beam of his flashlight illuminated the stencil-painted serial number he was looking for—*CG247*.

Here he would wait.

He turned the Maglite off and pressed the button on the side of his watch. The tiny light inside showed the time as 7:32.

Twenty-eight minutes until a new and better life. Then—

He hopped back, heart pounding.

Someone else was there, a few feet away.

A figure half consumed in the shadows next to the container. A tall man wearing all black and pointing a silenced Beretta in Burton's direction.

The man's height. His proportions. It was Pete Hudson.

Burton gasped.

The man stepped out of the shadows, and Burton felt both silly and relieved, despite the pistol pointed at him. It wasn't Pete Hudson. It was someone he'd never seen before. The man had a carved, angular face. Brown eyes. Dark straight hair, strands falling to his cheeks.

A hitman.

Someone had hired this gun, and Burton's mind instantly went to Glover, which would explain why Burton hadn't heard from Glover all day, not since he went out to buy some more pussy.

That piece of shit.

Burton never should have trusted the white trash troll. When this was over, he'd track Glover down and have him tortured to death.

But Burton wouldn't panic. Burton never panicked. That's how he kept progressing. Objectively. Without emotion.

"All right, friend," Burton said. "Who are you working for?"

The man said nothing, just motioned to the briefcase. *Hand it over.*

Burton laughed.

"Buddy, there are thirty passports in here." He gave the briefcase a shake. "Globalism: the wave of the future. The twenty-first century is almost here. It's all about bidders now, not borders." He pointed to *CG247*. "This briefcase is gonna slide right in there among a few hundred pounds of famous Pensacola brick. And when the container reaches Istanbul, my buyer is transporting the passports to an undisclosed spot in the Middle East, to some of his terrorist buddies who are just *dying* to get into the States." He paused. "But I'm guessing you knew all that, since you met me here at the right crate at the right time. Who was it? Glover?"

Still no reply.

"What, then? Are you a fed?"

No reply.

Their eyes locked. Waves lapped gently a few feet away. Distant sounds of revelry.

Then movement.

A quick blur of the man's arm. Burton flinched, body expecting to feel the burning tear of a bullet.

Instead, the man shot the briefcase.

It jolted twice in Burton's fingers, torquing his wrist painfully, making him shuffle back a step.

The briefcase swung back and forth on its handle, squeaking like an old, rusty sign. Two clean holes perforated it, bits of paper poking out.

Burton laughed. "Well, you might have ruined *a few* of the passports."

Then another flash of movement, so fast Burton didn't even have time to lose his smug grin.

A shock of pain to his cheek, chest, thighs.

He was on the pavement. The man had closed the gap in an instant, gotten his arm around him, threw him down, and snatched the briefcase.

He held the case for only a moment.

Before he heaved it.

It tumbled through the air.

There was a splash.

Burton understood why the man had shot it. Bubble holes, something to allow water to flow through the case, keep it from floating.

He lifted his chin from the concrete, looked to the bay. The briefcase bobbed gently in the inky water. For just a second. Then with a gurgle, it bubbled out of existence, one corner lingering above the waterline for a moment, his bright future waving goodbye.

The man moved closer, aiming the suppressed Beretta at him.

Burton whipped together a plan. An instantaneous plan. He always had a plan.

Keep the guy distracted. Just for a moment.

The Maglite had rolled to a stop against his hip in the commotion. He inched his thumb toward the rubber button.

"Clearly you're not a fed if you're about to execute me," Burton said. "Can you grant a dying wish and sate my curiosity? Who are you?"

The man stopped. A peculiar expression came to his hewn face.

Burton got his finger on the button. Was about to press it—

And stopped.

A wild thought came to him. An understanding, a recognition.

"Wait," he said. "For a moment there I thought you were ... It *is* you. Isn't it?"

It was Pete Hudson.

The hairs on Burton's arms stood up.

Pete Hudson...

The guy had different colored eyes—brown, not green. Contact lenses could change one's eye color easily enough. The height was the same, as were the general proportions, even if the man was a bit more powerful, more toned. But the face was all kinds of different.

Yet it wasn't the physicality that told Burton this man was Hudson. It was the presence. Something beyond appearances, beyond the tactile.

Then his suspicion was confirmed.

The man nodded.

No time to waste. Instant action. Burton pressed the button and flicked the Maglite up, shining the light in Hudson's eyes.

Hudson blinked, threw a hand over his face. And Burton swung a leg toward him, sweeping his feet from under him.

Hudson hit the pavement a few feet away. His Beretta slipped from his grasp, skittering into the darkness.

Burton hopped up. His Smith & Wesson was stashed in its holster behind his back.

But he didn't go for it.

Not yet.

He was going to get the most out of this. Burton milked all of life's moments for everything they were worth.

He smiled.

"Never thought I'd see you again, Pete."

CHAPTER SIXTY-NINE

"HE'S IN TROUBLE," Nakiri said and stabilized herself again.

The slope of the roof wouldn't have been a problem had the metal not also been wet from the earlier rain. The warehouse was one of the taller ones in the port, almost like a miniature hanger, about twenty feet. She'd used a grappling hook to reach the top.

She was prone, on the very edge of the building with the Remington Model 700P with which she'd so callously taunted Suppressor in the snowy woods in Virginia. The rifle's butt pressed into her shoulder, and a bipod held it steady in the front.

It was 250 yards to the shipping containers, and she'd watched all the action through her scope.

And now she saw Burton standing over Suppressor.

She'd worked this assignment for months.

She slept with that sack of shit, the man on whom her crosshairs rested. So many freaking times.

She could eliminate him right now.

She had the shot.

This was so goddamn stupid.

Especially since Suppressor was compromised.

"I said, he's in trouble!" she shouted to her cellular phone, sitting inches from her elbow, when Falcon didn't respond. "Burton has the upper hand. I have the shot. He's standing over Suppressor, motionless, like a big, freakin' bullseye."

"Hold," Falcon said. "Suppressor has completed the primary objective. If he can't complete the secondary, if Burton eliminates him first, then you put a bullet through Burton's skull. Until then, you do nothing but observe. Is that clear?"

"Suppressor's compromised, damn you!" she said. "He's lost his Beretta, and Burton's armed. He never goes anywhere without his Smith."

"I said hold, Nakiri."

She exhaled.

And her trigger finger trembled.

CHAPTER SEVENTY

TANNER PUT HIS BADGE AWAY, and the guard retreated into his shack and pressed a button. The red-and-white-striped boom gate arm in front of the Lincoln slowly raised. Tanner eased the car into the Port of Pensacola.

"Heck of a hunch you got here, Lieutenant," Pace said from the passenger seat.

Both of the Lincoln's front windows were down, and the fed had his stupid arm dangling outside as he looked into the port, drumming his fingers on the nice, freshly waxed paint. Every now and then, Tanner could hear the man's class ring tapping against his Lincoln.

Tanner's teeth ground together.

"Burton's meeting with someone connected to international terrorists," he said. "He won't be going to the airport, not with the security, especially on the night of a popular festival with people flying in from out of state and from other countries. I've called in units to both here and the airport, just in case, but this is where we'll find him—the port."

The sounds of the festival carried over from a few blocks

away. The air wasn't too warm, but it was thick and made his skin moist. They drove through the various buildings and patches of light. Tall metal things—spires and round tubes with pipes and electrical cords coming out of them.

"What exactly are we looking for?" Pace said as he continued to stare out the window.

Tanner's teeth clenched harder. He really wanted to tell this guy to shut up.

But before he could, he saw something. Motion at the cargo containers in the back corner.

He pointed. "There!"

In one of the aisles between the containers, two figures were silhouetted against the orangish glow of light. One of the men stood over the other, who was lying on the rain-slicked ground. Something was going down. Something bad.

They were just shadowy figures in the dark distance, but Tanner recognized them. He'd been studying them both for months.

The man standing was Lukas Burton.

And the man on the ground, the larger silhouette, was someone Tanner would recognize anywhere.

"Shit. It's Jake," Tanner said. "Doesn't look like his revenge turned out the way he'd hoped."

He flipped on the emergency light and floored the gas.

CHAPTER SEVENTY-ONE

"PLASTIC SURGERY." Burton said as he stared down at Hudson. "Is that it?"

Hudson nodded.

"Well, damn, you sure got your money's worth, Pete."

He cocked his head as a realization came to him.

"Why do I keep calling you Pete? I'm guessing 'Pete Hudson' was an alias, because you're clearly no more a car thief than you are a federal agent. You're a pro. An assassin. Are you working for one of my father's old enemies? Have you come to kill Jacques Sollier's son?"

No reply.

"I'm following in the old man's footsteps," he said, gesturing to the port surrounding them. "But I never even got to know the guy. Jacques met my mother here, at this port. This is where she worked."

He snickered and looked off, into the port. Memories of his mother working at the very place he was standing reminded him that he'd never left Pensacola. Unworthiness fell over him again. Momentarily. Then he straightened his back, remembered the bigger goal.

And returned his attention to the man on the ground.

This assassin was deadly, the sort you didn't turn your back on for a moment.

Burton continued. "He knocked her up and left, sent money every six months. Only visited twice before my mother was killed. No one ever figured out whether the murder was random or connected to Jacques. Regardless, from then on, I was on my own.

"I don't remember my first meeting with my father. I was only five. But I clearly recall the second visit, when I was eight, about a year before my mom died. Big guy. He had this sort of dignified power to him—the way he dressed and carried himself. Different from the Americans I was used to. Classy. He took me to a park, asked me about my studies, fed me at a fancy French restaurant downtown, taught me the history of a few buildings, and had me back to Mom before dinnertime. Last time I ever saw him. He was killed, too, a few years later.

"I was in and out of foster homes. Got in some trouble. Got arrested a few times. Then a chance meeting with Joey Farone changed my life. At a fruit market, of all places. He saw the potential in me, took me in as a ward for my last year of legal childhood. From then on, I was with the Farones, and I had a real poppa. Then you came in, posing as a car thief, and won the favor of my new father—and his beautiful daughter—*in a few months!*"

Burton stopped. He felt out of control. That wouldn't do. He was always composed. He took a deep breath before he continued.

"Whatever you were doing embedded with the Farones, you had us all fooled. Who are you?"

Still no reply.

Burton felt the corners of his standard grin twitch, ready to curl into a scowl. He took out his Smith.

"You'll forgive me for wanting to know a man's name before I blast him to Hell. *What's your name?*"

The man squinted those dark eyes at him, and his face screwed tight, eyebrows lowering. He locked eyes with Burton.

"Silence Jones."

Burton felt the gun dip in his hand. He gasped.

That voice...

So bizarre. Unnatural. Deep, crackling, and growly. Macabre and wicked. Inhuman—not so much animalistic as it was mechanical.

The voice jolted Burton back a few inches. He reaffirmed his grip on the Smith, brought it back up.

He realized his smile was gone. Revealing his shock. Lessening his dominance. So he smiled again.

"Well, Mr. Silence Jones, you've stolen so much from me —my poppa, his daughter, my funds in New Orleans, and the passports tonight, my chance at something bigger. It's finally time to even the score."

He pulled back the hammer.

CHAPTER SEVENTY-TWO

ON A NORMAL EVENING, Laswell would be enjoying his time at Pensacola Bayfront Auditorium.

It was a massive, squarish arena-style building—maybe fifty feet tall, brick, windowless, and with a gabled roof, built at the end of a pier, surrounded on three sides by Pensacola Bay. Gentle nighttime waves twinkled with city light as they lapped against the pier's concrete wall.

But while Laswell leaned against the decorative fence at the quiet walkway surrounding the building, he wasn't enjoying the splendid sights or the comfortable atmosphere. He was looking due east, the least glamorous direction, where, over a short stretch of water, was the Port of Pensacola.

A massive ship—big enough to have a helipad on top—was docked, bright lights making it's white-and-blue paint job shine out in the night. Just past the vessel was an area of shipping containers—that's where Laswell was staring, because that was where his new Asset would be attempting to stop an influx of terrorism.

Nakiri had phoned him, told him she'd finally heard from

Suppressor, that Suppressor knew where to find Burton, at the shipping containers at the Port of Pensacola, that they'd be going there to intercept him.

And now Laswell's two Assets were out there, hidden in the industrial complex on the other side of the water.

"Oh, shit!" Nakiri's voice came in scratchy through the phone. "Burton cocked his gun."

Though he couldn't see her, he knew she was perched on one of the warehouses in the distance, watching what was happening through a scope.

Laswell squinted. He still hadn't been able to find—

There.

There they were. Two figures. Faint outlines in a dark aisle between the shipping containers. The taller of the two men was on the ground.

That would be Suppressor.

The other figure had his arm extended, pointed downward, toward Suppressor.

Laswell's left hand clenched the fence, and his right hand smashed his cellular phone against his ear. Every bit of him was taut, muscles ready to explode.

Because the tone of Nakiri's voice had said she was getting the itch to interfere.

To defy him.

Like she had before.

"Hold," he said through his teeth.

"He's stepping closer. Oh, no..."

"I don't give a damn what Burton does," Laswell said, pulling the phone in front of his face to give it a proper shout.

A woman passing behind him shot him a look and hurried her young boy away.

"You let this play out, Nakiri!"

She didn't reply.

"*Nakiri!* I'm telling you to—"

He stopped suddenly. There had been a *beep-beep* in his ear.

He looked at the screen. The green multiplex LCD letters said:

CALL ENDED

"*Shit!*"

CHAPTER SEVENTY-THREE

SILENCE LOOKED UP.

At the revolver.

And beyond it, Burton's face. Not smiling for once. Grim.

Silence only then realized this was the closest he'd been to Burton since the punch to the throat.

The searing pain. The unnatural, impossible sensation that had coursed through his neck. The strange whiteness that had engulfed him. Death.

He'd accepted death.

It was about to happen again, death, once more at Burton's hands. He'd have to accept his demise for a second time.

"There's a lot I could do to you right now," Burton said, "to find out why you're here. But as you can guess, I'm running low on time. My friend will arrive any moment, and I need to explain to him why his passports are at the bottom of the bay. So we'll make this brief."

His finger tensed on the trigger.

Silence took a deep breath. From his stomach. A diaphragmatic breath. Just like C.C. had taught him.

He saw her face, smiling.

I love you, Cecilia.

Another deep breath.

CRACK!

Burton's shoulder exploded.

A cloud of mist, a snake of blood, and a chunk of flesh, all back-lit by one of the dim, orange streetlights in the distance.

Silence had only a split second to consider what had happened. It was all he needed.

She wasn't supposed to help him. She was only supposed to clean things up if he bungled.

Nakiri.

He blasted into action, not jumping to his feet but rolling straight toward Burton, a move Burton wouldn't expect.

The Smith & Wesson Model 29 flailed in Burton's hand as he stumbled, then the gun roared, muzzle flare blasting from the end of its barrel, strobing the surroundings with a flash of light.

Silence felt the bullet's impact tremor through the concrete. Debris peppered his back, hot pinpricks through the thick canvas of his jacket.

He crashed through Burton's shins, and Burton teetered over, his full frame collapsing onto Silence.

The momentum of their combined mass jolted to a sudden stop as they smashed into *CG247*. A hollow metallic thud rattled through the box.

Silence blinked his eyes open to find Burton's leg splayed on top of him. He grabbed the shoe and twisted hard, wrenching with that new strength that he'd trained for.

Snap.

The foot went backward.

Burton howled.

Silence scrambled closer, grabbing Burton's wrist below the gun. Even with a broken ankle, even with a destroyed shoulder, even with Silence torquing his arm with all he had, Burton held steady, muscles hard, quivering. Nothing but adrenaline and rage, the natural strength of a man who was born into a life of crime and violence.

Their locked arms quaked, making the metal wall of the container warble. Silence eased off, fractionally, feigning disadvantage. The Smith's barrel shook as it drew closer. Burton's sweaty smile became a sneering line of bared teeth.

Silence waited, then suddenly thrust forward. Explosiveness. Hard lessons learned with kettle bells and medicine balls. He smashed Burton's wrist into the container.

The Smith dropped, hit the concrete hard, clattered to a stop. Only inches away. Burton swiped for it, and Silence hooked him around the throat, rolling them a full revolution away on the wet pavement.

There was a twitch from Burton's hips, then a blurring knee met Silence's chin. His teeth cracked together, and his head snapped back.

Burton glanced to the gun. Several feet away now. Turned back to Silence.

Silence tried to focus, but Burton tilted in his vision, the teeth-cracking knee shot still echoing through his body. Burton slapped Silence's arms away, and wrapped his functioning hand around Silence's throat while the other dangled at his side.

Silence swung at the inside of Burton's elbow. No effect. A rock-solid pillar. Another swipe. Nothing. Burton was one powerful son of a bitch.

His eyes flicked to Burton's bloody shoulder.

Go for the wound, Nakiri had said while they watched a tape of Brazilian underground Vale Tudo fights. *Hit that weak spot. Relentlessly*.

Silence swung his torso to the side, momentarily lessening

the arm-pillar's grip on his neck, then smashed his head into the mess of Burton's shoulder.

He felt Burton's blood on his forehead, wet and warm. The impact was hard enough to send an electric quiver through his face, an instant headache.

Burton shrieked and dropped back. The grip on Silence's neck loosened.

That was all the space that Silence needed.

He shoved Burton back and rolled to his feet, a crouched position, his boots digging into the pavement. Burton looked up at him.

And Silence's foot thudded into the bloody shoulder.

Burton screamed again, shrill echoes shuddering through the alleys of shipping containers.

What else had Nakiri said?

Speed and power, dummy. Get rid of that energy you worked so hard to build. Give it to the scumbag.

He squared a fist, swung it down to Burton's face, a blur of speed and a flawless transfer of massive energy.

Burton's nose snapped. His eyes rolled back, cheeks slackened.

Silence grabbed a handful of Burton's hair and smashed his head into the concrete. A glob of blood shot from the corner of his mouth.

He gripped the hair tighter, and dragged Burton back to the shipping container. Adding his second hand to the hair, he reared back, and threw Burton face-first into the wall.

Bang!

The container thundered louder than when they'd both smashed into it moments earlier. Its sides shook. Burton slid down the corrugated wall, leaving a streak of blood dripping down the rusty metal.

He was a tangled pile. His face was all bumpy mounds of

flesh. Purples and reds and one swollen-shut eye. The other
eye blinked, looked up at Silence. Sputtering breaths.

Silence remembered C.C.'s mangled, dead face. Half a
face. Burton had stolen the rest of it, left it as flaps of skin.

He thought of his own ruined face. Falcon had told him
that Burton and his men had turned him into "hamburger."

Doughty's face. The street thug who had been harassing
Mrs. Enfield. Silence had smashed that face into the ground,
much as he'd just done to Burton.

But he'd halted abruptly.

Mrs. Enfield had come up behind him, put her wrinkled
hand on his shoulder, told him to stop.

Silence had then added mercy to his assassin's toolbox,
juxtaposing the Nakiri mainstays like stealth and intimidation.

Mercy.

He looked at Burton.

And his mind went to another image: Jake Rowe, in
Burton's living room, just before he was forced to watch the
video of C.C.'s murder. Jake had thought about how his
predicament—tied to a chair, surrounded by thugs, tortured
—bore similarities to a typical Hollywood action movie.

Burton stared back at Silence with his one functioning
eye.

In a typical action movie, this would be the point where
the good guy would show mercy on the villain, the man he's
been seeking revenge on the entire film. He would let the bad
guy go. Then the bad guy would reveal a hidden weapon, and
the good guy would defend himself, killing the villain. Our
hero would get his revenge but keep his honor.

Whenever Silence saw a revenge film with this sort of
climax, he felt unsatisfied. Cheated. That type of ending was
a copout.

In his new career as an assassin, Silence would need to know when a situation called for mercy.

But this was not one of those situations.

Burton continued to sputter, blinking rapidly now.

Still conscious.

Good.

Silence stepped to where his Beretta had disappeared and found it in the shadows, resting against a container wall.

He picked it up, went back to Burton, watched the man sputter for another moment or two.

Closed his eyes.

C.C., smiling at him from her spot on her favorite sofa in the library, book in hand.

Eyes open.

A one-second meditation.

He raised his gun.

And fired.

Two rounds to the forehead. A double tap.

In a typical action movie, the good guy would be overwhelmed with emotion at this moment. The soundtrack would swell to a thunderous crescendo.

But for Silence, his immediate reaction was anticipation of a delayed reaction. He knew the impact would come later, some time when he wasn't expecting it. For now, he was numb.

Just a simple thought.

Eight down; none to go.

It's done.

There was a flash of light, sudden and bright enough to make him jump. He looked up.

Bright blue, strobing.

A cop light.

An unmarked car approached, fast, turning a corner, the light pulsing out of its windshield.

For just a moment, he saw Tanner behind the wheel.

Headlights swung in his direction.

Silence threw a hand over his face and sprinted off.

CHAPTER SEVENTY-FOUR

"YOU'RE GONNA LOSE HIM!" Pace shouted.

"Shut up!" Tanner said as he swung the Lincoln back around, toward the front of the port.

But Pace was right. The tall silhouette had disappeared in between the shipping containers, and as they'd drawn closer, it had run past them, through a patch of shadows and into the belly of the port.

Finding Jake in this industrial maze would be next to impossible. But that didn't matter. All Tanner needed to do was head for the gate. Jake would be going toward the exit, of course, and there was only one way out.

The blue light flashed off the windshield in front of him, as the Lincoln's tires squealed. Tanner gritted his teeth, not so much in determination but at the thought of the damage to the tires. Brand-new Dunlops. He'd just had them installed last week. Martha would flip her lid if he ruined them in one night.

Hell with it.

He yanked the wheel hard, and the Dunlops screeched louder. The tangy smell of burnt rubber filled the cabin.

Jake Rowe was meeting a pair of handcuffs tonight.

A good man whom Tanner had trusted and taken under his wing.

And who then became a murderer.

With all the conflicting emotions running through Tanner's head, they all led back to one nice, logical conclusion: *catch Jake Rowe.*

That was the great thing about logic: it always trumps emotion.

The Lincoln's engine howled as they drove past an administration office on one side and a fenced-in area of barrels to the right.

But no sign of Jake.

Tanner slowed slightly, and he braced for another sarcastic comment from the passenger seat. Instead, Pace shouted, "There!"

Tanner followed Pace's finger. The shadows ahead. The tall figure of Jake Rowe, sprinting with all he had.

He was only yards from the exit.

Tanner floored the gas again. A *chirp* from the Dunlops.

At the gate, the guard emerged from his shack, into a pool of light, waving his arms at Jake, who sprinted even faster now, if that was possible, his long legs pumping furiously.

The guard reached out for him, and with one easy, swift move, Jake stiff-armed him, sending the guard to his ass.

"Holy crap," Tanner said as his eyes widened.

As big as Jake was, Tanner had never thought he was *that* strong. The guard wasn't a small man, and Jake had taken him down like he was cardboard.

Jake vaulted over the boom arm.

Tanner smashed the gas pedal. And he grimaced.

Because if Martha was gonna be mad about the tires...

She was going to be livid about this.

Pace shielded himself. "*What the hell are you doing?*"

And Tanner drove right into the boom arm.

SMASH!

The Lincoln's grill snapped the arm at the base. The big tube clunked over the hood, punched a crack in the windshield, and rolled off the trunk, clattering loudly on the pavement behind.

Tanner checked the rearview.

The guard was still on the ground, rubbing his head, but the arm had missed him entirely, rolling several feet away.

Steam trickled from the Lincoln's hood.

Busted radiator. Cracked windshield. And the bumper and grille were surely destroyed.

Out of the port. Onto the street. Ahead, Jake sprinted hard. He'd gotten a couple of blocks away from them, heading west toward Palafox Place.

Of course he was.

He was going for the anonymity of the crowd.

Damn, he was running fast. When the hell did he get in such good shape? He must have spent the entire time he vanished from Pensacola in the gym.

Out in the nighttime city light, Tanner could see now that Jake was wearing all black—jeans and a canvas jacket.

He shuddered at the preparations this guy had taken for his latest murder. Methodical.

Jake cut diagonally through a parking lot, weaving his way through the vehicles, shouldering past pods of laughing people coming and going from the festival.

Then he turned into an alley.

And was gone.

"*Shit!*" Tanner said.

They were back on Jefferson Street. Tanner hit the brakes, sending him and Pace jolting into their seatbelts.

Two cars in front of them, brake lights aglow. Parked cars

lined the opposite side of the street too. Chortling pedestrians weaved, stumbled through the vehicles.

There would be no more driving.

Tanner jumped out. Pace followed.

A quick glance back at the Lincoln. The front end was a jagged, steaming nightmare. Martha's impending wrath would be historic.

They ran into the crowd, heading for Palafox Place, one block over.

Down a side street lined with arts and crafts vendors. Paintings. Wire sculptures. Local honey. People turned to look at them. Some shocked faces, others drunken, laughing, pointing.

A mass of people had congealed at the corner, and Tanner shoved through a tangle of sweaty arms and onto Palafox.

Absolute pandemonium.

A giant, swarming mass of people, all shoulders and beer and sweat. Laughter. Joyful shouting.

Tanner wanted to go for his gun. He needed it in a situation like this, hunting down a murderer. But he couldn't. Not here. Not with people bumping into him from all directions. Not with thumping music that cut into his skull and pissed him off.

So many people.

So many that even a six-foot-three man could blend in. Hundreds of people. Thousands? Several of them six-foot-three or taller.

It was a lost cause...

Wait.

No, it wasn't.

There he was. Strolling away. Except...

He wasn't dressed in all black. This man wore a white shirt.

Tanner squinted, studied.

The dark hair. Identical. And the frame, the stature—just like Jake's, though harder, tauter, less gym-sculpted. Tanner's mind flashed on how much stronger Jake had looked when he pushed the guard over at the port.

The man wore black jeans. He could have easily torn off the black jacket to reveal a white shirt.

It was him.

It was Jake.

Tanner shot a quick glance over his shoulder. Pace had fallen back. There were several people between them. Tanner gave a quick nod of the head—*Follow me*—which Pace acknowledged.

He kept his eyes locked on the tall figure as he pushed through the crowd.

With every step, with every drunk he pushed past, Tanner was more certain it was Jake. Why else would the man be by himself in this massive party, casually working his way through the revelry, unaffected, unimpressed?

Ten feet behind the man.

A giggling twenty-something woman in a bright red wig and a green tutu jumped in front of Tanner, said something silly. He shouldered past her.

Five feet away.

Tanner stepped onto the sidewalk to avoid a cluster of middle-aged men, laughing loudly.

Back onto the street. Jake was right in front of him, no one between them, a foot away.

Tanner clamped his hand down on Jake's shoulder, yanked him around.

It wasn't Jake.

The man had sharp features, dark and almost exotic look-ing, like a really tall, really big Johnny Depp staring down at him with a perplexed look on his face.

Tanner removed his hand. "So sorry. I ... thought you were someone else."

The man continued to give him a confused stare. But he said nothing. There was a small twinkle in his eye, almost a smile.

He just kept staring.

Screaming and laughter and music pounded through the walls surrounding them.

The little smile grew a bit bigger. And almost kindly. Tranquil.

How much had this guy had to drink?

Tanner inched back.

Finally the man nodded, turned around, and slipped into the crowd.

Someone bumped into Tanner, and he diverted his attention to look.

It was Pace, panting.

Tanner turned back around.

And the man was gone.

Just ... vanished.

Tanner looked left, right.

Nothing.

Pace exhaled, catching his breath. "Wrong guy?"

"Obviously," Tanner said. He thought of the bizarre smile the man had given him. "Just some weirdo."

He scanned through the crowd, his focus bouncing from one tall man to the next. None of them looked remotely like Jake.

Tanner sighed.

"He's gone."

CHAPTER SEVENTY-FIVE

LASWELL LOOKED across the water at the police lights coming from the port. There were a half dozen cop cars, flapping yellow tape, and lots of milling personnel, but the energy was slow and methodical. It had been half an hour since the action had spiked.

"You're damn right," he said into his cellular phone. "Suppressor finished him off. Nakiri put a round through his shoulder first, so I guess it was a bit of a tag-team effort. Call it 70-30."

"Assets don't work in teams," Briggs said from a thousand miles away in D.C. "That was the whole point of this training assignment. It was meant to be Suppressor's final exam."

"So, he had a little helping hand. So what? You just don't wanna admit that I was right, that Silence Jones is Asset material. I'd say that's impossible for you to deny now, since he also led the FBI to Burton's contact, a guy with connections to terrorist cells all over the Middle East and Europe." He paused. "Sooooo ... does he have your approval?"

Laswell's fist clenched as he held his breath.

And he hoped to hell Briggs wouldn't do another one of his long, pensive pauses.

Thankfully, the pause was brief, only a second or so.

"He does," Briggs said.

Laswell released both his breath and his clenched fist. "Thank you, sir."

"Don't make me regret this decision. Good evening."

Laswell grinned. "Good evening, Senator."

He pressed the *END* button.

Footsteps behind him. He turned and found Nakiri approaching, her gray eyes waiting for him, staring coldly.

Always such a delight, she was.

He sighed.

She'd changed out of her tactical gear and now wore skin-tight jeans, black boots, a gray sweater, a bit of makeup. The same woman, but totally different. She was good at switching into and out of personas.

"Where is he?" Laswell said.

"Should be here any moment."

"He did it," Laswell said as Nakiri stopped a couple of feet away by the decorative hand railing.

She scoffed. "Not without my help. I loosened the lid for him."

"And he tore the damn thing right off. You think he's got what it takes?"

"Do you really give a shit about my opinion?"

He didn't reply. Laswell had a policy of not answering questions that were answers to his questions.

She groaned, looked across the water to the port. "Yeah, he's got the right stuff."

Laswell gave her a smartass grin. "I know he does. I told both you and Jupiter he has it. Told ya, told ya, told ya!"

Laswell felt a sudden presence behind him. He jumped.

There was Silence.

Materialized from the shadows.

"You scared the shit out of me," Laswell said, and then he grinned. "Stealth. Very nice."

"I taught him that," Nakiri said with the trademark dark twinkle in her eye. "And now that my instructing days are behind me, can you give me my *next* final assignment as soon as possible? As much as I like you, Falcon, I'm ready to never see you again."

"Nakiri, I never took away your final assignment. I only changed the parameters. I *told* you I took it away because I needed you to train Suppressor—ruthlessly, efficiently, and fast. I told you what you needed to hear to get the job done. And I also needed to see if you had it in you to do the right thing, one last test before I cut you loose into the free world again." He gave her a respectful nod, almost a bow. "You passed the test. Assignment complete, Nakiri. Go. Go live the rest of your life."

Nakiri turned to him. Her face melted, softening at the corners of her eyes, lips parting.

Laswell waved his hand back and forth between Nakiri and Silence. "You two never met, by the way."

Nakiri continued to look at him. She reached out and steadied herself on the hand railing.

Laswell swiped her hand away and shooed her off with a wave of the fingers. "What are you waiting for? Get out of here."

Her eyes remained fixed on him. Then, slowly, she turned to Silence. A moment of staring at the new Asset. Then she put her hand on Silence's shoulder, squeezed, and turned.

Her back was to them now.

A few steps at a slow pace, hips sashaying, the heels of her boots clicking on the concrete.

And then a brisk walk.

Then a jog.

Then she was running.

She disappeared into the night.

Laswell turned to Silence. "She's something else, isn't she?"

Silence nodded.

"I got something for you, Si," he said. "That's what I'm gonna call you, by the way. Si. I like nicknames. Okay by you?"

"Yes."

That voice. No matter how many times Laswell heard it, he still couldn't get used to it. Bizarre. Creepy.

Laswell smacked him on the shoulder. "You sound like a rusty chainsaw that's been fired up after sitting in the back corner of a barn for a decade or so."

Silence blinked.

"Anyway." Laswell reached into his pocket and pulled out the folded piece of paper. "I had a Specialist run the card you faxed me."

At the top of the sheet was a black-and-white image of the Alabama driver's license Silence had scanned.

"Manuel Doughty. Three prior arrests, one for murder. Not enough evidence to hold him. Our Specialist made a few adjustments in the computer, and some additional evidence just arrived via email at the Mobile Police Department. Doughty's been arrested again, and unless he gets the world's best public defender, he won't beat the rap this time. He'll never bother your neighbor again."

"Thank you."

Laswell nodded. "Walk with me, Si."

He started along the walkway. Silence fell into place beside him. Small waves lapped against the pier wall. Sounds of the festival in the distance. A seagull cackled as it floated on the thermals in the nighttime sky.

"I've given some thought to your debt," Laswell said. "And

I finally completed it yesterday. It's a damn good idea, if I say so myself."

He smiled, and his mustache twitched.

"You were all over the place as Jake Rowe. A few years of this, a few years of that—high school teacher, college professor, police officer. And I understand that Cecilia Farone was helping you to organize your headspace, that you have issues with concentration and focus. Now you've received a brand-new life with a new face, new voice, new name, and you've lost the love of your life."

Silence shrugged and offered him a bit of a frown. *Tell me something I don't know*, he seemed to say. He was getting eerily talented at non-verbal communication. Good. The guy was going to need it.

"So your debt is going to be this: one day, far down the line, you're going to come to me and tell me who you are, what you're all about. That's it. Of course, you could give me an answer tomorrow. Hell, you could come up with something right this second. But I know that's not your way. You have integrity, and you're a thinker, two of the many reasons I chose you. I know you won't give me an answer until you have a real one. Until then, you're going to kill people and right wrongs in this world."

Silence only nodded.

"Speaking of sticking to your word, you haven't visited her grave, have you?"

Laswell had made Silence promise not to visit Cecilia Farone's grave before he put him on a plane back to Pensacola a couple of weeks earlier.

Silence shook his head.

"Good. I'm sure you're itching to go, but no matter how different your appearance is to the old Jake Rowe face, there are only so many six-foot-three guys who'll visit her gravesite, and the Farone family surely has enemies still in the area. Give it some time."

"Okay," Silence said.

"How was it, your first assignment?"

"Challenging."

"Good answer." Laswell stopped, put his hands on the railing, and looked out into the dark water. "And the revenge? Killing Burton?"

A dark look swept over Silence's face. "Satisfying."

Laswell grinned. "I figured it would be."

He leaned off the railing, put his hands in his pockets, and faced Silence.

"I told Nakiri what she needed to hear to get you trained. A bit mischievous, but it got the job done. I did something similar with you when I brought you aboard. I offered you a choice: join the Watchers, or I'd turn you in to the authorities."

He paused.

"I was never going to turn you in. Should you have turned down the offer, I would have made you a Benevolent Cause, changed your identity, and given you a new life. Killing four men in one night was brutal, but so was what they did to Cecilia. I did what I had to do to get you to join. Maybe you want to rip my face off now, but I hope that shows how much I wanted you on the team, the faith I have in you."

Silence didn't respond.

Laswell took that as a good sign. So he just nodded.

He couldn't help but feel a tad guilty. He remembered what Briggs had said earlier in the day.

You can be a real manipulative son of a bitch, you know that?

Yes. Yes, he could.

His mustache twitched impishly.

"Chances are, this is the last time you'll see me in person. Assets rarely see their Prefects again beyond the initiation process. Nakiri only fell back into face-to-face contact with me again because of the weird circumstances that brought you to us. Most likely, from this point on, you'll know me as nothing but a voice on the phone, a valediction at the bottom of an email. Any final questions?"

"No."

Laswell nodded. "You've proven me right. You're an Asset. But you won't be just any Asset. There's something special about you. I can feel it. You're going to be a legend."

And Laswell wasn't exaggerating. No hyperbole. No embellishment. No sarcasm, for once.

Of all the Assets Laswell had pulled into the Watchers, this guy—this former teacher, this short-term police officer, this love-struck, heartbroken fool—was a step above. He had the X factor. The dark depths of tragedy and an endless pool of resourcefulness. He was the perfect storm, a giant mass of intangibilities.

Valuable, dangerous intangibilities.

"Good luck, Suppressor."

Laswell turned and left, leaving Silence Jones to his new reality.

CHAPTER SEVENTY-SIX

THE SUN WAS TOO BRIGHT. The sky was too blue. The temperature and humidity were too ideal, and the breeze felt too pleasant.

For what Silence was about to do, there needed to be solemnity. The sky should have been gray with a bitter chill and nagging drizzle.

He drove along the cemetery's neat, well-packed gravel path. When he left Virginia two weeks earlier, Falcon had told him he wasn't to visit C.C.'s grave. Last night, at the Auditorium, Falcon had reiterated the command, and, in the same conversation, had said he appreciated that Silence was a man of his word.

Silence *was* a man of his word. It was true. But Nakiri had said that bending rules was as useful a skill as any of the others she'd taught him when it was used judiciously and in situations that were entirely necessary.

This was necessary.

In the two weeks since he'd returned to Pensacola, he'd yet to visit C.C.'s grave. He'd been telling himself that it was because of the true-to-his-word quality that so defined him, that so impressed Falcon.

But that wasn't it. Not entirely.

There was also hesitance.

Dread.

He turned a corner and saw the grave just ahead. He pulled the car to the side, parked, and took out his binoculars.

Falcon was right. A six-foot-three guy shouldn't be hanging out at Cecilia Farone's grave site when a six-foot-three guy was wanted for her murder.

So he just observed it from a distance, seated in a vehicle, where no wandering eyes could discern his height.

A simple, unassuming gravestone. Granite. Sparkly new. Her full name at the top, *CECILIA NICOLE FARONE*, and dates at the bottom—a late 1960s date on the left and an early 1990s date on the right. The only other word was *DAUGHTER*.

The most special soul he'd ever known, summed up by *DAUGHTER*.

She spent most of her time in her books and in her mind. She had almost no friends, and her criminal family existed in a different realm than the one she soared upon. Her father hadn't known how special she was, not in his cogent days and certainly not after he slipped into dementia. Her brother loved her, but he was a lunatic.

Silence was the only person who would ever know who Cecilia Farone had been.

He stayed for two minutes looking through the binoculars. Then he left.

———

That evening, quiet had returned to East Hill. There were no festival noises from a few blocks over, no jet flyovers.

And no rattling, bass-pumping El Camino rolling past.

Silence watched Mrs. Enfield's hands, twisting against each other in the dip between her legs. Her blind eyes were apprehensive as they looked over the peaceful street in front of them. The two of them were on her porch swing. Baxter sat between them, purring and drooling.

"You're sure they're not coming back?" she said, her white eyes looking past him, to the end of the block.

She'd been fretting about her recent visitors since they sat down.

"I'm positive." Silence swallowed. "You're safe now."

He spoke as gently and reassuringly as his crackling voice would allow. He was getting better at controlling its intonations, evidenced by the way Mrs. Enfield leaned back in the swing and unknotted her fingers.

She exhaled. And nodded. Tension left her face as she fully accepted his words of reassurance. Silence wished he could let go that easily. He was working on that.

"God sent you to me," Mrs. Enfield said. "Right when I needed you. Lola, my last caretaker, left the state a few weeks before you moved in. I got no family left. Never had kids. Blind and alone, except for Baxter. But now I have a guardian angel next door."

Silence had never considered how difficult it would be to live alone with a disability. Nor had he ever thought he'd be someone's guardian angel.

"Yes, ma'am," he said.

"I can't very well go on calling you Silence. I give all my friends nicknames. I'm gonna call you Si. Work for you?"

That was two people in the last twenty-four hours who'd taken it upon themselves to shorten his name to Si. He really had no say in the matter at this point.

"Yes, ma'am."

The old woman tussled the fur on top of Baxter's head. The purring grew louder. "Will you tell me now what happened to you, why it is you won't talk to me?"

Silence didn't reply.

Mrs. Enfield nodded. "On your time, son. On your—"

"It was bad," he said and swallowed. A quick breath. He held it. Released. "My fiancée was..." He swallowed. "Murdered. Brutally."

Mrs. Enfield said nothing, just nodded again. She placed her hand on his knee and left it there.

He'd said it. Out loud. Through his ruined throat, with his monster voice. He'd put it out into the world, a simple fact that he'd kept entirely in his mind for months.

C.C. had been murdered.

In a typical action movie, after a revelation like this, the hero would receive his long-due relief. A look of serenity would fall over his face, as though it had been denial that had brought him such grief for so long.

But Silence had never denied that C.C. was gone. He'd not repressed the image of her mutilated face, the screams he'd heard when he'd been forced to watch the video of her murder.

For Silence, verbalizing that her incredible life had been cut short, that she'd suffered, that she'd been taken from him, was an act of solemn acceptance.

C.C. had told him he had control issues, that he desperately wanted to be in charge of his fate. But he couldn't, she'd said, and when he accepted that fact, things would get better for him.

She told him that he needed to stop trying to dictate the course of the future. She told him to stop thinking so much. She told him to relax.

She told him to let go.

So while he would never let go of her—*never*—he would
let go of her murder.

As much as he could.

He wouldn't see the destroyed face, his final image of her.
He wouldn't focus on the fact that the last thing she'd said to
him, in the answering machine message, was a bit of anger. A
swear word. A vile name, directed at him. *Asshole.*

He would see her beautiful smooth skin, dark eyes,
beaming smile that crackled with kindness and wisdom and
trivia and joy. He would hear her kind words. Like *love*. She
always called him "love."

For a few moments, he and Mrs. Enfield sat without
saying a word, just staring into the quiet street. No cars or
people passed. A solitary insomniac bird twittered in the
magnolia tree to their right.

Then Mrs. Enfield broke the hush, asking him a simple
but personal question: what was his favorite ice cream flavor?
Chocolate chip cookie dough. Mrs. Enfield hadn't tried that
flavor, nor any of the other "newfangled concoctions." Give
her good ol' strawberry. The next question was similar but
slightly more serious in tone: he was in such good shape that
she wondered if he might have some pointers for her. She was
trying to lose a couple of pounds. He looked over her tiny
frame and asked her where she planned on losing those
pounds from.

From that point, the conversation's seriousness level rose
no further. It was nearly an hour that they spoke, and Mrs.
Enfield was quite patient with Silence's constant pauses as his
throat became progressively sorer.

He didn't mind the pain.

When their conversation ended and Silence returned to
his own home, he found a FedEx delivery by the door.

Inside the house, he placed the small box on the marble
kitchen counter, cut the tape with a utility knife, and opened

the smaller box within, which was long, thin, and full of cards. He took one out, held it in his hand.

When he'd devised this plan, he'd never actually seen plastic business cards; he'd simply assumed—hoped—that they actually existed. A print shop downtown confirmed that plastic business cards were indeed a real thing, but he'd have to order them from a specialty business. The shop gave him the website of an out-of-state supplier.

It was one of the few times Silence had ever ordered something via the Internet, so he'd been apprehensive about the process. But as he looked at the card now in his hand, he was pleased.

Unlike most paper business cards, plastic ones had rounded corners. The proportions were slightly different too, creating an overall shape that, along with the thickness of the plastic, made plastic business cards identical to credit cards or other swipe cards—the only missing element was the magstripe.

The card in Silence's hand was opaque with a frosted, matte finish—like a glass shower door. He moved his fingers behind the card, watching the faint pinkish outlines through the plastic.

On the left side of the card were two dark blue geometric slashes, one slightly darker than the other. He couldn't help but grin. There had been several pre-designed templates, and while he could have gone with a completely blank card, he'd chosen one of the designs.

In hindsight, he couldn't say why he'd added a bit of flare to such a purposeful item. It seemed silly now. But he liked it.

It was a little bit of his future, looking back at him from the palm of his hand. Each time he would meet someone he was to help, he would hand the person a card. His voice was too damn jarring. The card would be his means of introduction.

Of course, once the introduction was made, he would ask for the card back. Couldn't have it floating around in the wide world.

Which meant he was going to have plenty of extras. The smallest order size available had been one hundred.

He put the card back in the box with the other ninety-nine.

———

Silence looked in the mirror.

He was drawing a much needed bath, and the air was getting chewy thick as piping hot water filled his old clawfoot bathtub. Whoever had taken the lead in redesigning Silence's 1955 home to his chic tastes had decided to leave certain retro-cool details intact, such as the clawfoot tub. He was impressed. The mystery person seemed to know him better than he knew himself.

Steam inched in from the edges of the mirror, tightening around his reflection. He felt moisture on his fingers and finally pulled his attention away, looked down. He saw that his fingers were clenched tight on either side of the vintage sink—another purposefully preserved detail—and his left hand pinned his PenPal to the porcelain. Moisture from the steamy air had condensed on its yellow plastic cover, tickling his fingertips.

He opened the notebook, flipped through the contents. The first several pages were leftovers from his Jake Rowe days. More precisely, the Pete Hudson days. As he continued turning, the notes evolved from his shorthand notes in the early days of the undercover investigation to the ones written on the fateful evening that led to the end of his former life. He saw the notes he'd written to Mayer, the mob doctor, when he got his leg stitched up.

Grab something for the pain, dickhead

A few of these notes, then there was the list of names—Burton and his men. All eight names were now crossed off. The previous night, after the events at the port, he'd put the final slash through Burton's name.

~~Cobb~~
~~Gamble~~
~~Hodges~~
~~Knox~~
~~McBride~~
~~Odom~~
~~Glover~~
~~Burton~~

Next was the five-word script he'd written for himself when he'd parked the Grand Prix, something he'd used to test his voice after the sight of C.C.'s body had given him selective mutism, literally scaring him speechless.

My name is Jake Rowe

He'd held the PenPal by the car's rearview mirror, read the note, tried to say the words—and nothing had come out.

Another flip revealed the message he'd shown Odom.

Did you hurt her?

Then the pages became filled with notes from Nakiri's training. Firearms data—cartridge types, muzzle velocities, effective firing ranges. Details about biomechanics and ortho-pedics. A reading list, exhaustive, years' worth of books.

He flipped to the last marked page, another list, one he'd written only moments earlier, after he'd turned on the water but before he'd faced the mirror.

It was a second list of names.

Identities.

Jake Rowe
Pete Hudson
Loudmouth
Asset 23
A-23
Suppressor
dummy
Si
Silence Jones

He pressed the PenPal against the mirror, into the encroaching steam. His eyes flicked back and forth between the list and his stern reflection.

Nine monikers in less than a year.

His fingers clenched the edges of the notebook, quivering, and for a moment, he wanted to throw it—out the door or into the filling bathtub or crashing through the thin awning window high on the wall near the ceiling.

Then C.C.'s voice came to him.

Life doesn't happen to you, love. It happens for you, she'd said. *One's identity is forged by the way one meets life's challenges.*

He took a deep breath, just like she would tell him to do. From the stomach. A diaphragmatic breath.

He tasted the thick, warm moisture in the air, felt it in his lungs. The water gurgled in the tub.

C.C. would tell him to meditate now, that he needed to, that one can meditate anywhere, anytime.

He closed his eyes.

Another deep breath, from the stomach. He monitored his body and became aware of the moment, of his presence. His legs, rather tight. His waist. His core. Up through his chest. His arms. Into his face. His jaw was clenched. C.C. used to tell him he carried a lot of his tension in his jaw muscles. He released it. The air felt cooler. The gurgling water echoed.

His eyes opened.

He blinked, felt the notebook in his hand. And something compelled him to look at one of the notes he'd studied moments earlier. He flipped back through the pages, found it.

My name is Jake Rowe

Months ago, he'd held this note beside the Grand Prix's rearview mirror and hadn't been able to say the words.

He looked at the old note, then quickly flipped through the pages, past all the other notes, past the list of names he'd written a few minutes earlier, to the first clean page. He pulled the mechanical pencil from the PenPal's spiral binding, scribbled out a note, and slapped it back on the wet mirror.

He looked at his reflection in the tiny bit of clean mirror

that the steam hadn't yet consumed. The muscles at the corners of his jaw—on this new, angular face of his—bulged taut and hard. He *did* carry his tension there, just like C.C. had always said. He released the strain again, and his eyes flicked over to the note he'd just written.

My name is Silence Jones

This was a second chance.

His throat was having a bad day, and he'd just run way too many syllables through it speaking with Mrs. Enfield. It throbbed, and as he swallowed, even the saliva hurt.

But he said it. All five words. No interruptions. No pauses to lubricate his throat. He forced himself through every sylla-ble, feeling all the slicing, all the ripping, all the red-hot burning until his eyes were bloodshot and wet.

"My name ... is Silence ... Jones."

His chest heaved. The muscles in his jaws tensed again. His nostrils flared.

A moment passed.

And then it was over.

C.C. would tell him to let go.

So he let go.

The steam clouded the last bit of his reflection as his jaw muscles slackened, eyes brightened, and a slight smile came to the corners of his lips.

He thought back to what Falcon had said the previous evening, before he turned and walked away, leaving Silence alone on the pier outside the Auditorium with police lights dancing off the water.

You're going to be a legend.

A legend.

Silence could live with that.

CHAPTER SEVENTY-SEVEN

Y EARS LATER.

The 1990s. Somewhere in Florida.

Walter Bowles tried to control his breathing, but the more he struggled to quiet himself, the more his breaths came out choppy, shuddering. Loud.

Shut up, shut up, shut up!

He rested his head against the concrete, cold on his crown of sweaty hair. Deep breaths. Slowly. He sucked in dust, nearly coughed.

The air in this goddamn place wasn't making it any easier to quiet his breathing. Dust everywhere, gray dust that marred his clothes, his face, his moist palms.

Everything around him was gray, not just the dust. Long flat planes of concrete broken by doorways and halls and endless columns. All of it was lines and angles, an exercise in geometry, an abstract painting come to life, drained of all vibrance until the only remaining color were patches of light coming in through the unfinished window openings, the sole source of light in the dark place, which illuminated particles of never-settling dust.

Walter managed to slow his breaths slightly. And he listened.

Nothing.

Dammit, he heard nothing. He couldn't believe it, but he would rather hear *something* than nothing. Because hearing nothing didn't mean that the man wasn't still out there somewhere in this partially completed concrete skeleton of a future office building.

No, the man was near. Hidden. Getting closer. Somewhere, moving through the angles of concrete, snaking through the shadows.

Walter knew this because he knew who the man was.

A man of myth among the criminal element.

Some people called him the Shadow. Others, the Quiet Man or Quiet Death. Walter had even heard him referred to as The Suppressor, both a clever play on his supposed persona and one of the ways in which he was said to dispose of his prey—a silenced pistol.

He'd heard rumors of the man appearing in Miami and Ocala and the Keys and the Panhandle. All over Florida. It had seemed to Walter and many of his associates that the man was some sort of vigilante protector of the Sunshine State.

But then a friend of his in Lincoln, Nebraska, of all places, shared a story. Gus sounded terrified when he told Walter that a group of pervs in his city were found dead in a motel room, all with two bullet holes in their foreheads. Their toy for the evening had been safely returned to her parents.

In the wake of the attack, the lowlifes of Lincoln had converged, compared their experiences. The collective conclusion was that a man had been snooping around the city, asking questions, breaking arms. A tall man. Pure muscle —not bulging but taut, hard. Dark, chiseled features. Cold eyes.

And those who were left alive reported that the man did very little speaking; he simply told them to, "Talk."

Talk. That's what the Florida legend was famously rumored to say! He wouldn't scream at you. He wouldn't throw a thousand questions at you to confuse you. He would simply say, "Talk."

And when he said that word, it came out through a horribly rough, deep, inhuman voice.

What did that mean, then, that Florida's killing shadow was also working in Nebraska? Could it simply be a case of blind, stupid regionalism that led people like Walter to believe the man was operating solely in Florida? Or could the man be tormenting the underworld of the whole country? The entire *world?*

No. No, that was crazy. All of it. Utter lunacy.

A man with a demon voice hunting down murderers and rapists and drug bosses? *Come on.*

Walter wasn't thinking right. There was no vigilante killer in Nebraska *or* Florida. There was no Shadow. No Quiet Man. No Suppressor.

Whoever was out there in the shadows wanted him dead. That was for sure. But he wasn't the boogeyman.

If Walter was going to make it out of this alive, he had to get his head on straight. And he had to walk straight as well, which was a challenge given the state of his ankle.

He put his hand on it, grimaced. Just the slightest touch, that's all it took to send ripples of electric pain up his calf. When he'd sprinted out of the alley and into the construction site, momentarily escaping the big man, he'd made a beeline for a room in the back corner, which was small and dark and seemed like the perfect place to lay low.

What he hadn't noticed were the rectangular cutouts in the concrete floor, future homes for heating and air conditioning components, assumedly. His shoe had caught in one, twisting his foot back and to the side. Walter had let out a scream that echoed off the empty corridors.

He'd limped through the labyrinth of walls for a minute or two after that, not going to the room he'd originally spotted, thinking that his scream might have alerted his pursuer to his destination.

Instead, he'd taken a circuitous path through hallways and empty doorways, up and down half flights of steps, dodging construction debris, until finally he could stand the pain no more and turned the corner into the next available room, which must have been a future closet or perhaps a tiny, windowless office for some menial, low-level employee. He'd collapsed against the wall, sliding down to his ass, taking the pressure off his ankle.

The room was too damn bright. There was an exterior window opening across the hall, and a golden rectangle of light spilled onto the floor beside Walter. After cramming himself into the corner, he was still barely outside the glow.

And that's where he'd sat, semi-immobilized, trying to control his breaths, frightening himself with tales of ghosts and goblins.

All of this was Constantino's fault. Damn him. Had Walter not gotten involved with the guy, had Walter simply kept his perversions to himself, had he continued his time-tested techniques of working alone, grabbing his own targets from schools and playgrounds and shopping malls far from where he lived, then none of this would have happened.

But Walter had gotten greedy. He'd broken his own rules, opened his big mouth. And that had led him to Constantino and his promise of a never-ending supply of treats.

Stupid! How could he have been so stupid? He'd had a good thing going. But now some cold-looking monster of a man was hunting him through a construction site. And Walter was hobbled. And unarmed.

He leaned his ear closer to the doorway.

And heard something. A slight scratching sound.

A rat? Or debris moving in the slight breeze that twisted languidly through the tunnels and holes of the structure?

Walter's mind flashed on the myth again. The Quiet Man. The Suppressor. The rational assurances he'd given himself a moment earlier vanished, and fear and superstition returned.

A few more of the scratching sounds. Closer. The cadence of footsteps.

Oh god. He was there. Just outside the room. Yes, he was, and—

A flurry of motion. Pressure on his shoulders. A wave of pain shuddered through his body from his ankle. A shift in his stomach, and he was upright. Another wave of pain as his back slapped against the wall.

The man was before him.

At about six-foot-three, he towered over Walter. He had sharp, attractive features. Dark hair. Dark clothes, too—jacket, button-up shirt, chinos. Eyes of death.

It was him. God, it was him.

How? How had the man gotten him off the floor? Walter wasn't very tall, but he weighed nearly two hundred pounds. Yet the man had yanked him up like a sack of groceries. The strength coming out of the man's fingers, pulsing into Walter's shoulders, was palpable.

The man swung his hands away and patted Walter down with machine precision and speed, so fast that when it was over, it took a moment for Walter to realize what had happened.

Finding Walter weaponless, the man stepped back, putting a few feet between them. He reached under his jacket and took out a pistol. Another flourish beneath the jacket, and he produced a silencer.

A suppressor...

The silencer joined the gun's barrel with the same speed as everything else the man had done, and in a blink the man now held the suppressed, lengthened pistol at his side.

Walter started to cry. He tried speaking, but his lips only sputtered. Popping sounds came from the back of his throat.

Warmth. On his left thigh. Spreading. He'd pissed himself. Oh, Jesus, he'd pissed himself.

The man stared at him, *into* him. Face not even twitching. A long moment.

Then he said, "Talk."

It *was* him.

The voice. When he'd said that one word, *Talk*, it perfectly matched the legendary descriptions. Deep, dark. Crackling and torn. Painful-sounding, even.

Demonic.

Walter tried to reply. No words, just the popping sounds again.

He swallowed. Cleared his throat. Tried again.

If he couldn't force himself to speak, this monster was going to kill him.

"I ... I can give you the man you're looking for. All the guys you've killed, they ... they're all connected to Jimmy Constantino. Over in Spring Hill. 1813 Elledge Boulevard. It's a storage facility. He owns the place. Pedos, man. You want it, Jimmy'll get it. That's all I know. I swear!"

He'd spilled it all. He'd ratted out Constantino. That should be enough to get him out of this situation.

The man didn't react. No nod. No shimmer across the eyes that showed a processing of the information. For the longest time, *he didn't even blink.* Just continued to stare at Walter.

With the gun hanging at his side.

Walter's lips trembled as he eyed the gun. The urine on his thigh grew cold.

He looked the man in the eye.

"Dude, I'm telling you, that's all I know!"

But what did *he* know, the killer man standing in front of him, looking at him so coldly?

Did the man know about Walter's adventures? Did he know about the eight-year-old, the one who started it all when Walter still lived in North Carolina? Did he know about the girl Constantino had gotten him just two weeks ago, the little blonde whose parents never locked her window?

Things suddenly grew quieter. The soft sound of the highway in the distance. Water dripping somewhere in a nearby room.

Walter couldn't take it. "I talked! You told me to talk, and I did!"

Finally, the blank expression on the man's face broke. A slight, dark grin appeared at the corners of his mouth. His lips parted, as though he had something else to say.

The man was going to speak again? No, this wasn't supposed to happen. He'd already said his word, his single word. *Talk.*

Yet he was about to say something else...

Walter inched away, cramming himself into the wall. "I talked!"

The man slowly raised his free hand, leaving the pistol dangling on the other side of his body.

"I talked, goddamnit! *What do you want from me?*"

The hand continued upward, to the man's face. A finger extended over his lips.

And the man *didn't* speak. What came out of his mouth was just a sound, not a word.

"*Shhhhhh...*" the man said.

He raised his gun.

And fired.

ALSO BY ERIK CARTER

Ty Draker Action Thrillers Series

Novels:

Novella:

Silence Jones Action Thrillers Series

Novels:

Novella:

Deadly Silence

Dale Conley Action Thrillers Series

Novels:

Stone Groove

Dream On

The Lowdown

Get Real

Talkin' Jive

Be Still

Jump Back

The Skinny

No Fake

Novella:

Get Down

ABOUT THE AUTHOR

ERIK CARTER is the author of multiple bestselling action thriller series.

To find out more, visit www.erikcarterbooks.com.

ACKNOWLEDGMENTS

For their involvement with *The Suppressor*, I would like to give a sincere thank you to:

My ARC readers, for providing reviews and catching typos. Thanks!

Aunt Amy, for medical expertise.

Ricky Cardenas, for some amazing editing polish on the first chapter.

April Snellings, for even more editing polish on Chapter 1.

Dad, for a bit of technical information.

Todd, for some historical information.

J, for name insight.

Made in the USA
Las Vegas, NV
14 November 2024